Ugly SECRETS

Ugly SECRETS

Little Hope Series, Book 6

LITTLE HOPE

HOME OF
SOME NOSEY FUCKERS

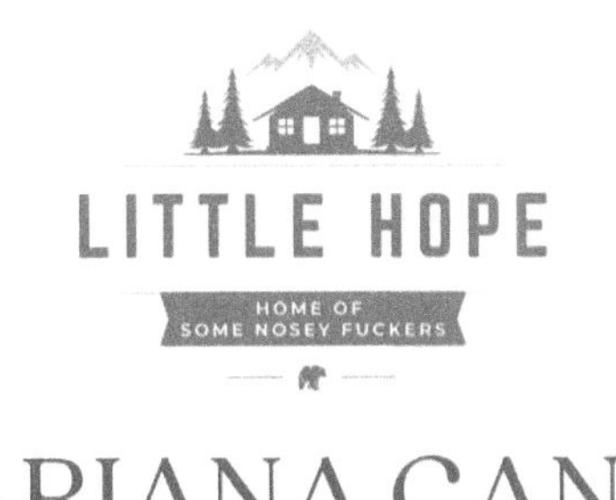

ARIANA CANE

"Because there will
be damage.
It's just a matter of
how much."

To those who still have faith in Jake,
this story is for you.
For those who don't,
this story is for you.
Every villain has a reason to be that way. Or a few.

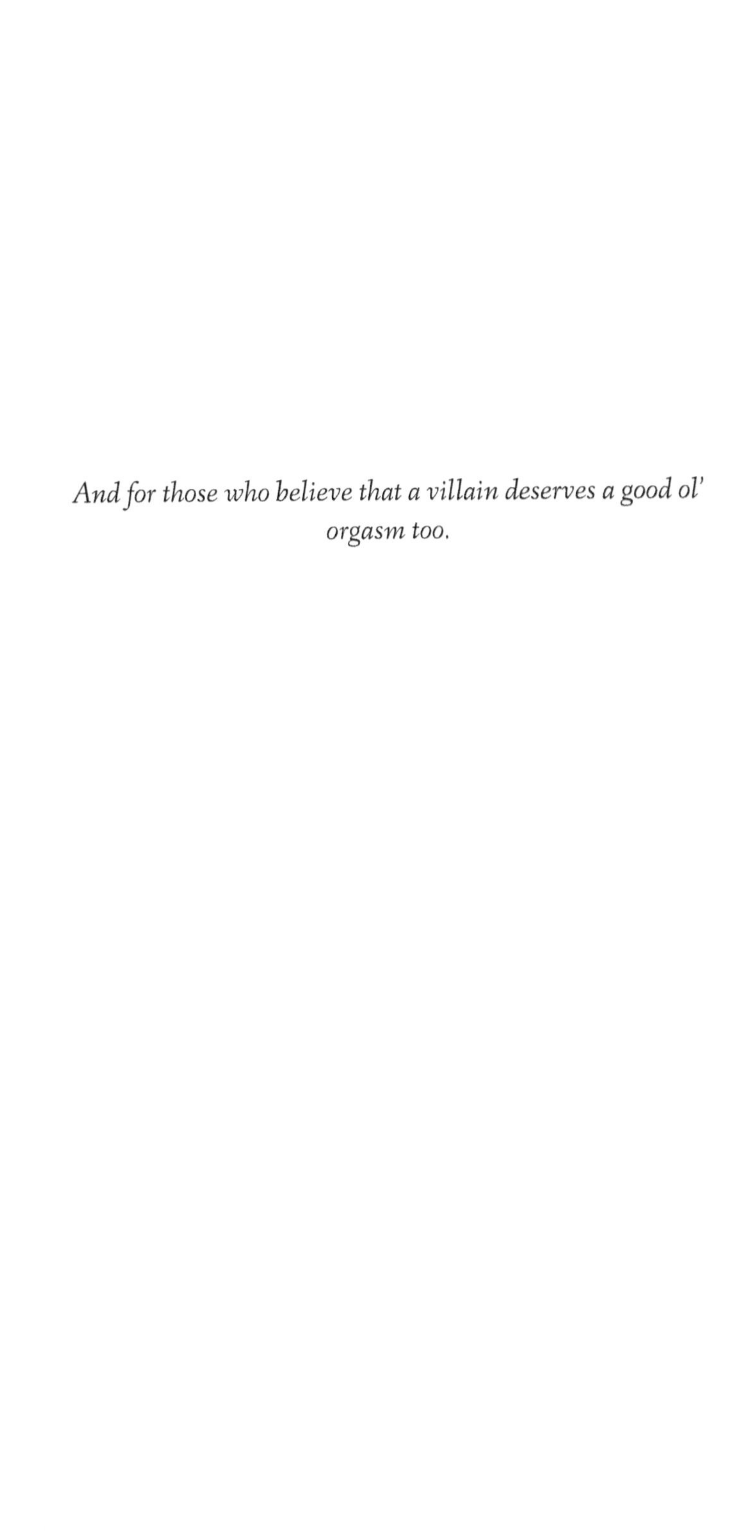

And for those who believe that a villain deserves a good ol' orgasm too.

Author's Note

Please read this first. It has some important information and trigger warnings.

Well, this is the last of the Little Hope era, and I'm emotional. I've been with this series for two years, and it has completely changed my life.

If you are here, then you probably have been with Little Hope since the beginning and want to see how Jake will get his life together. I am grateful that you are still here. Thank you! Even though it's supposed to be read as a stand-alone since it features a new couple, I wouldn't recommend doing so. There will be many flashbacks to scenes from previous books. If you haven't read them, they might not make any sense to you.

I don't know if you'll like this book, but this is exactly how Jake's story was meant to be told from the beginning. I knew what would happen to *and* with him. From Justin's book, I knew whom he'd end up with. At some point, you'll think the story turned crazy. And it might have. But this was always meant to be. This book was meant to explain all the blind spots from the previous ones. Since Little Hope is not exactly the most typical small-town romance, I always planned to go 'all in.'

This book was never meant to become a bestseller, it was always meant to give everyone closure—myself included. I needed to say goodbye to our couples so I could move on.

This book will have less spice than the previous books due to some topics and circumstances. Jake needs redeeming more than he needs orgasms, let's be honest. Don't fret though, there are some steamy moments here, I wouldn't do you that dirty!

What you'll see in this book:

- All the questions from all the books answered, including but not limited to: how Jake knew where to go in book one just in time to save the day, or how Mark knew how to find the bad guys in book three, etc.
- Groveling from everyone (seriously). Everyone in this series has some shit to apologize for.
- Emotional damage (I'm not responsible for your future therapy, ha-ha).
- Secrets that have their own secrets.
- Mega-super-duper slow burn (sorry! #iamnotsorry).
- A chocolate floor scene.
- Frank making an epic comeback.

Now, let's move on to the triggers. There are some pretty heavy ones in this book as well,

but I will separate them from the main body of this text with a ton of dots in case you don't want to accidentally skim over them. The triggers have some giant spoilers in them. Quite a few. But if you may be triggered by anything, I urge you to read them. Your mental health is more important than Jake. For those who can't read due to triggers but still want to know what happens, here's a spoiler for you: Jake gets his HEA. The end.

Anyhow, the TWs are below. If you decide to dive in, enjoy the ride. I'm bringing all the drama back!

With love,
Ariana

.

.

.

.

.

.

*TWs: drug addiction (all situations are different for everyone—I've made it this way, but every story deserves a voice), a scene of an active drug withdrawal, mention of SA (MMC's sister in the past), mention of the word r*pe, mention of guns, use of guns, physical assault, alcoholism, child neglect.*

Addiction is scary and most likely requires some sort of medical help. But in the book, I made this story about love. It might be realistic, or it might not be. Don't take it as a course of action either way. Remember, this is just a book where everyone gets their HEA. Even the villain.

Prologue

J**ake**

If someone was giving away the 'Most Hated Man' award, it'd go to me without even considering other candidates.

At this point, I don't even remember where it all started. It just snowballed out of my control along the way, making me question if it was all worth it in the end.

Spoiler alert—so far, it has not been.

Chapter One

J^{ake}

The wailing of a baby hasn't stopped for the past ten minutes.

"Shut it up! We're trying to sleep here!" someone yells from outside.

I'd agree with them if I didn't have insomnia—I've given up on the idea of sleep a long time ago, and now I just waste time lying in bed and staring at the ceiling.

"Shut it up or I'll shut it up myself!" the same voice bellows, raising my hackles. I might be an asshole, but I'll never tolerate threats to kids.

Please be quiet and don't say another word. Please be quiet and don't say another word.

"That's it, I'm coming out!"

. . . And he didn't listen. I hear the sound of a suddenly opened door banging on a wall, and the man's spiteful voice moves along the outside wall of my room in the shittiest motel I've ever stayed in.

I jump to my feet, quickly put boots on, and rush outside. It's fucking freezing, and this asshole's standing in an open robe and boxers. Poor fucker.

But when I take in the whole picture, my heart freezes. He's barging toward a woman who's backed into a car.

"Get the hell away from us, or I'll claw your eyes out," she hisses once he's about five feet away. She's way smaller than the man, but I'll put my money on her—she looks vicious and deadly with this determined look of raw fury.

"Shut your little spawn up. Or, if you're not capable of doing it yourself, I'll do it." The man moves forward. So do I.

Before he reaches the woman with the burning eyes, I grab him by his shoulders and pull him toward me. He stumbles but quickly regains his posture.

"Go about your business, man." His voice is full of arrogance. "I don't want any trouble with you."

"You've got it regardless. Go back to your room." I nod at the still open door right next to mine.

His back straightens as he squares his shoulders and takes a few steps away from me. "Oh, yeah?" His eyes narrow with an obvious threat. "I don't think so. Until this bitch," he points his index finger at the woman, "shuts it. I'm not leaving. I need to sleep." He spreads his arms wide. "We all do."

I take two steps toward him, grab the front hem of his robe, and pull him closer to me.

"Go. Inside." My voice drops. But my threats are on a different level. I can actually back them up. "And shut your door. I don't want to see your face again."

I can see the desire to fight in his eyes, but once our

unblinking eyes meet, he shakes off my hands and backs away. "Make it stop." He points at my chest and disappears into his room, loudly shutting the door behind him.

I turn toward the woman who stopped paying any attention to what was happening many threats ago. Instead, she pulls the hood of her sedan open and starts poking at something. The wailing child seems to be inside the car and indeed hasn't stopped crying for a while.

"You okay?" My voice comes out gruff and unwelcoming. Something I've tried to change but can't seem to shake even when I'm trying to be somewhat tolerable.

She lifts her face—it's stricken with dried tears. And I can't tell for sure, but I think they were that way before the asshole showed up. Her face is a little blotchy, eyes red.

"Thank you," she says quickly, glancing at where the jerk disappeared and going back to working on something under the hood.

I'm not used to being so easily dismissed after such an encounter, and she hasn't exactly answered my question, so I move toward her. She jumps when she notices me, so I instantly freeze, my hands held up in surrender.

It's probably the first time I can actually get a good look at her face and notice how beautiful she is.

Despite her eyes and nose being swollen, I can tell she's gorgeous. And very, very familiar. I have a feeling I've seen her dark eyes before. Her presence is also familiar. Even her wild, brown hair falling like curtains over her shoulders.

I catch myself staring at her like a creep on the street.

"I just want to make sure you and the kid are okay," I say as calmly as possible.

At the mention of the child, her shoulders drop with obvious defeat. "My car won't start, and I need to go to a hospital."

My stomach drops. "Are you hurt?"

She shakes her head quickly. "Brodie has a fever, and it's not going away. I've been trying to start the car for the past ten minutes, but it just won't." Her voice hitches at the end, her neck moving in a rough swallow, and I get the feeling those dried tears will soon be replenished with fresh ones.

"Let me see."

She quickly steps away, giving me space.

After a short glance, the problem is obvious. "It's the battery. You need a jump start."

"Do you have those things?" Her face lights up, like I'm her savior. "To start the car I mean."

I shake my head, and the hopeful look on her face dissolves into nothing.

"Wait here." I run to my room, grab my jacket, keys, and wallet, and run back to her. She's rummaging through her trunk, clearly looking for the cables she most likely doesn't have.

"C'mon," I call with a nod.

"What?" Her head pops out from behind the open trunk.

"I'll drive you to the hospital. You need to do the car seat 'cause I have no idea how this thing works." I move toward the back door of her car and open it. The small, wailing baby freezes when he sees me. His eyes are wide, and his cheeks are covered in angry, red blotches. "Hey, little man," I say out of nowhere, hoping like an idiot that a miracle will happen, and I'll calm the little dude with just my presence like Mary Poppins.

Naturally, he starts crying again. Even the baby sees right through me.

A hand gently pushes me out of the way, and her back

in a big, puffy jacket appears in front of me. She quickly removes the seat and pulls it out of the car.

"Let me help." I make a move to take the seat from her, but she steps back.

"I got it."

I nod with understanding and march toward my truck. When I open the back door, she quickly jumps inside and fixes the car seat for the little guy.

I turn my body toward her. "Are we ready?"

"Yes." She buckles herself up, and I take off. A few minutes later, the crying stops, and I hear the woman's loud sigh of relief. The atmosphere in the car should improve, but it's not happening.

It's snowing. We need to get to the hospital rather quickly, but I have a little person in the vehicle, and my palms are sweaty. I don't ever remember being so scared to drive, but I am now. Every turn I take, I drop the speed to five miles per hour.

"Thank you," comes a soft voice from the back seat. "Thank you for driving us. I don't know what I'd be doing. I tried calling Uber or a taxi or something, but there's nothing around here."

I glance at her in the rearview mirror. She's holding his tiny hand in hers, but her eyes are trained on me.

"No problem." Even to my own eyes, my tone comes out defensive. *She just thanked me, for fuck's sake. What's wrong with me?*

"Still. Thank you." She turns to the window. "I was scared."

"Of the man?"

"Hell no!" Her mildly offended look makes me smile. "I'd beat him to a pulp if he made a move."

"I believe that." I can barely keep from smiling.

"I was scared of not being able to get Brodie to a hospital. His fever spiked about five hours ago, and I tried just about every drug I could find at the drugstore, but it won't go down."

"At all?"

She shakes her head. "Fevers in babies are dangerous." Her gaze drops. "I'm really scared," she whispers, making my chest ache. I rub it with my hand because it feels like the beginning of a heart attack. I don't like the feeling.

"We'll get there."

I gently press on the accelerator, still trying to be careful on the snow-covered road. I want to ask her so many questions, like what the hell she's doing at a cheap motel in Vermont, but her mind is occupied with the kid right now, and even I know it's not the time.

And quite honestly, it's not my place. I'll drive her to the hospital and be on my merry way right after.

The hospital is run-down and clearly understaffed, which is not a big surprise around here—folks don't want to stick around once they get their fancy degree. A tired-looking nurse is sitting at the reception desk. There are a few people in the waiting room, all in a different sort of distress.

"You can go. Thank you," my passenger tells me when she notices me following her toward the reception.

"It's fine. I'll just make sure they'll see you, so we don't have to drive somewhere else."

"Oh," she sighs. "Right. Thank you."

"Stop thanking me," I say gruffly, making her eyes dart to mine. She gives me a short nod and steps toward the front desk.

"Hi, my son is nine months old, and he has a fever," she

says in a rather calm voice I sure wouldn't possess if I were in her place.

The tired woman lifts her eyes. "Kids get sick. Did you give him Tylenol?"

"Yes. And Motrin. But neither brought it down."

The woman pushes some papers toward my passenger. "Fill this out, please, and bring them back."

My passenger grabs the car seat from the floor and rushes to the waiting area. I don't have any choice but to follow her. She puts the seat by her feet, and the little guy starts crying. She tries pushing it with one foot like a swing and filling out the paperwork at the same time, but she keeps getting distracted. So I lean toward the seat and start moving it in a steady rhythm with my hand.

"I got it."

"Thank you," she breathes out, and starts to quickly move her pen about the papers on her lap. Once she's done, she rushes back to the reception desk. "Here," she says to the nurse.

"Wait for when you'll be called," the nurse replies automatically.

"Do you know how long that might take?"

"Those people are ahead of you." The nurse points at the general area where I'm sitting, surrounded by others.

My passenger turns around, and her eyes become even more worried. "That's a lot of people," she says to the woman. "My son is only nine months old, and his fever hasn't gone down with any of the medications. It's dangerous."

The nurse gives her a look of disregard. "Everyone here has an urgent matter. Please take a seat in the waiting area."

My passenger comes back to me and the wailing child and sits down.

"Do you think we can wait?" I ask her quietly, trying not to draw more attention to us than we already have. These people seem to be bored out of their minds, and it makes me wonder how long they've been here.

"We don't have a choice." She vigorously chews her lower lip, clearly thinking something.

"Do you know what this might be?" I nod at the kid in the seat I'm still rocking.

She shakes her head. "It's my first child, and I have no idea what I'm doing." Her teeth sink even deeper into the flesh of her lip for a moment before she keeps talking. "I googled the symptoms, and it might be pneumonia. I don't know; he's never been sick before." She pushes her hand into her wild hair, making it even wilder. By the look of her crazed, sparkling eyes, I'd say she's one word away from slipping into the abyss. "I really don't know."

I pull out my phone and google 'newborn pneumonia' while still rocking the seat. The move is automatic—almost calming to me. I don't even have to think about it anymore. After a few minutes of reading the internet results, I feel my blood draining from my face. I jump to my feet, push the car seat closer to the mother, and march toward the woman at the front desk.

"Can I help you?" she asks, unbothered.

"Yes, you can." My voice is stern. I used this voice when I was a cop and needed people to obey. "We need to admit a nine-month-old with pneumonia symptoms."

Her brows go up. "Yes?" She looks around and starts speaking louder. "Why would I give you and your son special treatment?"

I let the 'son' part slide and lean over the counter toward her. "Because if something happens to the child due to your refusal of care, I'll be here with a warrant tomorrow morning."

"Hey, you," one of the men from the sitting area calls out to me. "I'm here with a fuckin' broken arm, and I'm still here. Get in the damn line like everybody else."

Fuck, you shouldn't have opened your mouth.

I crack my neck, hoping it releases some tension and the man will go about his business in the meantime.

"Hey. Did you hear me or what?" he yells louder this time, making sure the whole lobby hears him.

I sigh—rather loudly—and shift my undivided attention toward the man. He stands up from the chair and puffs his chest out. *Here we go.*

His shoulders square back as he's waiting for my comeback. And there's only one comeback I'm ready to give him when I notice my passenger's rapidly paling face. When she notices me watching her, she subtly shakes her head, urging me to stop.

A shake of her head. That's what it takes to kill my pride and rage when my blood starts pumping. One fuckin' shake of her head.

Disgusted with myself and my reaction to all of it, I turn back toward the receptionist, still being aware of the man. He's too close to my passenger and her kid for my liking.

"Can we be seen?" I ask the nurse again.

Her face pales even more as she swallows and looks around at the onlookers.

"Hey!" The man's voice sounds closer.

The nurse rises to her feet and turns toward the yelling man as he nears. "The kid has pneumonia symptoms. He has to be admitted ASAP," she explains, stopping the man in his tracks. After a quick glance around, he retreats back to his seat.

The receptionist slowly grabs the stationary phone. After a beep, someone responds, and she starts talking. "We have a nine-month-old with severe pneumonia symptoms." She listens to something on the other end of the line before she says, "Okay," and puts the phone down.

"You can wait here. They'll come to get you."

"Thank you." I nod and take a couple steps away from her desk, so she doesn't hear us.

"Thank you, Jake." My passenger grabs my hand and squeezes it tightly. "Thank you so much."

I don't do well with gratitude, so I just nod like a dumb baboon.

Soon, another nurse appears from behind the double doors on the side and motions for us to come with her. Of course, I don't. I just pass the seat with the kid to his mother. "Good luck. I hope he'll be better soon."

"Yeah," she whispers and rushes toward the nurse.

I'm in my car when I remember that I drove them here, and that her car is still back at the motel with a dead battery. I probably should wait for them in the waiting room.

When I return, the woman at the reception desk gives me a dirty look, which I choose to ignore. I take a seat at the farthest corner of the room, prepared to wait to take them back home. Well, the motel, not home.

And only then do I remember that she called me Jake.

Which is my name. The name I never gave to her.

Chapter Two

O livia

"It's a good thing you brought your son in when you did. A couple more hours, and we might have been looking at a different story," the doctor says, as she checks my baby once again. "I heard your husband made quite a scene."

I feel the blood drain from my face but don't fix her words. "Yeah, he was worried."

"Well, good thing he was." She winks and goes to wash her hands. "A nurse will come to check on him in a few. If you need to step away, ask someone at the station to stay here."

"No need, I'll be fine." Walking around, enjoying coffee is the last thing I want while my child lies here, on this big bed, looking so small.

She turns to me with a stern look. "No need to be cooped up here for the next two days. No one will think you're a bad mom if you step away for a few minutes to get some fresh air. Or coffee." She points at the window. "There's a good coffee place right around the corner. Walk off your worry and come back refreshed. Your boy will need it." When I don't answer, she adds, "I mean it. If you're anxious, kids feel it. And he needs you strong and stoic, Mom."

With that, she leaves me alone with Brodie and the beeping machine. I curl up on the chair next to his bed and take his hand. The fever went down after the IV antibiotics they gave him, and now I can finally breathe.

And I start crying the moment I do. All the pent-up fear and helplessness was bound to come out. I bite the sleeve of my shirt, so I don't make a sound and wake him up. He's finally getting some rest after fighting this thing.

I can't sleep during the night, constantly checking on my son, so in the morning I need some coffee—the sweet doctor was right. Brodie woke up twice and went back to sleep, so I'm just left gazing at him as he sleeps. When the doctor comes back to check on him during the morning route, she sends me out of the room and on my merry way, saying that getting my feet under me is the best thing I can do for him right now.

The moment I walk out of the emergency room doors, I freeze. Because Jake is still there, on one of the chairs in the very corner with no one around him. Literally. People scattered away from him, and two seats on each side are empty in the overcrowded room.

I sigh and walk toward him. He's leaning on the back of his chair, scrolling through his phone.

"Hey," I say quietly as I sit next to him.

"Oh, hi." He instantly puts his phone into his pocket and looks around. "Where's the kid?"

"He stayed there. He has pneumonia, as we suspected, and they want to keep him for observation for at least twenty-four hours. I stepped out to get some coffee." I bite the inside of my cheek before braving myself to ask the question. "What are you doing here?"

He looks to the side, clearly feeling uncomfortable. "I wanted to leave but then wondered how you'd get back since you don't have your car and all that."

I shouldn't feel bad for him because it's Jake Attleborough, the asshole extraordinaire, but I do. I physically can't make myself hate him right now, not after he helped my son. All I feel is gratitude.

"Do you want to walk with me to get coffee? You might need some too," I offer with a sincere smile.

"Yeah, sure." He jumps to his feet, grabs his jacket, and gestures for me to lead the way.

On the way to the shop, he asks, "Is the boy okay now?"

The iceberg around my heart melts some more. "Yes, they put him on antibiotics, and the fever went down. He'll be good now."

"He will be." He nods, surprising me.

"Thank you, Jake," I say, trying to pour all the gratitude in my voice. "I mean it. I don't know how long it would have taken me to find transportation."

"I'm sure you'd find a way." His steps slow down. "How do you know my name?"

And here, right here, is the moment when the ice builds back up a little, protecting my poor heart.

"You really don't remember me?" I glance at him and find him watching me, unblinking. Like he's trying to solve some mysterious puzzle.

"No."

I sigh, expecting this answer, but hoping for another. "We went to school together."

"What?" His brows shoot into the stratosphere.

"We're here." I shift my focus on the building in front of us. "Let's get coffee before I fall face first on the floor."

We go inside, and the look the young barista sends Jake's way doesn't escape me. I mean, he's got the looks. His whole family does. A blond, perfect Greek god. So I don't blame her—I had a crush on Jake in school. Hence the iceberg around my heart.

"Hey." The barista fixes a lock of hair behind her ear and drops her eyes to the floor in a classic flirty gesture, making me roll my eyes. "What can I get for you?"

He turns toward me. "What do you want?"

The barista's face drops as she turns toward me—she clearly didn't know we were together. Well, not like *together* together, but she doesn't know how not together we are.

"Hi. Can I please have a venti, hot latte with a triple espresso and a pump of liquid sugar?" I could be petty about being 'disregarded,' but my child is recovering in the hospital right now, and I have plenty to be thankful for. As a strong believer of karma, I try to do no harm. Even verbally.

And this is precisely why us ordering coffee together seems even more surreal.

"Sure." The barista writes my order down and turns toward Jake. "And for you?" Her voice turns sugary, like the syrup I just ordered for myself.

"Large, black coffee."

"No cream?"

"Black," he repeats, clearly losing patience out of nowhere, showing a case of 'real Jake.' It, somehow, looks very amusing, and I don't find it even remotely rude.

"Alright." The barista rings up the order. "Anything else?" We both shake our heads. "It'll be ten-fifty."

I pull my wallet out, but Jake's already swiping his card.

"Please, let me at least buy you coffee," I beg sincerely because I don't know what else I can do to thank him for his help. He certainly won't accept gas money.

His eyes tick as he ignores me and puts his card away. We both move to the waiting area and lean on the bar. His eyes land on my face.

"You said we went to school together."

"Yep." I pop the *p*.

"Did I know you?" he continues his interrogation.

I shrug.

"Did you know me?"

I laugh. "Everyone knew you." The most popular guy in school, he took the baton from his older brother, Justin.

"What's your name?"

"Olivia," I reply, hoping his eyes will shine with recognition.

"I don't remember anyone with that name."

And there goes my hope.

I swallow the bitterness of his words down, along with my dreams that he knew and remembered me. "I was three years younger and had braces." His eyes dip to my mouth. "And no boobs." His eyes dip lower and instantly lift back up to my face while his cheeks turn a pretty pink color. "Yeah, I had no boobs." I can't help but chuckle.

"Sorry," he mumbles.

I wave him off, still chuckling. I needed this silly moment to relax.

"That's why you got into the car with me? Because you knew me?"

"That's why I doubted if I *should* get in the car with you." I quirk a brow, letting him know that I also know of his recent reputation.

The man is a menace to society. Everyone hates him. Everyone. Even his own brother for nearly ruining his relationship with his fiancé. Ask anyone in Little Hope, our hometown, what they think about Jake, and they'll tell you plenty of ugly stuff.

"I see." His face darkens as his shoulders turn completely rigid. He pushes away from the bar, takes his coffee, and makes a move to head toward the door when I grab his arm.

"Jake, stop."

He tries pulling his arm away, but my grip is strong—he either needs to cause a scene or use force to get rid of it. When he turns my way, I'm hit with a wave of such hatred, I feel for the first time what it's like to be on the receiving end of his rage.

"Don't be a drama queen," I try reasoning in a calm voice. "We're both from Little Hope, and it's no secret that you're not the most popular person there."

"Then you know to stay away from me." His voice is borderline threatening, but I'm not scared. First of all, I grew up in a trailer park, so not much scares me anymore. And second, I've seen this guy protect my child, and I know for a fact he's not a threat to us. To someone else—yeah, I can see it.

"What are you going to do?" I quirk a brow.

He leans closer to me. "Nothing, for a change." With that, he finally frees himself from me and marches away.

"Thank you, Jake! I mean it!" I yell to his back, but he doesn't turn around.

Well, that escalated rather quickly, but I shouldn't have expected less from Jake. There is a reason why he's so hated after all.

Chapter Three

T*wo weeks later*

Olivia

"Look at my nephew!" coos my brother, Mark, holding Brodie. "Who's gotten so big? Yeah, so big. Yes, you are. You're a very good boy," he continues with a warm smile.

"I think he thinks he's talking to Ghost," I chuckle, sitting next to Alicia, Mark's fiancé, at their breakfast table. It's a beautiful Saturday morning, eight past ten, and my life seems to be getting back on track. Brodie is on his last few days of oral antibiotics and looks so much better. The house I've been eyeing to rent will be available soon, and I'm going to look at a few spaces for my bakery today.

"Seems so to me. It's adorable though," Alicia sighs wistfully as she plants her chin on her hand to watch Mark playing with Brodie.

A wet nose nudges my hand. "Oh, hello, Ghost. Where have you been?" I start petting the German shepherd, my brother's dog. Though, ever since Alicia moved in, Ghost seems more like her dog, only pretending to listen to Mark sometimes. Watching their family dynamics is adorable. We've been here for ten days, and each day shows me how happy Mark is with Alicia, and how much he needed her in his life. I couldn't be happier for them.

I just wish she didn't come with a side of her brother Jake. I sigh to myself, recalling our last meeting, and immediately feel terrible. The man helped save my son. He showed a different side of himself, and there I was reminding him of his past. Or his present. I'm not sure—I don't know him well enough. I don't know him at all, but all his encounters with people close to me have been far from pleasant.

"When are you meeting with Jonah?" Mark asks, continuing to coo at Brodie.

I glance at the clock on the wall by the fridge. "In an hour. He says he has a special place to show me, which he thinks will be perfect, but it's a bit bigger than I expected, so —" I wince, letting the thought trail off.

"Do you think the down payment will be larger?" Alicia asks.

"Yeah," I reply, biting my lip—a habit of mine when thinking, which is why I always carry ChapStick in every pocket, due to my constantly dry lips.

Mark and Alicia exchange a look before she speaks again. "We can pause our project and lend you money."

"No!" I jump to my feet and rush to the kitchen to rinse my cup. "Absolutely not. You guys have been planning and saving for this addition for so long. You need it." I turn to them. "And besides, there must be a reason you decided to expand your place." I wiggle my brows, making Alicia's cheeks redden.

"We were thinking about starting a family," she admits shyly.

"Honey," I walk to her and touch her shoulder. "You *are* family. You don't need a child to become one, but if you're ready, I'm so happy for you."

Her face breaks into a wide, beautiful smile. "Can we practice with our nephew?"

I laugh, knowing she and Mark have been trying to steal Brodie since we arrived. "Go ahead. I can do my things faster. Are you sure it won't be too much trouble for you guys? I do appreciate your help, don't get me wrong. I don't know what I'd do without you. You're already letting us stay here, and now you're babysitting my kiddo."

"P-p-ph," Alicia hums, dismissing my concerns. "I'm in a writer's block and could use some distraction."

"And I miss my man so much," Mark adds, playfully tossing Brodie in the air, eliciting giggles from him and causing us to hold our breath in fear.

"Mark!" I cry out. "Be careful!"

"I've done it to you, and you were fine."

"I was almost eight years older, and you threw me off your shoulders in the water!"

He gives me a stink eye. "It's about the same."

I roll my eyes and head to the bathroom to change. Their house is very cozy and welcoming but very small, with only one bedroom, which they've given us while we stay here. They're both sleeping on a pull-out couch in the living room. I feel horrible for taking their space, but the local bed and breakfast doesn't have any rooms left—no big surprise there—and it's easier to find a unicorn than a place to rent in Little Hope.

Once changed from my flannel pajamas into jeans and a warm, white sweater, I wave goodbye to everyone, hug my baby, and head out.

Returning to the motel from the hospital nearly two weeks ago, I found my car miraculously working again. I didn't question my luck, but I have my suspicions that the local villain had a hand in it. I meant to thank him for that but was unsure how he'd take it—he doesn't seem to accept gratitude well, and I suspect the fine people of Little Hope have a lot to do with it. I don't blame them, honestly. Jake has never been a gift to society.

I don't need GPS to find the address given by Jonah, the realtor. I grew up in Little Hope and know every corner around here. The place he wants to show me is at the very end of Main Street, on one of the small side streets. Not the most ideal location for a bakery and a coffee shop but Main Street already has established businesses, including a coffee shop, so there's no place for me there. There's no place for me even here, on this side of town, but they all will have to deal with it. Mark has made a name for himself around here, so shall I. After living in a big city, I yearned to return to a small town and raise my child on its values, though some of those values need changing.

"Hey, Olivia." Jonah waves at me. He's dressed in a three-piece suit, his hair slicked back in stylish waves, and he smells like old Hollywood glamour.

I'll never be as cool as Jonah.

"Hey!" I reply, waving back.

"Are you excited? Because I am," he says, rubbing his hands together eagerly.

"I am," I admit with a smile. "But I'm also scared of how

much it will cost me." I half-ask, hoping he'll maybe give me a clue.

But he doesn't. Instead, he raises his hand, stopping further questioning. "First, see the place."

This isn't a good sign, so I follow him hesitantly.

"The place isn't here?" I look around, searching for a 'for sale' sign.

"Nope," he says with a secretive smile. "I want you to walk there and get the feel for the neighborhood first."

I stop, getting annoyed at him for wasting our time and making us freeze our bottoms off. "Jo-o-o-nah."

"Just trust me," he insists, rolling his eyes. "I know my real estate."

"Alright," I agree—not right away—and we continue walking down the small side street.

While we walk, he keeps looking at me from the side. When I'm tired of his side-eye, I turn toward him and ask, "What?"

He starts laughing. "I just can't believe how much you've changed."

"What do you mean?" I ask, confused.

"C'mon!" He laughs again. "You've seen yourself in a mirror. You were a very interesting *girl* when you were one," he quickly turns to me with raised hands, "if I was interested like that. But damn, girl." He clicks his tongue. "You've grown into Olivia Hardy. A woman who knows some shit."

I feel my cheeks heating up, not knowing what sort of 'shit' he's referring to. *Did I drop my vibrator somewhere?* Considering the possibility of deciphering his meaning to be nearly impossible, I decide to focus on the other part. "I was never an interesting girl, Jonah. Sweet of you to say though."

"Yes, you were." He nods, reinforcing his statement. "But every guy was too scared to come within twenty feet of you because of your brother."

I stop dead in my tracks. "What?"

He looks at my face in bewilderment for a few moments, then bends over and starts laughing.

"Are you done?" I ask, annoyed.

He smacks his thighs before straightening. "You seriously didn't know?"

I shake my head.

"Oli, everyone was *terrified* of Mark, so you were never on anyone's radar. He didn't even need to be around you to fend all of your suitors off."

I blink. Then blink some more.

"No one wanted to invite me to prom because of Mark?"

"They were scared of him. He was so much older than anyone in school and larger than anyone's brother. Or father." He raises his brows. "I'm afraid that's probably why you didn't have a date to prom."

"Not because of—"

He comes to me and gives me a quick side hug. "No, Oli. It's not because of where or how you grew up. Plus, all those posh boys love taking a poor girl out, thinking she'll be so," he blinks at me comically, "grateful."

My throat squeezes, and the pyramid of my insecurities gets a steady shake. Here I was, thinking that no one wanted to be seen with trailer trash, and Jonah just changed my world.

"And the girls?" I ask hopefully.

He waves the thought off dismissively. "Just bitches. You and I were never good enough for them."

The cackle that comes from my mouth would make any

hyena proud. Jonah giggles too and motions for me to continue walking, pointing left and right at the storefronts.

There are a lot of new places around here. I didn't even know we had so many businesses, but again, I haven't been in Little Hope for a long time. I'm happy to see the town growing.

"Over there," he points farther down the street, "is where the PTSD center is. The town extended the road, and now people from there have a direct access to town. A lot of people work there too, you know." He wiggles his brows. "Over there," he nods at a big—in Little Hope sizes—building with a sign 'Ms. Leah's Yoga Studio,' "is your best clientele."

"We have a yoga studio?" I ask in astonishment, feeling my joints suddenly starting to hurt. I've tried yoga and quickly figured out I wasn't ready for that.

"Yep. And it's awesome. They even have a Bikram yoga lesson. Leah, the owner, can put you into a pretzel and then untangle you without damage to your back." He makes a *poof* gesture in the air.

"Impressive," I reply with a giggle, still withdrawing my joints into my body like a turtle.

"You have no idea. I can audition for Cirque du Soleil after six months with her. And the classes are always sold out." He finds my gaze and holds it. "*Always.* She's so popular that a few other towns come to her classes since there's not much yoga going on anywhere else. And every time, we talk about how nice it'd be to have some sweets with a nice cup of fancy coffee afterward. And not all of us want to go to Donna's place to become the hot center for fresh gossip. You dig me?"

Donna. My competition. The *other* coffee shop. Even though they sell coffee under a famous brand, everyone knows she's dealing her own roast under the table. They don't have freshly baked goods though. My research says they resell stuff from the store, and people are fed up with the plastic cupcakes, so they drive thirty minutes away to Springfield, a bigger neighboring town, to satisfy their sweet cravings.

Little Hope used to have a bakery back when I was still in school, but the woman owning it has retired and moved to Florida, and no one took over after her. I wish I could buy her old bakery because it would require pretty much zero renovations, but Jonah shut the idea down right away, saying I don't want to deal with the building violations and the building owner. Even though the bakery is a separate unit, the building still belongs to an old guy who likes to cause problems for residents. Jonah even mentioned it might turn out to be even more expensive than actually building a kitchen from the ground up any place else.

Donna's shop is also the center of the local gossip mill with her standing as its queen. If you happen to fall on her bad side, you're doomed in Little Hope to years of suffering. I've never been on the receiving end of her fury, but I have my suspicion that's about to change. I've heard the local sheriff and his wife from the big city who moved to Little Hope a couple years ago still haven't recovered from the rumors Mrs. Roberts, their neighbor, spread around town about her, and the juiciest details were discussed at Donna's shop.

"So, you want to tell me that this side of Little Hope is new people, and the other one is old?" I ask, trying to sum up his speech.

"New, young." He rolls his eyes dramatically. "Call it whatever you want. The fact is the town is changing. The center has attracted a lot of new people since it opened.

New people bring more people and more money. The town is growing and becoming—" he clicks his fingers, looking for the right word, "more than just a small little town in the middle of nowhere."

"Is that a good thing though?" I ask. Changes aren't always good. I know that for a fact.

He shrugs. "Doesn't matter since we can't stop it. But what we can do is shape it into somewhere everyone would love to grow old."

His speech is so passionate, it strikes a chord in me. "Jonah, you're a genius."

"I know." His face stretches with a mischievous smile.

"And you are totally manipulating me," I say.

"And you are totally letting me." His smile grows even wider. "Imagine your son going to school where he won't be bullied because we've built a society we want where people are happy, and bullying isn't tolerated."

My heart cracks open and starts bleeding. "I can see that." A look of understanding passes between us. Jonah, being the only gay—out-of-the-closet and brave—kid at school in a small town, was bullied. It was a different time, and thank God, we're becoming better than that. But he knows what bullying means. Just like I do. A girl from the wrong side of town, being raised by a brother whose single father was always drunk. Not a good recipe for popularity.

The moment feels almost a little too intense. Almost too intimate. I smile awkwardly, looking at my shoes before he grabs my hand and pulls me with him.

"There," he says quietly. He doesn't point, but he doesn't have to. I see it.

The place I'll build my business. The place I'll lay down roots for my dreams and hopes. It's a small two-story brick building with floor-to-ceiling windows on the first floor and small, white windows on the second.

The giant, red door is beautifully carved. I bet it's the original from when the building was first built. The windows have black steel rods on them as an extra security measure.

Jonah drags me toward the entrance and unlocks it.

"Welcome to your very own bakery," he announces with a sly smile.

I give him a side-eye. "You can sell water to a drowning man."

"Well, thank you," he chuckles, and gestures for me to go inside. "It used to be some sort of diner back in the forties, and then they changed it into an insurance agency, but all the hookups are still in the back. So it shouldn't be a problem to remodel."

He turns the lights on, and I find a beautiful, open space I can work with. We walk to the back of the first floor, and I see that Jonah is indeed right—the place needs an update, but I don't need to spend a fortune moving or upgrading plumbing, electrical, or gas lines.

"You know what the best part about this place is?" His voice turns gleeful.

My brows merge with my hairline—I can almost feel them meet. "This isn't the best part?"

He pauses, a smirk playing at his lips. "It has a one-bedroom apartment on the second floor."

My eyes widen. "Get the hell outta here!"

He starts laughing. "The couple who owns the place used to live there, but they moved to Springfield a few months back due to their business relocating. And it doesn't need much work for you guys to move in. It's dated, yes," he admits with a slight wince, "but very clean."

"Say no more." I raise my hand and gesture for him to lead the way.

Jonah was wrong.

The place is ready for us to move in. It doesn't need any updates—he didn't see the last place we lived in. Being a single mom, paying for childcare and a place in a safe neighborhood is challenging. I chose a safe place over anything else. We had a very small and outdated home, and we were fine with it. It was twenty minutes away from my work, and my neighbor was a wonderful lady who babysat Brodie while I was working.

Opening a place of my own was always my goal, and I worked for the past three years to gain the experience I would need to do it.

Until Brodie came. My life changed forever. He became my priority, and I had to postpone my dreams of opening my own place until sometime in the future.

And that time has finally come.

"I'll take it," I say, despite knowing it's out of my budget.

Jonah's face brightens. "You have exquisite taste."

"And you have a very sleek tongue."

"You have no idea." He winks, making me laugh as he starts explaining the details of the listing.

The price is higher. Much higher.

Jonah's expression falls as he sees concern written on my face. "I know it's more than your budget."

"A lot more," I agree, chewing on my lip again.

"A lot more." He winces. "But you'll be saving on rent. Think about it that way," he suggests. Rather helpfully, I must add, since it's a very good point. This way, I'll be paying for something of my own at least, and maybe— *maybe*—I can break even.

"I need to think about it and see if I can pull any funds

from somewhere," I say, even though my heart is slowly sinking into the pit of my stomach with a heavy dread of unavoidable failure.

I don't have any funds to pull from anywhere, including my ass because I've already pulled everything I could from there, so I don't know why I'm requesting extra time. Nothing will change tomorrow or in a week.

"Take your time. I won't show it to anyone for now." His voice turns soft.

"Jonah, you don't have to—"

He raises his hand, silencing me. "I can't think of anyone who'd bring this place more good than you. I'll wait to hear from you."

His kind words dig inside my chest and squeeze my heart. "Thank you," I whisper sincerely. "But you really don't have to."

"Don't worry about it." He waves his hand dismissively. "Now, let's go and see what's around here."

We make another round through the property and walk outside. The weather is crispy cold, and I'm glad I brought a warm jacket. Glancing at Jonah, I wonder how he's not shivering in only his suit. I'm sure it's pure wool, but still, it's very cold.

After walking around a bit and seeing the neighborhood again from a different point of view as a potential business owner—I still can't believe I might become one—we say goodbyes and drive away.

When I open the door to Mark's house, I find a scene that nearly makes me go back to give them more time. Mark is on all fours, crawling around the room making horse noises while Alicia is firmly holding Brodie on top of Mark's back, making clicking noises and encouraging Mark to move faster. Brodie's giggling with so much happiness, it nearly breaks my heart. This is the first time ever I wonder if I'm making the right decision by separating him from his father. A boy needs a man in his life. I can't do what Mark's doing right now, no matter how much I try. It will never be enough.

Nope, it's a moment of weakness. His father is rather a violent person; we're better off without him.

"Look who's here!" Alicia laughs as she lifts Brodie off Mark's back. "Mommy's already back."

When he notices me, I can almost see his face fall. Fun with Uncle Mark is undoubtably better than a hug from Mom. I take my kid from Alicia, chuckling at Brodie's unhappy face.

"He didn't run you into the ground, did he?" I ask as I press my nose into his cheek, inhaling his calming baby scent I've used for the past nine months as an antidepressant.

"Are you kidding me?" Mark rises to his feet. "This has been just what we needed."

"Baby fever?" I laugh.

"That too." He wraps his arm around Alicia's shoulder, snickering as he does. "How did it go?"

I sigh and plant my ass on the couch. "It's gorgeous. Ouch!" Brodie pulls on my earring, nearly taking my ear off. "And it also has a one-bedroom apartment that would have been perfect for us to move into."

"You don't have to move anywhere. You can live here as long as you need," Alicia says with a serious face, making me smile at her sincerity.

"Thank you, guys. I appreciate it," I reply softly. "But we need to go and start our own chapter."

"Are you sure?" Mark doesn't sound convinced. "Because we're happy to have you here. Plus, who'll be watching Brodie while you're at work?"

"I'll find a nanny. Someone reliable and nice. It shouldn't be a problem in Little Hope, right?"

Mark and Alicia share a look and burst out laughing. "Good luck with that. It's either one or the other."

I think for a moment before replying. "I can work with that." Brodie pulls on my hair, drawing my attention to him. Once I'm met with his big, bright blue eyes, my heart melts. "I think I'll go with the kind ones first."

"My mom is free!" Alicia exclaims enthusiastically. "I think she can babysit."

"No!" I cry out too fast and too loud, scaring Brodie who starts crying. "I'm sorry, baby." I show him a stuffed animal and start rubbing his back. "Mommy got too excited."

When he's calm, Alicia continues. "Why? You don't trust my mom?" A note of defensiveness makes me feel like shit.

"No, Alicia," I try smoothing my rude tone. "It's not that. Even though I've never actually talked to your mom, I'm sure she's great if she raised a person like you. I'm just —" *How can I lie?* "I just don't want to bother her. I'm sure she has a lot going on."

She waves me off, wrinkling her nose. "She has nothing. In fact, she's been complaining about being bored. I think Brodie is exactly what she needs."

I swallow a giant, dry lump in my throat that's been preventing me from taking a breath since the moment Alicia made her generous offer. Her mom watching my kid. Jake's mom. Just great. Freaking great.

"Okay." I smile weakly, giving up since refusing means offending my dear sister-in-law. "I'll talk to her."

Mark sends an odd look my way, then glances at Alicia and back to me. "How much is the deposit on the place?"

I cover my face with Brodie's stuffed animal and groan into it. "Hmfmfmf."

"I didn't get that, but my guess is it's a lot," comes Mark's voice after a short pause.

"Ye-e-es," I groan again. Without the stuffed animal this time. "It's all I have. If I put this money down, I won't have a cent to my name and won't be able to do any renovations or even buy any supplies. So basically, I'll have a useless space with a mortgage I can't pay for because I can't work because I don't have anything because I put everything into the deposit." I'm hyperventilating at the end.

"Okay, calm down," Mark calls out in the voice he uses on me when I go into panic mode. "We will lend you money for the renovation."

"Absolutely not." I forcefully shake my head, sending my hair flying around. "I will find a way."

"Oli," Mark starts, but I raise my hand, silencing him.

"I will find a way, Mark." My voice is firm. So is my belief about not disrupting their plans more than I already have. "You and me, we always do."

His eyes turn sad—we both know what I'm referring to. Growing up the way we did wasn't easy. You don't trust people and you don't accept their help because it always comes with a price. Always.

Chapter Four

E *leven years ago*

Olivia

Today is the first day of school, and I'll see Jake again. He didn't notice me last year because I was just a kid, so it doesn't count. This year, I'm different. I've grown. I've got boobs now. Tony from our trailer park noticed them too, but when he talks about them, he's gross. I don't like it. I'm sure Jake will be different, more respectful.

Everyone sees him as a player. Quite literally. The quarterback of the football team and quite a panty dropper. He took over after his brother Justin graduated. But I see something more in him. I think he's good and just needs someone to show him that. Of course, that person will be me.

"What are you wearing?" Mark asks from the kitchen. I was hoping to sneak out before he saw me, but it seems that's not going to happen.

"Clothes. What else does it look like?" I retort.

He points at me with a spatula. "Those aren't clothes. It's practically underwear."

I roll my eyes at his overreaction. Such a drama queen. Sure, I have a crop top that I cut myself, but only because I've outgrown most of my shirts and they fit weirdly now. At least this way I look a little stylish. Somewhat. I can't ask for new clothes; Mark would go out of his way for me, even though we can't afford it. Especially now when he's training to be a firefighter and his pay is low. But if I say that to him, he'll sacrifice something important and drag me to the store. I can't do that to him, he's running thin as it is.

Plus, we don't have insurance, so he paid for my braces out of pocket. That's the only thing I didn't fight—I know that good smiles get you further in life, and I intend to get away from Little Hope. The farther the better. The moon will be too close.

So I'll just pretend to be a rebellious teenager, like more than half of my school. Those who have that luxury. Kids in our part of town don't have luxury—we're just trying to survive day by day with the resources we were given.

"It's fine, Mark," I dismiss him. "It's what kids at school wear these days."

"They do?" He raises a brow and pointedly looks at my skirt, which is admittedly too short. I already made a mental note to myself not to bend over in public places.

"Yes, it's the fashion this year, which you know nothing about." I smile and jog over to give him a kiss since I've been busted anyway.

He leans over so I can reach his cheek. My brother is a giant, which is why no one messes with me around here.

"Where's dad?" I ask, grabbing a pancake he just made.

"Who knows." He shrugs. "Probably sleeping it off somewhere."

I sigh and take a bite. Sometimes I wish our father wasn't a mean drunk, that he would just say he loves us and take care of us. But our reality is different; he's a total dickhead who used to beat Mark until he grew big enough to scare him off. Now he just comes here to drink or to sleep it off. And he does it quietly most of the time.

"Okay, gotta go," I say, heading out.

"Cover your butt, Oli. For real. Wear a sweater around your waist or something."

"I will," I laugh as I grab the door handle, but it flies open into my face. "Ouch!" I start rubbing the sore spot.

"Oh, shit, sorry!" Kayla, our neighbor rushes in and heads to the fridge for a bag of peas. "Here, Oli." She winces. "I'm sorry."

"Don't worry about it." I press the bag to my forehead. Great, my first day at school and I'll have a bump between my eyes. A sure way for Jake to notice me. "Your mom has friends over again?"

She looks away and nods.

"You can chill in my room," I offer with a smile, knowing this is painful for her.

She nods and waves goodbye. I hand the bag of peas back and head outside.

Kayla has been coming to our house for a long time. I don't even know when it started. She's a few years older than me and lives with her mom and sister. Her mom loves to bring her handsy boyfriends to their house, so Kayla hides here. When they come looking for her, they meet Mark and walk right back. Sometimes she stays overnight. Sometimes, even a couple of days. She's like family at this point, and Mark and I both know what it means to have shitty parents. Or a shitty parent in both our cases.

When I ask Mark about Kayla's mom, he always warns me to stay away from her and their trailer because 'something shady is going on there.' I cackle at his response every time—there's always something shady going on around here, so it's not news. But he's convinced her trailer is even shadier than most. I don't know what he means by that because Kayla seems like a great person, and he doesn't seem to have a problem with her.

When I go to unlock my bike from the ramp, I notice a new man heading inside their trailer. He does look shadier than the previous ones. Looking around before stepping inside, he notices me watching him, and an uncertain feeling settles in my belly. I rush away from there, pretending I didn't pay him any attention.

I always ride my bike to school while it's still warm outside. It's a far drive up the hill, but it beats walking. When it's cold, Mark will drive me in before work. Hopefully he'll finish this training soon and can become a real firefighter. I can't imagine anyone who'd fit a role better than my brother. Larger than life and kinder than a warm hug when you're sick.

I don't have anyone I can call friends, but trailer kids usually stick together if it gets too 'hot.' We don't eat lunches together or join marching bands, but we're pretty tight-knit with a bunch of shitty neighbors.

"When are you getting rid of your braces?"

I turn toward the voice. Jonah's leaning his preppy self on the side of the school. I bet his father dropped him off here—he's never sweaty in the morning from trying to get to school.

"I don't recall us being buddies, Jonah." He hit a nerve, and I can't help the snark that comes out of me. I've been wearing braces later and longer than anyone else, giving the bullies another reason to have fun.

"Well," he shrugs his bony shoulders covered in his red turtleneck—not exactly the best thing to wear when you want to disappear, "you don't have many options." He probably notices my hackles rise because he lets out a pitiful laugh. "Neither do I."

I sigh and keep walking toward the school entrance. Students usually leave their bikes on the side of the building and go all the way around using the sidewalk. But this two-minute walk seems too long with Jonah on my heels, so I cut it short between the trees and the building to get rid of him as soon as possible. I don't know why he decided that we're friends because we're not. I'm a trailer kid, and his father owns houses around Little Hope and other places from what I've heard. The likes of me and him don't mingle. I bet his sweater costs more than our monthly rent.

"Olivia," he calls out when I walk too fast.

I stop and turn toward him. "Look, Jonah, I gotta finish school and get the hell away from Little Hope. I don't plan on ever coming back, and you and your red turtleneck," I point my index finger at his chest, "you'll inherit your daddy's empire."

"It's not like I'm asking you to marry me." He puffs, looking down at himself. "And my mom told me this makes my eyes pop."

I let out a resigned sigh, somewhat agreeing with him about the color—his eyes really look brighter today. "Friendships don't work long distance."

He snorts. "Bullshit."

I shrug and am about to walk away when someone yells, "Hey, you. Using daddy's money to buy yourself some trailer trash, Johnny boy?"

Go, Olivia. Just go.

"I'm talking to you, Little Johnny," Brad the asshole continues. His family spends a lot of time making big money. But they totally don't waste it on their ill-mannered son.

"My name is Jonah, Brad. And you know that." Jonah sounds offended, which is exactly what Brad wants because he moves toward him with a wicked, evil smile on his acne-covered face.

"Oh, yeah?"

Mentally smacking myself on the forehead for getting involved—again—in a battle that isn't mine, I stand next to Jonah.

"Go about your day, Brad," I warn him, crossing my arms over my chest.

He pauses for a moment before proceeding with his supposedly scary walk. He can fool everyone all he wants—he knows he doesn't scare me.

"Or what?" he asks, subtly glancing around to see if we have an audience. We don't, so Brad will most likely leave Jonah alone. For now.

I cock a hip and quirk a brow. "Really, Brad? You really want to go there?"

He sighs, dropping his shoulders along with the tough act. "Go about your business, Trailer Trash. I don't have beef with you."

"Don't call her that!" Jonah cries out at the same time I say calmly, "Tough luck because I've got some with you."

It's hard to offend me with name-calling. *You've got to do better than that.*

"Go. Away." Brad is visibly losing his cool.

"Not today, buddy." I drop my arms to my sides. "This is your last warning before we have a repeat of what happened in the summer."

His cheeks turn bright red in a matter of a few seconds, and I feel a curious stare on the side of my face. Brad looks around one more time and takes a step back.

"Whatever." He throws his hands in the air in annoyance. "I don't need to be seen with two losers."

After a long, disgusted look, he turns and leaves us alone.

"Hmm," Jonah hums, trying to draw my attention, which I choose to ignore.

"What happened during the summer?" He grabs my shoulder.

"Nothing. Bye," I say, turning around to leave. I can feel a ton of silent, heavy questions in the air, but he shuts his mouth, sensing my mood.

"Thank you!" he yells to my back, and I give him a thumbs-up with my back to him.

I could probably use a friend. I should talk to him about the summer when I kneed Brad in the balls when he tried taking my hard-earned money from selling homemade cookies. He thought he was stronger because he was older and almost twice as big. He turned out to be wrong. Girls from the trailer park know how to pack a punch.

But if I mingle with Jonah, I'll eventually want a lifestyle I can never have. So not now.

Voices grow louder as I approach the entrance to the school. The jocks are coming. Jake is coming.

I quickly fix my hair, pulling it over my shoulder so my chest is on full display. I push them out because he's bound to notice me and my newly grown feature, right? It doesn't matter that he's three years older than me. Lauren from my grade was thirteen and her boyfriend was fifteen when I caught them behind the bleachers kissing each other's faces off. He seemed to know what he was doing, so that's another positive.

The crowd is moving my way, and I move toward them. Jake's in the middle like one of the Greek gods Mrs. Levinston told us about in history class. So perfect and bright. Commanding the crowds. Shining under the rays of sun.

He's coming my way. He's almost here.

I put a sexy—or what I think is sexy—smile on my face and push my chest out even further. I lift my face so I can find him watching me, of course . . .

But he's not. Watching me, that is. Instead, his eyes are on Ashley's sister's boobs, another popular girl who took over after her sister.

Well, today is not my day.

And the next day wasn't either. Or any other day for the next four years.

Jake graduated school and moved to Boston for college. Out of sight, out of mind.

He was my first crush, and he taught me a valuable lesson—I'm not good enough for the good boys of Little Hope. Maybe I'm good enough for the bad ones.

Chapter Five

J**ake**

I've been avoiding this day for a long time.

Today is the day I visit my parents.

I don't own or rent a place in Little Hope because it makes no sense. I barely spend any time there anyway.

I park my truck in front of the house without taking a spot in the driveway. I'll be leaving soon. I know things will go downhill the moment Justin arrives. He still hasn't forgiven me for nearly ruining his chances with Kayla, his now fiancé. I can't blame him, but I had my reasons. What's done is done. A giant snowball of actions and reasons has led me where I am now, and there's not much I can do to change that. I sleep in the bed I made. Alone. And I don't think that will change.

"Jakey, is that you?" Mom calls from the kitchen as soon as I open the door.

"Yeah," I call back.

"Come over here. We're just waiting for you," she scolds loudly.

Of course, I managed to mess up even being on time. I check my watch—I'm twenty minutes early. *Here we go.*

I walk toward the dining room where everyone's already around the table. Justin is hugging Kayla as she leans into him, both looking happy and content in each other's arms, and I feel a pang of guilt deep in my chest. I quickly look away.

Mark and Alicia are in a similar pose across from them. My dad is at the head of the table, and there are two empty spots available to me since Mom will take the other end of the table—one next to Justin and one next to Alicia. I choose the one next to Alicia. Always.

The moment Justin sees me, daggers fly my way with his glare. I ignore them. It's not his fault things are the way they are, but I think I'm past any redemption, so I just quietly take it, not wishing to get involved in any quarrels.

"Hello, everyone," I say as I take a seat.

"Hey," Alicia and Mark reply—the latter is less enthusiastic—followed by a polite "Hi, Jake" from Kayla, and nods from Dad and Justin. I've become a disappointment to my father ever since I was fired from the police force. Well, I was sent on leave, but everyone knows what that entitles.

"How have you been, Jakey?" Alicia asks, putting her hand on my forearm. I don't think anyone touches me of their own free will like this unless it's her or my mom. They're probably the only ones who still have faith in me— even when I don't.

"Good. You?" I reply, feeling uncomfortable. There's not much to say about myself.

"Good too. Been busy. Like, good busy." A warm smile

lightens her face. Alicia was always a ray of sunshine growing up, until that night. We thought we lost her to the darkness for good, but then Mark came into the picture. I was wrong about him. He's the only one who could pull her out of that bad place she'd been in. I owe Mark, and I'll be happy to take all the nasty looks he sends my way for as long as I live.

"How so?"

"Mark's sister and her son are staying with us for now until she can find her own place."

I pick up the glass of water in front of me and take a sip. "A hard task to do in Little Hope," I comment, smirking.

"True," she agrees easily. "She found this cute place though, a bit off Main Street."

"Yeah?" I ask, feigning interest.

She nods. "But I don't think she'll get it."

"Why?"

"Too expensive," Mark chimes in when no one asked him to.

"And she won't take money from us," Alicia adds.

"Do you know why?" Kayla inquires from across the table while refilling Justin's glass with Mom's lemonade.

"When she first arrived, we mentioned that we're saving for an addition. She doesn't want to take that away from us," she explains, shrugging sadly. "I'd give it to her in a heartbeat though. You guys should see Brodie—he's adorable. The poor kid has been recovering from horrible pneumonia." She sighs. "I feel so bad for Oli."

My ears perk up. Oli and Brodie who's recovering from pneumonia. What are the odds they're the same Olivia and Brodie I met in the parking lot of that random motel?

"What about a loan?" Dad suggests.

"She'll figure it out," Mark cuts off any further discussion about his sister's business—a move I respect.

"She will," Alicia agrees, starting to serve herself.

The conversation is flowing, thankfully leaving me out. They chat about Little Hope, someone's new baby, and the running joke about Kayla not setting up a wedding date, despite being engaged for about four or five years, I think. Then Alicia announces they're going to try to have a baby too.

Everyone's life is moving on but mine.

"Alicia," I whisper to her.

"Yeah?" she replies in the same half-whispered tone.

"I've got some money saved. You can lend it to Mark's sister."

She gives me a long look. "She won't take it from you. She's very independent."

"Tell her it's from your family budget or something. I won't miss it, and that way you won't be hurting either. It's a win-win."

She considers this for a moment. "Why?"

"What do you mean, why?" I return her stare.

"Why do you want to help?"

Et tu, Brute?

I clench my jaw, struggling to control my emotions. "Forget about it," I say, shoving tasteless food into my mouth.

"Jake," her voice softens, "I'm just proud of you, you know."

I keep chewing silently.

"I'd love to accept your help," she continues, knowing I'll be mute for the rest of the evening now. "Oli is such a wonderful woman, and I'll be happy we can help her."

I nod without looking at her. She takes it as the end of our conversation, lets out a loud sigh, and rejoins the table's conversation. Everyone else continues to ignore me. Mom tries to engage with me a few times but gives up after short, one-word answers.

That evening, I transfer the money to Alicia's account.

Chapter Six

O livia

"I just got an extra signing bonus, that's all," Alicia explains when I ask where she's suddenly gotten so much extra money. Her eyes dart to the side every time she repeats her answer, but she's gotten better at meeting my eyes. I know something is shady.

"Are you sure?" Beggars can't be choosers, and I'm at the point of being a beggar. But still, I have to make sure they won't be hurting lending me the money. I already tried a loan, but without any assets, my business plan wasn't met with as much enthusiasm as I expected. Turns out, banks tread a fine line with new ventures. Who knew life could be such a disappointment?

"Yes, I'm sure," she laughs, filling the kettle with water.

I sink back in my chair with relief. By now, I'd given up on the idea of opening a bakery and owning an apartment and even told Jonah that. He offered to loan me money too, but I feel weird taking it from an almost stranger. Yeah, yeah, I know it sounds hypocritical, but Jonah is a different sort of stranger than a bank. Despite how much he likes to act like one sometimes.

"I'll wire you the money so you can go to Jonah and sign that contract before someone else snatches the place." Her eyes shine with mischief.

A small feeling of hope starts blooming in my chest, and Brodie must feel it because he starts giggling. "Am I getting the bakery of my dreams?" I whisper.

"You're getting the bakery of your dreams!" Alicia jumps, clapping.

"I'm getting the bakery!" I grab Brodie and join Alicia.

A second later, Mark finds us just like that when he returns from his shift, jumping in the kitchen like happy maniacs.

"What's going on?" he asks as he drops his backpack on the floor.

"Oli's getting her own bakery!" Alicia announces loudly.

He quickly glances at her, which looks a bit . . . *odd* if I'm honest. "Is she?"

"Yep." Alicia's tone changes, and I feel weirdness thickening the air.

I suddenly feel like a third wheel. The suspicion that Alicia's giving me money they can't spare starts creeping on me. "Guys, if that's a problem—" I let it trail off.

"No, no. You're getting your bakery." When Mark sees my doubt, his whole demeanor changes from suspicious to caring. "C'mere." He opens his arms, and I walk into them with Brodie clinging to my chest. "I'm so proud of you," he says, giving me a gentle squeeze.

"Thank you." My nose tingles. Mark has practically raised me; he's a brother, mother, and father all in one, and to hear him say he's proud of me means more than I could imagine.

The next day, I load Brodie into the car and head to meet Jonah. Mark and Alicia asked me to leave my son with them, but Mark has a day off, and they need to spend some time together without extra people in the house. Despite how much they love my baby, they need to make their own, which is impossible while we're in the house, and they're sleeping on the couch in the living room. We've taken too much of their time and space as it is.

I'd be lying if I say I don't occasionally glance at the people on the sidewalks, hoping and dreading to see Jake at the same time. We finished on such a bad note when it shouldn't have been like that. I don't know what I'll do if I see him, but I know I have to reach out to him at some point to thank him again for helping me.

But Jake is nowhere to be seen, of course. I learned from Alicia that he doesn't live in Little Hope anymore, so I shouldn't be so anxious driving around town. Still, I keep imagining Jake's swagger and crooked smile. His ever-present sunglasses on his nose, which only add to the enigma of the asshole if I'm honest.

Jonah's office is located on one of the side streets, two blocks down from my soon-to-be building. Many little authentic small-town offices spread throughout the whole area, and the atmosphere here feels different from the rest of Little Hope. It almost feels how Jonah was describing in his vision of the perfect town.

I climb out of my car and look around. After a few days with Jonah, I'm not surprised he didn't take one of the larger buildings on Main Street for himself—he seeks authentic, small-town charm, even within a small town.

The door of his office flies open, and he steps outside, waving me in. "Come inside. It's so cold."

I grab Brodie's car seat and walk inside. "I thought you don't feel cold."

He shudders and shuts the door. "I'm always freezing, that's why I always have fleece undies on."

I raise my hand in front of me. "TMI, Jonah. Totally TMI."

"P-p-please." He rolls his eyes. "There's nothing there that will interest you."

"Thank goodness because from now on I will always be imagining your sweaty . . ." I point my finger at his lap, and his eyes follow it, "jewels."

"They are no—" He stops himself with a chuckle. "You know what, never mind." He walks closer and leans toward Brodie. "Hey, little man! I was wondering when I'd meet you."

Brodie makes a spit bubble and gives him a funny smile with his four teeth.

"You're just adorable! And I don't say that lightly." His voice drops. "I don't like your kind, but you seem to be alright."

I let out an involuntary snort and walk to Jonah's office. "He's not an alien."

"Might as well be. All his proportions are," he wrinkles his nose, "off."

I roll my eyes. "He's a baby."

"Doesn't change that fact," he says, raising a finger in the air.

"I see your charm hasn't changed," I deadpan.

He cackles. "Why waste it on you?"

"Your sales pitch is lacking."

He waves me off. "You're already sold," he says with laughter, making me join him too. Sometimes Jonah can be ridiculous. It's one of the reasons he couldn't find many friends—his sense of humor.

We sign all the papers, and I transfer the money to his firm's account right away, mentally thanking Alicia for what she's doing for us. The mortgage papers have been ready for a few days now—I've been hoping to figure out where I could find the money—so we call my adviser, and everything is fixed within a couple of hours.

I have to step into the bathroom to change Brodie's diaper and warm up his formula, and while I do so, Jonah is surprisingly willing to help despite him thinking that kids are aliens. Which is true, to a certain point.

When we get back to his dark mahogany desk, we finish what's left, and Jonah pulls the drawer open and produces the keys. I look at him with wide eyes.

"What are those?"

"Your keys." He pushes them toward me with a soft smile.

"Already?" I blink at him in confusion.

"Usually the deed needs to be recorded before I give you the keys, but," he looks around his empty office, "I trust you."

"Are you sure?" My voice drops to match his. "Because I can wait a couple of hours."

"It's fine. Go to your new home, homeowner."

I feel my face stretch into a wide, stupid smile. Rising to my feet, I walk toward Jonah and give him a hug.

"Thank you for everything."

"Don't mention it." He squeezes me back and steps away. "I'll stop by at some point if you don't mind." Averting his eyes, he adds almost shyly, "Could be the second chance at friendship, you know?"

"That'd be great, Jonah."

He looks at me sheepishly and smiles with a short nod. I take Brodie in his car seat and walk back to my car. My steps are light and eerie. This is what I've been working toward. Sure, I didn't plan to stay in Little Hope, but I also didn't plan to be a single mom. Life throws curveballs sometimes, and when it does, you just have to make the right move to catch it.

In what feels like no time, I'm parked in front of the building I now own. Is this what Mark felt when he held the keys to his house? Because this feels freaking amazing.

I look at the building in front of me and see the future. I see a little hope.

———

The next few days are a blur. Mark helps me move my stuff from their garage to my new place, and Alicia and her friend Josie help me clean it up. Josie is an interior designer or a house engineer—I haven't quite grasped it yet—and she seems to know a great deal about houses and everything related to them. It takes her a whole two minutes to find me a contractor who can help me fix the little things when Mark is too busy, and five more minutes to find me furniture since we have nothing. This place came with some stuff, but it's not enough. Especially with a kid.

Josie called her friend Freya who has two kids and a lot of stuff she could pass on to the next mom: me. Josie herself has twin girls but said all their stuff is too pink and girly. I don't doubt that—Josie is like a brunette Marilyn Monroe, stylish and feminine.

Soon, her husband, Kenneth, arrives to help with some things because she threatened him violence if he didn't. I'm sure the local sheriff has better things to do, but I'm not going to voice that. I'll take all the help I can get.

In all my life, I never thought Kenneth Benson, the local somewhat royalty would be in my kitchen cleaning the tile, but here he is. And it's because of Mark. I see how respectful the sheriff is to my brother, and my heart swells with pride. I've always known how awesome he is, and I'm happy now that everyone else sees it. I pause unboxing my dishes to glance at the bustling people and notice that here, right now, no one cares where we came from or what we've been through. All they see is us, and I couldn't have wished for more. This is how I've wanted Brodie to grow up.

My eyes dart to Alicia who's sending loving stares at my brother as she cleans the window in the living room. He reciprocates them when he thinks she isn't looking. It's adorable. My heart swells for a second time, this time with gratitude toward Alicia for what she has done for my brother.

Once all the moving is done, we spend our first night in our new home. And it feels good.

Brodie falls asleep right after I put him in his new bed that Mark made specifically for him. I was worried he'd be anxious in a new place, but he seems to have taken to the place right away.

When I lay my tired body onto the bed—*my* bed—my eyes well, and I feel tears falling down my cheeks. I don't wipe them. I don't want to. Because these are tears of exhaustion and happiness representing what belongs to me now, and I'll cry as much as I need to make this place our home.

Brodie and I will be fine.

Chapter Seven

Olivia

A couple days later, I'm working on little things in the bakery when I hear Jonah's quiet voice calling out from outside.

"Hey."

"Hey," I greet him with a warm smile, wiping my hands on a towel.

He looks a bit sheepish. Even his cheeks are pink. Maybe it's from the cold, but something tells me he's unsure about something.

"The place's looking good," he finally says.

"Thank you." I glance around, feeling proud of what we've done so far with the help of literally everyone. I'm putting finishing touches of paint on the trim above the cashier, and that's about it. The next stage is to order all the supplies and start baking. I wanted to order them earlier, but I wasn't sure everything was working properly and didn't want the food to spoil. Stinky butter sitting in a fridge for weeks doesn't make a perfect cream.

"Can I help with something?" he offers suddenly, stunning us both.

I blink at his three-piece gray suit. "Hmm, I mean, if you're not scared to get your really awesome suit dirty."

"I've got plenty of them." He walks to me, taking off the jacket and vest and hanging them over a clean chair. Then he proceeds to roll up his sleeves like he's about to get really dirty. "Put me where you want me."

I quirk a brow. "Why this sudden desire to help?"

He bites his lower lip while his brows draw in concentration. When he finally speaks, his voice is quiet but firm. "You were the only one who made my life in school bearable. So take it as a form of gratitude."

"Me?" My brows shoot into the stratosphere. "Jonah, I was a jerk to you, refusing your friendship. I don't see how that was helping."

He shifts his attention from the chair in front of him to my face. "You know what I mean."

Why does that sound like a question?

"A little emo gay was even less popular than folks from the trailer park." The corner of his lips lifts up in an unsure smile.

"Ouch." I wince. "But that's also true, I guess. I bet your life sucked."

His chuckle is sad. "You have no idea. You sometimes sitting with me during lunches was the highlight of my day."

How different our lives were back then, yet how similar.

"I've always liked you, Jonah. For being brave and," I scrunch my nose in concentration, looking for the right word, "very persistent."

"That's me." He smiles with pride.

I smile back sadly. "I just couldn't afford to have anything to tie me down to Little Hope."

"Because you were planning to leave?" he asks with understanding.

I nod.

"And now you're back."

I shrug. "Values change with the growth of wisdom."

He cackles like a hyena with a stuffed nose and walks past me to pick up my brush. "I've always wanted to paint houses. Find something else for yourself to do because this task is mine. I'm about to live my dream."

"You're so bossy," I say to his back with an open smile. He graces me with a raised middle finger.

"Everyone likes it."

Laughing, I put some music on, and we work for some time until the little bells of the dreamcatcher on top of the entrance door start their soft symphony.

I rise from behind the counter and freeze. In the doorway of my not-yet-officially-opened bakery is Jake. He has a blond beard without a single streak of white in it. It's more even and trimmed than when I saw him at the motel. His slightly sunken cheeks somehow make him look dangerous. The leather jacket he has on can't possibly protect him from the cold temperatures outside, and his signature aviator Ray-Bans perched on his nose are totally not needed indoors. But I can't imagine him without them. They're a part of the screen which separates him from the rest of the world.

"Oh." A loud sigh comes from the cashier area where Jonah has seemingly just lost his jaw on the floor. The paint is slowly dripping from the brush in his hand onto the same spot next to his jaw.

Jake must have heard the loudest sigh in the universe—because I'm sure Freya, living deep in the woods of Maine, heard it too—and turns toward Jonah. The moment Jake notices him, his posture changes. It turns rigid as his shoulders draw back. His lips thin, making his jaw pop even more.

"I didn't know you had someone here," he announces, taking a small step back. I take a step forward.

"Wait," I say, because I know he's about to run away, and for some inexplicable reason, I want him to stay and at least tell me why he's here.

He pauses, glancing between me and Jonah with an unspoken question in his eyes. Jonah, being a good sport, jumps to his feet and rushes toward the back staircase—the house is built that way so I can get to my apartment without going outside.

"I gotta get a new brush. I'll be back," he says loud enough for the folks on Main Street to hear.

In the awkward silence, we both watch him quickly disappear to the back. When there's nothing else to look at, I shift my gaze to Jake. He doesn't know what to do with his hands and sticks them in the front pockets of his jeans. I try to do the same.

But *crappy crap*, I don't have jeans. I'm wearing leggings with no pockets, so I awkwardly wipe the invisible dust away from my thighs and cross my arms over my chest. The pose makes me instantly closed off and a bit insecure. But this is how I'm bound to feel around Jake now.

We start talking at the same time.

"Look, Jake—"

"I'm sorry."

I freeze.

"What?" I ask, stunned.

He licks his lips before speaking. "I'm sorry for the way I reacted the last time we spoke." He rolls on his heels, looking like a fish out of water.

I feel a bit of embarrassment for myself when I remember how I was the one who ruined the good thing we had going with the coffee. "I should apologize for bringing it up."

"You told the truth," he says nonchalantly with a shrug. "No need to apologize for that."

I watch his face. "I still do." And there, right there, again, I see that Jake doesn't know how to be on the receiving end of an apology or gratitude. I might have been the closed-off one in the beginning, but the tables have turned. He looks like he's about to bolt. Maybe he knew kindness before, but he's forgotten about it. An invisible needle pinches my chest.

I drop my arms to my sides with a small sigh of defeat.

An awkward nod in return is all I get. His chest extends with a big inhale, and suddenly his shoulders aren't so rigid anymore. He pulls his hands out of his pockets as he starts glancing outside, clearly looking for an escape route.

"So, you're the new baker," he states the obvious while still staring out the window.

"Yep." I blow a lock of hair off my face. "And you get a full year of free baked goods."

His rough chuckle is totally unexpected. For the both of us. For him, because his eyes widen as if he didn't know he still could make that sound, and for me because the sound just ran through my body and settled in the pit of my belly. *Motherfucker.*

"Tempting." His lips stretch in a crooked smile—one I'm very familiar with. Well, teenage Oli was familiar with because she'd been dreaming about that wicked smile for years.

"Then it's settled." I clap my hands like a child, making his lips twitch. "You can stop by every morning when we open, and I'll save you a cheese Danish." I realize my slipup too late because his eyes widen before narrowing suspiciously.

"How do you know those are my favorite?"

I swallow, feeling my cheeks turning pink. "We went to school together."

"Yeah." He licks his lips again, and like an addict, my eyes follow the movement. "About that. I still don't remember you, and I know I would. Did you really go to school with me?"

"Well." I move the lock of my hair behind my ear because I suddenly feel nervous and out of place. "I was from the trailer side, so no wonder you didn't notice me. And I had giant braces for like fifty years. So I might look a little different," I explain, pushing a tiny speck of dust with my foot on the floor.

Jake ignores my self-pitying. "How many grades younger were you?"

"Three."

"I see." His eyes widen again, and he quickly scans the room. "Where's the little man?"

A ping of pleasure every mother feels when someone inquires about her child nearly makes me woozy. "With Alicia."

His brows shoot up. "My sister, Alicia?"

"Yeah. She and Mark have been trying to steal him away from me."

His face lightens out of nowhere. "I can see that happening. Alicia has been—" He cuts himself off before he says something I'm probably not privy to hear. "I'm glad she found Mark."

"Or Mark found her," I say with a gentle smile, because they are just good for each other.

The corner of his lips lifts up again. "Or that."

A sudden awkward silence follows as we look at each other without knowing what to say next. We've talked about my kid, school, and the bakery. Now what? Weather and books?

He gathers himself first and takes a step backward.

"Anyway, glad you're in town." He turns around and heads toward the door.

My feet move on their own accord. I don't even understand how I find myself grabbing his arm.

"Jake."

He stops and turns around. I'm so close that I can feel the height difference. I have to lift my head to see his face. He's silently waiting for me to talk without trying to pull his arm away.

A giant lump in my throat prevents me from speaking normally. "Thank you. Really." I swallow the sudden tears down. "I know what happened here. I know things can change."

His intense blue eyes are trained on me. His nostrils flare as his jaw clenches tight. Then he carefully pulls his arm away from my grip and steps outside without a single word.

"Holy motherfucking shit!" comes a very loud hiss from the general area of the back stairs.

I turn toward the voice and find Jonah peeping around the wall. His eyes are round.

"What?"

He looks around, making sure the coast is clear, and

walks toward me, pretending like he's wiping his forehead with the back of his hand.

"What do you mean 'what'? Jake talked to you. Like actually talked, without being a moron or a dick. I didn't even know he had it in him anymore." He rushes to the window and peeks outside, not even pretending to be discreet. "I think I just got pregnant a little."

I chuckle. "What are you talking about?"

He gives me a long look. "You know what else we have in common? Besides being outcasts as kids and all that?" He waves his hand between us.

"I don't," I say, rolling my eyes, "but I'm sure you'll tell me."

He blinks a few times before talking. "We both have a crush on the Big Bad Wolf of Little Hope."

At his words, my cheeks instantly heat up, and I feel the color creeping up my neck, so I quickly busy myself with tidying up whatever I can find. "I have no idea what you're talking about."

"Sure you don't," Jonah replies meaningfully, and goes back to painting while fanning his face. "So hot in here, oh. I might need to visit more often."

Chapter Eight

J^{ake}

Why the fuck did I go to the bakery when it's not even open?
I keep asking myself as I walk to my truck. And what the
hell am I even doing in Little Hope today on my own free
will? I wasn't summoned to a family dinner. Nor was I
summoned by Kenneth to deal with yet another problem
I've caused without even knowing it.

And yet, here I am, bright and early. Walking like a
fucking peacock, fresh out of a shower and with a new hair-
cut. I even trimmed my beard, for fuck's sake. I barely
remembered how to do it, and after a few tries, I had some
luck in the end.

When I stepped inside, I stumbled over my own feet for
a moment. Because I saw her. She's a beautiful woman,
don't get me wrong. But I've seen beautiful women before.
I've been with them. That's not it. She was standing there in

black leggings and a thin brown sweater, with paint splatters everywhere, including her right cheek. Her hair piled up on top of her head in something awfully messy but insanely cute.

I nearly spit when I catch myself on the word 'cute.' That's not my style. I don't do *that*.

The bakery was still a mess with paint jars and brushes everywhere, construction materials on the floor, and an unfinished mural on the window. But despite all of it, the place looked cozy. Like there might be things that need to be done, but the main features are there. The core of everything that holds it together. The soul. The woman herself. I've never been known to look into deeper meanings, but my past taught me to seek something else in life. I think Olivia found it. And I think I might be attracted to her like a moth to the light because of it.

But she reminded me not to get my hopes up. In case I've fucking forgotten what I am for a moment.

A villain. She sees me as one too.

What else did I want to hear, dumbass? A hero? Helping a woman once doesn't make someone a hero. I guess it was wishful thinking of me wanting someone to see me differently. At first, I thought she didn't know who I was, so maybe—*maybe*—I could start something new. Make a friend or something more, I don't fucking know. But I was quickly reminded that ship sailed a long time ago, and now faith just plays tricks on me.

Then, as another kick to the nuts, I find out she's Mark's sister. I know he tolerates my presence for Alicia's sake, but we all know he hates me. There's no way any friendship between me and her will ever exist while Mark is her brother. And I don't see this changing anytime. So I just need to forget about it and move on. Trying to find my own light is hard, and it might not be worth it in the end. She evoked some interest in me, but looking into the impossible future, I just need to forget about it.

"Jake?"

Fuckin' great. Just when I'm about to run away from this town as I've been doing for the past couple of years, my brother somehow spots me.

I don't have another choice but to stop and wait for him to catch up—there's no way I'm walking toward him. This conversation isn't welcome. So hopefully he gets offended and turns around, leaving me in peace.

He doesn't. Once he reaches me, he stops to rock on his heels, looking all types of doubtful. A disgusting look on his face.

"What?" I bark, because it's my default setting of talking to people, especially my brother.

"Can we talk?" He sounds even more unsure than he looks.

"We're talking," I state the obvious.

Completely ignoring my sarcasm, he looks to the side, where someone's calling his name, and waves at them in return with a weak smile. "Talk somewhere where no one will hear."

That can't be good.

"Alright," I say with a sigh. "I can stop by your shop in a few minutes."

"Cool." He nods. "I'll grab us coffee from Donna's."

Holy shit, this is not going to end well for me if he's planning to get me coffee. Unless it's poisoned.

I walk to my truck and drive to Justin's auto shop. He owns the only one in town, and it's gotten so popular that neighboring towns bring their cars here to fix them. He's doing good for himself.

His truck isn't here yet, meaning Donna's keeping him busy with the local gossip. I used to go there for my favorite blend she roasts right in the back, and I was her favorite Little Hope golden boy. But I haven't been there in months, so I'm sure my spot has been filled. Especially considering how unhappy she was to see me the last time I showed my face. It might have had something to do with my attitude since I had a horrible hangover that day and wasn't particularly pleasant. Donna can take a lot of my shit, but even she was fed up with me.

I'm mindlessly scrolling through my phone when I feel someone's stare on me. My blood always turns cold in cases like this for multiple reasons. I slowly lift my head, dreading what I might find.

But I find a big head poking from the side of the building where Justin has his shop set up. The damn moose the locals named Frank. A weird creature, and I've never gotten their fascination with him. I mean it's a moose, and we live in Maine. They're like squirrels around here.

So I go back to scrolling only to find that the intensity of the stare doesn't subside. Quite the opposite. It's like he's watching me even more thoroughly now he knows I'm aware of him.

I look at him with a sigh—the giant thing's still watching me from the side of the building, and his stare is judgmental.

Am I really going down that road? Rolling my eyes to myself, I go back to my phone, purposefully ignoring him. I won't be one of those people who make him out to be the local saint.

The damn moose watches me until Justin rolls his truck in and parks behind me. He comes to my car and knocks on the window.

"I see you've got some issues with Frank," he says, cackling.

I step outside, silently shooting them both a death glare that makes Justin laugh even louder.

"Let's go to my office. We should be fine there."

I follow him to the back of the building, past the stares of people who work here. I remembered he started with just two guys, and now it's like five or six.

When we get to his office, he gestures for me to sit and places a to-go cup in front of me. "Donna's personal blend. Black. No sugar."

I raise a brow. "Did you spit in it?"

He rolls his eyes and sits in his chair, smirking.

"Did she spit in it?" I keep probing.

He laughs with a twinkle in his eyes. "It'd only make it better."

It's rather humorous, and I know he's about to ask something really big. I take a sip of Donna's divine roast I've missed so much and put the cup on the table. "Spill, Justin."

He rolls his lips and looks to the side and then back at me. "I want to marry Kayla."

My brows go up. "And you need my blessing for that?"

"No, dipshit." His forehead wrinkles with concentration. "I asked her to marry me four and a half years ago."

"And?" I still don't know where this is going.

"And she accepted, but she won't set a date." His shoulders sag in defeat.

I lean back in my chair, not following his line of thinking. "And how do I play into that?"

He lifts his head and catches my eyes. His are intense and dark. And full of pain. My brother is full of fuckin' pain, and it feels like I'm the one responsible for that. He must be really desperate to have this conversation with me, so I feel obliged to do anything he'll ask before he even asks the question.

"I think she's stalling because of you."

"Me?" I rear back. I mean, I know I've been an asshole to her, but it was in the past, and I'm trying to be civil around her. How would I play into her refusing Justin? I'm not even in town anymore.

"Yes." His voice is gravelly. "Maybe she hasn't forgiven you since you've never actually, you know, apologized. And you're my brother." His voice drops at the end as if he's ashamed of it. Well, that's just another level of low for me. "So maybe she doesn't want to become a part of this family, you know?"

I know.

"What do you want me to do?"

He blinks as if I'm stupid. "Apologize to her."

"Do you really think my apology will change something?"

He leans back in his chair, puffing out air from his mouth. "I'm desperate, man. I'll take anything. Everyone's getting married and having babies, and we're stuck in the same place we've been for years."

"Have you tried talking to her?"

He covers his face with his hands. "I can't believe I'm talking about this with you of all people," he mumbles through his palms. "But yes, I have. And every time she says it's not the right time and lets just enjoy it and all that." After a loud groan, he drops his hands and looks at me. "Please, Jake. Just try."

Seeing his agony and true feelings toward Kayla, I can't believe I was blind enough to nearly ruin their relationship.

"I'll try." My promise is firm.

He lets out a loud sigh of relief. "Thank you."

I nod, grab my coffee because I'm not wasting this divine drink, and walk to my truck. Looks like I'll be staying a couple of days here—I sure as fuck need to get myself together before I meet Kayla head-on to do what Justin asked.

I pull my phone from my pocket and contemplate if I should call Emma from the B&B and ask for a room or call my parents and try to be a son.

After a heavy sign, I click 'dial.'

The *"Hello?"* comes after two rings.

"Hey, Mom."

Chapter Nine

J**ake**

It's been twenty-four hours since Justin asked me to talk to Kayla, and I found five hundred things to help my mom and dad with around the house, just so I can procrastinate and avoid the heaviest load.

I haven't taken a sip of alcohol for two days. A bottle or glass of beer at a bar are usually my evenings buddies, but it seemed wrong to get shitfaced before I came here, all shiny and shit, and then it seemed kind of fucked up to do it under my parents' roof when they're already disappointed in me beyond any measure.

But today, a drink of courage is much needed, and I can't keep hiding here.

After a long, hot shower, I towel dry myself and stare at the mirror. I look older. Older than twenty-nine. A frown line between my eyebrows for some unexplainable reason makes the bags under my eyes heavier.

I don't bother trimming or shaving my beard. No need. I'm not here to impress anyone. Not anymore. So I quickly dress and head outside.

"Jakey, where are you going?" Mom calls out from the living room where they're working on a puzzle together. They've been doing that for as long as I can remember.

"For a walk, Mom," I call back, totally lying. They won't be happy if I say I'm going to the bar to drown my sorrows in alcohol, probably getting into a fight in the process to let go of this all-consuming anger.

"Alright, honey. We won't be waiting up."

"Okay," I reply, even though I don't know why they'd need to wait for me.

I drive to the bar, thinking that if I need to get wasted, Rory will take my keys, and I'll just walk home. I don't worry about myself, but I don't want to kill anyone because of reckless drunk driving. I'm not planning to get shitfaced because I need to be coherent for the talk, but you never know.

I forgot how busy Cat and Stallion can get on a Friday night. When I lived here, it was a regular small-town bar. But times change, and so does this place. Since the PTSD center was opened around five years ago, I think, the bar gets busy nearly every night. I used to be one of those regulars.

The music and chatter washes over me the moment I open the door. Rory, the bartender, quirks a brow when I walk toward her and take one of the few empty seats at the bar.

"Haven't seen you here in a while," she starts as she places a glass in front of me.

"Yeah."

"Your usual?"

"Yeah."

She pours me a double, neat whiskey and leans over the counter. "Be a good boy and don't make me call the nice sheriff today."

"Yes, ma'am." I nod with a weak smile.

She taps her fingers on the counter, waiting for me to finish my glass so she can pour me another one right away per the established tradition, but I shake my head. Her brown brow shoots up.

"Really?"

"Need a clean head today."

She gives me a pitiful look. "A bit late for that, Jakey." With that, she departs to serve another person, leaving me alone with her words.

A bit late for that. Isn't she right? Everything is a bit late. I know, on a bigger scale, it's worth it in the end. I know it. But it's gotten too hard.

"Rory, do you have lotion? My hands are so dry, and I forgot mine at home," says the woman I expected to see here the least, coming from the corridor where the bathroom is and stumbling once she sees me.

Her hair falls over her shoulders in soft waves. She's wearing black skinny jeans and a thin, green sweater. Too thin for weather like this. Especially when she's feeding a kid. Is she feeding the kid? Are cold and feeding related? My eyes drop to her chest, and then I notice that it was uncontrolled. I quickly avert my eyes from her body to her face. She's smiling shyly. Fuckin' *shyly*. So far, I've only seen her as a mother bear protecting her cub and someone trying to be grateful. But not shy. I didn't even know she knew how to do 'shy.'

I feel my whole body go rigid, and the need to throw a glass back in one go is rapidly getting stronger.

"Hi." Her voice is higher than I remember.

I nod in response and stare back at my glass, figuring out how I can make it last.

"Here." Rory appears out of nowhere and pushes a tube of lotion over the counter toward Olivia.

"Thanks!" She grabs it and squeezes the lotion on the back of her hand. Then she starts spreading it over both her hands. With a massage. A slow and thorough massage.

Fuck me. This is the most inappropriate thought at the most inappropriate time. I probably need to get laid. Definitely. When was the last time I've been with anyone other than my hand? I can't even remember.

Rory pulls a half-full beer glass from under the counter and puts it in front of Olivia.

"You're a lifesaver." She takes the glass and takes a sip. The foam leaves residue on the top of her lip, and her tongue pokes out to wipe it clean.

Fuck it. I'm done.

I down the rest of my glass, stand up, and leave cash with the tip on the table.

"Are you leaving already?" Olivia's voice stops me, and I turn around. Only to find that it stopped not only me. Rory's standing a few feet away, watching Olivia curiously. That bartender witch always knows more than anyone else in town. That's why the sheriff is buddies with her.

I give Olivia a questioning look, and her tongue peeks out and wets her lips again. And it's maddening.

"I mean, I can get you another round. As a t-thank you." The little stutter at the end shows her nervousness.

I glance around, wondering if anyone has heard it, and of course find Rory with her brows totally merging with her hairline. Her face splits into a wide, wicked smile as she asks me, "Want another one, Jake?"

I shake my head and return my attention back to Olivia. "You shouldn't be here alone."

"Who said I'm alone?" Her eyes narrow at me while mine shoot around, looking for the asshole who brought her here and dared to leave her alone talking to another asshole.

"Who are you here with?" I hear the words but don't know how I'm saying them.

She grabs my forearm and pulls me back into the seat. "You. You'll be my companion for today."

Here lies my plan not to get shitfaced today.

"Rory, would you be kind enough to get us some ginger ale?"

We both look at Olivia as if she just grew a horn between her beautiful eyes.

Beautiful eyes? Who am I?

"What?" She blinks, looking between me and Rory. "I need to drive to pick up my child from Mark's, and you already had one."

I stare at the shelves full of liquor in front of me, not knowing how I got here in the first place and why the fuck I stayed. From the corner of my eye, I see Rory slightly tilting her head to the side before she dives under the bar and produces two glass bottles of ginger ale. I didn't even know she had those. Pouring each into a glass, she places them in front of us and disappears.

Olivia starts moving around, trying to get comfortable on a very uncomfortable high stool. Every time her body leans toward me, I get a strong whiff of vanilla and chocolate. She even smells delicious. So delicious, my mouth waters.

I definitely need to get laid if I get turned on by a simple foody scent.

We silently stare at our glasses until magical Rory appears again and pushes a plate with some brown balls on them.

"What's that?" I ask, mildly curious. I've never seen it here.

"A new item on the menu." She winks and retreats back to the depth of the bar to make her magic.

"Do you know what those are?" I ask Olivia.

"Looks like a protein snack to me," she replies nonchalantly.

I carefully grab one to inspect it. The more I look at it, the less appealing it looks. So I put it back.

"You don't wanna try?" she asks, sounding oddly upset.

I shake my head slightly. "It doesn't look . . . appealing."

She pushes the plate back toward me with the words, "Looks can be deceiving. Try one." Even I'm not dense enough not to get the hidden meaning behind her words. Plus, I'm hungry from her vanilla scent slowly surrounding my senses.

Sending the wish to survive this to my stomach, I take the same ball I already touched and take a careful bite so she can forget about that and move on, but the moment my tongue touches it, my taste buds explode, and I let out a moan.

"Wow," I mumble as I chew, taking another bite.

"You like it?" Her voice sounds pleased.

"Damn, yeah. It's good. What is it?" I take another ball of whatever the fuck it is and send it into my mouth.

"Looks like it's our new item on the menu," says Rory, appearing out of nowhere again like a ghost.

"Did Jim make those to try it out?" I refer to the cook at

the back whom I can hardly picture rolling sweet and sour balls for the bar patrons.

"She did." Rory points at my companion and extends her hand toward her. "Looks like we'll be partners."

Olivia lets out a tiny squeak and starts clapping her hands. "Oh, crap!" When she notices Rory's hand still in the air, she grabs it and starts shaking it like a maniac. "Thank you!"

"Thank Jake." She nods at me with a crooked smile. "He's a tough cookie to please. This boy has been spoiled by his momma's cooking."

"Thank you, Jake!" she exclaims and jumps from her stool. The next thing happens in a second; I don't even have time to think. Right from the chair, she jumps onto me, and I have to grab her waist so we both don't fall. Her warm, soft body feels nice next to my cold, rigid one. I don't remember the last time I was hugged. And I forgot how fucking good it feels.

Vanilla and chocolate envelop my senses, and I feel a false sense of security and calmness.

I let myself soak in this feeling for another second before I pull away and look down at her face.

"What was that?" I know my words sound gruff, but I can't help it.

"A thank you hug for helping me land Rory." She steps back and glances at the bartender. "She's a tough cookie to sell too."

Rory laughs. "We can start with a small delivery on Thursdays and Fridays and see how it goes."

"Sounds wonderful!" Olivia keeps smiling into Rory's back even when she doesn't see her anymore.

"What just happened?"

She grabs her glass. "I've been trying to sell my goods to

Rory, and she kept saying no one in a bar wants to eat croissants, so I decided to give her sweet and salty protein bars," she glances at the plate, "or balls to try and see if people will like them." Her forehead wrinkles. "I'll probably work on the shape though."

Now her presence here makes more sense. "It's good. I'd buy a lot of those," I say, sending another ball into my mouth. And yes, she should probably work on the name.

"Good thing you're getting free goods at my place for a long time."

Here, she said it again. Like she's expecting me to come back and get her baked things. Like *this* can be a constant. She's a contradiction to herself after she reminded me what sort of a villain I am. So I turn my head toward her.

"Why are you doing this?"

"What?"

"This." I nod between her and me.

"Talking to you?" She smiles.

"Stop it. You know what I mean."

Her brows draw together as she starts thinking what to reply. I can see the exact moment she can't come up with anything plausible because her shoulders sag a little, and she pushes her hands under her thighs.

"I don't know."

"Is it pity? Because I don't need pity. Yours or anyone's. I made my bed and I lie in it. Don't think that your magical friendship can change things. Because I won't change. I'm an asshole." I swallow before continuing. "What they say is true. I'm sure you know it yourself if you knew me in high school."

Her brows draw together. "I knew *of* you. But I never knew you were a bully."

"I've become one." My voice turns firm. "And you can't

change that. I don't even know how you can talk to me when you're Mark's sister."

"Beats me too," she mumbles and digs her hands deeper under her thighs. Now her body is bunched forward, looking like a slowly closing shell.

I stand up from my chair. "Don't waste time on me, Olivia. You have a kid to raise, and if I were you, I wouldn't want him anywhere close to me." I hold her gaze. "I mean it. He should be as far away from me as possible."

Her mouth forms a small *o* just as her nostrils flare. "I wasn't propositioning you, you know."

I lean closer. "We both know it would happen at some point because I don't see where else it might be going." I lean down so only she can hear my next words. "It's going toward me fucking you in a dirty bathroom of a damn bar. And then you'll end up being another notch on my belt." Her nostrils flare at my words. "Even I know you deserve better." Pushing away from her, I add a bit louder, "Good luck with your bakery."

I drop more cash on the counter and walk away.

Chapter Ten

J**ake**

She riled me up for the conversation I need to have with Kayla, and I'll find out soon enough if that's a good or bad thing.

Kayla's waitressing today at Marina's diner. I checked her schedule—she'll be leaving in about twenty minutes. Fuck knows why she still works there when there's a long waiting list to get inked by her.

I park at the back of the diner, waiting for her to come out. She does in thirty minutes. With her long, ash-blond hair around her shoulders, the green streaks of color in it faded, she looks like a ghost in the pale moonlight. She pauses when she notices my car, tilting her head slightly to the side and quickly glancing around. I don't blame her— I've been a dick to her on more occasions than not.

To ease her discomfort, I rush to step out of my truck and head her way.

"Jake?" Her voice is hesitant. "Is everything okay?"

I take a deep breath, feeling like a man before a hanging. "Yeah. Can we talk?"

She looks around once more, without fear this time. "Here?"

"Justin's back at your place, and I prefer to do it one-on-one."

She chews her lip before she turns around and gestures for me to follow her. "Let's go inside. It's freezing balls out here."

I don't want to hear about balls anymore this evening. Please.

"Wait. We can do it in the car. It won't take long."

She watches me before slowly nodding. "In my car."

My turn to nod and follow her to her Jeep. It's the same one she's had since she was still living in the trailer park. And the very same one I used to pull over on the road more than once. I heard Justin fixed it so it's safe. I sure hope he has two brain cells to rub together and doesn't let her drive this old can long distance. If I had a woman, she'd have the safest car in the world because I wouldn't want to wonder every single waking moment if she made it home safe from a grocery run.

I get into the passenger side and push the seat back because I can barely fit. She starts the car and turns to me expectantly.

"What happened?" she asks, her voice quiet, probably knowing where it's all going.

Truth be told, I've never actually apologized to her. I've been trying to help here and there on occasion when I see her carrying grocery bags and shit like that, showing that

I'm sorry with actions, but I'm not around often. Besides that, Kayla deserves a good apology. I was wrong about her. Plus, guilt is a powerful thing, and it's been eating me from the inside long enough.

I tap my fingers on my knees, not knowing how to start. I had this whole speech planned out which went out the window the moment I sat in this car.

"Jake?"

I take a deep breath and turn to her.

"I'm sorry, okay? Fuck." I wipe my face with my palm. "That sounded bad." I look out the passenger window before returning my attention to her. "I am sorry, Kayla."

Her eyes go round, and I continue.

"I am sorry for all the shit I put you through. I wish I could say it was justified. It was somewhat for me." Her breath hitches, and I know I'm totally fucking this whole thing up. "Fuck, that's not what I meant. I mean I *thought* I had a reason, and it was very legitimate to me at the time." I dig the heels of my palms into my eyes. "Fuck, I don't even know how to explain it. I really can't. But—" I swallow and look at the window again. "It was fuckin' horrible the way I acted toward you, and you didn't deserve it. And trust me, I'll live with this the rest of my life, so I hope you'll forgive me so at least one of us can move on."

I glance at her and find her watching me with a solemn look on her face. I wait for her to say something—anything—but she doesn't. My words are probably not enough. They *aren't* enough. Nothing will be enough for her to forgive me. Because I'm a petty asshole, and I wouldn't forgive myself.

"I forgive you." She stunts me into a stupor.

My mouth falls open, and I don't even know what to say

in response. *Thank you?* That'd be stupid. *I'm sorry again?* It doesn't make my apology any more valuable.

Her warm, small hand lands on top of my cold one as she says it again, "I forgive you, Jake. And you can move on too." I look at her bright eyes full of unshed tears and see exactly why my brother wants to marry her. She's a light to his hidden darkness. If my darkness is right here, on the surface, his is hidden deep beneath his humorous demeanor.

Fuck me, but I'll tie her up and drag her to the altar if I have to, but they're getting their happily ever after. It's probably not the best way to start the new era of our relationship, but he needs her. I don't think he can survive without her. So I'll help him make it happen. What's another forgiveness to ask for when I already have so many lined up? I've never been involved in the kidnapping of a bride, but it can't be that hard. Can it?

"Th—" I clear my throat because words don't come through. "Thank you," I croak, barely recognizing my own voice.

Her hand's still on mine, so she gently pushes it to flip over and interlaces our fingers together. It might seem intimate, and it is, but on a different level.

She sniffles before speaking. "Can you move on now, Jake?"

My eyes suddenly itch, and I silently shake my head.

"Why?"

It's my turn to sniffle because I'm turning into a fucking emotional mess. "I just can't, Kayla," I confess quietly. "I can't. I'm in too deep."

"Deep into what?" she asks in that quiet, understanding voice of hers.

I shake my head again and say, "I'm sorry again, Kayla. I really am."

"I know." She gives my hand a gentle squeeze. "Wanna get some extra points though?"

A note of humor returned to her voice, so I take that wave, grateful for it. "Sure."

"Let me ink you."

I feel my eyes bugging out of my skull as my head whips toward her. "Ink me?"

"Yep." She pops the *p* as if she has gum in her mouth. "And I know just what I'd do for you."

"Will you tell me before?" I narrow my eyes.

"Nope." She smiles like a wicked witch bent on doing evil, and I give up.

"Fine. Ink me."

Her whole face brightens up as she pulls her hand away from mine and starts clapping. "Yay! I'll tell you when the design's done."

I nod, knowing I just agreed to something awful by letting the woman I tortured for years choose a permanent image to put on my body. I don't want to think about it, so I avert attention from me to the question which has been bothering my brother. Her kidnapping situation will depend on her answer, so I'd better phrase it right.

But I've never been known to form my thoughts clearly, so I blurt out, "When will you set the date for the wedding?"

Her eyes turn into slits as she smacks my shoulder. "Jake, you jerk! Did Justin set you up to this?"

"No!" I say too loud and too soon.

"Why does he keep insisting on a damn date?" She throws her hands in the air in desperation, hitting the wheel with a loud 'ouch.'

"Why do you keep resisting it?" I'm genuinely curious now. It doesn't seem like she wants to dump him, which was my main theory on why she's avoiding setting the date. My brother is a slob—reason enough for anyone. His dirty underwear was aways everywhere around the house when we were growing up.

She deflates like a balloon and sags into her chair. Something's going on, Justin is right.

"Why, Kayla?" I push, feeling the time is right.

She sinks her teeth into her lower lip, and it turns pale. Contact worked on me, and maybe it will work on her too. So I carefully place my hand on her shoulder.

"Kayla?"

"It's just—" She groans. Then groans some more. "It's just everything's so perfect now. I don't know why we need to get married to be happy."

"Don't you want to get married?" I probe carefully. "Or you don't want to get married to my brother?"

"What?" Her head whips toward me so fast I'm sure she's given herself whiplash. "No! If I wanted to get married, it'd be to him and him only."

"Then what's the problem?"

She blows out air. "It's just, I feel like we can ruin a good thing if we get married, you know?" Kayla's eyes are staring at me with obvious hope that I understand what she means.

"I actually don't, I'm sorry. We grew up seeing our parents madly in love and groping each other around every corner." I mentally shudder. "Naturally, Justin wants it too."

"Oh," she exhales loudly. "You think he can't be happy without it?"

I pause to think. Can he be happy without it?

"I think he can," I say honestly. "It's just, for him, marriage is a way to ensure that you won't leave him, I think. He's probably insecure that one day you'll take the rose-colored glasses off and decide you've had enough with his slobby ass."

I can't believe I'm talking about it and convincing someone not to leave my brother. And Kayla of all people.

Her eyes fill with sorrow. "I don't want to leave him."

"So, you just don't like this whole institution of marriage? Because I think if you explain it to Justin, he'll understand. He's smart." Then I add with a smirk, "Sometimes."

She sighs. "It's not that. I want to marry him, but I fear that once we start prepping and all that, something awful will happen."

"What do you mean?"

She looks at me from under her lashes. "Do you know why Marina has never gotten married?"

I shake my head. I might have heard it at some point in the local rumor mill, but it slipped my attention. Which is a big surprise because I was Donna's regular, and she knows everything, and she made me aware of every little event in this town.

"Because when she set the date with her then soon-to-be husband, she found him in bed with Mrs. Roberts."

I feel my jaw drop to the floor. "No fucking way! Mrs. Roberts who lives next to the sheriff?"

This piece of information I sure would have remembered. Mrs. Roberts has been terrorizing Kenneth Benson since the moment he moved into that house years ago and found out how 'active' his new neighbor was. He used to come to work complaining about her early morning visits with new quirks nearly every single day.

"The one and only." She keeps nodding. "So, Marina kicked him to the curb, and he ended up moving to Springfield. Then my mother," at the mention of Kayla's mother, my jaw shuts so tight, I'm sure she hears the sound of teeth, "every time she brought someone new home and got serious with him, and they started talking about 'getting good' like everyone else—" she makes the quotation marks in the air with her fingers, not finishing the sentence. Her whole posture suddenly becomes small. And I feel like I want to have a conversation with every asshole her mother brought home. "Well, each time I ended up at Mark's house for a few days."

Hell. Her life was misery, and I was just adding to it. I'm a golden boy from a good family who ended up being a regular piece of shit, and she's a girl from the wrong side of town who ended up golden. Talk about life being unfair to good people.

"I'm sorry, Kayla," I say again, not knowing how to show her how fucking awful I really feel.

"I know you are, Jake. I do." She smiles. And it's so sincere that I decide to tell her something I never thought I'd tell anyone.

"That day at the police station?" I say, waiting for her to acknowledge that she remembers it. When she nods, I continue. "When I was—" *violent* "—aggressive. Remember?"

She smiles sadly. "Unfortunately."

I swallow a giant lump in my throat, not allowing myself to wallow in the shame. "I was in withdrawal."

"From what?" Her voice is barely audible.

"Some heavy shit." I glance at the windshield before looking back at her. "It's not an excuse for my behavior, but I want you to know."

The corners of her lips turn down. "Does Justin know?"

I shake my head.

She's quiet for some time. "Does anyone?"

Another shake. "And I prefer to keep it that way." This is the first time I'm voicing my problem to one of the people from my good ol' life. And it fuckin' hurts.

"Jake." Her voice turns to begging. "Are you still on something?"

"I'm sorry again, Kayla." I quickly squeeze her hand lying in her lap, ignoring her question, and rush out of the car. My nose is tingling. My eyes are itchy. Must be the cold getting to me.

I hope Kayla has truly forgiven me and can move on because I sure as fuck just dug myself even deeper.

Chapter Eleven

O livia

I stare at my glass after Jake ran away like his feet were on fire.

"Girl, where were you going with all that?" Rory asks, appearing out of nowhere. This woman is like a ghost, I swear.

"I'm not going anywhere." I stare back at her.

"Exactly." She throws a towel over her shoulder and crosses arms over her chest like an angry schoolteacher. "You're staying here, 'cause you really, and I mean *really*, don't want to get tangled in his mess."

I narrow my eyes. "And why is that?"

"The man's got issues, honey." She takes one of my protein balls and bites into it. "In and out of sheets, if you know what I mean."

I wish I could pull my protein ball right back from her

mouth, but I'm a grown woman who doesn't get jealous over a man who isn't even hers.

"You seem so familiar with his issues," I hiss angrily, even though I shouldn't talk like that to someone who just became my first customer.

"The whole town is familiar with them, honey. And you will be too once you settle in." Her face transforms from stern to kind with a one-sided smile. "Now, calm your feathers. Yes, we've slept together, but it's bound to happen in a small town. It's either that or Mrs. Roberts." I can't help my snort, imagining this kind of scenario. "All I'm saying is give yourself some time to get your good name set in stone because you sure won't do it with Jake by your side."

The information about them sleeping together is so not what I wanted to hear, but after the rage stage has passed, I actually hear genuine concern in her voice, so I just nod. There's a reason people go to this bar just to talk to her.

"He's good though." She winks at me. "Between the sheets."

I shoot her an angry glare, stand up from the stool, and march toward the exit, hearing her tinkling laughter to my back.

"I'm sorry, Oli! But it's true!"

I show her a middle finger without turning back, making her laugh even louder.

"Thursday, noon, bring your balls here. We'll see how it goes," she yells to my back through bursts of laughter, making every patron in the room send me a curious look.

As I step outside, I take a full breath in, trying to calm my rapid heartbeat. Since arriving back in Little Hope, I've been hearing about Rory being this wise owl of the town who sometimes turns into a therapist, and they were right. Up to the point when she said she slept with Jake. Sure, she did it to rile me up once the wise ol' owl saw my interest in him. She succeeded. The moment she mentioned them being together, a hand wiggled its way into my chest cavity and squeezed my heart until it started bleeding. I hate that I have such a reaction to a man, and this man in particular.

Rory is right unfortunately—I should think about my future, which is not with Jake, so I drag my feet to my car and drive to Mark's place to pick up my kiddo and go back home. The opening is soon, and I need to make sure everything is ready.

It's been three weeks since I landed my first customer who became my best customer. Despite how much I want to punch Rory in the tit sometimes, she brings me the most (and the only) money, and it's before I've even officially opened my bakery. My protein bars are a hit in her bar. I changed the shape and the color a little bit and added a bit of turmeric for a kick, and now it's the best snack on her menu. A week ago, I added a new kind with some Himalayan salt. She said people get them with their beer all the time now. Some people even order it to go, and she passes the orders to me, letting me keep all the profit. Unfortunately, I owe her one for that. Despite how much I get angry every time I remember her comment about her 'testing Jake between the sheets,' the woman has been a lifesaver. And to keep afloat is more important right now than dreaming about a man.

With her help and trust, Rory managed to give back something I'd lost about two weeks ago when everything started going to shit—she gave me hope.

It started when I was rearranging the furniture around

the dining area, trying to figure out the best way to accommodate the tables and chairs without sacrificing the intimacy of the place. The bells above the door chimed, and Donna came in, her snobby nose in the air as she entered my sacred space without knocking on the door, even with a *Closed* sign on it.

"Are you here to ruin my business?" she asked.

"No, of course not," I tried explaining at first. "I bake, and this is what I sell."

"But you sell coffee too," she stated the obvious.

"I do. To accompany the baked goods. People can get my croissants and go to your coffee shop to get your famous blend." I was totally ass-kissing, but I didn't have a choice.

"Hmm." She looked around. "I think I'll start baking too. Townsfolk are not accustomed to the fancy shit you have, so they'll come to me."

"You don't even know what I have?" I narrowed my eyes at her.

"Hmm." She waved me off. "You were in some big fancy city. Of course, you'd want us all to eat fancy foods. I give you a week before you go out of business." She wrinkled her nose, looking around my bakery, and then turned on her heel and strode out the way she came.

That was strike number one, followed by many others. People of Little Hope have been stopping by, saying how much they don't like my stuff before they even know what I'm selling. At first, I was determined to fight them. Then I was angry. Then I got sad, and sad is where I am right now.

So I'm very grateful to Rory for helping.

The opening is the week after Thanksgiving, and I still don't have a babysitter. The situation with people coming in and showing me their disapproval drastically decreased the number of applicants, and the only one who's come here so far is Mrs. Roberts. During the whole interview, she was complaining about Mr. Cricket, her neighbor, stealing her slippers and telling me how nasty and disgusting our sheriff's wife is. Josie is the sheriff's wife, the woman who helped me without asking anything in return. Yeah, no thank you. Besides that, I don't want to be the center of her rumors in the next living room she's sitting in.

I'm mopping the floor when someone knocks on the door. I lift my eyes only to drop the damn mop.

Jake's mom. Is here. Knocking on my door.

Run, Oli. Run.

I wipe my hands on my thighs and walk to unlock the door—I've become smarter and started locking it after enough people kept walking right in.

"Hello?" I ask, slowly pulling it open.

"Hello. Olivia, isn't it?" Her smile is warm and welcoming.

I nod.

"Can I come in?"

I instantly pull the door open because refusing her entrance would be very rude, and she's Alicia's mom. Among other Attleborough siblings. "Sure."

She walks inside and looks around. "I love what you've done to this place."

I quirk a brow, trying to figure out if it's some sarcastic remark because I've lost all faith in humanity, and she laughs at my reaction.

"I didn't mean it like that. I meant I really love it. It's so welcoming and cozy, and yet bright and eerie." When she turns to me, her eyes are full of wonder. "Does that make sense?"

"It does. And thank you." I wrap my arms around me, glancing in the corner where Brodie's sleeping in the playpen I set up for him because I've been spending a lot of time here recently, and I prefer to keep him next to me. "How can I help you, Mrs. Attleborough?"

"I was hoping I could help *you*," she replies with a smile.

"How so?"

"Alicia mentioned you haven't found a babysitter for your son, so I was hoping I could help you," she explains while her eyes dart around, assessing my place.

My heart skips a bit as I curse Alicia calling Jake's mom here. I know it's her mom too, but it's also Jake's. *Jake's.*

"You see, I've got so much free time on my hands and no grandchildren to spend it with, so I was hoping I could help you while you help me."

I clear my throat.

"And how would I help you?"

"By letting me spoil your son." She smiles. "It will be like a rehearsal before any of my kids grace us with a grandchild."

If the universe has a sense of humor, it sure is sharpening it with me now.

"He's a handful." I try to avert her desire from nannying my child even though he's a saint.

"They all are." Her smile grows bigger. "Can I see him?"

I swallow and nod. "He's sleeping."

"I'll be as quiet as a moth!"

She's already not. Good thing Brodie can sleep through a screaming fit during a football match.

Mrs. Attleborough tippytoes after me toward his pen like a very loud elephant in a fragile china cabinet, where Brodie's sleeping on his side with his little hands under his chubby cheek. He looks like a tiny angel with brown hair.

Mrs. Attleborough is quiet. Like really quiet while she's watching him. And she's not smiling.

"He's so precious," she whispers.

"He is," I agree easily.

"He's got his father's hair?" she asks, glancing at me. This is the most blatant 'father question' I've ever gotten.

"He's got mine," I reply a bit defensively, stating the obvious. Brodie's hair is exactly the same shade as mine. He even has soft waves when it's humid outside.

She looks up at me. "Your bakery is opening soon, and you don't have anyone lining up to babysit." She raises her hand in the air, silencing me when I'm about to open my mouth. "I know. I've checked. I'm your only hope."

I keep my mouth closed because I know she's right. But also. Mrs. Attleborough? Jake's mom? *Seriously, universe?*

"You can call me Mary, dear." It's like she read my mind.

"I mean—" I chew on my lip, not knowing what to do. She's right, I'm in a bit of a pickle here. "Okay. I'd love your help until I find someone."

She starts nodding rather quickly. "Of course. However long you need."

"But I can't pay you much."

She waves me off with her delicate hand covered in rings. "Don't worry about it, we'll figure something out."

I feel a giant weight being lifted from one of my shoulders.

Only to land on another.

As I watch her looking around with motherly attention, like she's proud to be here, I wonder what could have happened to Jake to make him the way he is when he grew up in a family with a loving mother like that.

Chapter Twelve

***A**bout six and a half years ago*

Jake

Typical. The first new woman in town who happens to pique my interest chooses the man who ruined my brother instead of me. If Alex hadn't gone in the Navy, Justin wouldn't have followed, and the shitstorm that came after could have been easily avoided.

Alex has always been a bad influence. He's one angry fuck. Always has been. Even at school, he was mean just because his morning water wasn't watery enough. At first, I tried to become friends with him too, hoping it would give me more opportunity to be with my brother because they seemed to be attached at the hip.

But soon, I realized they didn't need me. If Alex wasn't

there, Justin would have been a better brother. Yes, I'm younger, and there's not many common interests, but I tried following them everywhere. I looked up to my brother. We were so much alike, or so everyone told me. So I gravitated toward him like any kid would toward an older sibling.

Only to end up being thrown back like a damn unwanted puppy.

And then Alex decided that he hated his family and left for the Navy, dropping out of college and dragging my brother with him. It all went downhill from there.

So yeah, I've got beef with him. And now, with Freya in town, she seems to be mesmerized by the fucker.

My phone rings, pulling me out of the hatred I'm currently drowning in. An unknown number. I pick it up.

"If you want to save your girlfriend, you might want to go to Crawley's house." A small pause. *"And do it fast."*

A girlfriend? I don't have a girlfriend. Unless they mean Adison, who I've been sleeping with out of anger recently. I know Freya has beef with her, so naturally I thought it'd piss her off. And him. But she's the last person expected to be at Alex's house. Shit. They must mean Freya.

"Who is this?"

"A friend." And the line goes dead.

I look at my phone, trying to figure out if it was some sort of joke. But my gut tells me it's not. I grab my holster and keys and rush to my car.

"Jake, where're you going?" Mom asks from the kitchen where she's planning another remodeling with my dad. They do it every couple of years because Mom 'gets tired of tile colors.'

"I'll be back."

Sometimes I wish I didn't live with my parents, and today is one of those days.

I drive toward Alex's house, breaking all speed limits but still don't put the siren on. The call was shady, and yet here I am. Rushing to check the tip of an anonymous person about a woman who's not even mine. But I'm also a cop. One who's not on duty, but in a small town, you're sort of always on duty.

Why the fuck does Alex live in the middle of a fucking forest?

The closer I get to the cabin, the stronger the unease becomes. This feeling of lead settling in the pit of my stomach is getting heavier.

I park farther down the road and kill the lights. Something tells me I have to be cautious.

The lights in the cabin are on, and there are people inside. Freya and someone else. A man. Thank fuck Alex has giant windows in his tiny cabin.

They're talking. All right. I'll wait. I mean, I don't like Alex, so I don't judge Freya for bringing a dude to his house as some sort of a cosmic punishment, but it doesn't look like Freya is enjoying his company.

Something crinkles in the woods, and I get distracted for a moment. When I turn back, Freya is holding a gun in her hand, and it's pointed at the man who's now on the floor.

This, right here, is the reason for the lead in my stomach.

I rush toward the house as I pull my Ray-Bans from my pocket and put them on my nose. It's already dark, and shades are definitely not needed. But they help me detach from the world around me. From the noise that might distract me. They help me focus only on what's important: Freya.

As I run, the people in the house change positions. The

man hits Freya and knocks her down on the floor. His back is hiding her from view.

I'll never make it there in time.

I quickly pull my gun out and shoot. I've never needed time to aim, I've just always known where to shoot. Just like this time.

His back is a large target even from this distance, and my bullet finds it through the window. He goes down.

Now, nothing is covering Freya, and I can see her sitting on the floor, her hands at her face.

I've been working as a police officer for a couple of years now, but I've never shot a man. I mean, it's Little Hope, we've never had major crimes around here.

The movies make it seem easy. Shoot a man. What they don't tell you is that a part of your soul is getting ripped out. A small piece, but it's missing, and you'll always feel it. It doesn't matter that the man tried killing Freya in front of my very own eyes, he's still a human. Was. Was a human.

I bend over and vomit. And keep vomiting until nothing is left, including my guilty conscience. Or fear. Or pain.

I don't know how long I've been standing here when I hear nearing footsteps. I look up and find Alex walking toward me.

"I remember my first kill too," he surprises me in a quiet voice, bringing all the pain I just purged back.

My eyes itch.

He suddenly grabs my shoulders and pulls me into his arms. And I let him.

"I know," he whispers with *understanding*.

I think it's his voice that breaks me, and my body wretches with silent sobs.

A few days later, Freya's still in the bed and breakfast. I think she's waiting for Alex to show up. I don't think he will.

His last words before he left me that evening told me everything I needed to know. "I need help too."

That broke the damn of hatred I was holding toward him. He didn't need mine because he had plenty of his own. When he disappeared out of town, I knew he wasn't coming back until he got that help. But it's not my place to tell, so I'll just stay around Freya until she finds her own footing.

All romantic feelings I thought I had for her were a fluke. She was something new and something I couldn't have. Maybe she was older, and I was curious. Now, I'm her friend who'll stand by her until Alex gets the help he's looking for and comes back. He's got his own demons, and I can't tell what they are. The moment in the woods made me realize that he has something else underneath that tough demeanor, so I probably should let him off easy. Because I understand him too much.

———

Alex is still not back, and I've gotten even closer with Freya. She's like a long-lost cousin I didn't know I was missing. Maybe I'm trying to fill that void inside with her presence. The voice that has been there since our family cracked under the pressure of what happened to my sister.

I walk from the post office when two men in cheap, black suits walk up to me.

"We have a job proposition for you," one of them starts without any pleasantries. His smile is emotionless, so is his voice. And I recognize it. He called me to warn about Freya. He's in his early thirties. Dark, short hair. Bleak eyes. Easily forgettable face.

"Yeah?" I try to sound uninterested, even though all my internal alarms are going off.

"We know things," he continues, watching me. And I watch him back. If he has something to say, he'd better start now. "Alright." He smiles a very odd, dead smile. "We're from the Drug Enforcement Administration, and we want you to work for us."

My gaze darts between them before I let out a loud cackle. "What are folks from the DEA doing here?" I think I'm asking a funny question, but they don't smile in return.

"Someone is planning to move their kitchen to the nearby area." He finds my eyes and holds them. "And you don't want these neighbors."

I stop cackling. "Here? In Little Hope?"

"Yes. They have some things going on in Springfield. And we have a strong suspicion the individual you shot," I swallow at his words because it's not public information, "was a part of it."

"And he was here because of that?"

"Among other things." He nods. "There's another individual from this area who works with him. And this is where you come in."

They lay out the short version of what's going on, and I have to lean my ass on my truck because I'm getting unsteady. I don't want these things in our town.

After his speech, I still have questions because all of this story makes zero sense to me. "Why not recruit Benson? He's the sheriff and has actually been in a couple of tours. He has experience. Why the fuck do you need me?"

The first one smiles. "Benson is a good cop. Too good."

He doesn't say anything else, nor do I. Tired of waiting for me, I guess, they share a look with another man, and the first one graces me with an explanation. "Kenneth Benson is a rule follower, and we need someone who might bend them here and there."

"And you think it's me?"

He levels me with a stare. "We know it's you. In fact, you know it too. That's why you're perfect."

The heavy itchiness at the back of my head tells me it's not as simple as they make it seem.

"Was it some sort of a test?"

The first one shrugs with an easy smile—the good cop obviously.

"You do know that you could have cost a woman her life with your fuckin' test?" The rage in my chest is sudden and threatens to explode me from within.

"We were confident in the asset." Another fucking smile.

I clamp my mouth shut because if I say something, they'll say something, and it would all turn rather ugly rather quick. They understand it too because the good cop pulls a white card from his pocket and gives it to me.

"Call us when you have time to think about it."

"I won't." I drop the card on the ground and turn around to walk away when he speaks to my back. His first words make me freeze.

"This is your town, and they'll ruin it. It's not the first little paradise people like them have ruined, and yours will be just another notch on their belt. The young will succumb, they always do because life here is boring, and you know it. And when they do, the town will die out. But you have power to stop that. Don't disappoint me, Mr. Attleborough, I put a lot on you."

They leave me leaning on my car deep in my thoughts.

The next few days I spend doing my research on the information they left for me. Turns out, they weren't joking.

There's a lot going on around us I haven't even known existed.

The call comes in the morning.

I pick it up. "I'm in."

Soon after, I leave Little Hope for training. And because I can't share what I'm up to with anyone, I tell everyone I'm going to rehab for the next few months.

I wish I had. Because the first man I killed has been haunting me ever since. The things I've seen during training have changed my perspective on life.

The small assignments I start doing separate me further from my family with every passing day. The things I have to see, things I have to do, turn me into something dark. The more time I spend undercover, the blurrier lines become until I've lost the feeling of what's good and bad. The only line you can't cross is the one at the finish. While you still can see it, you have a chance.

Undercover work has changed me more than I care to admit. More than I thought I could change.

Or maybe the real me has finally come out, tired of hiding in the shadows.

And I don't like myself very much.

Chapter Thirteen

P *resent day*

Jake

With my apologies delivered, I leave Little Hope and return back home. I should be happy that I can spend some time nursing the bottle while wallowing in my solitude. But after a few days, it no longer sounds appealing. Fuck if I know why. All I want right now is to be around people. And not just any people but people I know.

I don't know what's happening, but I positively want to be in Little Hope right now. This change of mood gives me whiplash, but my body yearns to move.

So I pick up my phone and put a message together.

I'm taking a few days off. Don't call.

The reply is instant.

Okay.

I throw some clothes in a bag and jump into my truck. When a pop song from my childhood comes on the radio, I don't rush to switch it. Instead, I lean back in the seat and enjoy the ride for the first time in . . . *forever*. Just like that, driving my truck I used to love and pamper, with one hand on the wheel. Just chilling. Without rushing somewhere and just taking my time. There's no dark shit waiting for me at the end of my road, no assignment I won't be able to recover from. Just myself and the road.

With some lightness in my chest and some brightness on my mind, I'm suddenly starting to remember what hope feels like.

To say that Mom was surprised to hear my voice when I called and said that I plan on being in Little Hope for a few days—so close to Thanksgiving no less—and was wondering if I could stay at their place would be an understatement. But she was ecstatic, so here I am, dragging my feet into my parents' house, unsure of this whole visiting idea. It felt good on a whim, but the closer I get, the more doubt I felt. And now all this doubt is threatening to explode.

"Jakey, is that you?" Mom calls out from the kitchen the moment I open the door.

"Yes, Mom."

"Come here. I've got your favorite meatloaf."

Doubt starts to slowly dissolve. What I really miss about home is Mom's cooking and baking, she made me a diva where food is related. Nothing can replace it.

I walk into the kitchen to find my dad sitting at the island drinking coffee while Mom's stirring something on the stove. This is the view I'd been coming home to for many years, and this is how I grew up. I should have grown up a good person, but I clearly fucked up fate's plans.

"Hello, Son," my father surprises me right from the door. I usually get a nod and a grunt as a greeting, so this is something extraordinary. Hope shines brighter.

"Hi, Dad." I walk to the woman who wanted me to be a better man and give her a kiss. "Hi, Mom."

I walk to the fridge to get some OJ when I hear silence. No mug being put on the marble counter, no clicking of the wooden spoon over the frying pan. When I turn around, I find two pairs of slowly blinking eyes staring at me. Then they quickly go about their business as if woken up by something. *Strange.*

I pour myself some juice and go to the counter.

"Why are you cooking so much? Are you expecting guests?" I glance at the amount of food on the stove.

"You eat a lot." She chuckles and then suddenly sobers up. "Used to eat a lot anyway. But yes, I'm taking some of it to Oli's house. Poor girl has been working so hard to open that bakery that she doesn't have any time to cook for herself. Only for that adorable boy of hers." She turns to me with a stern stare full of meaning I can't quite grasp. "She's such a good mother, Jakey. It's so wonderful to see how good she's making it work when she didn't have any example in her life." She returns back to stirring. "I remember how she used to come to school with dirty clothes and tangled hair until Mark was old enough to understand how to do it all. It's heartbreaking really."

The heaviness is back on my chest. It's like something has been dropped onto it with the sole purpose of not letting me breathe.

"I'm so glad I can help her now," she keeps going, not seeing me struggling to get a lungful of air.

"Help her?"

"Yes." She sounds very excited. "I'm babysitting her son." I nearly spit the juice out. "Can you imagine that?"

"No, I can't," I deadpan.

"I don't know why your mother got it into her head that she needs to work when she can just enjoy her life." Dad doesn't sound happy about this arrangement, and I totally second that.

"It's not a job for me, honey. It's playing with a baby and spending some time with them. They're family now too. She's Mark's sister. It makes her one of us."

I clear my throat and stare at a black dot on the counter because I just got punched in the guts. Family? *Mom, please don't say it.* The last thought about Olivia I had was so not family-like. For some reason, this woman hasn't left my mind since the moment I saw her standing between the car door and the man in his robe, protecting her child. She was so fierce. So beautiful. So familiar. She looked like someone brave enough who wouldn't be scared to stand with me against the whole world.

The streetlight was illuminating half her face, adding to the mystery of her. And then her constant thanking and talking to me as if I was not me but an actual human being. All of that just made me wish I was someone else for a day so I could do things to her I was imagining alone in the shower.

My dad puts his mug on the counter. "Wait a minute, was she the same kid who was selling homemade cookies here every month?"

"The very same one." Mom smiles knowingly. "And I knew you loved her cookies more than mine. You always bought two batches."

Dad chuckles sheepishly without saying a word. *Smart man.*

"To be fair, her cookies were always good," Mom notes with a gentle smile.

"Was she raising money for something?" he asks.

"I guess for food." Mom's voice drops. Right next to where my heart already is. "I remember that poor Mark was doing some extra work here and there. He was older but he had to finish school and then he went to this firefighter training or whatever it's called. I think she started selling cookies to help him out when she was like, what, eleven?"

"About right." Dad nods, picking up his mug again.

"Every time she came to our house, and you opened the door, she blushed." Mom chuckles. "It was adorable."

This time, I do spit out my juice all over the counter. "What the fuck, Dad?"

"Not him, you big dumb boy!" Mom starts laughing hysterically while my father sends me an offended look.

"Who then?" I ask through the coughing fit.

"You!"

"Me?" I press my index finger between my pecs.

"You." She nods. "She had a huge crush on you. She usually circled twice with those cookies, making your dad always buy them. It was so very cute." She sighs wistfully, not noticing how my face probably pales right now.

"She had a crush on me?" I repeat like a dummy.

Dad laughs and takes a sip of his probably already cold coffee. "You sure didn't get my brains, Son."

"You have his brains," Mom confirms with a smile, and then mouths to me, "I told him about the crush. He didn't know."

Olivia had a crush on me in school while I didn't even know she existed. She was younger than me, so that could have been the reason. But still. How could I not notice a starry-eyed kid always looking at me? Was it because she was from the trailer park? Am I really that judgmental? She did seem familiar, but I couldn't place her face in my hormonal teenage memories.

"I'm so proud to see her opening her business and raising a wonderful child at the same time. She's so strong. Despite all the stuff our folks put her through."

I smack my glass on the counter, making them both raise their brows. "What stuff?"

They exchange a look before Mom goes into explanations. "Old local folks don't like her opening competition." She gives me a meaningful stare, letting me figure out on my own who's the catalyst for the war the locals have waged on her.

"Donna." I sigh.

Mom confirms it with a nod. "Wanna talk to her?"

"No one in this town listens to me anymore."

Dad rises to his feet, places a mug in the sink, and walks to me. "You're the only one who can change that, Son," he says, placing his hand on my shoulder. "Make them listen again."

Chapter Fourteen

Many, many years ago when Olivia started selling cookies

Olivia

I'm going to be a baker when I grow up, and I'm going to open my own bakery. But for now, I'm selling these cookies. And I'd better sell every single one of them because I spent all my saved money on the ingredients.

I've got a few batches here to see which ones will go first, but everyone says that Girl Scout cookies always make grown-ups teary, so here I am. I've never been a Girl Scout because we've never had it in school, but I'm sure if I were one, I'd show them more ways to survive without any money than they could ever teach me.

I'm dressed extra nice today in my favorite school skirt and shirt and even put a pink bow in my hair. Kayla lent it to me for the day. She said the cookies might sell better if I look cute. She was right. I'm almost out of everything, and I have a planned stop to make. This stop is far away from where I currently am, but I'll walk there. A few miles won't stop me from knocking on Jake's door.

Right before I ring the bell, I fix my hair and drape it evenly in the front, making sure my bow is still intact. I pick off a small piece of lint from my skirt, square my shoulders, and press the bell button.

The door opens a few seconds later. Jake.

I forgot what I came here for, so I just stare at him in his sleepy glory.

"Yes?" he asks, sounding rather annoyed.

"Hey, Jake!" I squeak.

His brows draw together. He turns and yells inside the house, "Mom, there's some kid here."

With that, he turns around and walks away, leaving the door open. Mrs. Attleborough rushes toward me.

"Hey, honey. How may I help you?" Her big, blue eyes are full of kindness and patience. Something I don't feel anymore after being rejected so openly. I mean, we go to the same school. How come he hasn't seen me even once?

"I—" I mumble, losing all interest in selling them anything.

"Are you selling homemade cookies?" She helps me find my words again.

"Yes," I sigh, stretching my arm with a basket of cookies toward her.

"Oh, how lovely!" She claps her hands like these cookies are the best thing she's ever seen. "Hold on a minute, I'll get my wallet."

She disappears, leaving the door open to my surprise.

Isn't she scared that I can just come inside and take something?

While she's looking for her wallet, I peep inside and see how different my and Jake's lives are. No wonder he's never noticed me at school.

I end up walking down the road toward the trailer park, and it's a long way. I stopped by Marina's diner and asked to use her phone to call Mark to see if he could get me, but he wasn't home, so the call went unanswered.

The first drop of rain falls onto my nose like a giant, heavy stone, washing away all hope I had in the morning. The second drop is even heavier, taking away with it every peace of joy I had from making my first dollar.

When it starts pouring, the only thing I worry about is that all that money will get destroyed by the water.

The tires of a screeching car make me jump to the side of the road, thinking I'm about to become roadkill.

"Oli, get inside!" Jonah's voice yells through the rain.

I turn toward the sound and find Jonah's head peeking from the open passenger window of his dad's car. He's rapidly getting soaked.

I look at their fancy car and then down at myself. I'll totally ruin their interior, and they'll make me pay. I can't afford that.

"Nah, I'm good. Thanks though!" I wave as if I'm not drenched to the bones—not so tired that I can't feel my feet anymore.

"Get inside, Olivia. We will give you a ride. It's a long walk," his father calls out, leaning forward so I can see him.

My shoulders drop because I very much want to accept their offer. "I can't. I'll ruin your car."

"It's just a car." Jonah rolls his eyes. "Get inside, I'm getting wet here."

With a shy smile, I run toward the back door and jump inside. It's dry and warm. The water drips around me, instantly creating a large puddle, and I hold my empty basket tighter on my lap.

"I'm sorry," I whisper.

"Don't even worry about it." Jonah's dad waves me off. "It's leather. It's easy to just wipe it off."

With that, he takes off. He doesn't need to ask where I live because everyone knows.

Jonah's chatting about something in the front seat, constantly turning to me. I just smile in return every time, because even though I'm dry and warm now, inside, I'm miserable. The difference between me and them is so obvious. Even though they're very kind and helping me, I feel like I'm a charity case.

And I vow to myself to never be that again. I'll get out of Little Hope. I will become a baker. And then I'll be famous and rich with my very own bakery where I'll make delicious goods that people will drive from miles away just to get.

Chapter Fifteen

P*resent day*

Jake

Grocery shopping was so not on the list of things I wanted to do when I was planning my trip to Little Hope. But here I am, rolling a full cart down the produce aisle, crossing off the items from Mom's never-ending list. She said she'd missed 'a few things' for her Thanksgiving dinner, and I thought, I don't know, a brick of butter and milk was it.

But clearly our definitions of 'a few' vary drastically since I just picked up corn from the floor because it fell from the overflowing cart.

"Watch where you're going," a hiss comes from my right.

I stand to my full height, totally dwarfing a little lady

with a nasty attitude. Mrs. Roberts, one of the locals who frequents the police station to snitch on her neighbors. I was always the one sheriff sent her to because I could charm the pants off her, and she usually forgot about her constant complaints about her neighbor who has dementia. After a talk with me, she always left without filing anything, therefore saving us a ton of paperwork. And sanity. Sheriff usually had enough of her in the morning when she knocked on his door to complain about something else.

She doesn't look so charmed anymore though.

"Such a disgrace to a wonderful family." She keeps going. "Got fired from the police force." Her voice goes higher, drawing attention from everyone around. "You must have done something awful if Sheriff Benson fired you. He's a very generous and fair man." She's totally enjoying being the star of the play she's performing. Ten minutes later, Benson will be the villain in her next story.

I grab my cart and want to move past her, but she places her foot right under the wheel. I try pulling back, and she grabs the cart as if for support. The only way I can get out of here is by going through her foot or making her lose her balance and fall if I pull it hard enough. I sigh to the ceiling and wait for her to get bored, so I can move the fuck on down the produce aisle, complete Mom's grocery list, and be a good son for one day.

"I heard your father talking about you. Such a well-respected man forced to bear your sins." She shakes her head, not noticing my jaw tick. This hits too close to home. "He's very ashamed of you."

I want to roll my cart over her foot so much that I nearly do it. One more word from her vile mouth, and I'll have another sin to add to my collection. But this one I'll welcome with open arms.

"Where did you hear that, Mrs. Roberts?" A voice I expected to hear the least is right behind me. I prefer her not to see this humiliation happening, but here she is. "Was it when you were rolling with Mr. Cricket under the bleachers perhaps?"

A few chuckles sound here and there while Mrs. Roberts brings her palm to her chest with a loud squeak. "How dare you?"

"Yep." The small woman comes to stand to my right. "I've heard that's the reason you don't like Mr. Cricket." She starts nodding to everyone gathered around us. "Because he rejected you *after* the bleachers," she says in a shushed voice so loud, I'm sure my parents could hear it in their house.

"That's not true!" Mrs. Roberts cries out.

"I don't know." Olivia shrugs one shoulder nonchalantly and starts picking her nails. "I heard quite a few people talking about it the other day."

"No!" Mrs. Roberts's head whips around, looking for support, but finds none. Because a chorus of voices has other things to say.

"True. I heard it too."

"Yeah, someone at Donna's mentioned it the other day."

"I saw them coming out of there. And she had her skirt *crooked*!" the last voice announces scandalously.

I glance down at the woman who came to my rescue and find her smirking at the quickly erupting chaos around us.

"Time to run," she whispers through the smile. "Before one of us gets involved again."

She takes my cart and pulls on it, not so gently, I might add, because Mrs. Roberts stumbles but quickly regains her footing, shooting Olivia an angry stare. Mrs. Roberts is the queen of gossip, and she can make someone's life pretty difficult since she works at town hall. Without thinking, I wrap my arm around Olivia's shoulder, grab the cart from her hands with another, and steer them away from the chattering crowd toward the cashier. Mom will have to do with what I've already gotten because I don't want to risk Olivia getting in the line of fire for me again.

"Where's your cart?"

"That way." She points in the direction of the dairy aisle. "I'll get it." She takes off, and I follow her. When she notices me, she waves her hand at me. "I still need some things, so you go ahead."

"I don't want you to stay here and deal with this wreckage."

"P-p-please." She rolls her eyes. "I've been dealing with this wreckage all my life. It just took a new turn once I announced my bakery opening." Something must have crossed her mind because her face darkens, and the corners of her lips drop. "I gotta go. Bye, Jake." With that, she rushes to grab her cart while I stand still with mine.

I'm not sure why she got so spooked, but it must have been something to do with the warning I gave her the last time we were together. I mean, not like *together* together, but in the bar, talking and all that. I probably shouldn't have mentioned the fucking I was planning to do with her in the dirty bar bathroom.

I drive the groceries home where my parents are already aware of the situation in the store. Mom's worried eyes meet me when I open the door.

"Are you okay?"

"Mom, for fuck's sake," I answer grouchily. "I'm a grown man."

"Language, Jakey!" Her brows draw together with a warning.

"Sorry."

"You're still my son, and I worry about you."

I soften my voice when I speak to her next. "You don't have to worry about townsfolk being meanies. I've dealt with worse."

Her mom-knows-all eyes drill a hole in my head, probably trying to pick my brain and see what I'm talking about.

I walk to her to give her a kiss on the cheek. "I'm fine, Mom. I'll be in my room."

As I pick up the book I've been rereading since I was a kid and go to lie on my bed, I feel the heaviness that has been sitting on my chest intensify. I got yet another reminder why Little Hope is not my home anymore and will never be. Benson was right to fire me, I deserved it. When I did what I did, I didn't know it'd follow me into the future. I don't know what I was thinking, but I told Kayla the truth. I was in a heavy fuckin' withdrawal. I didn't know I'd gotten so deep into it, and that was my fault. Things seemed to go downhill from there.

Chapter Sixteen

J^{ake}

It's past ten in the evening and I already know I won't be sleeping, so I grab my keys and go for a drive. That's what I've been doing for the past few years when insomnia hits too hard.

I don't notice how I'm automatically circling toward Main Street and then to the small street off it. The sign *'Sweet Dreams Are Made of This'* is bright and sunny despite the night. It's the brightest one on the street and has two little dancing cupcakes under it.

It was stupid to come here at night.

I don't even fuckin' know what I'm doing here when I notice the light in the window. I glance at the clock—it's fifteen past eleven. She can't be here. She's got a kid. I'm no expert, but I'd assume he'd be asleep by now upstairs in their apartment.

Maybe someone from today's encounter decided to fuck with her as a punishment? A few years ago, I wouldn't think they were capable of that, but times have changed. So have people. I don't want her to get between me and the fine people of Little Hope. I mean, I entertained for a moment the dream of her standing by me, but she's not really. By me. Where I could have protected her. She's as far as the fuckin' moon. Especially after my asshole behavior in the bar because I got spooked.

Clamping my jaw shut, I quietly drive by and park three houses down the street. Careful to not be noticed, I creep toward the window and peek inside. With no one in sight, there's still sounds of clanking dishes from somewhere, but no person to be seen. I try the door handle and find it easy to open. There's no way a sane person would leave it open at night unless they plan to run away soon.

I can just go inside guns blazing, but if the kid's sleeping upstairs, he'll get scared. I can take a lot on my conscience, but a traumatized kid is not one of them. So, still careful, I walk around the counter and toward the small kitchen area where the sound seems to be coming from.

A body rises from behind the stove.

"Holy fucking shit!" she yells, jumping backward. A huge metal bowl in her hands leaps along with her, spilling brown liquid on the floor. She looks down. "Sh-sh-shit," she hisses like a snake and makes a move to sit on her haunches.

But she slips on the liquid and falls backward with a yelp.

"Ouch!" she squeaks, trying to push away from the floor and get into a sitting position.

"Olivia!" I rush toward her while she's trying to stand up. The moment my feet step in the brown mess, I follow her down. I'm about to land and crush her with my weight, but I manage to get ahold of myself from completely squishing her.

My elbows are on the sides of her head, my palms splayed on the floor. The lower part of my body is on top of hers.

I look at her face. The brown mess that smells like chocolate from up close is all over her face and hair. Dark brown smudges on her cheeks and chin almost match the color of her silky hair. Her mouth is open, and she's breathing hard like a sprinter right after a run.

"What the hell, Jake? Why did you scare me like that?" she asks as her breathing doesn't slow down at all. Her nostrils flare when I make an accidental move with my body.

My eyes dart between hers. "I thought you were being robbed or something." Then I remember how I got in here. "Why the fuck don't you lock the door? It's night outside."

"Don't tell me what to do," she grinds through her teeth, making a weak attempt to wiggle out from under me. But I'm not done with her.

"I will if I need to explain simple fuckin' basics of self-preservation. You've got a kid here."

Her face turns into a mask of pure rage. "Brodie's upstairs in his bed, and I'm watching him through the camera. They'd have to get through me to get to him."

I lean closer. "And you're making it very easy for them by leaving the damn door open."

"From what I've heard, you're the one I should stay away from, and yet, here we are." Her nostrils flare as her eyes drop to my mouth for a brief moment before returning to shooting daggers at me.

"Exactly!" I hiss as I lean even closer. "You should have kept that fuckin' door locked."

It's hard to explain *how* what happens next comes to pass, but my lips press into hers. She sighs in surprise, and I quickly angle my head, shoving my tongue into her mouth. I'm not careful. I'm simply not capable of being careful now. I'm mad at her for endangering her and her kid's lives. I know who can be roaming the streets.

My kiss is her punishment and warning to be careful in the future. She should be scared. She should be.

But I don't think she is.

She suddenly digs her fingers into my hair and angles my head the way she wants it. Her tongue pushes into mine as she brings my head even closer to hers. Our teeth clack. Our tongues fight.

My pelvis rocks into her without my control. I'm hard. It's painful.

She frees her hand and brings it down, trying to push my thigh away.

Dread replaces passion, and I fear I might have scared her. I try to lift myself off her and let her go, but once her leg is free from the cage between my thighs, she drapes it around my ass. Quickly she does the same with her other leg and cages me in.

"More," she mumbles as her hands return to my hair, pulling on the strands.

I happily oblige, knowing this can never happen again, so I'm getting my fill for the rest of my life. Because that's how long I'll carry this memory with me.

I dive back into her mouth, sweet with her own taste and the chocolate batter. Our teeth keep clanking. We bite each other's lips as I attempt to get my fill. This is the dirtiest fuckin' kiss I've ever had. And the purest.

With every passing second, I know she'll remember who I am and pull away. I fear that moment.

So I rock my hips again, and she meets me halfway. With every thrust, she meets it double force, grinding over me. It's so fucking painful. It's so fucking good.

Her hands snake under my shirt, digging the nails into my flesh. I love the feeling. It grounds me to her like gravity.

But her movements slow down, and I just know the moment when reality starts slowly creeping in on her. Her legs stay wrapped around me while her tongue slows down its assault. I follow her lead. Her licks become slower and more deliberate, like she's getting her fill too, knowing it's coming to an end.

Soon, she bites my lower lip and freezes. I pull my face away but keep my body close to hers. I can get any fucking woman I want, I always could, but being here, on top of her, feels different. It's not about the release, well, it is, but also not. It's about the road there, and I know I'll enjoy it more than I should. Way more.

I open my eyes to find her slowly blinking. Her pupils are blown. Her cheeks flushed. Chocolate is everywhere. On her face, on her neck. On the floor and my hands. Our clothes are ruined.

Her chest's rising and falling, touching mine with every breath. She licks her lips and lets out a shuddering exhale.

I see in her eyes it's time to go. I carefully pull away, trying not to fall on the slippery floor again.

"I'm sorry," I say, but she just waves me off.

"It's fine. This batch was too sweet anyway." We both know that's not why I'm apologizing, but we both pretend it is.

I press my finger into the chocolate spot on my shirt and send it into my mouth. The perfect flavor hits my taste buds with an overwhelming need to fall on the floor and lick the remaining chocolate off the floor.

"It was perfect," I say and head toward the exit. Before I leave the kitchen, I turn back. "Lock the doors, Olivia. Always lock the doors."

She rolls her eyes. "It's Little Hope, Jake."

I wait till her attention is solely focused on me. "I'm not joking, Olivia. Lock the fucking doors."

With that, I walk away, leaving her standing in the middle of the room completely covered in chocolate with swollen lips and wild hair.

Chapter Seventeen

O livia

I blink. And then blink some more. And then again.

I just kissed Jake Attleborough and *lived to remember* it. Insanity.

I bring my hand to my mouth, still feeling him on my swollen lips. His touch on my body. My thighs are still shaking from holding him between them. I felt way more than I expected. His erection was right there, at my very core, eager to join its forces with my equally eager pussy. I groan remembering how hard I was squeezing his hips and how much I wanted him just to pull his pants down and make good on his promise from the bar.

Bad, bad Olivia.

I lick my lips, trying to memorize his taste. It was perfect. I need to replicate him in a cupcake and eat it every morning by myself. The chocolate sweetness mixed with coffee and his unmatched anger. A lethal combination. I'd get a Nobel Prize if I could just bottle it up.

A sound from the monitor on the counter shakes the stupor off me. Brodie's moving from side to side which means he'll wake up in about thirty minutes, asking for food. He's been sleeping mostly through the night but when he goes through growth spurts, he wakes up a couple of times, ravenous for food.

The floor is a mess, I am a mess, so I quickly clean the floor, cursing Jake with his crazy idea of scaring the ever-loving crap out of me. Then I rush into the shower, trying not to leave anything behind me.

After I feed Brodie formula and put him back to sleep, I'm contemplating if I should go back and try to make the perfect batch of chocolate, but it's well after midnight. My bakery's official opening is in a week, and Thanksgiving is in four days. And I'm tired. So I make the decision to have a few extra hours of sleep and drag my feet to my bed where I have awfully vivid dreams of Jake's cock out of his pants.

"What time are you coming?" Mark's voice booms through the phone.

"I don't know," I reply vaguely, hoping he'll let it slide, go to the Attleboroughs' house and have himself a very happy Thanksgiving. Without me there.

"Oli," he sighs heavily. *"You're not coming, are you?"*

"What do you mean she's not coming?" Mary cries out loud enough for me to hear over the phone.

Mark puts the phone away from his face because his next words are a bit muffled. *"She's not feeling her best, probably. It's okay. I'll check on her."*

"No!" I don't want Mark to lose this day with Alicia's family because of me being a chicken shit.

"*Nonsense!*" Mary says in the phone and clearly takes the phone from Mark's hands. "*Dear,*" her voice quiets down, "*he's not here.*"

"Why?" I catch myself too late and try to remedy my slip right away. "I mean, what do you mean?"

Her footsteps make me believe she walks away from Mark. "*He's just not here. Take your wonderful boy and bring him here. You both need to be with your family today.*"

I swallow and nod, knowing she can't see me.

"*Will you come?*"

"Yes," I say through my clogged throat.

"*Good. Mark!*" she yells, not moving the phone away from her mouth and making me wince on this end of the call. "*Here's your phone.*"

"*What was that about?*" Mark's curious voice replaces Mary's.

"We'll come."

Silence.

"Mark?"

"*Yeah.*"

"Should we not come?" I probe carefully, for the first time in forever not knowing what he might be thinking.

"*You should.*" A heavy sigh follows. "*And then you should tell me what the fuck is going on.*"

"I will." I will not.

"*Do you want me to come and pick you up?*"

"No." I roll my eyes—ever the big brother. "I'm totally capable of driving us, you know."

"*I know.*" His voice softens up. "*We'll see you soon.*"

The moment we hang up the phone, I dress Brodie in a cute turkey shirt and brown pants.

"Look at you! Your first Thanksgiving with family!"

It's always been Mark and me, and then it was just me. I couldn't come to visit every single holiday, at first because I didn't want to spend money on the plane ticket. He was busy working anyway during holidays since he didn't have a family, so I just stayed at the college and picked up a few shifts.

Then, when I was able to afford a ticket, Alicia happened, and I didn't want to impose, knowing that he was invited to the Attleboroughs' house. I didn't want to be a pity invite when they couldn't leave me hanging, so I just stayed at work, yet again, picking up shifts to save for the bakery.

Even though Mark would never make me feel like I'm a third wheel, I really didn't want to ruin a good thing he was building. Because knowing him, he'd sprint into big-brother mode the moment I stepped foot on the ground; he'd be caught between two stools, trying to make everyone happy. So I just removed myself from the occasion, making the choice easier for him. He'll always be my big brother, and nothing will change that. But he might never find someone like Alicia ever again. So he'd better make it work.

And today, I'll pretend that I belong too.

The nervousness about what to wear evaporated the moment I found out Jake wouldn't be there. Along with the desire to get dolled up. But it's Mark's family now, so I still have to try.

I find black skinny jeans and a beige baggy sweater. My shirt somewhat matches Brodie's in color, so we should look cute in the pictures. I want to show him everything when he grows up. I never had pictures taken of me when I was a kid in a home setting, and I'm remedying it by taking as many as I can, so he knows where he came from.

I let my hair down in soft waves when I finish my makeup consisting of mascara and some lip gloss. That's already more than I usually do—spending my days sweaty from baking in the kitchen, or painting said kitchen, is not the best recipe for a full makeup day.

Once we're both dressed and ready, I pack the formula, bottles, and diapers, and we head outside. In case we stay longer than expected—Brodie's still getting his weight back after being sick, so I'm very particular about the timing of his feedings.

When I open the door outside, a sudden feeling of gloom settles on me—it seemed so nice and cheery in the morning when the sun was up, but now, at four, it feels cold and unwelcoming. So the only desire of any human is to curl up in some cozy place with a cup of something steamy. But we've already made a commitment, plus I don't want to ruin it for Mark who'll feel uncomfortable with me being in Little Hope and spending holidays separately.

The whole street where the Attleboroughs live is packed with cars. People are visiting families, and the whole atmosphere is cheery despite the weather. Naturally, I get in the mood too. I grab Brodie and his pack and go to the door. I tried new cupcakes and cookies this morning, so I decided not to show up empty-handed and brought them with me.

I plaster a giant smile on my face and press the doorbell. The door flings open in a few seconds to reveal a grumpy-looking man standing before me. When he sees me, his eyes widen.

"What are you doing here?" he blurts out.

I open my mouth to say something, but nothing comes out, so I just open and close it like a fish on land.

"Jake! Don't be rude, let them in." Mary shoves Jake

aside and stretches her arms. "Give me that little gentleman."

I move inside automatically and pass a suddenly smiling Brodie to her. He took to her so fast, it's scary. Two minutes into their first interaction, and the boy was ready to drop me like a sack of potatoes every time she showed up in a room. I'm not going to lie, my feelings were a little hurt, considering it's always been him and me, and now he's so easily leaving me for another lady. And today is not an exception.

"Look at this guy!" she coos to him as she smooshes his cheek with kisses. "I missed you so much."

She heads away with my son in her arms, but before disappearing in the kitchen, she turns to me and mouths 'thank you.' *Was I set up? Or did he come unexpectedly?*

"Sorry, I didn't mean it like that." Jake scratches the back of his head. "I was just surprised."

"Me too," I mumble in return.

His brows jump up. "Why? It's my parents' house."

I give him a heavy stare. "Your mom said you wouldn't be here, otherwise I wouldn't have come."

He glances at the kitchen with narrowed eyes before returning back to me. "You shouldn't be scared of me."

I recoil back from the absurdity of his declaration. "I'm not scared of you." I never have been.

His brows furrow. "Then why didn't you want to come when I'm here?"

I look at him as if he just grew wings. "Because we," I look around, making sure no one can hear me, but it should be safe since everyone's busy with Brodie somewhere judging by the cooing and his laughter, "kissed and did other things," I add on a whisper.

His wide neck moves with a swallow. "Okay. Makes sense. If you feel uncomfortable, I can make something up and go." He sounds so sincere that my heart breaks. "Trust me, they won't be surprised."

"Jake." I soften my voice. "You shouldn't leave your own house because of me."

"Why?" He looks confused. "You and the kid should be comfortable here. I suspect it's his first Thanksgiving, right?" I nod, touched that he, out of everyone, thinks about that. "Then he should be stuffed with Mom's cooking just like everyone else."

I chuckle. "He's nine months, he can't eat much. I mush the majority of foods for him, so he won't choke. He barely has teeth."

He scratches the back of his head again, looking adorably lost. "Shit, sorry. I know nothing about kids."

"Oli, are you okay?" Mark's voice suddenly makes us both turn toward him. How long has he been standing here?

"Yeah." I smile back and glance at Jake whose face has changed in an instant. His eyes darken and his lips turn into a thin line. He turns and walks away down the corridor.

Mark's gaze follows him until he disappears. "What did he want?"

"He was just being friendly."

"He doesn't do friendly," Mark warns as he glances at the corridor where Jake just disappeared. "And I don't want him around Brodie."

I quirk a brow. "Really? The last time I checked, Brodie is *my* son."

"You're both my family, and I'm responsible for you," he states firmly, sending angry glares Jake's way.

My first reaction is to fight back, but then I think about why he's saying that. He's been taking care of me since I was born, and I'm pretty much his child. He fed me and taught me how to wipe my butt when I was a toddler. He found me used clothes from God knows where. He sacrificed a lot to send me to culinary school until I was able to support myself.

And he was taking care of Kayla when one of her mom's abusive boyfriends came to stay at their trailer, and he's always been treating her like a part of our tiny tribe. I grew up thinking Kayla was our relative until she moved out of the trailer park and got her life together. And then I left for college and didn't know much about what happened. Mark is not big on gossip, but he kept me in the loop about what'd been going on in Little Hope.

All his gruffness and roughness and ordering around come from a good place. I step closer to him and wrap my arms around his enormous torso. He's always been big, and all my life he's been shielding me from what could have gone down in the trailer park with his wide back so I couldn't see all the nastiness and dirt. One could even say I grew up somewhat sheltered.

"Thank you," I mumble into his chest, stunning him into silence for a second.

When he regains his composure, he returns the hug without a word.

When I pull away, I step back so I can see his eyes. "Thank you, Mark. I'm so grateful to you and I love you, but it's time you stop trying to protect everyone around you. I'm a grown woman, and I can protect myself and Brodie, so you don't have to."

"But I want to," he says quietly.

"I know you do." My smile is warm and sincere. "And you always can. But you don't have to baby me anymore. You have your own family to take care of now."

"You are my family too." His jaw clamps shut, and the muscle on his cheek jumps. He does it when he's mad.

"I know." I try to soften my voice, so his feathers won't go up. "But it's time to let me find my own footing." *And let you be free of the burden of me.*

I touch his shoulder one more time before striding toward the laughter and cheery voices.

When I enter the room, I find everyone on the floor laughing with Brodie who's trying to walk while Alicia holds his tiny hand. I pause as my heart skips a beat. This is what I wanted for him. This is what we've never had. A family who gathers together and celebrates moments in life.

A lump in my throat suddenly doesn't let me breathe. I look around the room. Kayla's sitting on the couch next to Justin, and they both are laughing when Brodie stumbles, scaring the ever-loving crap out of Alicia, who grabs him and her heart at the same time. Jake's standing in the corner of the room, silently leaning his shoulder on the wall. Mary's on the arm of a chair and she's hugging her awfully silent and not smiling husband. He's intensely watching Alicia and Brodie. His brows are furrowed, and his fingers are interlocked on his lap. I'm sure he's imagining her with her own kid playing in their living room.

"Fuckin' finally!" Justin says loudly when he sees me and Mark behind me. "We can eat now."

"Justin," Jake's warning voice comes from the corner, "watch your mouth."

Everyone freezes, and Justin slowly turns toward Jake. "What did you just say?"

"I said," Jake repeats slowly, turning to Justin, "watch your mouth. There's a kid in the room."

Justin looks at Brodie and then at me. "He doesn't even understand it, right?" he asks, sounding a bit apologetic.

"It doesn't matter. If it was your kid, you wouldn't like

anyone disrespecting him like that." Jake's voice is firm. Way firmer than I've ever heard.

The air is thick and silent. If a mosquito sneezed now, it would be as loud as a bomb. Another freaking lump in my throat silently grows and makes my eyes itchy. If I swallow it now, it would be as loud as thunder.

"Sorry, Oli," Justin says, wincing, and everyone lets out a chorus of exhales. We all feel like we've just dodged a bullet. Justin and Jake both have very similar explosive temperaments. Plus, Justin strongly dislikes Jake from what I've heard around town.

"It's okay." I try to sound confident, but it comes out as a squeak. I feel like I've just stepped into some sci-fi fantasy movie where Jake's protecting my child's honor because a sci-fi genre is the only one in which that would be possible.

Mary jumps from the chair, clapping her hands once. "Shall we go eat?"

"Fu—" Justin stops himself, shooting me a sideway glance. "I mean, yes."

Kayla chuckles and gives him a kiss on his cheek. "I'm so proud of you."

He turns to her. "Will you reward me tonight?" he whispers so loud, Donna in her coffee shop heard it.

Kayla giggles and whispers something into his ear as Alicia makes a loud gagging sound. "I need to bleach my ears. And my eyes." She covers said eyes with her hand. "And to think of it, my brain to."

Mary giggles too and tells Mark, "You need to up your game, boy."

Mark's cheeks turn beet red above his beard. I don't think I've ever seen them this shade.

"Mom!" Alicia cries out, and heads toward the big

dining room with Brodie in her arms and Mark hot on her heels, clearly rushing to avoid any more embarrassment.

Their dining room is beautiful. Something I'd love to have eventually. Nice, neutral tones with the perfect amount of furniture and decorations. Perfectly placed servings on the table make it look like a picture out of a magazine.

All the servings. Including a baby highchair. They don't have grandkids. *Why do they have a highchair?*

My question must be written all over my face because Mary's voice sounds next to my ear.

"My neighbor was giving it away, so I decided why not, you know? In case you ever need me to keep Brodie overnight or something." Her voice is apologetic and rushed.

I send her an angry stare, still mad about being set up because now I have zero doubt about that happening now. She forces a smile on her face, and I don't question why I would need her to keep Brodie overnight. I've already been doubting her helping me because she's so attached to my son on the one hand. But on the other, I don't think any other babysitter can love him the way she does because that woman loves my son, and it beats anything else in my book.

Feeling like this game is getting more dangerous, and after speedy consideration, I decide to look for other nanny candidates once the rush of the bakery opening subsides.

"That seat should be okay, right?" Mary's helpful voice wakes me up from the daydreaming.

"Which one?" I ask gruffly.

"Next to the baby-chair of course." She points at the seat between the highchair and Jake.

Sending her another glare, I sigh and head toward the seat, knowing I've been set up once again. That evil woman got something into her head that has no place being in there, and now she's trying to meddle in forces she doesn't understand.

Jake's sitting with a rigid back, staring at his empty plate while Alicia and Mark sit across from us, and Justin took a seat at the head of the table with Kayla on the side. Mary's empty chair is clearly next to George who is at the other head spot.

I give Jake a forced smile when I sit next to him. Even though it's the last thing I want to do, I also don't want anyone to be suspicious of what's going on. I feel like anyone can take one look at us and figure out that we kissed on the floor of my bakery with his coiled, strong body pressing mine. And something else very strong poking between my thighs.

Quietly clearing my throat, I carefully glance at Jake and notice him doing the same. He looks completely uncomfortable and out of place. In his own home where he grew up. And I suddenly feel like crap. My mere presence is adding to the tension of whatever is going on at the table. Justin is shooting glares at Jake every few seconds, and Mark is just staring him down. I don't think I've seen my brother blink—that's how intense he is.

Jake seems to be unfazed, and I feel an odd ping of pride. Very misplaced. Very. I mean, he's the villain of the story, so pride should be the very last thing on my mind when I look at him.

Feeling a hot stare on my face, I find Mark glaring at *me* now. He probably noticed my glances at Jake and now he's furious, especially after our short conversation. Mark has always been overprotective, but if he finds out that Jake's gotten 'a taste' of his sister, among other things, he'll have a stroke.

"Let's say what we're grateful for and eat already," Justin urges everyone, sniffing the lasagna right next to him.

"Good idea," George confirms, and takes Mary's hand who takes Brodie's hand.

Taking my son's other hand, I silently say how thankful I am to hold him. That pneumonia gave me such a scare that I found a newfound appreciation even in sleepless nights. He smiles as he usually does when I give him my finger to hold onto and makes cute bubbles with his mouth. My heart instantly melts and whatever doubts I had about having Mary as a babysitter evaporate. At least for today. I'll think about that tomorrow.

Someone carefully nudges my thigh to my right, and I find a big open palm waiting for my hand. The moment I place it into his, his giant hand swallows mine completely. It's dry and warm. And firm. Very firm. Calloused. Rough. Reliable.

The back of his hand rests on his thigh in a casual gesture like our handholding means nothing, while I imagine feeling the roughness of his callouses between my legs.

With such an inappropriate thought at the Thanksgiving table with the whole family present, I return focus on my kid and instantly forget about Jake.

George takes over as a head of the family should and says grace, making everyone's life easier—it's hard to open up when you don't feel particularly close to most of the people. I wouldn't have problems being sincere with Mark and Alicia, but every other adult at the table is not very close to me.

When he's done, Justin loudly claps his hands, clearly indicating that we should stop handholding and start eating.

A chatter around makes me believe that everyone caught on.

Excluding us. I'm still holding my boy's hand because I could sit like that forever and not get tired. And Jake probably feels the same because my hand is still in his. I gently pull it away, and he releases it after a ghost of a squeeze. It was so gentle and brief that I'm not even sure I haven't made it up.

Everyone talks as they fill their plates with food, and I look around for something Brodie might eat. Jake stands up, making me freeze. Did something go wrong that I'm not aware of? In the meantime, he scans the table, takes a plate, and places it in front of me.

Mashed potatoes.

"You said you mush food for him." He nods at Brodie, not looking me in the eye. "This is already mashed," he says it and sits down like nothing extraordinary just happened.

"Tha—" I can't finish it because it comes out as something incoherent, so I clear my throat before speaking again. "Thank you."

I take the potatoes and put some on a plate for Brodie. When Mary cuts turkey and asks me first which piece I want, I freeze and lift my eyes, blinking at her.

"Which piece, dear?" she repeats, waiting for my answer when I can't say a word. All our Thanksgivings consisted of Mark and me, and when I went to college, it was just me and maybe a friend or two sometimes who weren't fortunate enough to have a big family.

Everyone's eyes are on me, but mine land on Mark who's watching me with a soft, understanding look on his face.

"I'll take a drumstick, please," I finally say in a tight voice.

"Good choice. It's Jake and Justin's favorite too. They'll be lucky if Brodie won't want both legs, yeah? He looks like he can manage them better than you boys," she says, winking at Jake, making him let out a small chuckle.

While Mary's cutting the turkey for everyone, I shred it into nearly microscopic pieces and put it on Brodie's plate who's already stuffing his face with mashed potato, using a tiny teaspoon Mary placed for him. I saw him trying to use his fingers first, but he couldn't get much in, so he managed to grab the utensil and find a way to utilize it. My little guy makes me proud. But once he sees turkey on his plate, his eyes go round, and he drops the spoon, digging his little fingers into the meat.

A soft chuckle to my right makes my head whip toward Jake who's smiling looking at my son. Smiling. Like a big genuine smile that transforms his face. He even looks younger with those small wrinkles around his mouth. His big, blue eyes seem brighter than before.

"I see you've got a carnivore there, huh." His quiet tone is carefree and relaxed.

"Yeah." I smile back. "He loves it."

"Jake loved meat too," Mary voices delightfully, demonstrating how good her hearing really is. "He used to eat so much when he was about the same age. So much! He was a chubby little one, that's for sure. Justin ate vegetables and sweets. That little man could sense a candy a mile away and wobble to it. But Jake." She laughs. "He could do the same to my lasagna. It was hilarious."

"That's why Justin loves the sweetest latte in the universe of lattes," Alicia laughs. "When I try his coffee, I feel like I'm one sip away from diabetes."

"It's not so bad!" Justin cries out. "I love my lattes sweet."

"You're losing the point of drinking coffee," Mark snorts.

"Why? Because I don't drink that muddy shit you do?" Justin laughs in return, getting a nasty glare from Jake. Funny thing is that when Justin said the word 'shit,' every single head at the table turned toward Jake. Justin's cheeks pinken slightly, and he looks at me. "Sorry, Oli."

I giggle. Then I giggle some more. And then I start laughing.

"I'm s—" I laugh again. "I'm sorry, I don't know what came over me."

A few shared glances and smiles around the table tell me something I can't quite understand, but thank God, soon everyone moves on to their food and conversation again.

Jake's got the other drumstick he hasn't touched, which caused him another nasty stare from Justin who clearly hoped to get it. And every few minutes, Justin glares at Jake who still hasn't touched his piece. He literally ate everything at his plate but that thing. Maybe he doesn't like it that much after all, but the rivalry between them is too strong so they fight even over the drumstick.

"Does he want another one?"

I don't understand what he means and look at him with a question in my eyes. "What?"

"The kid." He nods at Brodie. "Does he want another one?" He nods at the lonely drumstick on his plate.

I glance at Brodie who's slowed down chewing because he's clearly full. He started playing with the leftovers on his plate, painting the mashed potatoes all over the highchair. Then I glance back at Jake's plate. That turkey leg is almost the size of Brodie's head. I want to laugh and say that he's okay, but when I find Jake's focused eyes, I stop myself before I say something that will ruin the moment.

"No, Jake. I think he's alright," I explain in a soft voice. "He ate a huge piece, and he's full."

"Do you want it?" His brows draw together in concentration as if he's trying to solve a world problem. He glances at my plate, where nearly ninety-five percent of the drumstick still lies on the plate because I can't make myself relax and start eating.

My eyes itch, and my nose stings.

"I'm good too, thank you," I croak, and he nods. Only after that, he takes the damn turkey leg and starts eating it.

I quickly avert my eyes from him and stare at my plate, scared a weird sniffling noise betrays me and escapes into the wild, letting everyone know what's going on in my head and my chest.

Chapter Eighteen

J^{ake}

Well, this was a total setup. I tried fishing for information from Mom before I came in, assuming that Olivia would be here since Mark has been coming to all family dinners for the past couple of years. I don't blame him—if I was married, I wouldn't want my wife out of my sight. But I am not and will never be, so I'm left only to assume.

I don't like kids. I really don't. They poop. They cry. They throw things at you. But somehow, Olivia's kid doesn't annoy me. Quite the opposite. I find myself constantly checking on him. He does this thing with his mouth that makes funny bubbles, and he does it when he's happy. The kid is always happy though, you can tell. It's probably Olivia's trait. I don't know who his father is, but the moment I think about his existence—and this is the first time the thought has occurred to me—I instantly hate him. She's never mentioned him in the handful of times we've seen each other, and one of those times we didn't talk much. Our tongues were too busy shoved down each other's throats.

The moment I remember the kiss and her body under mine, my dick twitches. While I'm sitting at family dinner. I'm trying to remind myself that I'm surrounded by people, and it seems to work. Until I glance at Olivia's finger which she's moving over her knee. She's clearly in her own thoughts, and I sure as fuck want to know what those thoughts are because the damn finger is a fucking tease. It slows down and then moves again, making tiny circles. *Does she do the same circles when she—*

"—more?"

"What?" I come out of the haze.

"Do you want more?" Kayla asks, stunning every single person at the table into silence. Myself more than anyone else. "I know you like wings too, and I haven't touched mine."

"Seriously?" Justin cries out like a baby. "He's got the leg, and now he's getting the wing too?"

"Yes." Kayla rolls her eyes and returns her attention back to me. "Do you want it?"

The silence at the table is loud. Everyone's eyes dart between me and Kayla. It's not just the offering of food, but it's Kayla who's doing the offering. And now everyone's waiting for my reaction. Is the fuse going to go off? Should they look for cover? Because Justin looks like a coiled cobra ready to attack if I say something wrong.

I don't have any desire to say anything wrong though. For the first time in forever, something inside me starts looking for purpose. I don't know where this came from, but that void inside suddenly *feels*, and I need to fill it with something.

"Yeah, I'll take it if you don't want it," I reply, knowing it sounds a bit gruff. But it's the best I can do now.

She pushes her fork into the soft of the wing and stretches it toward me. "Here you go."

"Thanks." I grab the piece off her fork and place it on my plate.

The chatter slowly comes back to life as I bite into the wing. I'm not hungry; in fact, I barely can breathe at this point, but I'll finish that wing even if I die here. After a few seconds of chewing, I feel someone's intense stare on me. Glancing around the table, I find Justin watching me. The two lines between his brows deepen while his arm is wrapped around Kayla's shoulder protectively.

When he notices my attention on him, he drags Kayla closer to him. She glances at him with a question and lets it slide. Obviously, Kayla has been smarter than any of us put together all along.

A child's whining to my left makes Olivia jump from her chair.

"Do you need help, my dear?" Mom asks as she rises to her feet too.

"No, I got it," Olivia replies a bit defensively. "He just needs a diaper change."

"You sure?" Mom keeps moving.

"Yes." Olivia's voice is stern. "Thank you."

"Okay. You can go to the bathroom or the guest bedroom down the corridor." She motions toward the hallway.

"Thanks." Olivia grabs her kid and the bag she brought with her and disappears from view.

Once she's out of sight, Mom starts talking to Mark.

"Your sister is a very strong woman."

"She is," he confirms, his voice full of pride. It's clear in the way he leans back in his chair, happy to talk about his sister.

"And she has a wonderful child," Mom coos, bringing her hands to her chest.

"Yeah, Brodie's awesome. We're totally getting baby fever from him." Mark chuckles, making Alicia's face turn pink.

"As you should." Mom's face stretches with a wide smile. "Does his father visit you often?" She shoots out of nowhere. Mark's eyes turn wide while Alicia cries out, "Mom!"

"Does he?" Our nosey mother totally ignores her.

Mark's jaw clamps shut as his neck moves in a rough swallow. "Why?"

"I'm just curious, that's all." She starts fidgeting with the plates. "Such a wonderful child and such a wonderful woman, and yet, I haven't seen the father. It's weird, you know."

Mark looks around the table, looking for support, but everyone's just as uncomfortable as he is.

"We should probably have invited him to dinner too," she continues, not seeing how much her questions are killing the mood. And, apparently, Mark too. I love my mom, but she can be like a seasoned detective, questioning someone with a lamp in their face without bothering how that may affect them. "Unless, you don't know who he is." She glances at Mark from under her lashes.

"Mom!" I call out with a loud warning. Yes, I want to know who the father is. I want to know who'll be a part of her life forever. But not this way. Not behind her back.

"He doesn't." Olivia's voice booms through the room, following mine. "If you wish to ask something, just do it to my face next time. I've been talked about behind my back my whole life, and I thought I outgrew it when we got out of the trailer park." She looks around the table. "But looks like I'll always be that girl."

And now we all know a new definition of a 'heavy silence.'

Olivia moves the kid from one side to another, hauls her bag over her free shoulder, and heads toward the exit. "Thank you for dinner, the food was amazing," she says without looking back.

Mark jumps to his feet and follows her, disapproval palpable in the air.

"Nice one, Mom," I say, causing Justin to snort loud enough for everyone to hear.

"Yeah?" He laughs sarcastically. "See who's talking. The asshole of the whole generation."

I open my mouth to shoot back but shut it just in time to compose myself. "I deserve that. But she doesn't." I point at the door. "She's just trying to live and raise her kid. Without others meddling." I shoot a stern glance at my mom. I love and respect her, but maybe I respect her a tiny bit less after her treating Olivia this way—like she's some sort of whore who sleeps around and accidentally gets knocked up. She might, but it's no one's business but hers. Even though I can't imagine Olivia like that. When Justin was doing the same, she was cheering him on for 'gaining experience,' and when it's Olivia, she's switched ships.

"But that's what you do, don't you? Meddle in others' business." Justin leans back, narrowing his eyes while I mentally roll mine. He wants a fight, and we both knew at some point today, we'd have a standoff. I'd just prefer it was any other time.

"I apologized for that."

"That's not enough," he cuts off. His cheek muscle jumps.

"That's all you're going to get. I can't change the past, but I'm trying to change the future. And I'm trying fuckin' hard."

His hand on the table curls into a fist. "I don't see you trying as hard as you think you are."

"Justin," Kayla's soft voice calls out to his sanity which has been lost at this point. I know my brother. Once his dark side emerges, there is no going back. Just like with mine.

"Not now." He shakes his head at her and shifts his attention back to me. He looks ready to attack. "You nearly cost me everything. My happiness, man. Her." He nods at Kayla. "And all because of what? Your pride? Prejudice?" His voice rises at the end. "What, Jake?"

I'm grinding my teeth because I want to tell him why. But saying it out loud also will mean admitting what sort of a giant idiot I am and all the fucked-up things I've done.

"Tell me why." He jumps to his feet and moves around the table toward me.

I stand to meet him but remain still. It was bound to happen sooner or later, and he deserves to land a few punches.

"Tell me!" He bellows, grabbing the front of my shirt.

I feel my nostrils flaring and my heart racing.

"Fuckin' tell me, Jake. Tell me what was so important that you decided it was worth losing your brother over." He gives me a slight shake, breathing like a bull.

My breathing matches his. My body wants to react and push back, but I'm holding it. I'm fighting like hell not to rip his hands off my shirt, breaking a few of his fingers in the process.

But he just admitted out loud what I suspected all along

—he'll never forgive me for what I've done. I glance around the table—none of them will.

Only Kayla's watching me with any sort of understanding, her face pleading. What for? To tell them what she thinks she knows? She doesn't know the half of it. And none of them ever will.

I look Justin straight in the eyes. "I can't. It was done, and I can't change that. You need to move on."

"I can't move on from it. Because of you, the woman of my dreams doesn't want to marry me."

"What?" Kayla cries out. "It's not because of him."

Justin's head whips toward her. "Why not then?"

Looking awfully nervous, she starts chewing on her lip. "Because I'm scared that when we get married, you'll stop loving me," she admits quietly, not looking at Justin.

"What?" Justin stumbles back. "What are you talking about?"

"What *what*?" She throws her hands in the air. "Everyone knows you're obsessed with things you can't have. Once you get it, you lose interest in them."

"Kay—" His voice hitches as he slowly walks toward her and drops to his knees in front of her. "Where did you get that stupid idea?"

Kayla sniffles, suddenly looking so small at this giant table with everyone's wide eyes on her. "Everyone knows it, Justin. You get obsessed with some car, you get it, you sell it right away 'cause you don't want it anymore. You find a new coffee flavor you love, you buy it, two days later, you trash the beans because you're over it. I live with you, remember? I see a lot." She wipes her nose with her hand. "I don't want to be those coffee beans."

Justin takes her hands in his—tenderly, I didn't know he could—and finds her gaze. "Kay, baby, this is a very, I mean, very silly idea. You are not a flavor to me. You are the actual definition of coffee."

Kayla starts giggling until she hiccups. Everyone who knows Justin knows how obsessed he is with coffee and lattes specifically. He has tons of coffee machines, and coffee is probably one thing he truly can't live without.

"Really?" she asks in a hopeful voice, like he just hasn't sounded like a cheesy fool. I mean, he was awful, but it seemed to work.

"Yeah." He drops her hands and brings his hand to frame her face. "Please marry me and be my coffee forever."

"You are so cheesy." She giggles again, wiping her now runny nose. "Okay. I will become your coffee forever."

Everyone starts cheering, and I take it as my cue to leave. I quietly slip away, grab my jacket, and head outside.

I don't make it far because I meet Mark on the porch. He's leaning against the wall and watching the road with his arms crossed over his giant chest. The dude is fucking enormous. He could take anyone if only for his sheer size of a small tank.

"What happened there?" he asks in a neutral tone.

I pause, surprised by his attempt to strike a conversation. "Kayla finally decided to marry my bro—" I stop just in time. "Justin."

Mark nods. "Thought so."

I linger for another moment before I move toward the steps.

"I appreciate you stepping up for my sister."

I pause without turning to him.

"But I don't want you around. She's been through a lot, and she doesn't need another burden."

I wince at his harsh words, but he's right. I'd be a burden to her, someone who's just starting her life.

"I'm not chasing anything," I say as I glance back at him.

"Not yet. But your interest is clear." His eyes are trained on me.

I let out a bitter laugh. "My desires mean nothing, Mark. I've already figured that."

His face turns confused, and I mentally smack myself for letting this self-pity slip.

"I've heard you. You can chill now." With that, I depart this joyful dinner, comprehending that it was probably the last time for a while I'll be welcomed here.

Chapter Nineteen

J^{ake}

As I drive away from Little Hope back home, or rather, the place I sleep, I find myself going off the road and making a U-turn. Then I find myself driving to Main Street and to one of the small side streets. Then I find myself parking next to the sign *'Sweet Dreams Are Made of This.'*

And somehow, I find my legs moving toward the door. The one on the right clearly leads to the bakery itself where I've already visited once, and the one identical door on the left most likely leads to her apartment.

I knock on that one. Nothing. I knock again.

It flies open.

"Mark, I told you, I'm fi—"

Her eyes go round when she sees me instead of Mark. Her wild hair falls around her shoulders like an untamed mane. She's changed into a light green sweater and leggings.

"What are you doing here?" she asks, hugging herself and looking around. *No need, honey, no one is near, so you won't be judged being seen with me.*

Suddenly I feel fucking bitter. *What am I doing here?*

"I—" I scratch the back of my head, trying to remember what made me come here but draw a blank. "I just wanted to see if you're okay."

She pulls the collar of her sweater higher, hiding her chin in it. "I'm fine."

I sigh. "Sorry about my mom. She means well, but she's nosey."

Her weak smile is a clear indication of what she thinks about my apology, and my mother for that matter. I don't even know why I'm apologizing for her because I sure as fuck can barely apologize for me, and I have a lot of atonements to make.

"Yeah," I say like an idiot, and stick my hands into the front pockets of my jeans because I don't know what else to do with them. It seems to be my motto these days.

Olivia starts chewing on her lips, looking at the street. Her left hand keeps pulling on her collar, and her right one is hidden behind her back. She rocks on her heels, looking unsure. She's probably weirded out by my presence here, and I can't blame her.

"Alright." I decide to make it less painful for everyone. "If you're fine, I guess I'll just, you know, go."

"Yeah, sure." She nods while the chewing of her lower lip intensifies.

"Gonna go then." I wave my hand at her, turn around, and head toward my truck, feeling like a complete moron. If I could facepalm myself without looking even dumber, I'd totally do that.

"Jake!"

Her voice makes me almost leap around in the air like a damn ballerina.

"Yeah?" I ask too eagerly.

She looks inside the house and then back at me, sinking her teeth into her lower lip. She's contemplating something. If she asks me to stand on the street and talk to her because she feels sad, I will. Even if my ass freezes to death and my balls start clinking like icicles.

She keeps watching me, worrying her lip. If she can't decide, she doesn't want it. So I'll save her the trouble.

"I'm gonna go," I say with a light smile, pointing at the door of my truck.

Her chest rises and falls with the deepest sigh, and her shoulders drop in defeat.

"Do you want to come in?" She nods at the stairs behind her. "Brodie's awake, so it might not be that fun for you, but I have coffee and hot chocolate. No beer or anything like that though."

I find her eyes and keep them steady, trying silently to communicate that it's okay to back out and I don't need her to be polite. But after she's made her decision, her gaze is steady.

"I was about to make myself a cup of hot chocolate anyway."

I nod and follow her inside. I'm not a fan of cocoa or sweet, cozy drinks, but she's making one, so I'll take it. It's the closest thing to *normal* I have nowadays.

Once I'm in, she closes the door and starts locking all three locks, sending me an odd look from under her lashes.

"I'm glad you've learned your lesson," I can't help but utter, enjoying how rosy her cheeks become in the moment.

I can almost see her rolling her big, soulful eyes, which

most likely look a little less soulful now that she's annoyed with me. "Don't let your head grow big."

I smile at her snarky tone and say something I probably —most likely—shouldn't have said. "Nothing will happen to you while I'm here. To either of you."

"Except, apparently, the bathroom fucking," she mumbles quietly under her breath—I don't think she meant for me to hear. Then her hand pauses for a moment while she says a little louder, "I know." Her words are so quiet, I can't even tell if I haven't made them up with my wishful thinking of being important to someone. "Let's go. Brodie's probably anxious I'm out of his sight," she adds, heading upstairs.

In front of me.

Up the stairs.

Where her leggings-clad ass ends up right in front of my face. I swallow the sudden tightness in my throat, hoping it'll somehow loosen the tightness in my pants. *What am I? A hormonal boy who just hit puberty?* I mean I love a good ass, but I shouldn't get hard by having one in front of my face. It's ridiculous.

Blinking the horny haze away, I try to focus on the steps in front of me, so I don't end up with my face hitting one of them.

When we get into her apartment, I'm hit with the smell of sweet baked cookies and coziness. At least, this is how I imagine 'cozy' to smell. The chaos is everywhere. Toys of all colors are scattered all over the place. Two worn-out couches are covered with mismatching pillows and throws. There's a giant stain of something yellowish on one of the cushions that oddly seems like a part of the interior.

A big window on the right shows the snowed in street

where my truck is parked. Warm fairy lights frame the window, making it look like a kid's fairytale dream.

The kitchen on the left is busy. The countertops are covered with bowls, plates, and boxes. A big thing—I think it's a mixer, though I'm not sure due to the complexity of the gadget—stands in the middle of a small island. It's pure chaos, and yet everything seems to be in its place. Paradox for sure. I've grown up in a busy kitchen where my mom cooked like she had an army to feed, so I understand the true meaning of a well-used kitchen.

While I'm ogling her space, she goes to a crib or whatever this thing's called.

Wait, it's not a crib. It's like a crib but on the floor and wider, and the kid is trapped inside without any possibility of escaping and causing a ruckus. Very handy.

"Look how big you are! Stayed by yourself without crying," she coos, taking him in her arms. "I'm so proud of you."

Another sudden lump in my throat out of nowhere. Legit out of nowhere. I don't even know why the fuck I'm so emotional. It's embarrassing at this point.

A loud whistle from the kitchen makes Olivia's head whip toward the sound.

"Oh, crap. Hold him."

She suddenly thrusts the kid into my arms without warning. I automatically accept him, and she runs to the kitchen.

"Don't curse!" I yell out of habit to her back, stunning myself into silence. She sends me a funny look and takes the kettle off the stove.

I look down at the tiny creature in my arms. He's watching me with his big, disturbingly blue eyes without blinking. His mouth is slightly open, and there're bubbles around it.

He blinks. I blink. He opens his mouth wider, and I brace myself for a cry. But instead, he starts giggling. Out of nowhere. This evening doesn't cease to wonder.

Then he wiggles, nearly making me drop him. My palms turn sweaty, and he feels like an eel, ready to wiggle his way out of my grip. So I tighten it. I wrap my arms around him, burying his whole body into my chest. This way he doesn't have a chance to escape and fall.

With him securely in my arms, I walk to the kitchen and find Olivia quietly cursing, wiping the stove.

"What happened?"

She groans. "I forgot that I put milk on with the water. Good thing the kettle whistles, or we'd be calling Mark's department."

I tighten my grip on the kid and come closer to the stove. It's a brown mess. The milk apparently escaped the pot and is now splattered all over everything, and she's trying to clean it.

"Need any help?"

"No. Just hold Brodie so he doesn't crawl here," she says, blowing a stray strand of hair out of her face.

"He doesn't walk yet?" I glance at the boy in my arms.

"No." She chuckles. "He just turned nine months. He crawls and tries walking when you hold his hand."

"Wanna walk, big man?" I ask the little guy, and he gives me a funny smile of a few teeth which I take as an agreement with my awesome idea. "Cool. Let's go."

I take him back to the living room and carefully place him on the floor. A few minutes later, we're walking around the coffee table which is clearly Mark's handiwork. I know because I used to have one of those at home even though I'll never admit it. He carves wooden furniture, and it looks dope.

"Do you have any preferences in your milk for hot chocolate?" Olivia calls out, clinking the dishes at the sink.

"No," I reply, wincing. I've always been scared of that question. Like when you go to a shop and ask for a cup of coffee, and they start asking you what sort of milk you want. I've always thought there's only one kind, which comes from a cow, but now there's all these types of milk a man can squeeze out of different plants. "Whatever you'll make for yourself."

"Then whole milk. It makes the cocoa creamier."

"Sounds good," I confirm without looking at her because I'm too busy watching the little man smiling as he conquers yet another loop around the table. He makes weird noises with every small step he takes, and I start quietly cheering him on.

Sometime later, Olivia brings two steaming mugs and places them in the middle of the coffee table.

"Make sure you don't leave it on the edge, so Brodie doesn't flip the hot liquid."

I nod and assess the threat. It would be better if those cups were standing on the island, far out of his reach. So I can fuckin' relax and drink the brown shit while ogling his mom. Instead, I'll be too busy watching the damn mugs.

Olivia walks up to me. "C'mon, Brodie, let's drink formula and go to sleep."

"What? Why?" I glance at the clock on the wall. "It's only past seven."

She takes the kid in her arms. "He's still small and needs to be in bed early."

"Why?" I'm still confused.

"He can't miss his melatonin window, or he'll never fall

asleep, and the night will turn into a nightmare pretty fast." Then she adds, wincing, "So is the next day."

"Oh, okay." I clear my throat and force myself to step away and relax. "I guess I'll go then."

"You don't have to. You can drink your hot cocoa while I feed Brodie. He already took a bath, so I'll just put him to bed after." She looks to the side, seemingly embarrassed with something. "But I get it. You have better things to do. I can get your chocolate into a to-go cup, if you want. And then I ca—"

"I'll wait," I stop her nervous mumbling.

She visibly relaxes. "Okay." With that, she sits on the couch with the kid in her arms and brings a full bottle to his mouth. His chubby hands grab it as he starts hungrily drinking it. So much unconscious desire to live in his little body that I feel inspired too.

I probably have been staring too intensely because she says giggling, "Yeah, he has a big appetite. I can't complain."

I laugh quietly. "I can tell."

Not knowing what else to say, I grab the steaming mug and take a sip.

"Holy sh—" I quickly clear my throat, making her let out a melodical laugh. "I mean holy cow. This is good."

"Bakery owner, remember?" She winks and adjusts the kid in her arms.

"Forgot for a second." I smile cheekily back, not knowing where this lightness has come from.

With the snow falling behind the window, a steaming mug in my hands of something I've never even liked but suddenly love—again, out of nowhere—and them peacefully sitting on the couch, I get a loud reminder that this is not my life. Even though I suddenly yearn for it very much.

Sobering up, I take my mug, walk to the kitchen, and rinse it.

"You don't have to," she calls out from the couch.

"Yeah," I reply like a fool and walk back. "I gotta go."

Her face falls as if she's unhappy with me leaving. Again, probably my wishful thinking. "Okay."

"Thanks for the cocoa. It was good."

She nods shortly. The edges of her lips point downward. I turn around and walk away. Away from their perfectly imperfect little family, back into the snow, making sure the locks are in place when I leave.

Chapter Twenty

Olivia

We're alone again. Every time I feel ready to talk to him, he reminds me of who he is. A lonely animal backed into a corner, snarling at everyone wishing to approach him.

I have to admit that I might have gotten my hopes up about him at some point, despite what everyone thinks of him. I've known Jake for a long time, and I've always seen something else in him. Something no one else does. But it's probably just my imagination, and Jake is exactly who everyone thinks he is.

I change Brodie's diaper and put him to bed. He's the best thing that ever happened to me, and I don't think anything else can ever top it. All regrets that Jake brought in are gone in an instant.

I give my sweet, little boy a kiss, take the baby monitor, and go back to the living room to put my ass flat on the couch and watch some mindless movie. I prefer to leave my kitchen clean for the night, but today has not been easy on me, and cleaning is the last thing on my mind now. So I warm up my already cold cocoa and put the TV on. It's eight forty-five, and Brodie is asleep. I have some time for myself before I go to bed and snuggle in too.

In the show, the female character is yelling at the contractor about getting out of her newly bought inn in a rural area while wearing just a towel and a nasty attitude when someone knocks at my door downstairs.

I pause the movie and walk to the window to peek outside. I'm not expecting any guests—Jake's visit was enough surprise for one day. Mark has called me before, and I assured him that I was fine and didn't need him to come to my rescue.

Pulling the curtain to the side, I stick my nose out to see who's there.

Jake's truck is parked at the same spot as when he first came in. If he ever left. Because his car is covered in snow, and there are no tire tracks in or out of the spot. I push my nose into the glass, trying to see if it's him who's knocking.

It's him.

Swallowing a lump of nerves down, I pad my feet down the stairs and unlock the door. He's behind it. His shoulders and head are covered in snow. His nose is red. His ears too. So are his cheeks.

"Hi," I squeak.

"Hi." His voice is rough. And cold. Yes, even his voice is cold. All of him looks cold.

"What are you still doing here?"

He watches my face before replying. "I don't know." He sounds sincere and lost.

I step to the side, opening the door wider. He walks

inside. I lock it and turn to him. He's like a snowman, but some of it has already started melting from the heat from upstairs. "You're freezing!" I bring my hands to his shoulders and wipe off the snow. Then I move them to his hair and rake my fingers through, shaking the snow away. When I accidentally touch his ears, I feel how freezing cold they are, so I press my open palms to them, trying to warm them up with my heat.

His icy-blue eyes are intensely watching me as I gently rub his frozen ears.

"Let's get upstairs before you freeze to death," I whisper, dropping my hands. He nods in response.

I take his cold hand and lead him to my apartment. It seems so surreal that I'm walking Jake Attleborough to my place by his hand. Teenage Olivia would have died from excitement on the spot.

"I'll make you something hot. One second."

He tightens his hold on my hand. "No. I'm okay."

I turn toward him. "Jake, you're freezing. You'll get pneumonia."

He shakes his head. "I'll be fine."

"Please." My voice hitches. "Let me do it. You look like a snowman. Even your nose is red."

The corner of his lips quirks up. "Okay."

I rush to the stove and put a kettle on. Then I quickly get the teapot ready with ginger, lemon, and honey. Sue me but I'm really worried about him. When I glance at him, I find him still standing at the same spot I left him.

"Take your jacket off. You can put it over there." I point at the radiator. "It will dry there."

He nods and rids himself of his jacket before coming to the kitchen. "Do you need any help?"

I chuckle, imagining Jake making tea. The picture is

hilarious. "No. Could you bring the baby monitor from the couch though? I feel better when it's here."

He speedwalks to the couch, grabs the monitor, and heads my way. His steps falter halfway as he stares at the monitor.

"What is he doing?" I ask, suddenly worried what could draw so much of his attention.

"Sleeping," he replies, still staring at the monitor. "He looks like you when he sleeps."

"Really?" I smile, feeling a ping of pride. I can't explain why but every time someone tells me that Brodie looks like me, I take it as a personal achievement.

"Yeah." He pauses. "When he's looking at me with his giant, blue eyes, it's almost unsettling. It's like the little guy is fifty years older than he is."

A knife in my hand slips, and I cut my finger. "Shit."

"Damn, sorry. That's a bad thing to say to a parent I guess." He comes to me and starts running water. "Where's your first aid kit?"

"In the cabinet over there." I point at the corner of the kitchen. He brings the kit while I keep my finger under the water. He totally picked the wrong time for his revelation.

"Let me see."

"I can patch it up myself." I nearly roll my eyes. I work in a kitchen, it's a miracle I still have all my fingers attached, so I'm well aware how to stop minor bleeding. No big deal.

"Let me see," he orders, stretching his arm toward me.

Well, when you asked so nicely. I pull my finger from under the water, and it instantly gets covered in blood. I guess the cut was deeper than I anticipated.

Jake takes my hand in his and pinches my fingers right under the cut, and the bleeding slows down. Then he pours peroxide all over it.

"Shit!" I hiss like a poisonous snake, ready to sink my teeth into him because he's the reason for my current pain. "I didn't expect that."

"Sorry." He doesn't sound sorry, and I'm about to say that he should stop enjoying my pain so much when he brings his face closer to my finger and blows on it. He blows on my booboo.

My throat closes up. But he doesn't notice it and keeps blowing.

"Is it better?" he asks a few moments later.

"Yeah," I croak.

He then cleans the wound—very professionally—and fixes the Band-Aid on top of it when it's nice and dry.

"Wow. You could be a kindergarten teacher," I announce, lifting my finger up in the air to inspect his work.

He lets out a surprised laugh and starts cleaning everything. I go to finish the tea. It doesn't take long because I was finishing up when Jake decided to drop a bomb in the middle of my kitchen. I pour water into the teapot and wait for the liquid to take a nice, golden color. Then I pour him and myself two cups and put one in front of him. The whole time I'm moving around, he leans his ass on my table, gripping the edge with his hands.

"Thanks." He picks up the cup and takes a sip.

"Careful!" I try warning him. "It's hot!"

"Hot is what I need now. You were right, I was a bit cold," he confesses with a smirk.

"A bit. Sure," I deadpan, and start carefully drinking my tea.

Now that all the action is done, we're left with the reality of him being in my kitchen after he stayed outside my door for an hour.

"How are you doing?" he asks, making me choke on the tea.

How am I doing? Seriously?

He comes closer and starts gently patting my back, not helping with the cough. I glance at the monitor, hoping my coughing fit didn't wake Brodie. A false alarm—the kid can sleep through everything. Definitely not my genetics.

"That's what you want to ask?" I ask sarcastically, but he just nods with a serious look on his face, so I guess we're going down this route. Taking a deep breath, I start talking. "I guess I'm fine. Considering people don't want me here."

"Who?" His voice drops an octave (when it was low to begin with) just as his eyes narrow.

"Hello?" I snort. "Nearly everyone. People around here don't like change. Especially made by someone from the wrong side of town."

His eyes turn cold. "People forget about that."

"Yeah? Like people forgot about Kayla?" I didn't mean it. I truly didn't.

But it's too late now. His face darkens, and he takes a step back. "Some people have never seen her as trailer trash if that's what you mean."

I watch him carefully, contemplating if I should continue down this path. "But you're not one of those people?"

"No," he states firmly.

"Why?" I'm genuinely curious because the Jake I see seems to differ from the Jake everyone else does. No matter how much I want to deny it.

He shakes his head. "Doesn't matter. I've never claimed to be a good guy, Olivia. With me, what you see is what you get."

I watch his face for any indication of doubt, but there is

none. He sees himself as a bad guy. Just like everyone else does. *Then why do I keep trying to convince myself that he's not?*

"Then why are you here? Because you want to do something bad?" Even as I ask this, I want to laugh. Even though I truly believe Jake is capable of doing awful things, I've never felt safer than in his presence. It's always been like that.

He carefully puts his mug back on the counter, trying not to make a sound, and looks at me. "It was a mistake coming here." He brings his hands to his face and digs the heels of his palms into his eyes. "Coming *back* here. It was a huge mistake."

He pushes away from the table and intends to walk past me, but I grab his hand, stopping his steps. He pauses but doesn't look my way.

"I don't know why I keep bringing up things that totally mess everything up," I say in a quiet voice, feeling sadness spreading through my very being.

His attention finally moves to me. His intense, blue eyes, which somehow seem even colder than they usually are, dart between mine for a few long breaths before he speaks. "Because you're my karma, Olivia."

"Karma?" I ask, confused. "What do you mean?"

His smile is the saddest thing I've ever seen. It nearly brings tears to my eyes.

He turns his body toward me and grabs my face between his hands. "With me, what you see is what you get. And I have nothing to give, Olivia." He touches his forehead to mine. "Nothing."

"You. You still have you."

He swallows. "I don't even have that," he barely whispers.

I cover his hands with mine. "Don't say that."

"I am exactly what they say I am. And you need to remember that. The next time I knock at your door, don't open."

"Why?" It comes out as a squeak.

"Because I will ruin everything you have."

My heart is beating in my neck now. The pulse is so strong that I hear it in my head.

"If I was alone, I wouldn't mind some ruining." I swallow the pulse down. "But I'm not."

"I know." He gently kisses my forehead. "And that seems to be one of the reasons I'm here."

His lips are so tender that an involuntary tear escapes my eye. He gently presses his lips to me one more time and pulls away.

"Jake." I clear my throat because it's now or never. "I need to tell yo—"

He presses his finger to my lips, silencing me. "Can you give me this one—" his neck moves with a rough swallow before he braves himself to continue, "—one time of *normal?*"

I watch as his eyes beg, and it's something I've never seen. So I nod.

He lifts his finger away from my lips and waits for me to continue, giving me an opportunity to back out. But I don't. I don't want to back out. I've been waiting for this moment for so long. I thought I was ready to tell him the truth, but fate said it's not the time. Today, we are having the night of normal.

"We have to be quiet," I whisper as I pull his face to mine. "Can you be quiet?"

His husky laughter tickles the back of my head. "Can you?"

My smile should say everything. Including the hunger I feel.

And then the shame kicks in. For my body. It's been nine months, but I didn't exactly have time to go to a gym or to even do basic stuff at home. Instead, I've been running around, trying to secure our future.

Feeling suddenly self-conscious of myself and him, the most gorgeous man I've ever known and had a crush on at school, I turn into a rigid statue. All laughter gone, I wrap my arms around my torso.

"What happened?" His voice is a bit hazy.

I look to the side, not knowing what to say.

"Olivia, what happened?" When I don't respond, he steps back. "You don't have to do anything. I was an idiot for coming here and asking . . ." He wipes his face with his hand. "Anything. Fuck. I gotta go."

"No!" I squeak. Seems it's all I do now. "It's not—" I clear my throat. "It's not you."

"What then?" He looks confused.

"It's just—" I chew on the inside of my cheek, wondering if I should say something or not. "It's just—" I take a deep breath and finally make an attempt to finish the sentence. "It's just I haven't been with anyone since I had the baby." No matter how much I try to stay strong and keep my voice steady, it wavers at the end.

Jake's forehead wrinkles in concentration. He looks in the general direction of the rooms. "But I thought—" back at me, "that you and—"

I shake my head. "I haven't had anyone since Brodie was born."

His face stretches into a mischievous smile. "I can assure you that the process is still about the same."

I look down at myself. "It's not that. No one has seen me. So . . ." I shrug.

"What do you mean 'so'?" he asks, dropping his playful smile.

"Oh, please." I nearly roll my eyes, losing a bit of that shame which is quickly getting replaced by annoyance. "Don't make me spell it out for you."

He blinks. Then blinks again. "Oh, yeah. You are going to spell it the fuck out to me because I don't understand shit."

Here we go, the old Jake rears his head.

"Yeah? Wanna know?" I ask with an ugly smirk. I know it's ugly, I've seen myself in a mirror with it. "I'm fat. And I have stretch marks. And my boobs are saggy. There." I spread my arms wide. "You have it." Then I glance down at myself. "I mean you don't have *it*, but you have the truth."

When I look back at him, I find him with a reddening face, biting his lips clearly trying not to laugh.

"Sure, laugh at my misery."

He lets out a chuckle, steps closer to me, and takes my face into his giant palms again. "Women are funny creatures."

I roll my eyes. "That's just what every woman wants to hear."

He waits for me to look him in the eye before speaking. "Every stretch mark. Every bruise." He grates out every word, making it quiet yet loud. "Every scar. It's all your story. It shows how strong you are and how much you've done to be where you are. A real man wants a real woman by his side." His words come out as an angry hiss. "So whoever the fuck ends up with you," his nose is almost touching mine now, "he'd better be a real man." His nostrils flare in obvious, barely restrained anger at something.

Someone. "Because you're the most real woman I've ever seen."

"Jake, I need to tell y—"

His mouth lands on mine. He was tender a few moments ago when he was touching my forehead, but all his tenderness is gone. He's angry at something. He's more like the Jake everyone sees. And he lets it all out.

His hands grab my ass, and he hauls me up on the counter. I spread my thighs wider, giving him space.

His already rock-hard cock is pressing on my core, and like a hungry hussy, I jerk my hips forward, not able to stop them. When my legging-clad pussy lands against him, he lets out a short and breathless groan into my mouth. Naturally, I do it again.

His grip on my hips and my ass intensifies. His fingers dig deeper into my flesh, definitely leaving bruises of ownership. I will look at them tomorrow in the secrecy of my bathroom as a reminder that this was not a dream.

His body coiled around mine feels so powerful. I've never felt so vulnerable before, faced with such sheer force.

I'm losing myself to something I'll never be able to recover from.

With every stroke of his tongue, with every brush of his hand over my skin, my mind descends deeper into the frenzy. I'm close to losing control. My hands snake between us, then down his torso—

When a tapping sound at the back of my head makes me ascend back to reality.

I pull away and try to blink the haze away.

"Is it—" Jake's voice is groggy. Husky. Scratchy. I feel it right in my own throat.

"Yeah," I croak. "Someone's knocking."

His eyes slowly widen as he stumbles back.

The sound that happens to be knocking intensifies. And it's coming from downstairs. From my door.

A sense of dread enters my body like lightning and lands in the pit of my stomach. I jump off the counter and rush to the window. On the street, right next to Jake's truck, is Mark's car.

Swallowing fear down, I move my gaze to my entrance downstairs and sure enough find my brother knocking his fist on it.

"Fuck!" I hiss, trying not to be loud because Mark's already plenty loud. "He'll scare Brodie. I'll be back."

I try fixing my hair while running downstairs and fling the door open. Once Mark's eyes land on me, they narrow into tiny, angry slits. One quick glance at me is enough to draw a conclusion.

"The fuck, Oli?" He shakes his head, pulling on his hair on the left side of his face with his fist. "Why the fuck is this asshole's truck parked next to your house?" He's nearly yelling, which says a lot about his level of anger because Mark doesn't raise his voice often.

I get into his face and hiss, "Calm down! You'll wake Brodie up."

"What were you doing?" He doesn't get my message and keeps yelling. And sure, right on cue, the cry upstairs begins.

"Good job, jerk." I rush upstairs, expecting Jake to be climbing out the window on tied-together sheets. But I don't find him anywhere in the kitchen or the living room. Or any window.

Instead, I find him in Brodie's room with my son in his arms, cooing in a soothing voice I've never heard from Jake before. His wide back is turned to me, and his head is tilted toward Brodie's face where he's singing him "Twinkle,

Twinkle, Little Star." I freeze, not able to speak or breathe. My throat is closed because Brodie's responding to him by quieting down.

"What the fuck?" booms a loud voice behind me, instantly making Brodie wail again.

Jake's body instantly whips around as he cradles Brodie closer. "Calm down. You'll have a chance to talk to me outside," he declares with a calm but firm tone.

"Don't tell me what to do!" My brother is angry. Very, very angry.

Jake's face turns vicious. I mean *vicious*. It's scary. Something sinister peeks its head out, and this might be the first time I recognize the villain everyone's talking about.

"Lower. Your. Voice." His eyes are trained on my brother, and for a second, I see Mark stunned. Not many people have the courage to tell him what to do in a pleasant manner, let alone order him around, so he doesn't know how to react.

In the meantime, Jake uses it to his advantage. He passes Brodie to me and marches out of the room. A few moments later, when Mark starts blinking again, he follows him, and I'm left consoling my baby. I know I need to go and make sure none of them die during their 'talk,' but I can't leave my kid. So I tighten my grip on my baby and plant my ass in the chair.

When I start quietly singing a lullaby, I also silently pray that I won't need to clean blood from the walls in the morning when I come downstairs to assess the damage. Because there will be damage, it's just a matter of how much.

Chapter Twenty-One

Jake

The fucker scared the poor kid to death.

The rage inside me keeps boiling to the point where I can barely restrain myself from turning around and smashing this idiot's face into the wall. Apparently, he can't control his emotions since he let himself loose in front of a child. Even when he saw the boy crying, he didn't shut up. The kid's presence is the only thing holding me grounded now. The only thing.

When I saw Brodie in his crib wailing, my first instinct was to pick him up. I don't know what came over me since today was probably the first time I've ever held a baby. But once his weightless, little body was pressed to me, my chest tightened with something new. Something I haven't experienced, this tightness. This urge to protect.

"Hey!" Mark yells behind my back, but I ignore him and keep walking. "I'm talking to you, asshole!"

I whip around to hiss into his face. "Lower your voice."

He stops dead halfway down the stairs. "Yeah?" His eyes narrow. "Or what?"

"Or you're gonna scare your nephew even more than you already have."

His jaw clamps shut, and he starts grinding his teeth but doesn't say anything and rushes past me outside. The moment he opens the door, the cold air takes away all the warmth that Olivia put in me. I shiver, silently cursing myself for letting this weakness into me.

"Are you good now? Or need me to wait a bit and lower my voice even more?" Mark sounds sarcastic, probably thinking I care about his opinion.

"What do you want?" I ask calmly.

"Me? I want to know what *you* want."

"I don't want trouble, that's for sure," I mumble, knowing well enough we're past that point.

"Yeah." He laughs. "A little too late for that," he confirms what I already know without his smartass. "Should have thought about that before you came here to—" His lips pinch together.

"To do what?" I ask, barely containing my sudden enjoyment in his misery. I don't like it. I never have. It may have something to do with prejudice which I'm not proud of. But once the seed is planted, it's hard to get rid of it.

His demeanor changes from unsure to vicious. "Yes, Jake. To do what? We both know you're an asshole who doesn't think twice about anyone else."

You don't know how far that is from the truth.

"I care about my family," I hiss through gritted teeth.

He laughs. "Yeah, I see how much you care about your

family. Disappearing from town, making your mother go insane with worry."

That hits harder than I expected. I didn't know my mother cared much if I'm honest. Once I became the local villain, she seemed to be ashamed of me, and when I moved out of Little Hope, I thought she took a breath of relief. Everyone else had.

"Oh, wait." He smacks his palm over his thigh. "I also love how you care about Justin. It's so fucking awesome. You almost ruined his life, Jake. I remember how you treated Kayla." He takes a step forward. "Do you think I don't remember how you faked his 'sleepover' or how you talked to her when she was just trying to escape?"

Every word hits harder and harder, and I could tell him I had a reason. I thought I was protecting my brother. Even if it would be half the truth.

Another step toward me. A small one. Feels like he's prolonging it to either give me time to reciprocate or back down. Neither will be happening. He has things to say, and I have time to listen.

"Why the fuck are you quiet, Jake? You always have so much to say." He looks like he's losing patience. "What's changed?"

"I have nothing to say. But you do. So go ahead."

He looks stunned for a moment, clearly not expecting this answer. "Yes, I do." He blinks. "Let's start with the most important question. What were you doing in my sister's house?"

I can tell him to go to hell, but he seems to genuinely care for Olivia, and she doesn't have anyone else. So fuck it.

"I came to check on her."

Another moment of silence. I seem to keep surprising him according to the shocked look on his face.

"Why?"

"Because she was really upset, and I felt responsible."

"Why the fuck would you feel responsible?" His forehead wrinkles in confusion.

"Because my mother wasn't exactly nice."

"Must run in the family," he mumbles, but I hear it. And even though it's my mother he's talking about, I can't say if he actually means it in a disrespectful way. Mark seems to be a decent brute with a soft underbelly who might have more social anxiety than I do.

I keep my mouth shut, not wanting to make the situation worse. It will escalate at some point anyway, and I don't want to paint the snow under Olivia's windows red right before the opening of her bakery, still hoping to resolve everything with words.

Seeing me still quiet, Mark finally gives up on trying to stare me down and exhales loudly.

"Look. Oli's been through a lot. I don't know if you knew, but we both have abandonment issues. We've never had decent parents. Nor did we have a decent home. We tried to build it. And while you were playing ball in high school, she was taking a bus to Springfield to work as a waitress in the diner in the evenings. Alright? She didn't have it easy. And yes, everyone fucking knows about her crush on you in school. And you," he points his finger at me, "showing up there," his finger moves toward the window with the fairy lights, "disturbs her more than you think." Another deep sigh. "Fuck, it's even more than she thinks. I know my sister, Jake. She can't take it. Especially, not now. Not when her life seems to be getting back on track."

I swallow down the guilt I'm feeling. *Did I just make it all worse?*

I just recently discovered that this gorgeous woman had

a crush on me when we were really young, and I nearly bit off my elbows, blaming myself for being a blind dickhead. And now he's adding to the pitiful story my mother has painted about Olivia's life.

Fucking hell. I have to stay away from here, as far as possible.

"What about the father of the kid?" I blurt out.

His eyes narrow. "Why the fuck do you care? Are you auditioning?"

Am I?

I clear my throat and look to the side. "I just want to know if it wasn't—" I cough again. "Something, you know, like violent or something." My eyes keep darting from side to side, not able to meet his.

He's quiet for some time before he speaks. "I don't think so."

My head whips to him. "What? You don't know?"

He sighs deeply. "I don't know who the father is. But I know she wasn't upset or something. Like in *that* way, you know. Look." He scratches his beard. "It's not your business. Or even mine, no matter how much I want to know. But Brodie is not a child of violence."

I let out a deep breath of relief. I didn't know how much I needed to hear that. For some reason, I can't bear the thought of Olivia suffering the way my sister had. I can't even think about any woman suffering that way, but when I think about Olivia in that capacity, the red comes over my eyes, blinding me with pure rage.

"Why were you here, Jake?" he asks again after giving me some time to process the knowledge.

"I came to check on her," I repeat the truth.

"You left dinner more than three hours ago. The drive here is ten minutes."

"And?" I raise a brow.

He rolls his eyes. "And what the fuck were you doing here for so long?"

I level him with a stare because even though he cares about Olivia and her kid, she's a grown woman, and I don't have to tell her brother how my tongue was down her throat and my hands were on her gorgeous ass.

"Jake." His teeth grind. "I'm losing my patience here. What the fuck were you doing here for so long?"

"Drinking hot chocolate, asshole. Happy now?" I snap because I've never been known for otherworldly patience, and he's already wasted my yearly resolve.

He blinks at me. Then blinks some more and then starts laughing. "You? Hot chocolate?" He laughs even louder, probably waking every single neighbor on the block. The last thing Olivia needs is a drama scene under her window. Rumors in this town can be vicious. Just ask Kenneth, the local sheriff. The last time I was here, I heard he was going down on his wife on the floor of the local store in the produce aisle.

"Are you done? Or do you want me to call you an ambulance?" I deadpan as he keeps getting louder.

When he's done laughing, he wipes his face, while still cackling. "Oh, asshole. That was a good one." Suddenly, his face morphs, his eyes narrowing and his jaw ticking. "Listen here, Jake. No matter what you've built in that head of yours, thinking that you can hurt Olivia and get back at everyone this way, I'm warning you. Do not come close to her. We both know you're no good for her. You're no good for anyone. And if you thought you could prey on a woman in a moment of weakness when she's down, you're wro—"

I push onto his chest with my hands. "Shut the fuck up. Shut. The fuck. Up."

He barely stumbles back but blinks at me in astonishment. I get into his face.

"Stop painting me like a fuckin' dickhead who preys on women." I point my finger in his face, feeling the rapidly building rage threatening to spill out. "You know better than anyone else. Fucking' hell." I step back, shaking my head. "Fuckin' asshole. After what happened to my sister, do you really think I could do something like that?"

He seems lost and maybe even a bit embarrassed because he doesn't know how to respond.

I shake my head again. "You're lucky you're good to my sister. It's the only thing keeping your teeth in your fuckin' mouth right now."

Then I head toward my car. My bones are freezing but my blood is boiling. I left my jacket in Olivia's place, but I'm not going back. Ever.

When I'm in the confines of my truck, my phone pings. The message that pops on the screen makes me breathe a sigh of relief.

Your vacation is over. Tomorrow morning NM.

I start the engine. I think I have finally figured out where I belong. And it's not in Little Hope anymore.

Chapter Twenty-Two

T*wo years ago*

Jake

A big perk of working for these assholes is the access to their database. Just starting off on the force, I didn't have the credentials. But I've finally gotten them. I don't have an office, but I have access, which is more than I could hope for. It took me a shitload of years, in fact, way longer than I anticipated. I needed to know the truth.

I figure once I learn what I need to, I'll leave.

With the access key, I type my password and then open up the search bar.

Eighteen hours, hundreds of searches, and about twenty cups of coffee later, I find them.

The names of the people who assaulted my sister.

The reports pop up—dozens of them throughout Maine, New Hampshire, and Massachusetts. Assaults reported but never investigated properly. Seventy-five percent of them being pushed under the rug because the assholes had relatives in high places.

The more I find, the more hairs I pull from my head. These reports will give me nightmares for years. There's no fucking way no one knows they're connected because it took me one long night to put them together; I'm sure someone else has done it too.

I stare at the mug shots of the two monsters who changed my sister's life forever. I want to kill them with my bare hands. I want to rip their heads off and burn their fucking bodies so there's no memory on this planet that they ever existed.

I want to end them.

But I can't. Everything will crumble if I do.

Because the reports say that every single time, they had the same drug in their system. The very same drug that started slowly deteriorating the younger generation of Little Hope.

So I do the only thing that can work. I grab my phone and call one of my new contacts from the wrong sides of every town I go to. Some people I've grown acquainted with when I was sucked deeper into that other life. I dial a number and tell them everything I need them to know because there's someone out there who wants Alicia's attackers to suffer as much as I do. Mark. He'll be my hand of justice.

"Send a hint through your people. I've heard he's been poking around so he might not look at it with suspicion. Make sure he knows they will be at the same club tomorrow night."

"Will do. You owe me a favor after this," one of my moles says.

"Yeah."

Justice will be served tomorrow. I hope Mark will be smart about it and won't get into trouble. *Fuck.* He's not going to be smart. He'll want to kill them.

Fuck!

So I dial another number.

"Hey, pretty."

"Jakey-y-y," she drawls. *"Long time no hear from your sweet mouth. I miss that mouth."*

"Yeah." I laugh, trying to not let my rage slip through my voice. "I have some information for your friend."

"Kenney the Hungy?" she cackles. He hates that nickname his old fuck buddy has given him. She's been trying to get me into this weird dynamic she has with men, but I steer clear of that. She's too much of an asset to ruin it with a casual fuck.

"Yep. Him."

Her voice turns giddy. *"Gimme, gimme. I'm dying to have a reason to get him all bothered. He's been kind of odd with me recently. I don't like it."* I can hear her pout on the other side of the call.

"He can't know where it came from."

A pause before she speaks again. *"Alright. You got me intrigued."*

"I have two names and a place. And one of Sheriff's friends will be there." I start before relaying everything, hoping she'll follow my instructions and make the tip anonymous. I don't want Benson in this shit that's happening in town behind his back. He's too much of a good guy not to get involved, and it might get too complicated.

That's why I'm here, after all.

Chapter Twenty-Three

P*resent day*

Olivia

When Brodie completely calms down and falls asleep, I carefully transfer him into his crib, take a deep breath, and walk toward the window. It's been about twenty minutes since Mark chased Jake downstairs, and I'm scared. Carefully peeking from behind the curtain, I expect a dead body on the sidewalk but find nothing. I mean it—nothing. Not a speck of blood, not a body print on the freshly fallen snow.

Not Jake's car either. Only Mark's truck is still parked where I saw it before. The headlights are off, which means he's probably sitting on my steps. Otherwise, he's been freezing his ass in the cold truck.

I check on Brodie one more time and head to the stairs. When I open the door, I hear nothing.

"Mark?" I call out quietly.

"Yeah."

Exhaling loud enough for him to hear down there, I say, "Come upstairs."

A few moments of silence tell me that he's unsure if he should come up or just leave. Which means he's mad, and we're going to have a conversation I'm not going to like. But soon, his nearing footsteps give me hope that it might not be so bad.

Then I see his face, not making eye contact with me. *Nope, it's bad. Can't wait to have this talk.*

"Do you want something to drink?"

"Hot chocolate?" he half asks, half suggests with too much sarcasm in his voice. So I just roll my eyes and flip him off.

We both walk to the kitchen where he leans on the very same spot Jake was leaning on and crosses his arms over his chest. Another eye roll from me.

"Stop rolling your eyes or they'll get stuck there," he says grouchily.

I start making his cocoa while shooting daggers at him. "Say it so we can move on."

"Say what, Oli?"

"Whatever you came here to say," I reply with a sigh.

"I came here to check on you because I'm a good brother who worries about you. But you didn't need checking, did you? You were fine with Jake here." The amount of sarcasm in his voice makes me grind my teeth.

I want to slam the damn pot on the table, but it will wake my baby up, and he's had enough scares for one evening. So I place it gently, even though my insides are screaming.

"Yes, Mark. He came here to check on me. And you know what? I feel better after his visit."

"Yeah?" His eyes narrow. "What did he do that helped you so much?"

I quirk a brow. "Do you really wanna know?"

"Fuck, Oli!" he cries out, and I instantly jump next to him and cover his mouth with my palm.

"Sh-sh-sh!" I hiss angrily. "You'll scare Brodie again!"

"Msory," he muffles, and I take my hand away. "Sorry," he repeats. "I'm just mad, you know?"

I look at his face. "Why?"

"What do you mean why?" He looks flabbergasted. "Because Jake Attleborough, the king of all assholes, was here, that's why."

"And why do you think he's so bad, huh?"

His face turns serious. "Because he is bad, Oli. Really bad. All he does is hurt people. Even those he loves. Even, and I mean it, even if you have any dumb idea in your head that he will love you, he will hurt you ten times more at the end."

"Jeez, thanks." I take the steaming milk off the stove. "'Dumb idea that he will love you,'" I parrot his words, shaking my head. "Just what everyone wants to hear."

He sighs. "I didn't mean it like that."

"Yeah?" I glance at him as I stir the cocoa mix into the milk. "To me it sounded exactly like that."

"No." He moves his hand toward the mug, but I smack it.

"Not yet."

He quickly pulls his hand away, shaking it as my fly-swat was painful. "I meant it in the way that Jake can't love anyone. Not really."

I want to tell him that he's wrong, but it'd only open a new can of worms I'm not ready to discuss. We need to tackle this one first.

"Keep going," I urge him to get it over with.

"He's no good for you."

"How do you know?" I ask, as I take one of the mugs filled with steaming hot chocolate and push it toward him while still holding the handle.

"He's bad, Oli. Just trust me." He makes a move to grab the mug from me, but I pull it away. His eyes narrow.

"How do you know?" I ask, knowing I'm on the direct path of annoying him to the point where he'll explode. I can't stop though—it's in my job description as younger sister to annoy my older brother.

"Oli." His voice takes a warning tone. "Give me the cup." Now I know I've reached my goal.

"I will." I push it a little toward him but still out of reach. "When you tell me why you hate Jake so much."

He looks at the ceiling with a loud groan. "Because he's a total dickhead, and he's the last person I'd want around Brodie."

I swallow. "Why?"

He groans louder. "Because he's violent, alright? He's a psychopath who goes from zero to sixty in one second flat. He's been in a fight every single time he comes to Little Hope. Every single time. He goes to the bar, gets wasted, and picks a fight. I'm surprised he doesn't have assault charges lined up waiting for him when he enters the town." He clicks his fingers in the air. "Oh yeah, and he has alcoholism issues. For sure. Want that around your son?"

I shake my head, not able to talk due to the giant lump in my throat.

"Thought so." He nods to himself. "And he's a dick. I mean, look at how he's been treating Kayla all this time. He thinks she's inferior because of where she grew up."

"How do you know it's because of that?" I ask quietly.

"Everyone knows it. That's why he hates me. And that's what he thinks about you too in case you have any doubts about that." He wipes his face with his hands. "He's only normal to Alicia, and that's why I tolerate him. She seems to be the only person he treats as a human being. Anyone else is fair game to him."

If Mark could punch me in the face, it probably wouldn't have felt so bad. Because what he's saying hurts worse. Much, much worse.

"The point is," Mark scratches his beard, "you have a child to think about now. When you had this stupid crush on him in high school and I didn't say anything, it was because I knew you'd outgrow it. But now you have to think about someone else too." He steps closer to me, puts his hands on my shoulder, and finds my eyes. "You really, and I mean it, really don't want him around your kid. He's unstable to begin with, but when he's drunk, he's a whole other level of violent. Do you understand what I'm saying, Oli?"

I feel my lower lip start trembling, so I just nod.

"Oh, hell," Mark sighs and pulls me into his chest. "I know, Oli. I know you've been crushing on him since forever. But it was a teenage thing to do, you know? You'll get over it. I promise," he tries convincing me in a soothing voice while holding me tight.

Soon, I feel my body start shuddering from the silent cries. I let go of all the silly ideas I've ever had. All the stupid dreams. And go back to the reality where I have responsibilities, and my love life is not the priority. It's not even on the radar at all. And if I had any hopes that I might get a happily ever after with Jake, someone from my horrible school years, I need to let go of them because a person like him will never be good enough for my son.

As I cry, I think that it was a good thing Jake stopped me from talking with his stupid kiss. He might have saved us all some big-time pain.

Chapter Twenty-Four

Olivia

Today is opening day. The dream I've had since I was a kid is about to become reality.

The first weekday after Thanksgiving seemed like a smart business idea at first, but I didn't count on Little Hope being a small town where everyone bakes their own goods. Kudos to me for being a 'smart' businesswoman. It's ten in the morning, and no one is here.

It's Mark's shift today, and Alicia's on a deadline. She's about to send her book to the publisher and is running behind, so I don't think she's showered for about a week. Mrs. Attleborough is out of sight. She hasn't set foot in my place since the dinner, and I'm grateful for that. I'm not ready to face her just yet.

It's ten fifteen, and still no one. I'm on my third cup of coffee because I didn't sleep a minute last night, making sure everything was perfect and all the pastries were ready for the opening. *Such a waste of resources,* I think, taking a bit of my perfected éclair and shoving it down with a giant sip of coffee when the door bells chime. They're hung right next to the door, so every time it opens, the ring creates a sweet melody. I knew it would become one of my favorite sounds in the whole planet as a sound of hope.

And just like that, hope is awake.

My head whips toward the entrance. Mark's standing in the doorway in his full firefighter gear, smiling from ear to ear. And behind him, more people. More firefighters.

He comes inside and walks straight to the counter. Four other men follow him.

"Where can a man get a decent cup of coffee and a sugar fix around here?" a very young-looking guy, probably even younger than me, asks, leaning on the counter. His smile is flirty, and his demeanor as friendly as they come.

"Why, you're in the right place, wonderful sir." I curtsy and point at the chalk-drawn menu of drinks on the wall. I spent twenty minutes drawing and erasing it to make it look pretty. "Anything your heart desires is here."

He winks and leans his other elbow too, now with his face directly in front of me. "I bet it is."

I giggle like a schoolgirl and take a few large cups to go. "Anything specific for anyone?"

"I want my coffee as sweet as your smile," he says, grinning like the Cheshire Cat.

Another older-looking man pushes him to the side, nearly making the guy fall. "That was cringy, I'm sorry, hun. We're working on Roy's manners."

"What?" Roy cries out mockingly. "It was not!" He turns to me. "Was it?"

I press my lips, trying not to laugh, and shrug.

Roy sighs. "I'll take a sweet latte. Surprise me, sweetness." He winks again, unable not to flirt apparently.

I start working on his coffee, laughing. This guy can't help himself.

"Anything else for anyone?"

"My regular for me," Mark says, and goes to check out the pastries.

"What's he getting?" the older guy asks.

"Americano with cream," I reply, as I start frothing the milk for Roy's latte.

"Same for me then," he says.

"And me." The third guy raises his hand.

"Me too. Three sugars for mine though," the fourth adds.

"Coming right up!" I finish Roy's latte and place the cup on the counter. "Here you go."

"What's inside, sugar?" He takes it and sniffs through the little hole in the lid.

"Love. It's all about love," I answer with a wink, making him smile even wider. As I start the coffees for the others, I keep an eye on Roy, trying to catch his reaction to the first sip. And I see it. I know coffee is not exactly my specialty, but I have some mean homemade syrups I have high hopes for. And Roy happens to have one of those in his coffee.

"Holy crap," he says, licking his lip. "I freakin' love it. What's that? For real so I know what to order."

"It's a chestnut praline latte. A seasonal drink."

He places his hand to his heart and says with a slight bow, "You've got a loyal customer in me, lass."

Every man in the room rolls his eyes in unison, and it's almost loud.

They bought half of what I had. Some of it for the firehouse, and some of it for their families. While I pack their pastries to go, Mark asks me how Brodie's doing in this new daycare he found. Turns out, there's a small daycare for local kids. A baby boom has been going on for a few years, so one of the local teachers decided to branch out and make a small daycare. A couple weeks ago, her daughter came back from school in Boston and now helps her. So they were able to extend the age range and they had a spot left.

Mark was the one who helped this lady when she fell on ice and broke her arm last year, and she knew Mark had a nephew who was the perfect age they were looking for. She called him, and I dropped Brodie off for a couple hours on Friday just to see how he'd do. And he was perfect, so she said I could bring him today for a full day. It's been one of those few times when fate smiled at me with good intentions.

"He's doing great," I say, feeling my steps becoming lighter every time someone asks about my son. "Mrs. Levy sent me a few pictures already, and he seems to be thriving. Not a tear in his eyes."

"That's our genetics," Mark says with pride. "Fearless folks."

I glance at him with a smile—Mark's as proud of Brodie as any father could be. With an uncle like that, Brodie will never feel the lack of a man figure in his life.

While Roy's batting his eyelashes at me, the door chimes again.

"Dang, I thought I'd catch something, but looks like after you boys, the counter will be cleared out," Sheriff Benson laughs as he shakes the snow off his hair.

"Why do the police folks always come last?" Roy asks their captain, who is the same older-looking gentleman.

"Beats me," he shrugs with a cackle.

Kenneth chuckles and proceeds to the counter. The

door opens again, and a bronze-skinned goddess in a police uniform follows the sheriff.

"Jennica, my love," Roy switches his tone right away. "Let me get you a cup of joe."

"Roy, you'll get in trouble with my hubby one day." She walks up to him and pinches his cheek. You'd think this is where his flirting stops because the tall goddess just placed him in the 'baby' category. But the man doesn't lose his footing, instead he intensifies it.

"My sweet, sweet Jennica," he bats his eyelashes at her the same way he just did a few minutes ago at me. "There is no force strong enough to stop me from pursuing you."

Everyone cackles, including Jennica. "Roy, one day you'll find someone who will make you lose all of that." She circles her finger around his face. "And I can't wait to see it unfold."

"Not in this lifetime, Jennica." He leans his elbow on my counter again. "Because you're already taken." His smile is so wide, I'm sure his ears are about to fall off.

"If you're done flirting with my deputy," Kenneth inserts himself between Jennica and Roy, "then I'd love to order our stuff so we can go and, you know, actually work." He shoulders him away.

"What? Need to give some old, poor grandma a speeding ticket?" Roy clicks his tongue.

"Yep." Sheriff pops the *p*. "The very same grandma whose cat you've saved five times this morning."

"Ouch." The captain puts his open palm to his heart. "I'm wounded."

Everyone shares a laugh, confirming my suspicion that rivalry between cops and firefighters is real, even in small towns.

"Those are divine, Olivia!" One of the guys comes up to

the counter, chewing his éclair. "Are you planning on making those every day? I want to get some for my girlfriend's birthday. She's coming from Springfield soon, and I want to make it, you know, special."

"Yes!" I reply excitedly. "I'll be making them every day. It's one of my staples."

"It's awesome." He salutes the pastry in the air, making everyone curious. Now, they dig into their baked goods too, and the room erupts into loud moans.

Mark's head whips around. "You all would make some good porn stars."

"You say that," Kenneth says through chewing, "because you're used to all of this." He nods at the counter with pastries. "And we're new." He takes another bite. "Give us a break."

A few nods and hums follow, making Mark chuckle. Even though he made a joke of them, I see how his eyes shine with pride every time he looks at the people here. He loves that they love it. He's proud of my success.

We chat a few more minutes before everyone pays and leaves. Even though I offer an 'opening' discount, they all refuse it, and now my register is almost full. Well, not physically, some of it was paid with cards, but I didn't plan to sell so much just for two groups of people.

In the next hour, my door never closes. People come and go. Some of them are just curious, some actually want to try my creations.

At about eleven, Jonah comes in with a giant bouquet of red roses.

"Look at my favorite business owner making waves on her first day!" He walks behind the counter and wraps his arms around me without warning. I freeze for a moment because first of all, it's unexpected, and second, there is a giant bouquet squashed between us. But soon I relax into his embrace, not knowing how much I needed that.

"Thank you," I mumble into his jacket, and he gives a gentle pat to my back.

"You are doing great, Oli. I'm proud of you," he says quietly.

My throat closes up. I didn't know someone other than Mark can be proud of me. I didn't know anyone cared enough.

"Thank you," I squeak and pull away, scared that I'll cry on my very first day here. "These are my first flowers."

"Ever?" he asks with round eyes, and I nod. "Oh, honey." The corners of his lips turn down like I've just told him the saddest story in the world. "We need to remedy that." He places the flowers on the counter and takes off his jacket. "I'm gonna find something to put those in."

With that, he takes off toward the back and up the stairs to my apartment, feeling awfully at home. I should be annoyed. Shouldn't I? I don't know. I can't find the strength to be mad at Jonah when all he's doing is trying to help.

I serve two more customers who come here with cups from Donna's shop but wanted some baked sweets to pair with it. I think to myself that it could be the perfect thing if I want to coexist with Donna in this town. I need to explain to her one more time that we can even actually run some sort of a promotion together and up our sales. Of course, I'll have to sacrifice selling coffee. Otherwise, it wouldn't be fair to her. But if she continues being difficult, I'll have to push my homemade syrups more.

Moments later, Jonah comes back with a vase I didn't know I had, fills it with water, and places the roses on top of the pastry display. Right next to the cake pops. Then he goes to wash his hands and comes back to me.

"I have a free hour, so I can help you."

"With what?" I blink.

"See over there?" He points at the yoga studio across the road. "They are about to finish the first class of the day—they started late today. You just wait." He nods and crosses his arms over his chest with a satisfying smile. "Better go and put more stuff in the oven if you don't want to lose their business."

I glance at the display. I have a few cupcakes left, some pastries and small cakes. "Do you think it won't be enough?"

"You never know." He shrugs his wide shoulders. "Better be prepared."

"Oh, crap." I rush to the kitchen and yell to him. "Hold the front."

"Aye, aye, captain." He salutes and turns toward the new customer who just walked in.

I place the prepped doughs on the tray and stick them into the oven. After setting the timer, I check what I have left and rush to Jonah who's chatting with two more people, convincing them to try my éclairs.

"I've heard someone nearly orgasmed from them," he whispers with a conspiratorial smile.

"Jonah!" A woman in her fifties rears back, clutching her imaginary pearls.

"We'll take two!" her companion of the same age says. "Each."

"Wise choice, Mrs. Tulicle." Jonah nods his head approvingly, shooting the prude lady a wink. The poor woman turns a bright shade of a ripe beet. "Oh, here is the queen of orgasms," he says, nodding his head at me.

"Jonah!" I cry out in horror, looking around like I've just been caught naked.

"We will be the judge of that." The lady who requested éclairs giggles and pays for the pastries.

After a few more shared giggles, they leave, and Jonah meets me with a shit-eating grin. "Why the sour look on your face? I'm creating you a brand here. Be merry, woman!"

I glance around, making sure there're no ears around. "Jonah," I hiss, "you're ruining me before I've even started. It's a small town, for God's sake. That's not what people need to talk about in my bakery."

"P-p-please," he waves me off like an annoying fly. "That's precisely what they need. Well, hello there," he suddenly purrs, staring at the door. I follow his gaze and freeze. Actually freeze without any ability to move or speak. I seem to be doing that a lot nowadays.

It might have been embarrassing, but I can't even blame myself because right at the door I see a person from my childhood. The very same Jake who looks younger than he was a week ago. The same boyish half-smirk on his face. The same Ray-Bans he takes off the moment he steps inside and hooks them on the front of his collar. His cheeks are rosy from the cold. A few specks of snow cover his shoulders and hair. His beard is longer and messier than I remember.

He slowly takes off toward us, and this is when I notice that the chatter in the room has stopped. Every single pair of eyes is trained on his deliberately slow movements. It's like he's contemplating if he should leave or continue and can't quiet decide.

"Hello, Jakey," Jonah announces loudly, deciding for him. Now escape would look cowardly.

"Hi," Jake replies, not sounding as enthusiastic as Jonah.

Even his demeanor is slowly changing from happy to sullen when he notices my talkative friend.

"What can Olivia get you? Because I'm leaving to check on the pastries in the back. Be right back." He gives Jake a small wave and rushes to the kitchen, stunning us both. Then his head pokes for a second as he yells. "Do you love the flowers Oli's admirer brought this morning? He must be something." He wiggles his brows as I cry out, "Jonah!"

He chuckles and disappears in the kitchen.

I turn toward Jake and mutter a forced "Hey."

"Hey." Jake's voice turns cold. "A secret admirer, huh. Fast."

I narrow my eyes at him. "What can I get you?"

He looks around. "Coffee, I guess."

"Coming right up." I crank the music in the shop a bit louder, and everyone takes it as a sign to go back to their damn business. Then I start making him coffee, not asking which one he wants. I don't think he wants any, but he's here.

"Who got you flowers?" Jake's voice behind my back turns colder with every word.

I glance at him. "Why does it matter?"

His nostrils flare as the muscle on his left cheek starts moving under his skin. "I want to know who else has been where I have? Was it at the same time?"

"Be quiet," I warn him with a hiss while looking around to make sure no one else heard the hammerhead.

"Why? Scared your reputation will get tainted?" His eyes narrow, the villain Jake is back. The very same one who bullied Kayla for years.

I drop what I'm doing and walk back to the counter where he's standing. "Why are you so interested in that, Jake?" I narrow my eyes. "Are you jealous?"

His nostrils flare for a moment again before they go back to normal. His shoulders rise and fall with a deep sigh. "Yes," he grinds out, surprising me.

Did he just admit to being jealous? I was just being pitiful and didn't expect this answer. So I give up on this stupid idea Jonah has planted.

"Jonah brought the flowers to congratulate me on the opening."

He blinks. Then blinks some more. Then, after exhaling loudly, he looks toward the kitchen. "You don't say." Chewing on the inside of his cheek and suddenly looking unsure, he turns toward me. "Then I guess I have to apologize. Don't I?"

I smile, disregarding the situation. I need to process his confession before I can say something I'll regret. Like how I've always been jealous. That every time he sat with a beautiful girl at the lunch table at school, I couldn't even eat my PB&J sandwich because I had acid rising up my throat—that's how jealous I was. Or when Mark casually mentioned on the phone that Jake was shacking up with Adison. Or any other times I've seen women throwing themselves at him while I could never do that because he didn't even know about my existence. And I've tried to be one of those women, but every time, his nose scrunched up and his eyes turned glassy when he stopped seeing me and shifted his attention someplace else.

"How have you been?" I ask while I'm grinding the beans while beating myself up for going down this awful memory lane. "You know, since we've—" I clear my throat. "I mean we—"

His lips curve in a smile. "Tested your countertop?" His voice turns even gruffer.

My cheeks heat up in a second flat. "Yeah, that."

"It's been alright. Considering."

"What?" I ask, not meeting his eyes.

"Considering the state I've been left in," he confesses in a husky voice, making my head whip toward him so fast, my hair creates wind behind it.

"The state?" I ask, swallowing.

He laughs in that scratchy, mega-attractive tone every single one of us secretly loves. "Yes, Olivia. And it's been *hard* to deal with."

I nearly drop the cup I just grabbed. I want to look at him, I really do, but what if I find something I like. Because this Jake is even more than I saw in my kitchen.

"What's going on with you?" I whisper, glancing at him from under my lashes.

His facial expression turns sober. No flirting or humor left in him anymore. "I just wanted to see you before—" He looks to the side. "I just wanted to see you."

"Why?" My voice is unsure and doubtful of myself. *Can I even ask that? Am I dreaming?*

He's silent, and after a few moments, I place a cup on the counter for him. He's watching me with a solemn look on his face. And I don't like it.

The door chimes again, and a few young women come inside. They are bright and cheerful and very, very happy. They must be the new people I was expecting according to Jonah. And I trust him now, they sure can bring a joyful mood to this place.

"Hey! You must be Olivia! Everyone's talking about your new place!" one of them exclaims before they even reach me. She sounds like a happy person who wants to fill the world with happiness. I can get behind that.

They all rush toward the counter and start talking among themselves, deciding which ones they want to try.

One of them comes closer to where Jake's standing and asks him, "What would you recommend?" Her voice suggests a lot of flirting coming his way in the near future.

Jake looks at her without sharing her obvious interest but replies, rather politely, "Anything Olivia makes is good."

"Oh, yeah?" She glances at me and then back at him. "*Everything* Olivia makes is good?" she asks suggestively, finding his eyes.

He holds her stare. "Everything."

She smiles an easy smile, not a note of flirting left in her eyes. "Alright, then." Then she looks at me. "Can you get us three different things we can share with the smallest amount of calories. We don't want to waste too much of the workout." She pats her jacket where her belly is.

"Sure," I nod with a smile, trying to remind myself that they're my paying customers who will help me keep my head afloat, and I absolutely cannot dig my nails into their eyes for flirting with Jake.

I grab the box when the second lady joins the first. "Can we also get some coffee? I heard from my boyfriend that your chestnut praline latte is to die for."

I smile, thinking that her boyfriend is probably one of the men who saw Roy drinking his latte today.

When the third one joins, she leans her chin on the shoulder of the first one and starts openly looking up and down at Jake. Everyone knows she's satisfied with what she sees, because she pushes away from her friend and cocks her legging-clad hip to the side. "Hey, I'm Kaira, and I haven't seen you around town yet."

The first lady pats her shoulder, smiling. "Chill, Kaira, he's taken."

My head whips at her while I'm writing the order on the cup. "What?"

The first lady gives me a funny look. "Oh, yeah. He's very taken." Then she glances at Jake with the same smile. He's holding steady though. Not a note of humor on his face.

"Oh, Margo, ladies," Jonah's voice sounds right behind my back, "I'm so glad you guys could come!" He shoulders me to the side. "Let me help. I've always wanted to ring this thing." He starts punching something in at the register.

"But you've already d—"

"Jake, it's Oli's break time, but she won't take five." He points at the empty table. "Take her over there, away from my bleeding eyes. Can't look at her saggy, tired face anymore."

Everyone laughs at his unfunny joke, but Jake gets it.

"Let's go," he gently orders me, and nods in the direction where Jonah pointed.

I look around, not sure if it's a good time to drop my business and join Jake. But the ladies start waving their hands at me.

"It was nice meeting you, Olivia! We will be coming Monday, Wednesday, and Friday." They don't look offended by Jonah's sudden appearance and more than awkward situation, so I smile back at them.

"Likewise," I say as cheerfully as I can. "Thank you for stopping by and supporting my business!"

They start nodding their heads with wide smiles, and I follow Jake to the table.

"That was weird," I admit when we're both seated.

The corner of his lips quirks up for a moment.

"Do you want anything else?"

He shakes his head, yet again not making a sound. *Well, it's going to be a delightful conversation.*

I start tapping my fingers on the table when I don't

know what to do with my hands. Every pair of eyes is secretly glancing our way. Including the Judas, Jonah, who sold me out. Twice in the past fifteen minutes.

Yet, Jake doesn't utter a word. I'm beginning to lose my patience and am about to stand up and walk back because I don't have time today for quiet sittings like that, when he probably notices me being edgy and grabs my hand, stopping me.

I look down at where our hands are connected and relax back onto the chair.

"What's happening, Jake? Why did you want to see me?"

His eyes dart between mine, digging deep into my soul. Way deeper than anyone has even looked. "Because I think the next time you see me, I'll be a different person."

I lean over the table closer to him, ignoring the curious looks people send my way.

"What's going on, Jake? Please tell me." Something is changing, and it's slipping from my fingertips. This trail we've somehow created is quickly winding out of my sight. "Are you in trouble?"

He doesn't respond. Nor does he let his eyes leave my face. He licks his lips as if he wants to say something, but then he clamps like a shell and completely withdraws. Then, he grabs his coffee, drops cash on the table—a hundred for a cup of coffee I'm not even sure I didn't burn— and starts walking backward.

"Take care, Oli. Take care of yourself and your boy."

Turning away, he ignores me calling his name. He walks away from the bakery, and somehow, it feels different this time. It feels final before it even started.

Chapter Twenty-Five

J^{ake}

I don't know why I keep coming back. I can't explain it.

Every time I feel like I'm beginning to slip away, I remind myself of her face. Of her body in my arms. Of the feeling I can never have. My imagination can run just fine, alright. I know what I could have felt if we had continued with what her asshole of a brother interrupted. And that could have been the memory I'd be living with for the rest of my life.

But I don't have that memory. I just have a moment of normal I haven't had for a while.

Imagining different scenarios about how I would pursue her is like some sort of punishment I've been implementing on myself since the moment I met her. In each one of them, her long, brown hair is wild after I run my hands through it. Her eyes are crazed after my kisses. Her cheeks rosy from her desire. Desire is definitely something we don't lack. That woman lights up like a fire.

I throw my head back and groan. *What am I doing to myself?*

What is it in her that drives me crazy? Is it the way she looks? No doubt, she's beautiful with that quiet, sure beauty that will last forever. Is it how fiercely she loves her kid and tries to make the best for him? I've seen plenty of that in my life—my mom was one of those mothers.

Or maybe it's the way she makes me feel. Like I'm larger than life. Like I can be her protector. And there's nothing I wish for more. This is precisely why I'm driving away. I'm too messed up beyond repair to be around a woman and her kid. I don't know if I'm safe. I don't know if or when I'll slip up. My own future is too unpredictable to insert myself into someone's life when that person is looking for stability. I can't imagine why else she would be back in Little Hope other than that. The more big cities I see, the more sure I become of them not being the best choice for raising kids. If I had one, I'd want him here, where my family is. Where I can teach him how to ride a bike and go fishing.

Suddenly, my chest tightens with pain, and I can't breathe. I pull off to the side of the road and clutch my chest, thinking I might be having a heart attack. But I'm not. I'm just getting a taste of real regret.

I park next to the building where I rent a one-bedroom apartment and go upstairs. I grab a bottle of bourbon from the cabinet and go to the couch. I don't bother with a glass— at this point I need much more than that to not feel anything. Alcohol replaced the drugs. It's either one or the other.

I stare at the white ceiling in the complete silence of the

cold room. There's no one to call me from another room to come and watch TV together. No one to ask me how my day was. No one to share anything. And I did it all to myself.

This is why I started doing more assignments. Why I chose the most dangerous ones. I get desperate in the heavy silence of my solitude and the bottle. I look for any gratification in the life I'm sending down the drain every single day.

Maybe one day we will do what we're sent to. Then I can go back and try to have a normal life.

If I'm not too broken by then.

And if she's still not taken. Because I don't see any other way I can have *normal* now.

Chapter Twenty-Six

O livia

When Jake walks out the door of my bakery, he leaves me with an unsettling feeling in my chest. The feeling that I might not see him again. And I think that it's the first time I've truly felt the meaning of regret. I wish I had talked to him—told him the truth. Because his goodbye feels too final.

Do I need to worry about him? Do we all need to?

When I look at Jake, I see what other people see too—an easy to anger person who's quick to respond with violence. Someone who hates the world and the world hates him back.

But I also see a lost man who's maybe even a little broken. I remember Jake when he was young, so I really think there was a moment when the trajectory of his life changed. I don't argue the fact that he's always been a little mean, but Jake right now is a whole different level.

Even though I've seen tiredness in his eyes. As if he wants to change—something or himself—but can't. Or won't. I don't know.

One thing I do know is that I can't bring this instability to my son's life. He proves that time after time.

When the giggling sounds of the yoga ladies move toward the exit, I go back to the counter, ready to scold Jonah for dear life. He's waiting for me, leaning one hip on the side of the counter with a shit-eating grin on his face.

"You're welcome," he says, wiggling his manicured eyebrows.

"For what, jerk?" I meet him with hands on my hips.

"For stirring the pot a little." He nods toward the street. "He needs it."

"He doesn't. Nor do I." Looking up at the ceiling, I sigh loudly. "Why did you get this crazy idea in your marble head that I need to hook up with Jake?"

"I hope you mean marble as in stoic perfection." He dramatically moves hair off his face. "Because my skin is flawless. Anywho. We both know there is a shit ton of chemistry going on between you guys—we've all gotten a little pregnant around here," he fans his face with his hand. "And you have unresolved feelings from high school. Why not give it a go?" He shrugs his shoulders. "Maybe he just needs to get laid, and all his anger will disappear in the nothing of this wonderful world. Along with his load." He waves his hands in the air, widening his eyes. Is that supposed to be the nothing, the wonderful world, or the load?

"Jonah, even if I wanted to hook up with Jake, I have a son to think about."

Jonah's back straightens as all the humor disappears from his face. "Oh."

"Yeah, oh," I mimic him sarcastically. "I have a child, and I want him to have a healthy and stable life."

Understanding dawns in his eyes. "And Jake's anything but those things."

"Unfortunately." I cross my arms over my chest and longingly look at the street. "That ass though."

Jonah chuckles and follows my gaze. "Oh, yes. That ass." He shifts his attention to me. "I don't have much of a family, but I'm pretty stable." He looks like the same kid who asked me to be his friend all those years ago. And last time I rejected the offer. "I can't give you what Jake can." He wiggles his brows. "But I can help when you need it."

I look to the side because for the love of everything, I can't meet his eyes.

He comes closer and gently places his hand on my shoulder, waiting for me to look at him. "I mean it, Oli." He smiles sadly. "You might think I have it all figured out, but I'm just as lost as everyone else. And I'm lonely." His smile is heartbroken. "I need a friend who can pick up my pieces when I fall apart. And I can pick up yours. You know, in case you decide to go for the tight ass." His face takes on a rebellious expression. "I might even fight Mark for it. I mean I'll lose for sure, and this gorgeous skin will be ruined, but I'll try. You're worth it."

I chuckle. "Why fight Mark?"

"Duh." He rolls his eyes. "Once he knows about Jake sniffing around, he'll come guns blazing."

He probably sees my face changing because his eyes widen. "Do spill!"

I contemplate if I should share with him at least some things that have been going on. I have a brother whom I can come to with any problem. But for some things, I just need a friend. Jonah is right. I rejected him when we were kids, but I'm not going to make the same mistake by disregarding one of the few people who's tried to be around even when I had nothing. My biggest fear was to get stuck in Little Hope, and here I am, years later, back in Little Hope of my own free will. So I move closer to him and tell him the events of the night when Mark found me and Jake.

The next four hours before closing are busy. I text back and forth with Brodie's daycare, who says that my boy's doing great and even makes attempts to walk on his own because he sees other kids doing so. After every picture she sends, I feel lighter and lighter.

Josie and Freya come with their kids who create chaos I'm very familiar with. And I make myself a mental note to make this place more mom and kid friendly. Once my budget allows, I'll buy more toys and activities for the little guys, so their moms can enjoy an éclair with a cup of coffee.

Around two, Alicia barges in, buys an americano with a double espresso shot and a few pastries, gives me a big, stinky hug, and rushes back to finish her book. I'm positive she still hasn't showered.

Freya's husband, Alex, stops by at some point to buy éclairs for Freya and the kids. And even though I tell him they were already here, he insists on buying more.

Kayla comes in for a second before driving to work. She grabs a cupcake and rushes out because she's late to her appointment.

The people keep coming in, and by the end of the day, I'm almost sold out of everything.

A little past three, when my shop has been empty for the past twenty minutes, Justin walks in. He's cautious, though I have no idea why. We've never really known each other. We'd never even talked before I moved back to Little

Hope, but now we're pretty much forced to be in the same circle.

He looks around and nods approvingly to himself. As if he's surprised this place is not a rat's nest? I don't know. I might be overthinking a little, but I've heard Justin isn't a very nice fella. And even though Jake is nastier—according to rumors—I look past it in him, while in Justin, I see all his imperfections, big or small.

"The place looks great," he says, somewhat surprised as he walks up to the counter with his hands in the front pockets of his jeans.

"Thank you," I reply genuinely, even though I want to quirk a brow and ask him what he expected.

"I came to congratulate you on the opening." He looks out of place.

"Thanks, Justin." I try to sound casual. "Want a cupcake? I've got some left."

"Nah. I'm not a fan of those. But I'll get something else."

"Well," I say as I walk to the pastry stand, "I've got some éclairs left. A feta pita. Some pigs in a blanket. And that's about it."

"Really?" His brows shoot up to his hairline. "You're out of everything?"

"Don't sound so surprised," I deadpan.

His cheeks pinken a bit. "I didn't mean it like that."

I laugh, waving my hand at him. "Relax, I'm just messing with you. I didn't expect it either. I think it's a one-day wonder though since people came today to support me on opening day, so it might slow down tomorrow."

"I hope it won't." He smiles cheekily.

"You and me both. Are you in the mood for sweet or salty?" I point at the stand.

"Pigs in a blanket sound good. Are they big?" He leans down with a stretched neck to find them.

"Not very." I grab the tray from the stand and pull it out. "Like that."

"They're tiny," he says, scrunching his nose.

"To a normal-sized human, they're alright." I laugh, looking him up and down. Justin is one of the big guys of Little Hope, the same size as Jake. Even though Jake is leaner. More coiled. Angrier.

How come every single thought of mine comes down to Jake? It's exhausting.

He laughs. "I'm a normal-sized human. You're the pint-sized one."

I roll my eyes, feeling him and me slipping into a more comfortable place where we can joke without sensing this odd dread over our heads. And not knowing where this dread comes from makes it even odder.

"I'll take all of those over there." He points at the tray. "The guys will love those."

"The guys?"

"Yeah. The boys at my shop. I hired a couple more people."

I forgot that Justin owns the auto shop in town. "How many people work there?"

"Five now. Plus myself."

"Wow." I whistle under my nose. "That's a lot for a small town."

"It used to be just two, but now, the town is growing, plus people from Springfield travel here since I hired a guy who works with fancy cars." A note of pride in his voice makes me smile wide.

"Fancy cars, huh? Little Hope is changing."

He laughs. "Can't stop progress." His facial expression

shifts to a solemn one a moment later. "I also wanted to apologize for acting like a Neanderthal around your kid. I'm so used to swearing at the garage that I didn't even think, you know?"

I raise my hand in the air, stopping him. "No need, Justin. It's all good." When he opens his mouth to argue, I stop him again. "No, really. It's fine."

"Okay." He nods and takes out his credit card to pay. "Also." He moves his jaw from side to side. "I don't know what's going on between you and Ja—"

I smack the box with the pastries on the table, making his eyebrows rise in a silent question. "Why is everyone so interested in that?"

He watches my face. "Because he's not good for you or for your kid. Alicia and my mom are obsessed with Brodie. He's family now, and I don't want him to get hurt."

"He is your brother, for fuck's sake." I shake my head disappointedly. "Aren't you supposed to be on his side?"

"This is exactly why I'm warning you against him, Olivia." He finds my eyes and holds them. "Because he *is* my brother, and I know him more than anyone else."

"He seems to care about Alicia," I say stubbornly, feeling offended on Jake's behalf since he doesn't have anyone in his corner.

"Yes, he does," he confirms with a short nod. "But it's because he feels guilty."

"For what?"

He blinks, so I repeat my question.

"Why does he feel guilty, Justin?"

He grinds his molars, probably shaving some of his teeth in the process. "Because she wouldn't tell him what happened."

I feel anger rising in my chest. "Maybe it's because he was a kid?"

"What?" Justin blinks his stupid blue eyes at me.

I stand straight. "You were the older brother. She came to you. He was still a kid when it happened, wasn't he?"

He's quiet, but his molar grinding slows down.

"Why did no one tell him it was fine? Why did no one tell him it wasn't his fault?"

"He knows," he hisses.

"Does he?" I ask with a stubbornly raised brow.

Justin's neck moves with a swallow—he can't say for sure. Because no one questioned how other kids felt. Especially, not the rebellious younger brother.

I throw my hands in the air in a surrendering gesture because Justin already looks like a kitten in a cold ditch.

"All I'm saying is that I don't believe people are born villains. I think people are made into them. Something happened to Jake. Just like to you." I point my finger at him, waiting for him to understand. And I can see he does when his cheeks turn a slight pink color. "But you've found your way out, haven't you?"

With a sad face, he replies, "I have, and it was hard." Then Justin turns around to look at the street for a few moments before returning to me. "But I think Jake is too far gone to come back from there. There's only this," he swallows, "darkness left in him."

I lean over the counter to be closer to his face. "Where you see only darkness, I see a spark of light."

His eyes are sad when he speaks. "I think you might be the only one."

I meet his stare with my unblinking one. "And that is enough."

The next week flies by in a blur. My time is divided between caring for Brodie and running the bakery. Turns out, the demand didn't die the next day—the people are coming in. Some curious to see what the hype is about, and some are already returning customers.

Donna hasn't stopped by.

Nor did Mrs. Attleborough. I'm sure she's aware of Brodie being in the daycare now. I still don't think I want to see her just yet. Being nosy is one thing, being nosy behind my back when she's taking care of my kid is another.

I'm not going to lie, every time the door chimes, I lift my head in hopes of seeing Jake walk into the bakery. Even though I know we can't be anything. Even though we're totally toxic for each other. Even though I'm not even sure why I'm having these thoughts while I can count our interactions on one hand.

Almost a month later, the bakery business is booming. With Christmas and New Year and visitors coming into town to see their relatives, along with the regulars and randos, I had to increase the number of pastries I prep each day. People from the yoga studio come in almost every day. They love when I predict their usual orders and start coffees before they even say anything. It not only makes them feel special, but also makes me feel like part of the community. Jonah was right, the people of this street and I are good for each other.

Jake hasn't stopped by yet. Nor has he stopped at his parents' house. When I carefully ask around if anyone has seen him, I just get a shake of their heads. Jake has officially disappeared.

Today is a usual day when I start pastries early in the morning while Brodie's still sleeping, then I get him downstairs with me and wait until Jonah comes in to replace me at the counter for twenty minutes while I drop off Brodie at daycare. Jonah's been doing this every day since the opening like a true friend and a lifesaver. I pay him with breakfast and pastries to go. Sometimes he stops by at lunch and gives me a small break. If I have this constant stream of customers for another month, I might be able to hire someone to help me part-time and free Jonah from his early morning imprisonment.

Sometimes he stops by in the evening to spend some time with me and my kid, and Brodie has come to love him like another uncle. Every time he comes in, he brings a toy, and every time I warn him to stop spoiling my child. But he just waves me off and keeps on spoiling. I can see that Jonah wants a kid of his own, and he will be an awesome dad. I just hope he can find someone good enough to become his partner so they can become parents together. Because quite honestly? I don't think there's anyone good enough for Jonah—that's how amazing of a human being he is.

And today, just like any other day, I pay him with breakfast, and he leaves, promising to come back during lunch.

Around nine, Justin comes in.

"Hey, Oli. Can I have some pigs in blankets to go?"

I go to grab a box, smiling all the way. "You've become an addict, I see."

"You've made me." He smiles cheekily. "And the boys. They're gonna make me broke, always requesting the same." He looks at me pleadingly. "You gotta give me a discount as a regular customer. Or a family discount! That'd be cool."

I laugh. "I'll think about that. Hey, have you talked to Jake recently?" I ask while swiping his card.

"No." His cheerful demeanor clouds instantly. "We don't talk on the phone or text. We don't do that."

I chew on my lower lip, contemplating if I should ask something else.

"Why? Was he around? Did he do something?"

"No." I place the box in front of him and lean my elbows on the counter. "That's the point. No one has seen him. So, I'd think at least someone from his family talked to him, you know."

His eyes turn wary. "What about Alicia?"

"She hasn't heard from him since Thanksgiving."

He looks at me with newfound worry in his eyes. "I'll ask Mom."

"Can you text me when you talk to her?"

"You still at odds with her?" he asks, smiling understandingly.

I nod, not wanting to elaborate.

"I will. Thanks, Oli." He salutes, takes the box, and leaves while I stare at the slowly falling snow outside.

Jake's last visit was worrisome, and it left a bad taste in my mouth. Ever since, I can't stop thinking about him and his vague words.

Soon, Jonah comes for lunch, and we actually get a chance to talk since there aren't a lot of people today. The weather has been weird, and everyone prefers to stay home rather than driving on the icy roads.

"What is *that*?" I ask, pointing at his face where a thin mustache has appeared seemingly overnight.

"You like?" He pouts his lips and makes the hair above them dance a little.

"Sure, Jonathio," I say, laughing as I begin to whip us up two off-the-menu sandwiches. He looks like an old man.

"I look good!" he insists, checking himself in the reflection of the espresso machine. He makes us coffee, then we both take a seat at the window table.

"Have you heard anything about Jake?" I ask randomly.

He stops chewing. "No. Should I?"

I shrug. "No, but you know everyone. So maybe you heard something."

He places his sandwich back on the plate. "Do you want me to find something out?"

I look out the window at the icy, disgusting snow, and think about my child I'll be picking up soon and how he doesn't need any complications like an unstable figure in his life. So maybe, it's fate's way of telling me I need to stop digging and just let it go. Finally.

"No." I take a sip of my coffee. "It's fine."

"You sure?" His ever-attentive eyes drill holes in my face. "I don't mind asking around. I just didn't know you decided to pursue him after all. The last conversation we had about Mr. Attleborough Jr. and his double junior left me with the impression you didn't want him around Brodie." He glances to the side before returning back to me. "And quite honestly, after spending time with Brodie, I don't want Jake around him either. That little man is so full of happiness. I feel like bringing Jake around will dull it in some way, you know?"

I give him a death stare. "Sometimes I don't see the benefit of my kid having another uncle."

He chuckles, waving me off like an annoying fly. "Oh, please, you love me."

"Unfortunately," I mumble, making him laugh louder.

"Just in case you change your mind, let me know. The offer is on the table."

"Thanks, Jonathio."

He rolls his eyes, grabbing the sandwich from the plate. "When will you drop this stupid nickname?"

"When you shave that porn mustache off," I reply, pointing at his face.

"I'm at the Top Gun stage, woman. Leave me alone," he warns me with his index finger in the air.

"Whatever you say, Jonathio. You don't look like the actor from the movie though. You look like an Italian man from an eighties porn," I say, quickly digging into my own sandwich.

He chokes on a bite but still shows me a middle finger.

Chapter Twenty-Seven

Olivia

Another month goes by, and we're completely settled into the Little Hope life.

The bakery continues to do great. In fact, way better than I expected. Even after the holidays, I have a steady income from regulars and a few new people here and there. I didn't even know Little Hope had so many.

I've ventured into baking fresh bread, and people love it. It takes me some extra time for the preparation in the evening, and I have to get up an hour early in the morning because I have only one oven. But it brings in money, and I'm happy.

I'm always tired, but who isn't? I'm thinking about hiring someone, but at this point, I can't afford it yet. I'm trying to pay off as much of my mortgage as I can and put money aside for Brodie's daycare, because the more hours I get for him, the more expensive it becomes, plus we desperately need a new car. Mine is making awful sounds, and I need to drop it off at Justin's place to see what's happening. I can ask Mark to take a look at it, but he's still recovering from the holidays, and I don't want to stress him out even more. Plus, taking care of my own car is another step to becoming fully independent.

I talked to Alicia about arranging a schedule for that extra money she lent me, but she refuses to take it, saying it can wait. Every time we talk about it, she changes the topic. I'd be lying if I said it doesn't make me suspicious. Did she really give away something she couldn't, and now they are suffering because of it? I need to grill Mark about the matter.

I'm heading out of town today to meet some new suppliers. It'll be my first night ever away from Brodie and I don't know how I can survive this. He's staying with Alicia and Mark—the only people I truly trust with my son. Mark wanted to come with me, but Alicia made a funny face—she looked scared at the thought of staying with Brodie alone, and I don't blame her. I was scared to be with him alone at first too.

I still remember the night I left the hospital with him and didn't have anyone yet. Mark was on the plane, but the first night I was alone, not knowing what to do and how to cope with my life changing overnight. I had been trying to get myself ready for the change, but no one can really prepare you for what your hormone-flooded body and overwhelmed mind will do to you when you stay with a little human one-on-one. I guess this would have been the time when it would be nice to have his father in my life. But I made the decision to keep him away, and I have to stick to it.

Which I'm currently doubting as I drive to Montreal in Mark's truck—alone—because my car is not exactly safe for this road. A couple weeks ago, I sat with a calculator and did the math of what I had in stock. Turned out, I spend way more money on supplies than I should, and it's time I find a good deal somewhere since I have an established business now. Though to me, it sounds like a joke. I've been open for like two and a half months, but Josie keeps telling me to change my attitude about this venture and make it more serious. She says it's all about the right mindset. Plus she told me that I needed to get out of Little Hope to breathe some fresh air so I can come back with more energy. She does that all the time, leaving Kenneth alone in the house with the kids.

I trust her—she's built her business from the ground, and now she's a successful owner of a developing company. I think that's what it's called.

She showed me the best way to search for good and cheap suppliers, and that's how I find myself on the road, drinking crappy gas station coffee after crossing the border as I fill up Mark's truck for the zillionth time—this thing devours gas. But at least I get all the pee breaks I need from the constant crappy coffee.

Looking around the surrounding snowy fields, I see how similar Canada is to Maine or Vermont so far. Feels like I'm still home.

Despite the familiar picture, my heart aches the farther away from home I drive. I've never been this far away from my son and don't know how I'll be sleeping tonight without him moving in his crib by my side. Freya told me I should take this opportunity as a fun trip for myself and even maybe do some shopping while I'm in the city. I nodded when she said that but laughed to myself that I would never spend money on clothing when I don't have a need for it. That's not how my life works.

The first stop is a farm on the way to Montreal. The owners are extremely nice, and they have way better cheese prices than my current supplier from Vermont, even with the shipping included. Now that I have a better offer in hand, I can try negotiating a deal with my current supplier.

Feeling energized after my first meeting, I drive on and find my hotel in Montreal, change shoes into more comfortable ones for walking, and rush outside to see the city. Not having visited many places, everything impresses me. Even buried under the snow, the city is alive. Beautiful streets with nice cafés inside, friendly people and dogs with frozen noses. I'm loving everything I see.

Until I get lost. Completely and totally lost. The buildings turn dark and unkempt, the people are fewer and fewer in between. Smiles are nowhere to be found. I have no idea how I managed to take a wrong turn.

I quickly pull up the maps on my phone so it can direct me anywhere other than here and start looking around for street signs when something catches my attention. After being raised in a trailer park, I'm very familiar with what a deal looks like. And what I'm witnessing right now is a drug deal in the dark corner of one alley. Every person here is looking behind their shoulder. Everyone's alert.

But that's not what catches my attention. The person doing the deal does.

His black, puffy jacket is open. He doesn't have a hat on, his blond hair and longish beard are a mess. He's barely recognizable, but I know it's him. His arm stretches toward another very shady-looking man, and after a quick handshake, he retreats it back into his pocket. Two other men are standing around without doing much. From what I'm seeing, I don't even know who looks shadier, and if I didn't know him, I'd consider him the most dangerous of the bunch.

"Jake." I can't help but whisper his name.

Maybe a little too loud and not at all under my breath as I thought at first. Because his head quickly whips toward me. His eyes turn sharp, despite him looking like a damn junkie just a second ago. Giant circles under his eyes and sunken cheeks confirm the picture I've suspected at first— he's high or has been.

"Who's that?" the little less shady man asks, following Jake's gaze. "Who's Jake?"

My eyes dart between them, and I understand that the man I'm looking at is *my* Jake. I mean, Jake. But his calculating eyes warn me not to say another word. His lips are pursed tightly together. His flared nostrils finish the picture of cold fury.

I blink, trying to erase *this* face from my future memory. "Sorry, I thought you were someone else." I give them a forced, closed-off smile and turn around to quickly walk away.

"Hold on," the man yells a bit louder to my back, but I ignore him and keep walking. "I said, wait!" he yells this time.

But I pick up speed and start running.

I don't know how long I've been running as fast as I can, but the streets have changed at some point. They become brighter, and from here, I think I can actually get a cab and just drive to my hotel without any add-on adventures.

The light at the end of the tunnel seems like a reality, and I finally stop to take a brea—

A hand covers my mouth from the back and drags me into an alley adjacent to where I decided to stop. It didn't seem dangerous or even dark enough outside, but with someone's presence behind my back, this spot now seems pretty lethal.

I start fighting for dear life, trying to shake the man off me by using the self-defense tactics Mark drilled into my brain when I was a kid. But this man is a true giant, his hand is around my throat, pressing into my windpipe, and I'm exhausted from running and can't get his paws off me as he drags me deeper into the alley.

"Get her in here," a male voice hisses from somewhere.

"I'm trying," another one says right near my ear. "The bitch is putting up a fight."

"Get her over here!" The first voice gets angrier, and I understand I need to fight harder if I want to survive these two attackers. I fight and wiggle and thrash my body around.

Until he lets go, and I fall face first on the ground, snow getting into my eyes and mouth. I'm trying to get my bearings as fast as I can while I hear a couple of baffled hits and then the sound of a heavy body dropping on the ground. Yelling. A string of exchanged profanities. Another thud.

"Fuck." A worried voice I know stops next to me, falling on his knees. "Are you alright?"

I wipe the snow out of my eyes now and can see Jake's worried face in front of me. His eyes quickly run about my body, assessing the damage.

"Are you alright?" he repeats the question firmer.

"Yes," I cough out. "I am."

He rises to his feet and takes my elbow, dragging me up. Not gentler than the asshole before if I may say so.

"What are you doing here?" His voice is full of barely restrained anger as he's towing me toward the light outside the dark alley.

"Me? ME!" I nearly yell into his face. "What are *you* doing here?"

He glances at the unconscious men on the ground and shoves me to move forward. "Let's go. The rest are coming."

I'm happy to get away from this place, so I gladly follow his lead without any more questioning or fighting. There's always a right time for both, and it's not now.

"Where are you staying?" he asks in a clipped tone, getting angrier with every breath.

I tell him the address, and he steers me onto a busy street where he catches a taxi and shoves me inside. I expect him to close the door, but he climbs inside right after me, so I have to scoot over. He tells the address to the driver and stares out the window without saying a word.

"Jake?" I call out when the silence becomes unbearable, but he ignores me. So I call out louder. "Jake?"

He ignores me again.

"For fuck's sake, Jake." I smack my thighs with my hands. "Answer me! What were you doing back there?"

He turns his eyes toward me, the coldest I've ever seen them. Looking positively murderous right now, even with those giant dark circles underneath them. "Years," he clips out. "Years, Olivia." My name feels like poison on his lips. "And you managed to fuck it all up in one minute."

"What?" I rear back. "What do you mean? I didn't do anything other than try to get the hell away from there."

"Not now." He shakes his head and stares back at the window. The atmosphere is so heavy I can barely breathe.

When we arrive at my hotel, he silently passes cash to the driver, gets out, and waits for me to follow him. Then he nods to me to lead the way, and I trot inside the hotel like a puppy who just peed in someone's shoes. This is how easy I turn into someone being bullied. I've never been known to bend my knees when facing life.

My room is on the third floor. We walk into the elevator —silently, of course—and then to my room. I put the key card into the slot, and Jake pushes me to the side and steps inside the room first. And not just steps, he does it like some dude from an action movie. Carefully, watching every-where. Only then does he motion for me to follow him.

I go inside, half expecting a robber to jump on me from under the bed, then I take off my jacket and hat and drop them on the chair by the TV. Jake's already next to the window, carefully pulling the curtain to the side and looking at the street.

I drill a hole into the side of his face with my stare. "Want to tell me what's going on?"

He completely ignores my question and shoots me back with one of his own. "What are you doing here, Olivia?"

I grit my teeth together, dreaming of sinking them into his neck to pull out a chunk of those stubborn, pronounced muscles.

"You answer my question first, and then I'll answer yours."

He sighs and finally turns to me. "You've made me. Years in the making, and you just showed up right there. With your big eyes," he waves his hand in front of my face as if my big eyes are offensive to him, "and all that. And boom, everything's gone."

I quirk a brow, choosing it to be the only way I show my displeasure because I need to focus on the other part.

"Made you? What are you talking about?"

Another deep sigh. "I've been undercover for years. And it was supposed to be the last time I did it." He quickly turns back to the streets.

"Did what?" I take a step toward him.

"All of that," he replies, crossing his arms over his chest.

"Jake." I step even closer and place my hand on his arm. His jacket is still so cold from the freezing air outside, I assume his body doesn't feel any warmer either. "I don't understand."

He turns to me. "I know." He sounds detached, not offering the explanation I'm so eager to hear, and he knows it.

"Are you on drugs?" I ask half jokingly, half expecting him to laugh it off.

"I am," he confirms calmly instead. "And we need to get you out of here before I go into withdrawal."

"What?" I rear back. It's not the answer I expected if I'm honest.

"Yeah, princess. Surprise." His smile is weak. "I'm an addict, and what you witnessed," he throws his thumb behind his back, "was a drug deal. With me selling the shit, in case you got that part fucked up in your head. A couple more weeks, and I'd go higher up the chain and finally get actual names. But now, it's all gone."

I take another step back. "You're a drug dealer?"

"Scared now?" He quirks a brow, looking satisfied with himself.

But none of that makes sense to me. Jake, a drug dealer? Yes, he's an asshole, but I've always seen him as a righteous one. I can't wrap my head around him getting involved into selling drugs and poisoning other people.

"I don't know," I reply honestly, and see the moment his face becomes surprised too. He didn't expect this answer from me. I didn't either. When someone tells you they're dealing drugs, confusion wouldn't be the first reaction, I don't think. But I'm confused. Confused with him being the bad guy everyone sees him as and worse. What do I do with this knowledge?

"You should kick me out of here, Olivia." He nods at the door.

I stare at him point-blank. "Will you go if I do?"

"No." His chuckle is sad. "I can't at this point. Those guys heard you call me by my real name, so I can't leave you now."

"Why?"

He glances outside. "You've made them suspicious. They'll come after you to find the truth."

I swallow the sudden fear down—it's about time the damn thing showed up. "Who will come after me?"

"Them." Now, he nods at the streets.

"And you're not one of them?"

He watches my face with a new intensity. "What do you think?"

It's a good question, and before I answer it, I want to be sure. So I stare at his eyes, trying to see what sort of dark demons he's hiding in that blue coldness . . . But all I find is loneliness and fear. And tiredness. Bone-dead tiredness. So I say honestly, "I don't think you are."

He licks his lips, trying to avoid my eyes. This seems to be another thing I manage to surprise him with.

"Fuck, Olivia." He covers his face with his hands. "What the hell are you doing?"

I pat on the bed and sit on it. "I don't know," I answer truthfully, because a drug addict is the very last thing I need in my life right now. It was bad enough when he was pronounced the town alcoholic, but I seem to look for other 'adventures.' "Are you really on drugs?"

He digs the heels of his palms into his eye sockets. "Yes. And I'm gonna go into some serious withdrawal soon if I don't get anything. I was supposed to meet with some people and get high, hoping the party will move on to their location, but now I can't."

"So you can sell more drugs?" I can't hide the disappointment from my voice. Nor do I want to.

"No." His laugh is dark. "So I can find the name of the people at the top and pass them to the fucking government, so I never have to think about this ever again. Maybe even move to fucking Mexico when everything's done."

"What?" I feel my eyes widening to an unnatural size.

"Moving to Mexico. You know, where problems don't exist anymore, and I can just live on a beach sipping margaritas." One side of his lips quirks up a little in the ghost of a smile.

"Not that, Jake!" I wave him off, annoyed that he's thinking about Mexico when he just dropped a bomb the size of Australia on me. "The part about the government and all that."

"Oh, that." He sounds totally disappointed. "I'm undercover. *Been* undercover for the past who the fuck knows how many years."

Now my eyes are about to bulge out of eye sockets. "Like in the movies?"

He chuckles. "No, not like in the movies." Then he peeks outside one more time and walks to sit on the only chair in the room. "Not so fancy."

"No way," I gasp mockingly. "You don't run around, guns blazing?"

"No." He crosses his arms over his chest. "It's a shitty job really."

"What do you do exactly?" I squint my eyes.

"It's complicated." He glances to the side. "And it might

take a lot of time which we don't have right now, so I need you to get ready so we can go."

"Go? Go where?"

"Back to Little Hope," he explains. "They know you know me. Now they want to know who I really am." His face turns dark. "I can't go back. And you can't go outside." He pushes away from the chair. "Is that enough information for now so you can get a move on and get ready? I'll help you."

"I haven't even unpacked." I point at my bag. "I just came and changed shoes, that's it."

"Good." He walks to grab my duffel bag. "Get your shoes, and let's go."

"I can't go. I have a meeting tomorrow."

"You can't stay, Olivia." He walks up to me. "It's not safe."

"Why?" I feel my forehead scrunch in concentration. "I can just hide here, in the hotel, and go tomorrow in a taxi. Then I can get back here the same way and go to Little Hope after." To me, it sounds like an awfully detailed plan any spy would be proud of. Totally bulletproof.

He watches me, slowly blinking. Then he looks at the ceiling before putting his free hand on my shoulder. "I don't think you understand the severity of the situation. Those people are dangerous, Oli. They control the whole coastal drug system. And now that they have a suspicion I'm not the one they thought I was. They'll stop at nothing to get to me."

"Are you in danger too?" My voice sounds scared, but I'm not embarrassed of that.

He sighs. "I'm fine, Oli. Let's just get you out of here, okay?"

My eyes dart between his, and when I find genuine fear, I finally whisper, "Okay."

He gently turns me around and ushers me toward the door. We take the elevator down and head toward the reception area. Then we head outside to the parking garage to get Mark's truck.

"Why didn't you flash your badge at the receptionist, and didn't, I dunno," I shrug, "ask her not to give our information to anyone?"

He looks around the garage while ushering me to move faster. "It would only draw unnecessary attention because she'll start gossiping with everyone the moment we're out of sight. Plus, they'd get what they need from her anyway. This way, she won't need to make something up and put herself in danger because of that."

"Makes sense. I guess," I reply, quite impressed with his caring for other people. In movies, they make it seem like collateral damage is a sure and obvious thing. But when I hear his simple explanation, I see there might be another truth to it.

Jake stops for a second and turns to me. "Do you trust me?"

I look into his eyes, trying to get a good read from him. But a moment later, I understand that I don't even need to search for anything because I already know the answer.

"I do."

The look in his eyes softens. "Then know that if I had even the slightest hope that telling the receptionist not to say a word would do us any favors, I would. I don't give a flying fuck about anyone's safety but yours where you're concerned. I just dropped an operation we've been developing for a few years."

Well, or that. Looks like I have my very own morally gray hero Alicia loves to portray in her books so much.

"You were mad," I remind him about his reaction to finding me in the dark alley.

"Yes, I was." The muscles on his jaw move. "Because it was you who made me. Which meant you were on their radar now too." He leans closer to me. "Believe me, Oli, if it was someone else, I'd throw them under the bus because the stakes are fuckin' high. This operation took fuckin' forever and a whole lot of me. But none of it matters now. Do you understand?" He's trying to communicate something he doesn't say with words, I can feel that. Even though he's pretty clear in his explanation, there's something else in there, between the lines and his concerned face.

But I don't know what exactly. So all I can do is silently nod to his statement.

"Good. Now, we need to get the fuck away. Where's your car?"

We reach the truck while Jake's head is moving three-sixty like in a horror movie. He watches every corner, every shadow. Every speck of light coming our way. Every sound makes him jumpy.

I'm about to ask if he should drive and then remember the drugs, before climbing into the driver's seat.

He turns even jumpier. He's pale. A thin layer of sweat covers his forehead. It doesn't look like fear anymore.

"Are you okay?" I can't hide my own fear from my voice.

"Yes. Drive."

I shift gears and pull onto the street while he takes out a handgun and checks the magazine. I eye it but don't question. If what he's saying is true, a gun makes a lot of sense.

The Canadian streets during winter are pretty much

Maine streets with a few extra inches on top—nothing extraordinary, so I'm used to navigating a vehicle in heavy snow. What I'm not accustomed to is driving with a gripping fear in the bottom of my belly.

Jake's body is coiled next to me. His presence is *felt* not only with his big, menacing body, but with the heaviest aura I've yet felt around him. His pierced together lips and a deep line between his eyebrows are the sure definition of concentration. If someone googled the name, they'd find his picture next to it in the results tab.

The more I look at him, the more sweat covers his face. His breathing turns a bit shallow and ragged.

"Jake, are you sure you're okay?"

"I'm going into withdrawal." His voice is ragged too. "We need to get as far away as possible from the city."

With that, he pulls a small bag of pills from his pocket and seemingly starts counting them.

"What are those?"

"Plan B." His tone is clipped.

"Jake," I raise my voice, "what the fuck are those? Please, tell me you don't have drugs in my brother's car."

His sweaty, pale face turns to me. "Oli, I'll need to take this so I can protect you until Benson can or they send someone else until I recover."

My next move is sudden—I stretch my body toward him and smack his hand, making all the pills fly on the floor.

"What the fuck?" he yells.

"Those are evil, and you know that!" I yell back.

"I know that!" He matches my tone. "Don't you think I fucking know that when it literally ruined my life? I hate that shit more than anyone ever will, but more lives are at stake. And now, it's your life. The only fucking life that matters to me now. And I can't fuckin' protect you when

I'm a vomiting mess, Oli. Don't you understand that?" The desperation in his voice is as clear as the determination against the evil pills in mine.

I shoot him a glare, even though I'm mad at myself for calling him out on using. At his words, I don't feel like he actually ever wanted to do it. "I know how to use a gun. And I'll hold it until you get better," I try reasoning with the stubborn man.

"Oli." His voice turns pleading. "It's not a game. They're dangerous people, and you have a son to think about."

"Do you think I don't fuckin' know that?" I blow up. "And this is precisely why you won't be taking that shit ever again. Because if I'm bringing you around my son, you'd better be squeaky clean!"

After stunning him into a weighted silence, I pull my phone away from my pocket and dial Mark.

"*Sup, big shot. Got any good deals?*" His happy voice, mixed with Brodie's laughter in the background, fills the space from the speaker.

"Yes!" I try to sound happy. "In fact, I got so much good stuff going on that I was wondering if you could watch Brodie for a couple more days."

A moment of silence tells me everything I need to know —Mark has doubts. He knows me too well, and he's very protective. Which means I have to up my game. "*Is everything okay?*"

"Fine, you caught me," I singsong. "I just want to take Freya's advice and spend some time for myself, you know?"

"*Okay, Oli.*" His voice drops an octave, but the doubt is still there. "*I know. And yes, take all the time you need. In fact, I don't think you can take Brodie away from Alicia when you come back anyway.*"

Alicia's happy laughter rings through the phone. *"That's a fact! Is that right, mah man?"* She probably tickles Brodie because he starts giggling too.

"I miss him so much," I say sincerely, letting sadness envelop me for a moment.

"He misses you too," Mark replies. *"Are you sure you're okay?"* I can almost imagine him narrowing his eyes as he asks.

"Yeah. I'm fine."

I feel a heavy stare on the side of my face.

"Alright then. Have fun!"

"Tell Brodie I love him." This is where the tears swell in my eyes, clouding my vision. Quite literally.

"I will. Be safe."

"I will be."

When we hang up, I grip the wheel tighter and press the accelerator a bit harder. My emotions are all over the place. My mind is busy trying to figure out if I've made the right decision.

"What was that?" he asks quietly. "Why did you do that?"

"Do what?" I stare ahead.

"Don't be a smartass. You know what." Jake sounds annoyed.

"Because you're not taking this stuff, Jake," I scold him, like I do Brodie when he does something he's not supposed to.

"Yeah?" He's full of very loud sarcasm. "What do we do then, Ms. Know-It-All?"

"We're going to a motel to get you clean."

He looks at me like I just told him I had intimate intercourse with an alien, and then he bursts out laughing.

"What's so funny?" It's my turn to be annoyed.

"You want me to get clean with you?"

My knuckles turn white as I grip the wheel with all my anger. "Is that such a bad thing?"

"It's ugly. It's long. It's fucked up." With each word, his tone darkens.

"What are you on?"

"What?" he asks, sounding confused even though I've asked a pretty clear question.

"What drugs are you on, Jake?" I repeat, losing my patience.

"Why?"

"Jake! Just freaking answer me." My knuckles turn white from gripping the wheel too tight.

After a short pause, he says, "Stimulants."

"Okay." I nod to myself. "Once we're in a hotel, I'll google how to get you clean."

His following laugh is very annoying. "Oli, I'll never let you see me getting clean. It's a fuckin' horrible thing to watch. Never, Oli. You'll never see it."

Chapter Twenty-Eight

J_{ake}

As I puke my guts out for the millionth time in the past hour, I stop feeling anything other than need. I was embarrassed the first few times, but now all I can feel is pain. In my head, in my body, even in my blood. How many withdrawals can I go through before it becomes easier to just give up and succumb to the pain for good?

"Drink it," Olivia orders as she pushes a plastic bottle to my mouth. I turn away. "Drink it, Jake, or I'll pour it down your throat."

I try to laugh. "I'd like to see you tr—" But I can't finish because a coughing fit takes my breath hostage.

"Yep, that's what I'm saying." She pushes the bottle to my lips again once I'm done coughing. "Drink it."

I obey and swallow a few sips before a shudder runs through my body, and I black out. Through the shudders, I think I feel her hand on my head and hear her voice. "You'll be fine, Jake. I'm here. Google says stimulant withdrawals are brutal, but you'll live. And I want you to live. We have some unfinished business. So you'd better hurry up and make those five days three. Or two. Please, Jake. Do it for me and my kid."

Those words get burned into my subconscious. *Do it for me and my kid.*

I will, Oli. I will.

<hr>

I come back to the sound of a running shower and try looking around. My smart cookie put a stool under the door handle and shut all the blinds. A quick check of my night-stand leaves me with dissatisfaction—she took my gun. I feel naked without it.

Another smart move on her end, but still, I don't like feeling vulnerable.

Speaking of naked. I glance down and find myself covered with a blanket with no clothes on. I'm weak. I barely have energy to pull the blanket up to check that she undressed me down to my underwear and most likely cleaned me with a washcloth.

Such a fuckin' embarrassment not only for my masculinity, but humility in general. I've dropped so low that the most gorgeous woman I've ever met had to go and wash my fuckin' puke and sweat-covered body. I won't recover from that.

The water stops, followed by the sound of her light foot-steps. A vision comes to my hazy mind, and for a moment, I feel another sort of hunger. A very unexpected one. When

I'm in withdrawal, sex is the very last thing on my mind. But times are changing or so it seems.

Water is dripping from her long hair, she's wrapped into something that used to be a white towel, and now it's somewhat gray. She's holding the front of it together over her chest.

She falters when she notices me watching her.

"I didn't know you were awake." Her voice sounds gravelly and tired.

"Unfortunately," I manage to croak.

"Hold on. I'll get you something to drink." She runs to the dresser and grabs a water bottle from it.

"No need," I whisper because my throat is dry. "It will just come right back out."

She walks to the bed and kneels in front of me. "Something will stay. Drink," she says, pushing the bottle to my lips. I try drinking it but can't. Swallowing is too painful. Breathing is too painful. I pull my face away from the bottle, but her surprisingly strong hand digs into my shoulder and holds me still.

"Drink, Jake. I'm not asking."

I try cackling at her bossiness but again, I can't. So I swallow a couple of sips and fall back on the bed. I want to keep looking at her because she's become my anchor to reality and to all the good that might still be waiting for me. When another wave of pain and need knocks me down, I know the next time I wake it will be the worst.

***

I wake up to the same dingy motel room, my body wrecked in pain and my mind clouded by a relentless craving. My throat is parched, and I can feel the sweat drenching the sheets beneath me. It's another hour—day?—of hellish detox, and this time it seems to be worse than before.

I blink the dryness of my eyes away. And when I can see, I find Olivia on the chair next to bed. She's asleep in a sitting position, leaning her head on the back of the chair. When she hears my weak attempts to move, she becomes wide awake in a second.

The need is overwhelming, and her presence is the only thing tethering me to reality in this nightmare. I think I'm at the worst of it now. It should get better after. If I don't succumb to the call.

It's all so unfair to her, but I don't think I'd be able to do it without her help this time. She's been with me every moment, quite literally holding my hand through the agony of withdrawal.

I look at her, her eyes tired but determined, and I know I don't deserve her. I don't deserve this thing she's offering without asking anything in return.

"Jake," she whispers, her voice soft and soothing. "It's going to be okay. I promise."

I try to nod, but even that small movement feels like an unreachable task. The nausea washes over me, and I lurch toward the edge of the bed, retching into a bucket Olivia has placed for me. The sound is guttural, and I can feel the tears streaming down my cheeks. It's humiliating, but Olivia doesn't flinch. Now, she's seen me at my worst, yet she's still here.

And I don't know why.

"Just a bit longer, Jake," she says, brushing my hair gently. "I think it'll be over soon."

"Yeah, I'll fuckin' die," I croak in an inhuman voice, and she laughs. Even though it sounds sad.

"You'll be fine."

I want to believe her. I want to believe that this agony will end, that I can beat this demon holding me hostage again. But every cell in my body is screaming for relief, for that familiar numbness that drugs used to bring.

As the hours drag by, I figure I was right when I thought this part would be the worst. Because it fuckin' is. Even with Olivia by my side, it seems impossible now. She holds me when the chills rack my body, and she talks to me when anxiety threatens to consume me. Her words are a lifeline, pulling me back from the brink of despair.

And then, the darkest hour comes . . . The room is claustrophobic. It's filled with the echoes of my regrets and bad decisions. The walls seem to close in on me, and every muscle in my body throbs with pain. When I think I can't take it anymore and am going to run away from this fuckin' room to find the pills Olivia knocked from my hands in the car even if I have to lick them with my tongue, she climbs into the bed with me. Then she positions herself behind my back and pushes my head to her chest.

And she hugs me. Tightly. So tightly, I don't think I can escape. Even if I wanted. Which I don't. She starts raking her fingers through my hair and humming a lullaby she probably sings for Brodie.

Brodie. Fuck. Her kid. Her kid who's waiting for her at home while I'm holding her here along with my misery. I have to hurry the fuck up with this withdrawal thing.

Then I remember what she asked me to do. To do it for her and her boy.

"You have to do this, Jake," she whispers, causing tingles. "You have to do it for the last time and never go through this again."

I swallow bile down my throat and nod. *I'll do it for you.*

Chapter Twenty-Nine

O livia

I didn't know we'd make it through. Watching him go through *this* was the worst thing I've ever witnessed.

I could almost feel his pain in my own body. And then, after the chills racking his body reached the peak, he grabbed my hand while I was still holding him on my chest. His grip was strong, and I wasn't sure my hand would survive. But here I am, using the very same hand to stroke his wet hair while he sleeps.

I think we're past the worst part. He's not feverish anymore, and his sleep doesn't seem nightmarish. In fact, he's snoozing rather peacefully while still holding my hand. I could use another shower because I'm drenched in Jake's sweat, but the moment I try pulling away, his grip intensifies. So I give up and find a more comfortable position to sleep.

When we arrived at the hotel, I googled types of withdrawals and what I should do to help him through. The main advice seemed to be to keep him from himself. And that's what I've been doing for the past two days, which honestly have felt like a full month. I read online some scary stories about people in withdrawal and how violent they can turn. I'm not going to lie, they scared me, and I half expected Jake to turn into a feral animal at some point. But he turned out much stronger than I gave him credit for. Every time he was slipping away into rage, I thought my time was near. So I called out to him. When he heard my voice, he immediately calmed down like some sort of magic spell. There was one time when he didn't become calm, so I did the next most natural thing I could think of—I took his hand in mine. I still remember how peaceful his face became. And how fast he dropped back on the bed, dragging me with him. And how he pressed my hand into his chest while returning to a fetal position.

To some, he might have looked miserable. To me, he looked *mine*.

I check my phone one more time in case Alicia sent me anything else. Yesterday—or was it this morning—I called her and asked her if they could take care of Brodie for a little longer. She was suspicious, and I had to tell her the truth that I'm with Jake, and he needs my help. I didn't elaborate the details, and she understood why. It's his story to tell. She assured me that she'd take care of Brodie and would try to ease Mark's murderous tendencies once he learns what's causing my delay. And the last part will be very hard. Mark will kill me and then he will kill Jake. That's a given.

Not finding any new pictures of my boy on the phone, I

put it aside and fall asleep, not able to fight my own body anymore and stay awake.

When I come to, I'm alone in bed.

Shit! I jump to the floor and rush to the door. I don't know how he got out! I was holding him the whole night. Wasn't I?

When I'm feverishly unlocking the door, a low, grouchy but oh-so-normal voice asks from behind my back, "What are you doing?"

"Shit!" I jump, startled, with a hand pressed to my chest. "You scared me."

His face changes with his old signature half-smile. "You thought I left." He has a towel wrapped around his waist. And it's low. Very low. My traitorous eyes dip down his chest and torso. He's smooth. His skin is golden. That color you can never reach with tanning. The color that comes only naturally. His shoulders are wide. His ribcage is extensive. His muscles have muscles. He's incredibly lean but the coiled power in his body is almost scary. Almost. Not enough for me not to swallow sudden thirst in my mouth.

For goodness' sake, Olivia! The man just came out of hell, and you're ogling him like he's the last meal on the planet.

Suddenly, I feel irritated and tired. "Can you blame me?" I ask, walking by him, hair flying behind my back.

"I can't," he replies quietly. Not what I expected to hear if I'm honest, so I pause in my path of bitching.

"Are you okay?"

"I am now." He's watching me with newfound intensity. Like something heavy and deeply meaningful is hiding behind his eyes, but I can't figure out what. "Thank you, Oli."

"Yeah," I reply, not knowing what else to say. I mean

what do you say to a person who's been puking his guts out on you for the past few days, and yet, you're still here because it didn't scare you, and you still find him mega-attractive? Isn't that intense? I'm not an expert, but I don't think this is what he needs right now.

"We need to go."

"Now?" I ask, lost in my thoughts about wanting Jake for myself in different capacities. It's like a floodgate has been opened in my mind, allowing these stupid thoughts to flow into every corner of it. "You just got better."

"And now we need to go," he confirms with a nod. "I don't know if they're on our track, and I want to warn Benson about what might be coming. I'm not even sure why they're not here yet. I'm sure one lousy bodyguard." His cheeks above his beard turn pink.

"Okay," I reply weakly, trying not to stare at his body. "You might wanna get dressed, you know. I took your clothes to the hotel's laundry room. They should be dry by now." I've undressed him and washed him, but he was sick then, and not even one naughty thought entered my mind while he was weak. All of that seemed to change, and now my imagination has no limits.

He looks down at himself and goes back to the bathroom, chuckling, while I run around the room and gather all my belongings. A moment later, he comes out with another towel around his shoulders and heads toward the door.

"Where are you going?"

He pauses next to the door. "I need to run to the laundry and grab my clothes." He looks down at himself. "This's all I have now."

I groan into the sky and go to push him out of the way. "I'll get it. Wait here."

"No fucking way," he says, grabbing my arm. "You're not going there alone."

"Why?"

"For fuck's sake, Olivia." He sounds angry. "Haven't you heard a thing I've told you before? They'll be coming after you."

I cross my arms over my chest. "And what do you propose to do? You can't go out there in a towel. You'll catch pneumonia."

He sighs loudly and walks to the stationary phone. When someone replies on the other end, he says, "If you get me my shit from the laundry room, you'll get a good tip." He listens before he explains what someone needs to bring.

A few minutes later, someone knocks on the door. I rush to open it, but Jake stops me silently and gestures at me to go to the bathroom. I want to ask what's going on, but he signals for me to be quiet, takes his gun from the place I hid it before—the sneak must have found it before I woke up—and slowly moves to the door.

I peak from inside the bathroom, but Jake firmly suggests with his very heavy stare for me to get lost. I do just that.

When I hear him opening the door, I hear another male voice. "Here you go, man." A rustling of a plastic bag.

"Cool. Thanks."

A moment of silence.

"Cool, man!" The voice sounds very excited—probably Jake leaving him a good tip.

The door closes, and I ask with unhidden sarcasm, "Am I allowed to show my face now?"

His husky chuckle is delicious. "Yes, you may come out."

I walk out of the bathroom only to find him dropping

the towel from his shoulders, and the next towel is about to follow, but he pauses with a raised brow.

I glance down at him, somewhat upset to find the towel still intact. "You can use the bathroom," I say, pointing behind my back.

He nods and disappears, leaving me to finish gathering everything.

"Can I take a quick shower?" I ask loudly, so he can hear me through the closed door.

"No," comes his loud and firm answer.

"What?" I ask, sure I just misheard him.

"No," he repeats, coming out of the bathroom.

"What the hell, Jake?"

He finds my glare and holds it. "If you go into that bathroom and get naked there, I'm walking in there with you to fuck you until we both can't move. And we can't do that right now."

My mouth falls open. It probably hit the floor, I just didn't hear it. Did he just say he'd fuck me if I get naked?

He comes closer. "I remember you coming out of there before with a towel around your wet body." His eyes dart between mine while he taps his index finger on his temple. "And it is all I remember. This is all I *will ever* remember."

I want to tell him that I don't mind being fucked by him until we both can't move anymore, but he's right. Not here. Not in this filthy motel room drenched with regrets and revelations. If we ever do that, I want it to be clean. In all aspects. And at this point, I think it's safe to say the fucking will be happening one way or another.

"We should go," I whisper, looking at his face.

"We should." He nods and goes to grab the bags.

Jake goes to the motel office, letting me breathe some fresh air for a whole minute by myself. When he comes out, we go to Mark's truck and get ready for the drive. It's a few hours left to Little Hope, but it might snow again soon, so it might take a little longer.

Jake's driving, and I pull out my phone. No messages from Mark, no calls. And this is very frightening. I expected him to blow up my phone once Alicia told him whom I'm staying with, but nothing from him. Which means someone will probably die when we come home.

I text Alicia that we are on our way, and she sends me my boy's picture with a signature 'can't wait to see you.'

"Who is your kid with?" Jake suddenly asks, startling me.

"With Alicia and Mark."

He nods. "Do they know?"

"They know I stayed with you, but nothing else."

"Thank you," he says, sighing.

"You have to tell them, Jake."

"I know." His face turns cold. "There's a lot to tell, and they're not going to like it."

"I can be there if you want," I offer, despite all the horrors coming my way from Mark's rage when he finds out.

His giant hand suddenly covers mine. "Thank you."

I flip my hand and let our finger intertwine together. It's comfortable. It's fitting. It's meant to be.

We stop at a gas station to get some gas, snacks, and coffee. When I whip my credit card to pay for everything, Jake pushes me to the side with an offended look on his face.

The rest of the ride is surprisingly calm. At least for me. Paranoid Jake keeps looking at the rearview mirror for some bad guys to come and chase us.

When we pass the 'Welcome to Little Hope' sign, I decide it's time to crack an egg.

"I think you should know that Mark is probably going to kill you."

He cackles, relaxing into his chair. "He can try."

I turn my body to face him. "I mean it, Jake. He's really mad, but I couldn't not tell them where I was. I have a child and can't be irresponsible."

The muscle on his jaw ticks, and he nods. "I wouldn't want you to lie to your family. It's not right."

I snort so loudly that he gives me a side-eye but keeps his opinion to himself.

When we turn on my street, I see the end. Quite literally. Alicia's car is parked next to my house, and I'm one hundred percent positive it's not her.

"Here we go," I mumble under my breath, glancing at Jake, whose knuckles on the steering wheel turn white. Shit, I should have driven here so at least Mark wouldn't take even more offense. But it's too late.

Jake parks the truck, and I rush outside.

"Wait," he calls out, following me.

"No," I reply, slightly turning to him while I keep walking. "I'd rather you wait here until I figure out the mood inside."

He speedwalks to catch up with me and grabs my hand. "I don't want you to go there alone," he says, looking into my eyes. "It's not your fault you've been held up."

"Yeah, but Mark doesn't see any reason right now. All he knows is that I've been with you. Therefore, he wants to kill you now more than he wants to kill me. And I didn't spend the last two days stroking your beard for you to be killed before you can taste my éclairs."

He looks at the building before turning his attention back to me. "You're not going there alone, Olivia."

I try reading his face and see if I can at least reason with him because it's not the time or place for his macho stuff, but he's dead set on coming with me. So I just sigh, accepting the fate of a foreseeable funeral, and nod for him to come with me.

And sure thing, Mark's waiting for us in the kitchen. He's sitting at my island with a cup of something obviously cold in it. He's probably been here for a long time.

His eyes are trained on the door when we walk in. He doesn't move, nor does he say a word. This is bad.

"Hey, Mark," I start. "Where's Brodie?"

"Nice for you to remember you have a son."

"Mark!" I cry out, not expecting him to say such a nasty thing.

"Don't do that, man," Jake says, slightly shaking his head. "Don't go down that road. It's ugly."

"You'd know, right?" my brother asks sarcastically, probably expecting Jake to blow up so they can go into a good ol' brawl. But Jake surprises us both by being the level-headed one. You'd never think he just went through a brutal detox, and all his nerves were in pain. He's so calm and collected. And strong. He looks strong despite losing a few pounds pretty much overnight.

"I know that, and this is precisely why I'm telling you not to say anything. Olivia is a great mother." Jake's voice is just as firm as his body.

Chapter Thirty

J_{ake}

"And you'd know that, right? You know her so well by now?" Mark shifts his attention from me to Olivia. "Why did you choose to spend some sweet time with this asshole without telling us? Did you know already that you were going to meet with him while you were talking to your 'suppliers'?" he finishes the nasty message with air quotes.

"Mark!" Olivia cries out, pressing her hand to her chest. She's wide-eyed and looks completely offended. "You know me better than that."

"Do I?" He leans back in his chair, looking completely relaxed. "I thought I did too. You went off to college and never visited."

"We called and texted nearly every day." Olivia's voice turns small.

Mark completely ignores what she says and continues.

"And then one day, you tell me you are pregnant, and that's it. I don't even fuckin' know who the father is. Don't I deserve the truth? I fuckin' raised you, and now you're sneaking around with this asshole," he says, pointing at me. "I'm your brother, Oli. Your family. And you're choosing him over me."

"I'm not choosing him." Olivia's tone is harsh. "Because I didn't know I had to make a choice."

I glance at Olivia and find her smooth throat moving with a long swallow. The corners of her lips point downward. She's very upset. And that kicks in some protective instinct in me that very few people could evoke. My sister, Alicia, being one of them, but even my desire to protect her wasn't so strong. What I'm feeling now is feral. Uncontrollable. Needed.

"Get up," I say to him.

He slowly shifts his attention to me with a raised brow.

"Get up, Mark," I order, trying to keep my cool in front of Olivia. "You're coming with me."

"Am I?" He leans back on the stool with a cold smile.

"Do you want to clean up the mess here after?" I nod at the general area of the living room.

He's up in a second.

"This conversation is not over," he says to Olivia, who doesn't turn to even look at him anymore.

"Oli," I call out, but she doesn't respond. She's standing with her back to me, her shoulders down. "Oli," I call her again. "Don't bring Brodie here until I'm back. I'll call someone to come here until then. For now, go lock the door behind us."

She's quiet.

"Olivia, do you understand?" I put more force into my voice, dropping all the gentleness.

"Yes." Her reply is quiet.

"Good." Satisfaction from her agreeing to my ask is strong. Unexpectedly strong. I thought I liked her defiant. Turns out I like her agreeable too. "I'll be back."

"The fuck you will!" Mark bellows from the hallway, and I rush toward him, shutting the door behind me.

"Wait," I stop him by pulling my phone from my pocket and dialing my brother for the very first time in many years. Mark looks totally stunned. Either by my shushing or my weird action, but he's just standing and watching me through a few very slow blinks.

"*What?*" comes a sleepy voice on the phone.

"Can you come to Olivia's place and stay with her for a couple of hours? And get that shit you store in your safe."

I give him a moment to think about it. He knows I'm referring to his weapon he keeps in his safe in his apartment in case bears come too close—we've had a few encounters before. If I ask that, he knows I mean business.

Now, when the silence is too long, I ask again. "Can you do that?"

"*I'll be there in ten.*"

"Thanks, Jus."

He disconnects without saying a word. But I didn't expect him to. Justin can be an asshole to me all he wants, but he knows something is going on, and his protective instincts are close to mine. He'll be here guarding Oli like a watchdog.

"What just happened?" Mark asks dumbfounded.

I nod for him to follow me downstairs. He does. When we are in the small hallway, I turn to him.

"We can go outside and make a scene, or we can—"

I don't have a chance to finish because a giant fist connects to my jaw. I'm not sure how it's not dislocated. His punch throws me to the wall. It's like being fuckin' hammered in the head from two sides. Now I see why everyone's fuckin' scared of him—his size sure rivals his damn power.

Before I can fully comprehend what just happened, a second punch lands in the same place, surely cracking a tooth or two. *Alright, I'll give you another one, and if I'm still standing, we talk.*

The third one comes to my stomach, and I'm sure there is a kidney falling out somewhere from my back. Olivia will probably find it tomorrow.

"This is for fucking my sister, asshole," he says, readying for another punch, but I stop this one with a block and try to stand straight. It's hard to do when you've just been hammered by a building.

"I haven't fucked your sister," I hiss, blocking another punch. "You've got three in, and that's all you're ever getting."

"Yeah, you've been in a damn library all this time," he says, trying to land a hit.

"We haven't slept together." I pause, forgetting to block. "Well, we did sleep together, but—"

It was clearly the wrong thing to say because he bellows in rage and punches his wrecking ball of a fist into my face again.

"Shit!" I hiss. "I need my eyes to watch out for them, motherfucker."

His next blow, I block his arm and swing him around—something I learned how to do undercover. In that world, fighting is nasty and doesn't have rules, but it does the job. And now, he's pressed with his face in the wall with his arm nearly out of its socket behind his back.

"Calm down. You've landed. A lot," I admit with

respect, wincing from the pain of a rapidly growing bruise on my face. "I haven't *slept* slept with Olivia. She's been," I take a deep breath and add, "helping me detox. So she might have fallen asleep in the same bed, that's all I meant."

He turns his head toward me. Well, as much as he can. "How is that better?" he nearly yells. "Are you a damn addict?"

"Yes, and no." I sigh again. "It's complicated. Can I let you go without you smashing my face again? I don't think I can take another without being out of commission for a few hours, and I need to be fresh."

He contemplates this for a second before nodding, so I slowly release him and step back. His weary eyes roam over me, looking for something. This is a typical reaction when you tell someone you're on drugs. Everyone is weary of you, as they should be honestly.

"I need to go to Benson's office. And I think it's best if you come with me."

He eyes me for a few seconds before shaking his hand in the air. "Damn, Jake. Your jaw is very stubborn."

I snort loudly because of the unexpected remark. "And your fist is like a damn hammer."

Mark's turn to cackle. "I expected you to be out after the first punch."

"Stubborn jaw, as you said," I say, rubbing it with my hand. "I don't have a car here. Can you give me a ride to the station?"

"Yeah. We have to use Alicia's car though." He looks up at the door upstairs. "I don't think Oli wants to see me now to give me the keys back."

I pull the keys I still have in my pocket and throw them at him. "I've got them."

He catches them in the air and narrows his eyes at me. "Did you drive my truck?"

I can't help but enjoy his anger this time. "I did. Nice wheels."

His nostrils flare, and his jaw starts ticking. My own jaw may not survive, so I remove myself from the situation and walk outside, congratulating myself on annoying the asshole for what he said to Olivia. I'll make sure to annoy him even more when the danger subsides.

In the car, Mark asks, "Do you wanna tell me what the fuck happened?"

"Later. When Benson is there. I'm telling this story only one time."

After a long and painful side-eye, he shifts into gear and takes off toward the station. When we arrive, I close the door and walk toward the entrance only to be yelled to my back, "Don't smack my door!"

I show him my middle finger without turning back, and I swear I hear his growl. Good. Another annoying moment he deserves for the way he spoke to Oli.

"As I live and breathe! Jakey is here!" Jennica, Benson's deputy, greets me when I walk inside. She's always been loyal and law-abiding—something Benson loves and respects in people. While I've always teetered on the edge with the law. But to me, she's always been nice. Even when I was a total dick. I think she's always known how to put me in my place, so maybe she saw right through me.

"Hey, Jennica," I say, coming to give her a hug because she spreads her arms wide without giving me a choice.

"We've missed you," she announces quietly, giving me a tight squeeze.

"You have not," I laugh back.

"What are you doing here?" Sheriff Benson asks,

coming out of his room and leaning his side on the doorframe.

"We need to talk."

"Do we?" He raises a brow. "Too late for that, don't you think?"

When Mark follows me inside—who the hell knows what he was doing outside all this time, probably cooling off —Benson's brows draw together.

I notice two sets of curious eyes poking out from the break room. One belongs to a girl I don't know, and the other to Brad Dudley, the mayor's son and one of the addicts I found in a shitty place when I was undercover. He got mixed up with the wrong crowd and started hanging out in the areas where the drugs were cooked and distributed. I dragged him out of there and brought him home. And that's how our not so wonderful mayor came to owe me a favor, and I'm an asshole enough to collect it. Considering it was to save my sister's boyfriend from jail, I'd say it was worth it.

When Brad sees me, his eyes go wide, and he quickly retreats back into the lunchroom. I don't blame him. If I were him, I wouldn't be flashing this part of my life around either.

"Let's hear him out," Mark announces, walking past the sheriff into his office.

"And what exactly are you doing here?" Benson asks him, looking surprised.

"Don't even ask." Mark waves him off and plants his ass on the leather couch by the window.

"Boss?" Jennica asks, without actually asking a question. I've always envied how perfectly they fit as work partners.

"Hold the front," he replies and nods to me, inviting me inside. Once I'm in, he shuts the door and goes to his desk. "Talk."

I take the seat across from him and turn my chair so I can see them both at the same time. My phone chimes in with a message.

I'm here. She's fine.

Knowing I can rely on Justin in a situation like that, I push my phone back into my pocket and start.

"I work for the DEA as an undercover agent."

Kenneth and Mark look at each other, and a second later erupt in guffaws. I can't say I'm not surprised, but also can't say I'm not offended a little bit.

When they don't stop laughing for who the hell knows how long, I ask, "Are you done? So we can get to the issue?"

Benson smacks the desk, still laughing, and wipes tears from his eyes. "An undercover agent," he repeats, and starts laughing again.

Mark's laughing too but he's slowly stopping. In fact, his face's turning solemn with every passing second. A minute later, he's not even smiling anymore. Instead, his face is trained on me.

"Did you get my sister into this shit?"

Now, Benson stops laughing too. "What?"

"This asshole," Mark points at me, "came back to town with my sister. After he was apparently detoxing."

"What?" Kenneth's head whips to me. I'm sure he cracked a spine there.

"Are you both done dicking around so we can have a talk?"

"How about you do—"

Kenneth doesn't let Mark finish because he shuts him with a loud "Mark" and then turns to me. "Go on."

I look at both of them, and when I know I have their attention, I start.

"Seven years ago, when Freya's ex came to town, he didn't come alone. The DEA followed him. He was selling drugs, laundering money, and doing a lot of other shit you don't even wanna know about. But he came here for many reasons, her only being one of them."

"What could he want from a small town?"

"Small towns are not noticeable and don't have a big force. So small towns are often used to hide big things," I explain, something I've come to learn. "He came here to find Freya, but the DEA found out he was communicating with his people about moving his big operation here."

"How big are we talking about?" Kenneth asks.

"Cooking. And cooking a lot of it."

He leans back on the chair, scratching his beard.

"Cooking? What the hell are you talking about?" Mark asks.

"Drugs," Benson explains.

"Drugs? Here, in Little Hope?" Mark chuckles. "I know guys in the trailer park smoked weed, but that's about it."

"Before, yes." I nod. "But times are changing. And that place would be the first to get hit."

"Desperate people," he whispers.

"Yeah," I confirm solemnly. "And Kayla's mother was working with Freya's ex. That's how he knew how to find her. She, apparently, still has her people here."

Sheriff whistles, leans to grab something out of the cabinet of his desk, and retrieves a whiskey bottle. Then he walks to another cabinet and pulls out three glasses.

"I didn't know it back then, but the DEA gave me a giant folder with her name across them all."

"Stop," Benson raises his finger in the air. "Not yet."

He walks to the table, pours three glasses, and downs one in one go. Then he pushes one toward Mark who comes to take it and one toward me. I shake my head, refusing it. I just went through a damn detox. Alcohol is the last thing I need. Despite how much I want it. Then Benson grabs my glass and downs it too.

"Go ahead," he says, sitting back in his chair.

"At first, I thought Kayla was part of it too."

"That started way before Freya came to town," Mark notices, making me wince with guilt.

"Yeah, I had my reasons. I might have gone too far."

"Might have?" Kenneth's brow goes up.

"I went too far," I state firmly. "But I truly believed she was a part of it."

"A part of what?" Mark asks, leaning forward. "I work in the fire department. You'd think I'd know if drugs were circulating in town."

"You wouldn't if they were just being cooked in the woods and distributed someplace else. Plus, the quantities are not large yet. They were testing."

"Where did they move it to?" Sheriff asks.

"Canada," I reply, eyeing Mark, who's turning redder by the second.

"And you dragged my sister there?" His voice can barely contain all the hatred he's feeling toward me. And the worst part? I can't even blame him.

"Wait, hold on." Benson raises his hand in the air, stopping my staring contest with Mark. "What does your sister have to do with anything?"

I shift my attention to the sheriff, not willing to see the

judgment from Mark. "She saw me in Montreal doing a deal. Obviously, she didn't know I was undercover, so she called my name."

"And they didn't know it?"

"Of course not," I say, nearly rolling my eyes. It's such an obvious thing. "The DEA recruited me here and sent me to a bunch of places to track the drugs. I had to become one of them so they could trust me. And I've gone too far," I admit, swallowing a giant lump in my throat. "But they trusted me. And we were about to take them down."

"How?" Mark sounds curious now. Like he's watching some sort of TV show and not lives being ruined in real time. Including mine.

"I was about to get promoted and get closer to the top to find out where and how they move it in big quantities. I was making my last deal before the introduction when Olivia saw me on a street."

"Fuckin' coincidence," Kenneth mumbles, pouring himself another glass.

"Hold on." Mark moves on his chair. "Can anyone explain to me how that shit works? Because I'm not getting it. How no one knew who he was?" He points at me. "And where is all of it happening?"

"Kayla's mother is the only one so far from the town who's connected to it. She's never seen me. At least, not since I was like nine. Freya's ex didn't have a chance to find out who I was for obvious reasons. But he was here for a few days. Long enough to find out that the woods behind Alex's cabin would be a perfect secluded location for their operations. Cooking, storing. No people on a random hike. No electricity or cameras. No civilization. So the DEA caught their communication about setting everything up here. Once Freya's ex was dead, Kayla's mother—"

"Can we call her anything else?" Mark asks.

"Let's call her S?" Bensons suggests, agreeing with Mark too fast. Both are so sensitive, I want to nearly roll my eyes.

"That's better. Not much, but better." Mark nods and gestures for the sheriff to pour him another glass. At this rate, they'll get shitfaced before I even finish the story.

"So when he died, Ka—" I quickly fix the misstep because both their faces change, "S decided to pause moving here and focused on their regular work."

"And how do you play into that?" Kenneth's face is clouded.

"They approached me after the ex incident."

"How did you know about him in the first place?" he asks, narrowing his eyes. "I've always wondered."

"I got a call from them with a 'suggestion' to go to the cabin. No mystery there."

"I see." He starts scratching his beard very intensely. "Why did you agree?"

I look out the window before replying. "Who the fuck knows. I was looking for a purpose in life. I was young. And it seemed like something worth fighting for."

"Does it still look the same?" His voice is quiet.

I turn to look at him and answer truthfully. "Less and less with every passing day."

"Where is Ka—" Mark quickly clears his throat, "S now?"

"In Canada. Presumedly, Montreal. I was hoping I would be taken, if not to her, at least one of her closest people. Once I recorded everything, that'd be game over. A fucking celebration for closing a giant operation we've been working on for years."

"Until Oli," Mark notices calmly.

"Until her," I confirm.

"And you said you were detoxing?"

"Yeah." I wince at the painful memory, pressed under the weight of shame over my head. "But they saw her calling my name, so I couldn't leave her. They'd be coming after her too to find out about me. I had some shit with me to get me here, but Oli didn't let me use. We stayed in a motel until I got clean. Not a good decision, but the one we made at the time." I wince at the memory of what might have happened if they'd found us there while I was incapacitated. "So here we are." I walk to the window and stare outside, not able to bear their heavy, judgmental stares.

"Is she in danger?" Mark asks worriedly.

"We presume that yes, she is," I confirm his fears. "So I'm staying with her."

"What?" he bellows like a wounded animal, jumping from the couch. "You are not staying in the same house with my sister!"

"Is that wise, Jake?" Benson asks quietly, completely ignoring Mark's outburst.

"That's all we can do until another agent arrives to back me up. I've sent word, and someone will be on the way just in case. In the meantime, I'm staying with her." And mentally I add that I'll be staying with them after as well.

"I can stay with her," Mark says, pushing his chest forward.

"You can. Who will stay with my sister then?"

He chews on his lips. "She'll come with me."

"No, no," Benson says, standing up. "You will be staying in your house," he orders to Mark and turns to me, "and you'll be at your parents'. I'll stay with Olivia until the agent arrives. And then we will keep one of us patrolling the outside."

I give him a death stare. "Patrolling the street won't do shit. They're not amateurs."

"Then we'll be inside the building."

I sigh. "Kenneth," I start, calling out to his common sense, "we both know when it can happen. Today, tomorrow, or the next year. You can't be spending all your time there."

"My sister needs protection!" Mark cries out, walking around with squeezed fists.

"Yes," I reply, turning to him. "And that's why I'll be with her. Since my cover's blown up, I basically don't have a job. So my main goal will be protecting Olivia. I'm trained. I know them."

"No fucking way," he says, shaking his head like a stubborn bull.

"Mark," Benson calls out in a calm voice, "Jake's onto something there. He's a good shot, I've seen it myself. He's trained. And he can protect Olivia and the baby."

"No." Mark crosses his giant arms over his chest. "No way."

"How about moving her someplace else?" Benson suggests.

"They'll find her anyway," I stop this train of thought. It's not happening. It doesn't matter where she is. Besides that, they don't even know who she is or where she's from. It will take them time to figure it out, and we don't know how long. She can't put life on hold forever."

"See?" Mark blows up. "You bring only trouble. If she hadn't seen you, she'd be fine."

"I know that," I grind out.

"Mark, that's unfair," Benson says, surprising me. "Undercover work is shit as it is. Don't add this guilt to it."

"But—"

"Just don't," he stops him with a shake of his head. Then he tells me, "Alright, let's discuss the plan. And I'll need to speak to your supervisor or commanding officer, whatever you call them."

I nod. "I'll text you his info."

"Good. Now," his face stretches with a wide smile, "you missed quite a few punches thrown at you over there." He points at my face.

"Exactly," Mark chimes in, sounding enthusiastic. "So I don't think he's a good fit for a protector role."

"Are you?" Sheriff asks me, barely containing his laughter.

I flip him off and start talking about the plan.

Chapter Thirty-One

A

Jake

My brother is shacking up with her. I'm sure of it now. He has disgustingly dreamy eyes every time her name is mentioned. Fucking Kayla Adams. The spawn of the woman who's turning my life into a living hell.

Fuck. I am the one turning it into hell. When they offered that shit, I could have said no. But I haven't.

I've been on my 'trips' four times now, and only this time they turned suspicious. If you're one of us, they said, surely you wouldn't mind tasting it yourself. They said it would make them trust me more. I could have said no. I could have come up with a lie. But I haven't. I agreed too easily, and they took me right in. I got some new information that night because I was 'one of them' now. I've come places I'd spent years trying to get into. The next day, the same thing happened, and it was easier to say 'yes.' I thought I did it once, and it wouldn't be a problem the second time. Then, I'd just come up with a lie.

But there were more times. And the shit got heavier. While I'd go deeper. I'd learn more. I'd see more. I'd gotten more information by then than anyone on my team had.

I've also received confirmation that Kayla's mother is one hundred percent involved. The only question I have now is if Kayla herself is involved. And I sure as fuck don't want her around my brother if she is. They say a person is innocent until proven otherwise. For me, it's the opposite. After my sister's incident, everyone is fucking guilty until they prove to me that they're not.

I've gotten too rough with Kayla perhaps. While I was arresting her for some made up shit. But I need her here. I need her out of sight until the deal is done. If it still goes through, she's not involved. That will be my proof either way it goes.

I scratch my chin for the tenth time in the past five minutes. My skin is itchy. I'm edgy. I thought the active withdrawal was the worst of it, but looks like this shit will last for a long time. The craving is no joke. Everything is annoying. Everything puts me on edge. Everyone's voice is like gravel deep inside my head, scratching and itching on my skull.

Kayla's sitting in the cell, alone. Her knees up to her chest. She looks fucking miserable, and a ping of remorse knocks on my stomach. Just another hour, and I'll let her go. The longer she's here, the more I know she's innocent.

Another ping. Guilt this time.

I scratch my chin again, thinking about never doing this

shit again. Doing drugs and arresting Kayla while behaving like a damn Neanderthal.

"Jake!" Justin bellows as he barges in the station.

"What?" I bark, walking toward him with a cup of steaming coffee in my hands.

"What is she doing here?" He jerks at the cell where Kayla's still sitting in the same position.

I can't tell him the truth, so for the next five minutes I fuck around and piss him off to the point where his face turns red. I know I've pushed too far. I know I am in the wrong. Especially when the time of the deal has passed, and Kayla Adams is officially not involved. But Justin's reaction makes me mad. He was the one who put this hatred inside me. He told me about how Kayla snitched on him after the fight eight years ago resulting in him being stopped by a cop so he couldn't get to our sister in time to save her. He told me it was Kayla's fault. I could choose to hate Justin too for not making it there, but I couldn't. He was my brother, he still is. He's an asshole, but it seems to be the genetic trait I inherited as well.

"You're gonna let Kenneth know about that," he hisses through gritted teeth. I can see his desire to strangle me right now, and I won't stop him if he tries.

"Or what?" I ask with a raised brow, knowing I'm just digging this hole even deeper than it already is.

"Or I will," he promises with a solemn look on his face, thinking it should scare me.

It doesn't. I know my days on the police force are done. I've known it since the moment I accepted the pill. The only reason I'm here is habit. And maybe something like a desire for normalcy. This job has been my happy place for a few years, and I thought I was good at it. Until the DEA showed up to send me into a spiral.

Or maybe they didn't do it, and I was spiraling on my own already, and they just gave me a little push to open the real Pandora's box I'd been carrying by then.

As Kayla leaves the station with Justin following her shortly after, I get the feeling this is the day I'm truly losing my brother. I've had my suspicion that Kayla wasn't part of it all, but my hatred toward her was too strong to see the logic.

I look around the station where I suddenly feel lonely. Or is it the town? It doesn't feel like home anymore, and this job feels like something I don't deserve anymore. Guilt has been weighing on me for a few months now. Maybe since the moment I decided to emerge into the drug world deeper by accepting their offering.

Guilt is a powerful thing. Sabotaging one's life just to feed it seems like the only way to go. And the life in this case is mine.

Chapter Thirty-Two

P*resent day*

Olivia

Justin's staring at me from across my kitchen island. His arms are crossed over his chest as he's drilling a hole in my face.

"What?" I ask when I can't take it anymore.

"Let me get it straight. You," he points at me, "literally found Jake working undercover, and now he's made, and the bad guys are after you?"

I shrug. "Pretty much."

"And you are telling me my brother is working for the DEA?" He sounds like the definition of a doubter. He even snorts a little at the end of his question.

"If that's what they're called, then yes."

"Shit," he says, planting his ass on a stool. "Who would have thought?"

"Yep." I pop the *p*.

He narrows his eyes at me suspiciously. "And what were you doing in the motel for days?"

I squint back at him. "Ask him."

The footsteps downstairs make Justin jump from his stool. He takes the gun I didn't even know he had out of his belt and moves toward the door.

"It's me!" Jake's loud voice makes Justin relax, and he hides his weapon. When Jake opens the door, he tells Justin, "Thank you. I owe you."

"You don't. Not for that," Justin replies, looking lost. I can understand why—his whole world just crumbled, and the brother he painted as a villain must have some redeeming qualities after all.

When Jake turns to me, I cry out. "What happened to your face?" I ask, rushing to check him.

The right side of his face is a mess. It's red, and blue, and purple, and getting more colorful by the second. His eye is half shut. His nose is swollen. I bring my hand to check if it's broken. It's way too swollen not to be.

"Stop fussing over him," Mark says grouchily, passing us by and heading toward the sink.

I send him a warning to stay quiet and rush to the freezer to grab a few ice packs. Throwing one to Mark with the words "For your hand" and making him smirk, I return to Jake and carefully press ice to his cheek. But the damage is too much so I end up not knowing where it's the worst.

"Oh, stop, Oli." Mark sounds like a big baby, but his words work because Jake pulls away.

"I'm fine." His quiet words pierce me right through the heart.

"Be quiet," I order firmly, leading him to the stool where Justin was just sitting.

"Ouch, man. That looks painful." Justin doesn't sound happy or sarcastic to everyone's surprise. Quite the opposite. I'd say he's empathetic.

"It is," Jake admits with a chuckle. "You got lucky you avoided his hammers." He nods at Mark, making him smirk even more.

A chorus of weak but friendly laughs makes me think that men are indeed a different species who resolve all their issues with fists. If women had a fight like that, there'd be a war till the end of times. Mentally shaking my head, I take Jake's hand and press it to the ice, showing him to hold the pack, and go to the medicine cabinet where I have some arnica gel.

Everyone is quiet. The only sounds are my footsteps and the soft crackling of the ice packs in their hands.

When I get back to Jake, he pulls the ice away from his face, giving me access to the injury. I pour the gel into my hand and press it to his cheek. His eye twitches for a moment, betraying the pain, and I take some pressure away. I'm too angry to be gentle, but his face has suffered enough.

"Are you satisfied, Mark?" I ask.

"We will revisit it," he mumbles, earning another glare from me.

Justin chuckles, leaning his elbows on the island. "I'd love to see that."

After a glare his way as well, he stops chuckling and starts talking. "When were you gonna tell us what you were doing?"

"I wasn't going to." Jake's tone turns cold. It's like they've never broken that thick ice.

"Why?" Justin asks, sounding puzzled. "It's better than *any* shit you were doing."

"It's not." Jake's voice is sad. He carefully pushes my hand away and steps back. "I will stay here for some time."

"Here?" I parrot, blinking at him in confusion.

"Yeah," Mark clears his throat. "The situation is not ideal." He speedwalks toward me. "But if you are uncomfortable with him being here, even a little bit, you tell me now, and he won't step foot into your house."

"What?" I look between him and Jake. "What the hell are you both talking about?"

"Someone needs to stay with you," Jake explains.

"I can stay with her," Mark says, glaring at him.

"Someone with training," Jake adds with clear sarcasm in his voice.

Mark's head whips to him. "I've got plenty of training in the trailer park."

"Oh," I sigh, finally understanding what's happening. "I see."

"Please tell me if you do because I'm sure as fuck lost," Justin says, raising his hand like a good pupil.

"Someone needs to protect me," I explain to the only unsuspecting person in the room.

Justin starts laughing. "And y'all chose Jake for that?" He smacks the counter in a fit of laughter. "What did you smoke there in the station?" he asks Mark, whose cheek muscle starts slowly twitching.

"Justin," I grit out.

"Don't," Jake warns me quietly.

After squinting my eyes at him with a silent warning to shut up, I whip my whole body toward Justin. "I appreciate your coming here to bodyguard me, and I thank you for that. But I think it's time for you to go."

"What?" Justin pauses, blinking slowly without any indication that he understood a word I just said.

I sigh. "You need to go, Justin. We're all tired. And soon, someone will say something they'll regret. So let's just all go to bed."

"Not together!" Mark exclaims, earning a stare from me. "What? I don't want you sleeping with Jake *together*." He says the last mockingly like an unfunny comedian.

"Jake will be sleeping on the couch because I don't have another bed." I turn to him. "I hope it's okay?"

He nods. "It's much better than some places I've slept."

"Yeah?" Justin chimes in. "Like Adison's bed?"

Awkward.

"Justin." Warning is clear in Mark's voice. I'm surprised he's on Jake's side. I think.

"What?" Justin's rapidly raising voice doesn't leave any doubts where this is all going. "Do you think this little piece of information is going to change all the shit he's done to everyone?" A few moments ago, he was slowly warming up to Jake. But looks like he just reminded himself why he didn't like him in the first place.

I quickly glance at Jake only to find his jaw clamped shut.

"This is why I wasn't going to tell anyone anything." He's so tight-lipped, I'm not even sure it was him speaking.

"Yeah? Like a coward?" Justin walks past him, hitting his shoulder on Jake's. "I bet you were going to disappear like you usually do. And when our family needs you, when I need you, you just leave without a trace."

"And where were you when I needed you?" Jake's quiet question, asked in an exceptionally calm voice, makes Justin pause. "Where were you when I needed my brother?"

Justin turns around. "You were bullying the woman I loved."

"So were you." Jake slowly moves toward Justin. "You planted that hate into me. You told me she was the reason Alicia was raped."

The word sounds like a slap in the silence. We all turn toward Mark who's watching the scene unfold with a pale face.

Jake's chest rises and falls in a fast rhythm. After a few breaths in, he tells Mark, "I'm sorry."

Mark nods in acknowledgment but doesn't add anything.

"I told you to back off of Kayla, and you didn't," Justin keeps going. "Why the fuck couldn't you just leave her alone?"

Jake's mouth closes shut so loud, he's like a pit bull. Only he doesn't have anything stuck between his teeth.

"Why, Jake?" Justin's voice sounds more tired now. Resigned. "Just tell me why. It can't go on like that. This new," he waves his hand around Jake, "*you* gives me nothing. You are still the asshole who bullied my fiancé. You nearly cost us our happiness. Why? Why did you hate me so much? What the fuck did I do to you?"

Jake's silence only makes Justin burn hotter.

"I was your brother." His voice breaks at the end.

"You stopped being my brother after Alicia," Jake finally cracks.

"What?" Justin rears back.

"Oh, c'mon." Jake quickly pulls on his hair as the only sign of stress he's shown since he arrived. "You were so focused on self-loathing you didn't see shit under your nose. I was a kid. And you were taking your misery out on anyone."

"But what happened to Alicia—"

"Happened to all of us," Jake finishes. "You should have all come together to help her, but instead you separated yourself from everyone. That's why I took the job with the DEA. The assholes who did this to our sister," at these words, I hear Mark's loud air intake, "were stopped on that night on a fucking road by cops for reckless driving. The bloodwork showed they had a bouquet of drugs in their system. It was all swept under the rug because the judge was their relative or some shit. But the drugs were there. Twenty minutes away from Little Hope. Our home, Justin. And it was moving our way."

Justin listens to all of it with an unwavering stare.

"It doesn't explain why you were such a shit to Kayla."

I can see in the way Jake's jaw is moving that he's contemplating if he should say something or not. I'm almost ready to hear it because I'm curious to know the reason too. But Jake chooses not to say anything. His shoulders deflate while Justin gets pumped.

"For fuck's sake, Jake. You're a coward," Justin hisses, and turns away to leave.

"Kayla's mother is a drug dealer, and he didn't know if Kayla was involved too," Mark says in one big breath, causing Jake to whip his head toward him with a warning, which Mark chooses to ignore completely because he keeps going. "Yeah, so even right now, he's trying to protect—" he turns to Jake. "Who are you trying to protect?"

Jake laughs, shaking his head. I wonder which part he finds funnier—Mark's desire to step up for him or the blindness of the newborn kitten he's operating with.

"Anyway. There is your truth." Mark spreads his arms wide and walks to the fridge to grab himself a can of sparkling water.

To say Justin's eyes widen would be an understatement. They are practically bulging out of his eye sockets. "Is that true?"

"Yeah. But Kayla got cleared soon after," Jake clears his throat, "the jail incident."

Justin whistles, raking his hand through his hair. Funny how similar they act yet they don't notice it. "You could have fuckin' asked me, and I'd tell you she was innocent."

"And your head was so clear when you were thinking with your dick?" Jake's brow quirks, making Justin avert his gaze for a moment. "That's the reason I kept on hating—I didn't want to get into her pants and could think with my head between my shoulders."

Justin chews on his lips. "Where is her mother now?"

"In Canada. She's moving some big shit."

Justin keeps chewing on his lower lip, and at this point, I'm scared he's actually going to take a chunk out of it. When he's done destroying his lips, he looks between Mark and Jake while totally ignoring me. "We don't say a word to Kayla."

"No shit," Jake says. "This is precisely why I kept this information to myself." His side-eyes could kill a lesser man, but Mark is still standing with a smug look on his face.

Suddenly, Justin turns around and starts walking toward the exit. "I have to go."

We all watch him leave, but everyone with a different feeling. I can't say for Mark, but Jake has a look of longing on his face, and I get a suspicion that Jake misses his brother more than he lets on.

"I need to pick up Brodie," I say after a long silence.

"He's probably asleep," Mark says, glancing at his wristwatch. "You can get him tomorrow."

"So you can accuse me of being a bad mother one more

time? No, thank you." I grab my jacket and go outside. "Coming?" I ask them both.

Jake rushes to the door first, Mark follows slowly behind. He can drag his feet all he wants—I know how to find his house without his directions.

"Oli." His sad voice is meant to stop me in my tracks, but it doesn't. "Oli, wait," he repeats louder.

"What?" I finally stop on the bottom step.

"I'm sorry, Oli," he sighs out. "It was a dick move."

I cross my arms over my chest. "It was."

"You are a good mother, Oli. And I'm proud of you." His voice turns softer with every word he says. "I was mad at Jake and you. But mostly at Jake for seducing my little sister."

I roll my eyes. "He didn't seduce me."

"I know that now." He walks past me so he's not towering over me so much. "And I can't believe I'm saying it, but I think he can protect you while I'm away. But the moment you feel frightened, or uncomfortable, or anything—"

"I'll call you," I finish for him.

"Yes, you call me." He smiles. "I'll always come."

"I know." I smile back, happy that we moved that elephant away from the room. I've never had a big fight with Mark, and I wouldn't want to start now.

"Let's go get Brodie. Alicia will be heartbroken." He chuckles.

"You guys can always come and visit."

"Oh, trust me, she's planning to. But also, Oli, don't forget," he pauses and turns to me, "I'll have another round with Jake."

I roll my eyes and flip him the bird. His shaking shoulders are a clear indication what he thinks of that.

Chapter Thirty-Three

J^{ake}

When we get to Mark's house, Alicia doesn't ask any questions—she knows better than anyone that sometimes you just can't answer. I'm sure Mark will bring her up to speed tonight when we leave. So she just gives me a tight hug while Olivia gets Brodie together.

"I think you will get better now," she whispers, slowly releasing me from her hug. Her eyes dart at Olivia who's emerging from the room with the kid in her arms. And I have to agree that my sister might be onto something here.

"Do you want me to carry him?" I ask, surprising Alicia. And myself, if I'm honest.

"No," she replies quietly, hugging him tighter. "I'm good."

"Here." Alicia rushes to the kitchen and brings a big backpack which she passes to me. "Bring me my baby soon," she coos, coming to carefully pat Brodie's head. That makes Olivia smile. I'm not sure about dynamics with a kid in a family setting, but she's smiling, so it must be good.

We say goodbyes while Mark is being a stoic stone statue with his arms crossed over his chest and brows pinched neatly together.

When we are outside, Olivia goes to buckle up the kid's seat, and I'm about to walk to the driver's side when I hear my name being called quietly. Mark's standing on his porch, the door closed behind him.

"Can you come here for a second?" he asks, coming down the steps.

I walk to him, slightly surprised with his very polite request. When I'm in front of him, I see how troubled he is. How blown his pupils are. How sunken his cheeks.

"Yeah?"

"Did you—" He sighs and looks at the sky before getting himself back together and trying again. "Was it you?"

My questioning look might be a good indication that I don't get what he means because he rephrases it. "Did I find them because of you?"

I watch him with a blank stare. "I don't know what you mean."

"Jake." He sighs again. "I need to know."

"You don't," I say, turning away to go back to the car. He is the hero who slayed my sister's monsters. He saved her. The end.

There's a pinching in the middle of my chest, and I don't know where it's coming from. But every time I glance in the rearview mirror of Olivia's car where she's sitting in the back seat, holding the tiny hand of her sleeping kid, I get another ping out of pattern.

At her house, she gets still-sleeping Brodie from the seat while I grab the bag and run to unlock the door.

Inside, she goes to the bedroom to put him to bed while I'm left standing awkwardly in the middle of the living room. I don't have any clothes or any shit really. I might need to run to the store tomorrow to grab some things or just go to my parents' house.

Sometime later, Olivia comes out, looking tired. She goes to the kitchen, grabs a tube of something, and walks to me. "Put this gel on your face. It'll help the bruising go down quicker."

"I don't—"

"Just take the damn thing, Jake." She sounds so defeated that I don't fight anymore. Instead, I squeeze the gel into my hand and start rubbing it all over my face. I glanced at it in the mirror in the car, and it made me wince. I bet Mark had a lot of fun.

"Are you hungry?"

"No, thank you."

"Okay," she sighs and goes back to the bedroom.

I guess this is my cue, and I plant my ass on the couch where I'll be camping for the next who knows how long, lean on the back, and close my eyes.

Her quiet footsteps wake me a moment later. She's padding toward me with a comforter and pillows which almost completely cover her face. I jump to help her. She passes half of it to me, and we start putting sheets on the couch.

"You didn't have to. I'd be fine just on the couch."

"Don't be like that, Jake. I thought you know me by now."

I stop moving and look at her. "I think I do."

Her cheeks turn rosy, and her movements quicken. "I

have to wake up early tomorrow—the bakery has been closed for a long time, and I need to catch up. I'll try to be quiet, but I might accidentally wake you up."

"Don't even worry about it, do what you need. In fact, try to pretend I'm not even here."

She pauses and gives me an odd look I can't pinpoint. "That'd be hard to do, Jake."

I don't know what she means but refrain from asking. She looks too exhausted for any kind of talk.

Olivia woke up at three. I'm not even sure she slept at all. She crept past me toward the back stairs and left the door open. I'm sure she did it so she can hear the kid.

I could use some sleep, and so could she. But she can't afford this luxury. So I go to the bathroom and quickly get ready for the day. I found a spare toothbrush so that's a bonus. I hope she won't mind.

Soon, I'm walking into the kitchen downstairs where Olivia's already running around, looking panicked.

I warn her from afar about my presence. "Hey."

"Hi!" she squeaks, pushing her hair back into some sort of a hat on her head. "Did I wake you?"

"No," I lie. "I don't sleep well." Not a lie. I'm not sure how I fell asleep in the first place.

"Oh. Okay." And then she goes back to running.

"Can I help you?" I look around, not sure how I can do that. But if she points me in the right direction, I might be of use.

She stops mid run and looks at me with wide eyes. "Do you really want to help?" There's so much hope in her voice that I know there's no way I'll say no.

"Of course."

"Okay." She grabs my arm and tows me to the sink. "Wash your hands—thoroughly," she adds with a stern look. "And then you'll be kneading the dough."

"W-what?"

"The dough. Hands first," she bosses, pointing her index finger at the sink.

I quickly wash my hands. "What now?"

"Put this on." She passes me an apron and a similar hat she's wearing. I eye the things in her hands like they're going to bite me. "Jake!" she rushes me. "If you want to help, put this on."

Sighing, I do as she says, and soon I'm met with trembling lips and averting eyes. The little minx is trying to hide her laughter!

"Alright, come over here."

I follow her to the steel counter where she was apparently kneading the dough before I interrupted her.

"You gotta make it smooth," she says.

"How?" I look between her and the dough like the latter is going to literally attack me.

"Just like you'd be giving it a massage."

"The dough?" I blink at her, not sure if I heard her correctly.

"Yes, Jake! Stop repeating everything I say. We got no time for that. Now," she does something unexpected—smacks me on my butt, making me jump, "go and make this dough happy."

I laugh and start the process—the smack definitely worked. At some point, I begin getting the hang of it and, quite frankly, even start enjoying it. It's a mindless task that makes me look at myself from outside my body. No brain power required, no extra skill. Just working my hands into the dough. The smoother and fluffier it becomes, the more gratification I feel.

While I'm kneading the giant batch of dough, Olivia flies around like a hummingbird around a flower. When I come back from my trance, I find tons of different batches surround me, and the oven is puffing with something inside.

"I wish I had another one," she mumbles, shaking her hand after she pulls something out of it.

"Another what?"

"An oven," she sighs.

"You have one, no?"

"I do, and it's not enough. Some of these things need to be baked at different settings, so I have to wait. Which means I have to wake up extra early to get everything ready on time for opening. If I had more ovens, I'd be able to prep everything in the evening and just stick it inside in the morning. Plus, I'll be able to bake more." She sounds so wistful that I make a mental note to myself to get this damn oven for her, whatever it takes. "Let me see." She comes to check on the dough. "Wow, Jake. You made it better than I could."

"Yeah, right." I step aside, scratching the back of my head, fully understanding the compliment was meant just to cheer me up. "Can I do anything else?"

She gives me an odd look. "Do you really want to help more? I thought you were traumatized by the dough."

"No, I'm fine," I chuckle. "I really want to help." My desire to help is sincere, but my desire to stay around her is stronger. I'm a selfish bastard after all.

"Alright." She smiles, and for the next hour, she gives me small tasks here and there, and I run around the kitchen like a little bell boy, sweating into the hat she gave me from the heat of the kitchen. By the time the clock hits six, I can barely stand. And the bakery isn't even open yet.

Right on the dot, the camera screen on the table makes a noise.

"Brodie's waking up. I have to get him ready for daycare," Olivia says, washing her hands.

"When will you be opening?"

She glances at the clock on the wall. "A little later today. I usually open it, then Jonah comes in to replace me for fifteen minutes or so until I get back."

"Jonah?" I can't help but let annoyance slip into my voice. I don't know if Jonah plays both teams, and the idea of him sniffing around Olivia doesn't sound appealing. The thought of anyone rolling their dicks around her doesn't sound good at all.

"Yes, he's been a huge help to me." There's so much gratitude and respect in her voice, I want to vomit.

"I'm here now. You don't need him," I spurt out, not able to bite my tongue.

Olivia's smile looks funny. "I need him because he's my friend."

"Just friend?" I ask, swallowing.

Her smile turns even funnier. "Yes, just a friend. You know that he's gay, right?" she asks with squinted eyes.

"Yeah. I didn't mean it like that." Suddenly, I feel like a giant idiot.

"Sure," she laughs. "I'm gonna go upstairs."

Trying to erase the painfully embarrassing moment, I ask, "Do you want me to open the bakery?"

She pauses half-step with wide eyes. "Can you do it?"

"I mean, I can. We already put everything up there. I can read the prices and I'll figure out how the register works. I might scare your customers though," I add with a cheeky smile, trying to sound nonchalant even though I'm scared myself to face the people of this town.

"They'll have to get used to you if you are planning on staying here anyway. Might as well start now." She shrugs and runs upstairs where Brodie started waking up.

Through the monitor she left on the table, I see how she leans to take him from the crib and starts mumbling something sweet to him. He makes funny noises in return. And my throat clogs. It's getting so tight I can barely breathe.

For some unexplainable reason, I want to go there and join them. I want to hear the coos and the mumbling. I want to get the hugs. I want to belong to them.

I don't know where this newfound longing for a family of my own came from, but the more time I spend with Olivia watching her interact with her boy, the more I wish they were mine.

Chapter Thirty-Four

O livia

I drop Brodie off at daycare and rush back to the bakery. To my surprise, I find it indeed open. A few cars are parked along the street, but I don't pay attention to any of them because no one knows I'm back or if the bakery is open.

I go through the front bakery door and find it packed. Jonah's leaning his side on the wall with a giant smile on his face, watching grumpy Jake serve customers. A lot of customers.

Jonah ditched his ever-present jacket and rolled his sleeves like he usually does when he's helping me.

I run behind the counter, wash my hands, pull an apron on, and come to the register.

"Thanks," I mutter to Jake.

"No problem. Look at all these people who came to see

the new monkey in the circus," he whispers back without his usual annoyance, making me chuckle.

"You are the old monkey."

"Semantics." He smiles back as he walks to the éclairs. "What do you want to get this early morning, Mrs. Roberts?"

And his usual annoyance creeps back. He's trying to mask it with a smile, and Mrs. Roberts doesn't seem to notice. I can't blame the man—this lady can play on everyone's nerves, especially when she brings the gossip in. I don't want my place to become the second Donna's shop. I've always dreamed it to be a safe and judgment-free zone where everyone is welcome. Even Mrs. Roberts. Even after the supermarket incident.

"You are here, thank God," the girl from the yoga shop rushes through the door. "I'm opening early today, and I didn't have a good cup of coffee since you went on your mini vacation with your hot boyfriend."

"He's not—"

"Can you blame her?" Jonah chimes in with a raised brow.

After a long look at Jake, she starts laughing. "No, I can't really."

I laugh too even though I don't feel joyful. Somehow, I feel like a mouse in a glue trap. "What can I get you?"

"Your latte please. Any special flavor of the day. Large. I mean it, large large."

I giggle and go to the coffee maker, completely ignoring smiling Jonah who hasn't moved from the wall. His stare hasn't left my face, and his smile only seems to grow bigger.

While I'm finishing the coffee, Jake rings up Mrs. Roberts who's chastising him for his behavior and asks the girl if she wants any pastries. She points at two things, and he gets them ready for her, ignoring Mrs. Roberts's chattering. I walk up to them, passing the yoga girl her coffee and ring up her purchase.

"Have a good day, Mrs. Roberts!" I say with a smile, officially dismissing her. She snorts, turning around to leave. Looks like we've survived this encounter without spilled blood.

"Watch her heading to Mr. Cricket to invite him to the bleachers," a low but quiet voice tickles my ear. I glance at the smiling Jake and giggle like a schoolgirl. He quickly rushes to the next customer while I'm left at the register with a giant smile and a stupid beating heart.

A soft clearing of someone's throat brings my attention back from dreamland to reality where the girl is looking at me with a look of understanding on her face. "Thanks, Oli. Please don't leave anymore." She pauses and glances at Jake. "On second thought, leave and come back happy. See ya!" She cheers her coffee and rushes out the door.

Soon, we ring up the rest of the line and now we can take a breath. And I can get my inevitable grilling from Jonah. There is a young couple sitting by the window quietly chatting. I haven't seen them before, so they are probably someone new I haven't met yet.

Jonah pushes away from the wall and moves to lean his elbows on the counter in front of me.

"Well, well, well." He sounds gleeful. Just like the Jonah who loves to bring new gossip here, and to my shame, I always listen to it. "Look who the cat dragged in. Olivia and Jake. Working together. Where have you been, dear?" Behind his humorous tone, I hear genuine concern. He remembers our last conversation, so my little trip with Jake might seem off to him.

"It's a long story," I sigh, glancing at Jake. "I'm not even sure I'm allowed to say it."

"I'll find out anyway. You know me." Jonah brings up a valid point. He can figure out anything he puts his mind to.

"Jake?" I ask, making Jonah's brow draw together in worry.

"Don't tell me he wrapped you around his magic dick."

Jake was trying to take a sip of coffee when Jonah said that, and now, he's coughing as the hot liquid clearly went down the wrong pipe.

"I mean," Jonah eyes Jake's legs, "it's probably truly magnificent. But c'mon, girl," he turns to me, "we just talked about it. You have Brodie to think about."

"And how is that of your concern?" Jake asks, walking to stand by my side with arms crossed over his chest. His humorous demeanor is instantly replaced by a tough one.

"It is my concern," Jonah says, straightening to his full height, "because I was here when the whole town treated her like a pariah. She made it through, but now, she might crumble back down."

"Because of me?" Jake's voice turns dark.

"Yes, Jake. Because of you. What will she do when you just up and go as you usually do, huh? What will she have then?"

I eye Jonah, completely dazzled by his stance. He's on my side. But he doesn't know the whole truth. And I am the one feeling bad at the end.

"Jonah," I sigh tiredly, noticing the curious stares of the couple by the window.

He completely ignores me and keeps staring Jake down who seems unbothered.

"I still don't see how any of this is your business."

"Jake," I call out to his sanity which is long gone. If it

ever was present. "Jonah is my friend, and he will be here. So you have to deal with it." The glare I get from the man could burn someone to the ground. "Don't give me that look. He's my friend, and if you're planning to stay here, you have to learn how to coexist." I turn to Jonah. "Both of you."

"You want to tell me he's staying at your place?" He smacks his forehead with his open palm. "Olivia, you're so stupid."

"Don't say that," Jake grits out a very loud warning that makes the couple by the window ditch their éclairs and become totally attuned to the show.

I give them an apologetic smile, trying to remember their faces to offer a free cupcake the next time they visit. If they ever visit again after that. All this drama is not good for business.

"Alright, you both gotta stop." I grab the front of Jonah's shirt and pull him toward me over the counter. He's almost lying on top of it now. "I'm going to tell you something, but you have to keep your mouth shut. Deal?"

His eyes dart between me and Jake before he finally gives a slow nod. I whisper to him a short version of the story. The more I say, the more his eyes go round. At the end of the story, he pulls back from the counter with a puzzled look on his face.

"I can hire a bodyguard for you."

"Jake will be here."

"Oh, I mean on top of Jake." Then he eyes Jake and lets out a loud giggle. "That'd be something to see."

I feel my eyes widening, and I quickly look at Jake whose nostrils flare.

Jonah continues giggling. "I mean to stay here at all times."

I expect Jake to blow up and start yelling profanities

and push Jonah out of the bakery, but he surprises me. Again.

"Maybe it's not such a bad idea."

My head whips toward him. "What do you mean? I already have you." Is he trying to bail on me? Once I'd slept on the idea of Jake being a constant of my life, it didn't seem like such a bad idea after all.

"And I will be here. But if he knows someone good for hire, I'll take it. I don't want to take chances with your and your kid's life."

"No freakin' way." I put my foot on the ground before these two run me down. "I don't need some stranger following my every step. Jake is more than enough." When they both try to protest, I raise my hand, silencing them both. "This conversation is done. No strangers in my house. I trust Jake to take care of us."

Feeling a pressuring stare on the side of my face, I choose to ignore Jonah because, apparently, he has something to say, which I for sure don't want to hear. He does this all the time when he has a loud opinion.

"I need to think about it." Jonah quickly collects his jacket and rushes toward the door. "Do you need me during lunch today?"

"Only if you want to," I reply gently, not wanting him to feel like he's not needed anymore once I've got some help.

He nods. "I'll see if I have time." Then, looking at Jake, "Take care of her."

With that, he's out of the bakery onto the street.

"I'm sorry I told him," I say quietly to Jake, knowing I probably shouldn't be yelling left and right about him being an undercover agent.

"You did the right thing," he replies, still watching

where Jonah disappeared. "I didn't know you were such close friends."

"We are. Well," I add as I start filling the coffee machine with beans, "we've become ones. Again."

"Again?"

"We tried in school, but it didn't work out. So here we are. Our second chance." I shrug.

Jake nods with understanding and goes toward the back. "If you don't mind, I have a few calls to make."

"Sure," I reply with a smile, even though I suddenly feel lonely with the prospect of him leaving me here alone in my own bakery I love dearly. "Thank you for the help, Jake. Really."

He nods and disappears up the back stairs.

Chapter Thirty-Five

J**ake**

Did it kill me to agree to let another man protect Olivia? Sure as fuck it did. But I swallowed my pride and agreed to let another man help me protect her. Until she said she trusts me and wants only me. It ignited something inside me. To be honest, that thing was ignited a long time ago, but today, it was refreshed with gasoline. I didn't know how much I wanted her trust in me. I didn't know how much I *needed* it. In the place where no one else takes me seriously anymore, I need her support more than I could imagine.

Another thing that's been bothering me since we arrived is my cravings. They haven't left. They are here, always at the back of my head. Like an ever-present evil whispering into my ear. I want to say I'm strong enough not to give in, and I won't. Until Olivia is safe. Then, when I'm not needed anymore, all bets are off.

I fuckin' need rehab if I want a shot with her. The more time I spend with her, the more I want one. Even when I don't deserve it. I mean, who needs an addict in their life, especially when they have a kid to think about. I've got to find my backbone if I want to be worthy of them. And fast.

When I'm upstairs, I pull out my phone and dial my boss, Silent.

"What happened?" He doesn't sound happy. Obviously.

After I tell him the whole story because it's useless to hide anything from him, he's quiet—his namesake. Thinking. Planning.

"They'll come after her to find out about you. Stay with her, you're right. We'll be around, waiting too. It's Little Hope after all. Maybe she'll feel obligated to visit."

I sigh, knowing nothing will change his mind now. "You want to use Olivia as bait."

"That's our best chance in finishing the operation and saving your girlfriend. They'll come after her anyway. We just can make it shorter. I'll send the word out. Or she'll be living in fear for months or years to come. I'm doing you a favor here."

"You're an asshole."

"An asshole who told you not to get involved with anyone. And see how that turned out for you."

"I wasn't involved with anyone."

"Say that to the one who's coming after your sweet little bakery owner."

And just like that, I know he knows more than he lets on. As usual.

His dark chuckle grates on my nerves. *"We will be in touch. They'll come soon, be prepared."*

Every single conversation with Silent, the chief of this operation, leaves a bad taste in my mouth. He's always hiding something. He always knows more than anyone else. And today, it's the same. After every call, I want to go to the bar and get shitfaced.

So I grab my jacket and head outside, planning to do just that.

Only on the stairs, I remember I'm not alone anymore. At least, for now. I don't have the luxury of doing what I want, when I want it. I have other people to think about. People who rely on me. Fuck, I thought being an undercover agent was hard. Turns out, being a family man is harder.

Wait. I pause midstep. *Am I a family man now?* I'm not. But I can pretend to be. And these people are coming after my family. A fake one, but it doesn't matter.

I rush upstairs and start checking the apartment, seeing what I can do to make it more secure. In the process, I start cleaning as well. I'm walking around anyway, why not pick up a few things here and there?

Then I go to the kitchen and notice some dirty dishes and other stuff lying around. Olivia dropped her life to stay and help me get clean. The least I can do is clean her house in return.

It takes me about three hours, but the place is spotless. I even vacuumed. I'm sure I could wipe the floors too but to be honest, I'd do more damage than good if I tried. So I leave it as it is.

I don't expect the bad guys to come here guns blazing during the daylight when the bakery is open and people are everywhere, and besides that, they don't know where to look yet. My boss would send word out, and then, hopefully, in a few days we hear something. I can live in constant state of danger, I'm used to it, but I don't want this state for Olivia because eventually it will get to her too. She'll start getting nervous and aggravated, on edge around new people, jumpy when the door of her bakery would open. And this is not the life I want for her.

Soon, her light footsteps on the back stairs tell me she's coming here. And I get nervous like a schoolgirl. I jump to my feet and wipe my suddenly wet palms on my jeans. Which reminds me that I haven't had a decent shower or fresh clothes in days.

I expect her to show up any second, but she's still walking. Her slow footsteps sound tired.

When she shows up in the hallway, her face is sunken, and her arms are at her sides like useless noodles. When she sees me on the couch, she moves to me and falls on it with a loud groan.

"Are you okay?" I sound like a complete dumbass. Of course she's not. She can barely walk.

"Yeah." She groans again. "Everything hurts." She checks her wristwatch and pushes away from the couch. "I have to go pick up Brodie."

"Do you want me to go?'

"No, he probably won't come with you and start crying." Then she walks to the kitchen in a zombie-like state and takes a glass from a cabinet. She goes to the sink, and then she pauses. Her head starts slowly moving around, checking the apartment, and I feel my cheeks getting heated a bit to my utter embarrassment. Good thing I haven't shaved my beard, so that's a plus. "Wow!" She sounds a little more awake. "Did a fairy come while I was gone?"

"Probably," I chuckle, standing up to go to her. "Let's go, I'll drive you, so you won't fall asleep behind the wheel."

"Jake." She totally ignores it. "Thank you so much." Her voice breaks a little bit. "Thank you." She sniffles. "You just —" Another sniffle. "You just can't—" Then she sighs loudly and cuts the space between us in two giant steps. She throws her body at me, wrapping her arms around my torso. "Thank you, Jake." She can't stop sniffling now into my shirt.

"I didn't know you'd get so upset," I say sincerely, not knowing what I'm supposed to do. I mean, I grew up with a sister, but she's never been so emotional, so I don't know how to behave properly in this situation.

"I'm not upset," she mumbles. "I'm happy."

My heart drops to the pit of my stomach. I can't breathe. I can't move.

"I'm really happy." She nails the coffin shut.

I look at the ceiling, hoping to see the sky, wrap my arms around her, and hold her tightly. I don't think I could release her if she even asked.

"Why are you crying if you're happy?" I ask, her hair tingling my nose, but I will not move my head for all the gold in the world. She smells so damn good, like cinnamon and chocolate wrapped in a vanilla package. It's mouth-watering.

"Because," her words sound even more muffled because she digs her face deeper into my chest, "no one has done that for me for a long time. Besides Mark, I mean." A loud sniffle. "I didn't think anyone else would be interested enough to do something for me."

I pull away to look at her face. "What do you mean?"

She wipes her nose with her sleeve, leaving it red and absolutely cute. "It's always been Mark and me. And now, he has his own family." Her eyes suddenly go wide. "I mean, don't get me wrong, I love that he found Alicia and they're happy together. But there's no place there for me anymore."

"I don't understand." I feel my brows meeting together

in confusion. "You are family no matter what. Whether he's married or not, it doesn't change the fact that your brother loves you." I can't believe I'm fuckin' saying that.

"I know." She deflates. "But I can't keep asking him for help when he has his own family to take care of. You know, like this." She waves her hand at the kitchen. "I wouldn't ask him to come and do all this stuff. But someone who would be *my* family, would see it." She looks around again. "I want a family of my own."

My stomach tightens, and I don't know what to say. The truth is I kind of like playing house too, even though we've just started. What am I going to do when the bad guys are caught? What will be my purpose in life?

"Speaking about family." I smile. "Let's go get Brodie."

"Shoot!" She jumps on the spot like a cartoon character and rushes to the door to grab her jacket.

I follow her, chuckling and reminding myself that I should really stop at my parents' house to grab some clothes for myself.

Chapter Thirty-Six

J ake

Olivia told me to be 'useful' and passed Brodie to me, and now I'm trying to figure out what to do with a little dude who can't even walk on his own.

He's on my lap, smiling and trying to pull on my beard, while I'm sitting on the couch with a straight back, scared to move and drop him. Moments later, someone knocks on the door downstairs.

I'm instantly alert.

Gripping the boy to my left side, I quickly move to the window and carefully pull the curtain to the side. When I find Jonah waiting by the door, I relax, shift Brodie in my arms, and go to open the door.

When he sees me, his eyes go wide. "I see you've made yourself comfortable," he says, trying to take the kid from me. But I move to the side.

"Olivia is in the shower. Go."

He rolls his eyes and rushes upstairs, jumping over two steps. My turn to roll my eyes and follow him.

When I get to the apartment, Jonah is rampaging through the fridge like he's in the comfort of his own house. "I can eat a damn cow, so hungry, and the baker's got nothing."

"She's tired," I snap at him. "Go get some pizza."

He stops destroying the pretty empty fridge and looks at me. "Good idea. Want some too?"

I'm starving, so I nod, thinking this is not the time for pride. We wanted to stop by the store and get something, but it was late, and Oli said Brodie needed to get dinner and go to bed soon. So we just quickly grabbed my clothes—she didn't go inside—and came right here. She's hungry too, and I'm mad at myself for not thinking to order pizza myself.

"Cool. I'll get something."

I nod again and make a mental note to go tomorrow to the store to stock up the fridge, so Olivia doesn't have to think about that.

He clicks something on his phone and puts it face down on the counter while I'm helping the little man walk around the island. He seems to be liking getting exercise, and I'm better at doing something than standing and waiting.

"So." Jonah clears his throat and stares at me. "What are your intentions?"

"Intentions?" I look back at him with way less attitude.

"Yeah." He crosses his arms over his chest, puffing it up. "Regarding *my* Oli." His brow quirks up, and my eye twitches. He did it intentionally, and he managed to hit the mark.

"My intention is to keep her safe." That's not my *only* intention though.

"Really?" He squints his eyes. "I swear I thought you wanted to get in her pants."

I want to punch him in the face, but he's also right. So it feels kind of douchey, even for me.

"She is a beautiful woman," he keeps going, pushing on the same sore spot he's discovered.

"What do you want, Jonah?" I ask, resigned. He's not going to leave until he takes a chunk of life out of me. Might as well do it now.

The air around him instantly shifts. He drops the humorous persona and turns into another Mark. "Oli had a crush on you. We all know that. You know that. When you fuck it all up and leave, it will kill her. And she can't afford it. She has a child. She's more fragile than she looks."

"I'm not going to leave." I feel anger boiling in my chest, but I'm trying to keep under the hood and prove to him that I'm not as violent as everyone thinks I am. At least, not here, not where Olivia is concerned.

His face saddens. "You probably truly think that, but you will. One way or another, you'll fuck it up. You always do. I sure as fuck want to have some hope in you, but I don't." He presses his open palm to his chest. "Besides that, how are you planning on being around while drugs still have a hold on you?" He raises a brow. It's not mockingly per se, but the truthfulness of his question makes it sound a bit sarcastic.

My teeth grind. "I'm not thinking about that now."

"I know you're not." He sighs, dropping his arms by his sides. "Look, Jake. I'm going to be honest with you. You are hot as sin, with all of that," he waves his finger in the direction of my face, "bad-boy thing going on. And you probably will be good for her to roll around in the hay." He winces. "It could be good for the both of you, actually. You sure could use some pressure release with all that stiffness. But that's it. Catch your bad guy and be on your merry way. And try to do it faster so she doesn't fall in love with you." His face turns softer. "She has a big heart, and it's very open to opportunities. She's like a kid in an amusement park, all starry eyed, despite living a tough life. We don't know what she's been through. You and me, we've had it easy. We've had family and money and love and support. She had only Mark. I don't think you can understand how truly fragile she is."

I swallow, not able to take a full breath in.

"My point is, don't break her heart, Jake. Or I'll break your legs." His gaze drops to my lower half for a moment before returning to my face. "I'm planning on becoming a godfather to this boy and forever stay in their lives. And I'll be watching, Jake. My reach is way farther than you think."

Any other man threatening my life would end up with fewer teeth after a few more words, but he means well. He's become another member of Oli's family, and I have to take him seriously. Especially after seeing how fiercely he's trying to protect her. She has way more people in her corner than she thinks she does.

"I'm staying, Jonah," I state firmly.

He's watching me with narrowed eyes for a few seconds before letting his face stretch into a wide smile. "You've come far, Jake. Others might think you've degraded, but you've grown. I can see it." He walks up to me and gives me an unexpected smack on my back. "You'll be alright."

I didn't know how much I needed to hear someone else having faith in me other than Oli. That's two people in the whole world now. Maybe Jonah is okay after all.

When I relax a little and look at Jonah, I notice him moving around the kitchen and chirping about a company he can hire for Olivia. All his animosity is gone out the window after his last words. How is that possible? He was like a guard dog before.

I groan. Loud. And his head whips toward me. "What was that?" With a lifted brow, he presses his hand to his chest.

"Was it some sort of a test?" I ask, ignoring his question I don't even know what he asked about.

"What?"

I almost growl this time. "You know what."

An evil smile creeps on his face. "And I knew you'd pass with flying colors."

Just great. I have another meddler in my life. At least, this one truly has Olivia's happiness at heart.

Chapter Thirty-Seven

J^{ake}

Olivia comes back into the living room soon after the pizza gets here, and we eat in a comfortable atmosphere. When Jonah first came here, he was dead set on hating me, but something has shifted after our conversation, and now he's joking around like we've been friends for years. He's the only one who's joking though. Olivia's face looks worried, and I'm too alert to let myself relax. Plus, I haven't had friends or anyone to talk to for years, and switching into a friendly gear is not easy.

When Jonah leaves, we clean the table together. Oli's quiet. Too quiet and too focused.

"Hey," I call out. "Are you okay?"

She drops the wet sponge into the sink and looks at me. "Do I need to leave town, Jake? Is Brodie in danger?"

I walk up to her, and she has to lift her chin up to look me in the eyes.

"It crossed my mind, but it's easier to protect you here. We know everyone." I fix a lock of her silky hair behind her ear. "A new face will stir everyone's attention. We have Kenneth and Mark. The DEA is sending someone to stay on the street for the whole time. I am here. I will not let anything happen to you." I take her face into my hands. "I will not, Olivia. You can trust me on that."

"I know," she whispers without hesitation.

I lean forward and press my forehead to hers. "I don't know what's going on with me. I don't have a name for it, but I'm all in. Whatever this thing is. As long as you need me here."

"What if I need you longer than you can give?" Her voice is barely audible. Her warm breath fans my chin.

"That's impossible, Oli. Because I'm very addicted to you."

I hear her swallow. "I think you will leave me. My life is not glamorous, and I have a baby. He's my priority."

"I know." I press a soft kiss to her lips. "And I respect you so much for that. But I believe your heart is so big that you can find space for everyone in it."

I'm so close to her lips, I can feel her smile.

"I've got space," she says.

"I know you do." Another kiss. "I've got plenty of it. For the both of you."

"Okay," she breathes out.

"Okay," I repeat with a smile.

"Are you going to kiss me harder?"

I let out a soft chuckle. "Do you want me to?"

"I want you to stop talking and do that thing you promised to do when we were at Cat and Stallion." Her gentle laugh is challenging. The moment we're having is tender. I want to cherish every second of my time with her, but what she's suggesting we do is anything but tender. She's asking me to fuck her because that's what I told her I'd do to her in the bar.

"Not today, Oli. Today you've had too much stress." It pains me to say it, but it's the right thing to do. And I want to do what's good for her.

"You're right," she agrees too easily, and my quickly rising dick weeps in disappointment. "I've had a lot of stress today, and sex could be a really good release." She pulls away from me. "But you're right. I'll get my vibrator and hide in the bathroom."

"What the hell." I grab her hand and pull her toward me. She smacks into my chest with a laugh. "Fuckin' witch."

I grab her ass and lift her up. She slides over my hard dick and giggles. With her in my arms, I march toward the couch on a mission of delivering good on my promise. I fall onto the couch with her on top of me.

I pull away for a moment to look into her eyes. "Are you sure?"

"I've been sure for a long time." She watches my face with a small smile.

I swallow. "You saw me back in that motel." I don't need to explain anything else—she knows what I'm talking about.

"You promised you wouldn't do it again."

"Everyone promises, Oli. You have to be careful trusting people." *Why the fuck am I talking about this now?*

Her turn to take my face into her warm hands. "You're not just everyone. You're Jake. My Jake."

This, right here, is enough to break any man. And build him back up. This is better than any therapy. Better than rehab. This is the support of a strong woman. This is all a man needs to conquer anything. Including addiction. Now, I have something to live for, and I sure as fuck won't let drugs get in the way.

"I think I might be in love with you," I whisper.

"I think I might be too," she says quietly back.

I press my lips to hers. Gently. Savoring every moment. Every breath. She smiles into the kiss. She *feels* happy. I'm happy.

I let my hands roam to her back, hugging her closer to me. Feeling her better. More.

Her scent, a delicate mix of her own smell and ever-present vanilla with chocolate envelops me, pulling me deeper into the moment.

I place my hand gently on the side of her neck, wanting to feel her pulse under my fingers. It's rapid. It's erratic. She's in the moment too. Even when the kiss is soft and tender, she's aroused. More than I expected her to be. I've always thought sex and kisses needed to be rough to be good. Hard enough to break sweat. But what I'm—what *we* are feeling now is more than that. I'm not sweating, I'm not panting, but my own heart is about to jump out of my ribcage. My dick is as hard as steel. If someone told me to stop now, I wouldn't be able to. It's easier to stop breathing.

Each touch of our lips is a silent promise. A declaration of this thing between us that we can show with our bodies better than we can say with our words.

Her fingers tangle in my hair, pulling me closer. She lets her tongue slip into my mouth. And the moment it touches mine, the pit in my stomach explodes with a zip. I exhale, not able to control it. The *want* just became the *need*.

She must be feeling it too because she presses her hips into me. An unspoken request for more.

I deepen the kiss, angling her head the way I want it.

She's like clay in my hands, obedient to everything I silently ask her to do.

I love kissing her. I love touching her. But this contact is not enough. I want her skin on mine. So I pull away from the kiss, and slightly turning to the side, I grab my shirt and take it off.

"Oh," she sighs and does the same with her shirt. She's left in a sports bra with a small stain on the right side. The stain makes me smile. It's so much of Olivia to not give a shit about it. She probably thought no one would see it, and it makes me feel better. She wasn't planning on showing it to anyone anytime soon. *Good.* This just became my favorite part of her wardrobe.

While I'm staring at her bra, she's staring at my chest. Then, carefully, she presses her index finger into my left pec.

"What are you doing?" I ask, quietly laughing.

"I've always wanted to do that." She pokes at it again, giggling. "It's hard."

I laugh again. "That's not the only thing that's hard."

She wiggles her ass over my lap and notices playfully, "I know."

"Come over here." I grab the back of her neck and pull her toward me. Diving into this kiss is easier this time. Faster. She meets with the same enthusiasm as poking at my chest.

Our tongues switch to a tango, skillful and electrifying. The dance never ends.

I pull away from her lips to trail kisses along her jawline, tasting the sweetness of her skin. Vanilla and chocolate make my mouth water. My hands roam around her body, tracing the curves, tangling in her hair. My movements turn chaotic. I don't know which part of her I want to focus on because I want to taste and touch everything.

I press her into me, my body flush against hers as we become lost in this. With every trace of our tongues, I forget about the world around us. Nothing else exists but her.

"Jake," she whimpers, and I take it as a course of action.

Grabbing her by her waist, I drop her next to me on the couch and quickly rid myself of the clothes, standing in front of her fully naked. She looks down at me, licking her swollen lips, and starts quickly pulling away the leftovers of her own clothes.

Then she suddenly pauses when she's about to pull away her panties. Her hand goes to cover her tits while she looks around.

"What just happened?" I ask with a rough voice because I'm barely able to speak at this moment. All my blood is not anywhere near my head.

"Can we turn off the light?" she asks, not meeting my eyes.

"Why?"

"Can we?" she insists, while still trying to cover her body.

At this moment, I think I begin to understand what's going on. I remember she mentioned before that she hasn't had anyone since Brodie was born. So I drop to my knees in front of her.

"Oli," I call her while she's actively avoiding eye contact. "Look at me, Oli. I'm sitting on my knees in front of you with my dick hard as a rock. Don't do that to me."

She snorts and finally shifts her attention to me. "What?"

"You are beautiful," I say, knowing I sound sincere because I'm telling the truth. "You are the most beautiful woman I've ever seen. This," I trace a dark line on the side of her stomach, "is beautiful. So is this." I trace another one. "When I look at you, all I see is you."

"Exactly." She rolls her eyes, making me laugh.

"No, Oli, I see you. Those little things you see as imperfections I see as you. You are not you without them, and you are beautiful." I sigh and shift myself closer, slightly pushing her legs apart. "And I'm in pain because I need to taste this beauty."

She giggles again, letting her legs relax, so I crawl flush to her. I press my finger on her panties, right where it's hot. "And I need to taste that."

She bites her lips. "I've never liked this underwear."

This is all I need to hear. I grab her panties with both hands and rip them apart, trying not to hurt her. I don't want them to snap and hit her anywhere. Once I have full access to her, I dive in. The moment my mouth touches her flesh, she gasps and quickly covers her mouth with her hand. I want it to be my hand. But this is the next thing. For now, I focus on her.

With every sweep of my tongue, I push my finger inside. With every push of my finger, she lifts her hips from the couch. This is what I call a success.

"Jake," she breathes out. Loudly. "Now, Jake. Now."

I pull away, wipe my mouth with the back of my hand, and move on top of her. Quickly shifting her to lie on the couch, I position myself between her legs.

"Now?" I ask, teasing her entrance with the tip of my cock.

"Now," she whimpers, pushing her hips onto me. I love how eager she is. I love how responsive.

"Now," I finally agree when I see her reaching a point where she can't even see me anymore. I slowly push myself into her, letting her adjust to my size. I mean, a child's head went through this place, I'm sure my dick can fit. But it's on the larger size, and I don't think she had much fun pushing a human out of it. So I wait.

When she starts wiggling again, I take it as a good sign and let myself go deeper while lowering myself on top of her. I wasn't lying when I said she was beautiful, and I could look at her all night long. But I also want to feel her.

So I press my mouth to her neck and start kissing it. While moving my lower body on top of her. She meets my every thrust halfway, completely forgetting about her insecurities. I love that. I love that she trusts me. I love how that makes me feel.

I'd love to say I could do it all night long, and I can, but not today, and not with her. Sweat covers my body. My arms begin shaking. The lower part of my stomach is getting tighter. I haven't had anyone for a long time. And I've never had Olivia. If I thought I could control myself around her before, all my control went to shit the moment her tight, wet pussy wrapped around my cock. I stick my hand between our bodies and find her clit. I know the moment I do because she gasps, and I have to cover her mouth with my hand. Her eyes go wide, and I pause, listening to her reaction. *Is it a good wide or a bad wide?*

When her hot tongue touches my palm, I get my answer and keep moving. But this time, I make circles over her clit, making every nerve of her body sing. I feel that. It's like a tight string in my hands. I have to let go of her mouth because otherwise we would end up in a very odd position.

When I see her nearing the peak, her breathing becomes ragged. Her cheeks and chest are red. She's clinging onto me like her lifeline. This is the time when I go all in. Holding myself with my hands propped on the side of her face, I make my amplitude deep. Hitting all the way in and out with every thrust.

She comes apart. Her mouth falls open, and I'm scared she'll make too much noise. I love noise, but we have a kid in the house, so we have to be careful. I cover her mouth with my hand again, and it seems to send her over the edge. Shudders rack her body while I help her ride each wave until I hit a wall of my own.

I drop on top of her, scared that it was too intense. For her. For me. It was too intense. She'll probably run away now.

"Can we do it again?" she whispers into my neck, making me shake with silent laughter.

No danger of her running here. I've met my match.

Chapter Thirty Eight

O livia

I knew Jake would be good in bed. I remember, I think.

When his breathing returns to normal, he lifts himself up in his full naked glory and offers me his hand, which I take. Once I'm on my feet, he bends and grabs me bride-style.

"Oh!" I exclaim, surprised by his actions. "What are you doing?"

"We're going to clean up and then we repeat it again. As you requested," he says, looking smug. His facial expression of a self-satisfied man makes me giggle. He bends a little next to the coffee table with me still in his arms. "Grab the monitor."

I do as instructed, letting my heart feel all the love I'm feeling for him now. Even now, after all of that, he remembers that I come with a package. This is the best possible package, but not everyone sees it this way. But Jake is not everyone.

In the shower, he carefully puts me on my feet and starts the water. When it's warm, he steps inside and, with a crooked smile, he nods for me to join him.

And I do as I'm told. For a change.

When we're totally spent and barely able to move after another round, we help each other to dry off, get dressed, and walk out of the bathroom. Jake heads toward the living room.

"Where are you going?"

He turns back with a funny look on his face. "If you want another round, you need to give me a second, Oli." Humor makes his words jumpy and light. I love this Jake.

"No, silly. Why are you going this way? The bed is here." I nod at my bedroom.

He looks between me and the door. "You want me to sleep with you?"

"Duh." I roll my eyes and walk up to him to grab his hand. "Let's go. You're warm and cozy, and I'm getting cold."

Without saying a word, he follows me into my room. Hesitant at first. And even more so when he sees the bed and Brodie's crib by the wall.

"You sure he won't mind?" he asks sincerely, making me snort. But he doesn't get the joke—he's truly concerned. So I soften my voice.

"No, he won't mind. Let's go."

I climb into the bed, on the side closer to the crib, and gesture for him to join me on the other one. Still hesitant, he slowly and carefully gets on the bed, trying not to make a noise. It's actually adorable and shows more than words could. He cares about the well-being of my son, and I get the feeling that I might be actually doing the right thing.

He lies on his back, with hands on his chest, like an Egyptian mummy. A far cry from the confident man walking around the house with his dick out. I scoot over to him and lay my head on his shoulder. My contact seems to relax him a little because he takes a full breath in and shifts his body so his arm is under my neck, and his hand is on my shoulder.

"Thank you."

I'm not even sure he said it out loud, but I don't think he wants me to respond even if he did. I plant a feather of a kiss on his chest and instantly fall asleep.

I wake up fully rested. I don't remember when I've felt so good before.

Fully rested.

Fully fucking rested . . .

I jump from the bed in horror and rush to the crib only to find it empty. My blood runs cold.

I sprint to the kitchen and stop dead in my tracks. Jake's standing at the kitchen island, his face and shirt covered in some sort of yellowish goo, while he's holding a spoon and a pack of baby food in his hands, trying to negotiate with Brodie who's sitting in his highchair too, covered in the same substance.

"Look what you did. You woke your mommy up," he chastises Brodie who doesn't have the slightest idea what's going on.

And what's going on is my heart is melting to my feet

and crawling its way toward Jake to forever imprint itself on him.

I glance at the clock on the wall and gasp in horror—it's fifteen past seven. I haven't slept this long in years.

"Jake! Why didn't you wake me up?"

"You needed your rest," he says, looking at me with a quirked brow. "You spent a lot of energy yesterday." When he sees my mortified face, he adds with a smile, "With all the worrying I mean."

"Sure, that's what you meant," I reply grouchily and go to my son to give him a kiss. "But you really should have woken me up. I have a bakery to run, and now the whole day is wasted."

"I put stuff in the oven. Whatever I found in there. And googled some instructions," he says with a cheeky smile, making me open my mouth and pinch my own thigh. "What are you doing?" he asks, noticing my gesture.

"Pinching myself to know if it's real."

"It's very real. You could just ask me to give you a kiss as proof of reality." He leans toward the table to look at his phone. "In fact, the timer is about to run out. I put the note on the door that you'll be opening a bit later today. And later is about in ten minutes."

I blink at this picture of ideality I never could have even imagined in my head. Jake with Brodie in my kitchen while I have a bakery to run which he already set up before I even opened my eyes. Who the hell would call Jake a villain?

I check the timer and see that I have about five minutes left, so I rush to brush my teeth, then give Brodie a hug and a kiss before I can run downstairs. Right as I reach the doors, I remember that I forgot to do something I've never done before. So I turn around, run up to Jake and kiss his cheek too, making him open his mouth, and Brodie giggles like he usually does when he's happy. Only now can I go downstairs, just when the timer goes off.

I'm scared to see what's going on in my kitchen if I'm completely honest. I remember Jake looking helpless the last time he was trying to help me in there, so my hopes are low.

I get a big surprise though. Cupcakes and little layered cakes are in the oven, not burned, not flipped over, but raised and baked the right way. I pull them out and place them on the table to inspect. Perfect. They are perfect. And I can clearly tell he didn't put them into the oven while it was cold. No. He waited for the right temperature to stick the trays inside.

Sighing loudly like an old grandma, I pinch myself one more time just in case and start making creams for the pastries.

Sometime later, Jake joins me in the kitchen with Brodie in his arms.

"I'll drive him to daycare in a second if you can just stay here and turn off this button," I point at the blender, "when it's done."

Jake shifts Brodie from side to side. "I think it's best if he stays around until we figure this thing out."

"Oh." I feel my arms turning into noodles because another part of reality hovers over me like doom. "Yes, let's keep him here."

This part of reality is scary, and I'm glad Jake is here with me. Even if he's partially responsible for me being here.

The next few hours run by. The bakery is busy; I opened later today and have to multitask to catch up, like making creams for all types of pastries at the same time, and by midday I can barely stand. The extra sleep was worth it though—I don't remember when my brain was functioning at a hundred percent like today. I think I'm getting addicted to having Jake around, and it's been only a day.

We walk outside and toward Jake's truck, which he somehow got here from his place—wherever that is. While Jake fixes Brodie's seat into the back, I run across the street and knock on the heavily tinted window of a parked sedan. It rolls down to reveal one of three men constantly camping here for the past two weeks.

"Here you go," I say, passing him a cup of hot chocolate.

He silently accepts it with a smile and rolls the window back up. Neither of the three people talk, but I make a point to bring them something hot to drink at least twice a day. They're there to protect my family after all. Of course, they might have some secret missions of their own like catching bad guys and using me as bait—I've seen movies—but they're here, and it makes me feel better. I can tell that it makes Jake feel better too because he seems more relaxed since they've been posted outside our door.

We're driving to the store, and while he's staring ahead on the road, I can't stop staring at him. He's shaved and got some of his weight back. I mean, he was sexy as hell as a lean guy, but with his cheeks not so sunken anymore, he looks . . . healthy. Happy. Content.

"Sh—" Jake clears his throat, pressing the sudden breaks.

"What happened?" I grab the dashboard, scared to find bad guys rushing at us.

"The damn moose," Jake explains grouchily, nodding to the front. And then I see him too.

The local legend, Frank the Moose. I mean, I'm not sure everyone sees the same moose because we're in Maine, but this is my first time encountering one after I've come back.

"Is that Frank?" I ask in awe.

Jake gives me a disgusted look. "Please, don't tell me you're one of those."

I laugh because I know how strongly Jake feels about people who think of Frank as some sort of local saint. "I'm not," I reply with a wide smile on my face.

"Oh no." He wipes his face with his hand, groaning loudly.

"He's gorgeous. Look at him! He's smiling!" I shake Jake's arm, so he finally stops complaining and looks at Frank.

"He is a moose. He can't smile," he grinds out, losing patience.

"Isn't your brother his friend?" I ask with a cheeky smile. Everyone knows Justin and Frank are rivals for Kayla's attention. I've heard stories about it. "And he's like a part of Kayla's family?"

Jake looks at me like I'm a lost cause. "And this is the only reason she still stays with him. She's loony. No one in their right mind would stay with Justin."

I throw my head back with laughter and smack his shoulder lightly. "Just look at him. He's smiling. Seriously." I keep laughing because the moose sure as hell is smiling.

Grinding his teeth, Jake slowly pulls his attention away from the steering wheel and looks up. "I'll be damned."

"Told you," I laugh.

"The damn thing is smiling," he whispers, clearly not believing what he's seeing.

"Yes, he is."

Then Frank starts slowly walking toward the car, and I

expect Jake to hit the gas. Instead, he's watching the animal, mesmerized by his gracious movements. It's a ride or die moment. Animals can be unpredictable, so I don't know how Jake will react. Frank is clearly a gentleman, so I don't have doubts about him.

The moose comes up to Jake's window and licks it. I burst out laughing, and Brodie joins me a second later. I don't think he understands what's going on. He's only one, but when mommy's having fun, something good must be happening.

Then Frank leans forward and pushes his giant eyes against the glass. He blinks a few times, licks the window again, and departs. With a smile on his big, velvety lips, I swear.

Jake's not moving. I don't even think he's breathing, so I gently touch his hand. "You've been approved. Let's go."

He shakes his head with some sort of disgust at himself, making me laugh again, and finally shifts into gear.

This is not our first trip to the grocery store together, but it's the first one after Frank's approval. It's like some cosmic dome hovers over us, telling people to be polite. Since I've started showing up with Jake, people have not been kind to me. But today, things are different.

Jake has Brodie strapped to his chest and is pushing the cart. As I load the cart, Donna rises in front of us like a facial cyst overnight. The corners of her lips point downward, and her hands are on her hips.

"So it's true," she says snarkily.

"What is?" I ask, trying to appear calm.

"That you're taking all my customers."

"Donna," I start with a sigh. "I already told you—I don't take your customers. I want to do some sort of promotion together so we can make the most out of it. But if you won't be friendly, I don't think we can coexist here together."

"I was here first," she hisses. And she's not wrong, but it doesn't mean she can monopolize the coffee industry of Little Hope. We all need to eat and pay our bills.

"Hi, Donna," Jake's drawl comes right behind me. "You're looking good."

"Oh, Jakey." Donna giggles, switching her persona one-eighty. "I haven't seen you in a while."

"And I haven't seen you either, and here you are, looking as good as ever."

Donna giggles again, fixing her short hair behind her ear.

"Olivia told me you must be doing some voodoo because you look younger than before she left town."

"Did she?" Donna sends an odd look my way, less hostile this time for sure.

"Have you met Brodie?" Jake pushes past me toward Donna. You can rely on my kid to smile and be happy to charm everyone, and this is clearly what Jake's been doing by sticking Brodie into Donna's face.

"Awe, look at you," Donna coos and pushes our cart away from her path to touch my son's hand. I'm not exactly a fan of that, but Jake warns me to keep my mouth shut with a slight shake of his head. I sigh and clamp my jaws together, so I don't say something I'll regret and jump at her.

"Look at him!" Jake says in awe. "He never smiles like that with anyone. He must be sensing something good in you."

Donna's face stretches into the queen of all smiles. Her cheeks pinken, and her shoulders drop.

"Maybe." She shrugs shyly. "Anyway, I've tried those

famous éclairs of yours," she announces without looking at me. "They're alright, I guess."

I try not to smile but can't.

"I'll stop by to say hi to this wonderful, young man," she touches Brodie's cheek this time, nearly making me jump out of my skin. I get a stern look from Jake just in time to take a deep breath and calm down. "And I'll see what else you've got."

With a short nod to me, she pats Jake's shoulder and walks past us while we both turn around to see her go.

"What just happened?" I ask.

"Brodie and I just tag-teamed her into becoming an ally rather than enemy." He turns to me. "Donna is one of the gossip queens who knows everyone. She's been here longer than you've been alive, and you need to make good with her."

"But I—"

"You need to make good with her," he repeats firmly, hugging Brodie with one hand. "I'll help you," he promises with a loud reassurance.

It's so good not to fight the world alone anymore.

Chapter Thirty-Nine

J**ake**

I can truly say that I'm happy. For the first time in many years.

And I see hope. I have a lot of shit to figure out and fix, but I'll get there. I have a reason to do it now.

"Jake!" Olivia yells from the back stairs. "Can you bring me my phone please? I think I forgot it on the table."

"Yeah, one second," I yell back and go to get it.

It's on the table, right where she said it was. I take it in my hand, and the screen lights up. There is a memory popped up of a certain day, and the pictures keep slowly changing. And I can't stop looking because the Olivia in the photos is different. She seems so young and so carefree. She's grinning at me from one of them. And then she's sending me a kiss.

It's this Olivia—the woman who seemed so familiar to

me when we first met at the motel. When I couldn't place her in my past. She's right here.

And then she's with a man, cheek to cheek. They're both smiling at the camera. Both their eyes glassy, I'm not even sure they're coherent, but they both look happy.

That man is me.

My heart drops to the bottom of my stomach and settles there like a giant stone.

I click on the picture.

It's Olivia and me, in a bar, drunk out of our minds. I click on the picture, and it sends me right to this day from the same gallery.

I fuckin' wish she had a password on her goddamn phone.

The next picture is her kissing my cheek. The next is us taking shots. And then more shots. Until we both turn into two animals who are taking pictures of their dancing and kissing.

And then I see the date on the top of the picture. Almost two years ago. Almost.

I scroll through the pictures and find more of them. I am so drunk, I'm not even sure I know I'm awake in them. Olivia is about the same. I've never seen her drunk, but she looks pretty plastered in these photos. Which move to a hotel room in Chicago.

Where I was on an assignment that didn't go well, so I got wasted. I have a giant blank spot in my memory from that day, but I know I've been there. This is my go-to bar when I need an escape when I'm in the city.

"Jake," Olivia calls out. "Are you coming?"

I don't respond.

"Jake."

The sound of my shuttering heart is her only response.

"Jake." Her voice sounds closer. Right next to me. "Jake," she whispers.

I lift my face away from her phone and look at her with different eyes. Her face is pale.

"I didn't know how to tell you." Her voice is small.

"You've had plenty of fuckin' opportunities to do it." Mine is ominous.

Her neck drops with a swallow. "I know. I tried a few times—"

I step closer to her. "You should have fuckin' tried harder to tell me that I have a son. That the kid I love is mine," I hiss.

Her lower lip trembles, but I don't give a shit.

"I'm sorry, Jake. I was going to. I just didn't know how. Or when."

"Any fucking day I've been living here would be just fine."

"I'm sorry," she whispers.

I take a deep breath. "How the fuck did it happen? I don't remember shit. I think I'd fucking remember that I fucked you before."

She winces at my crude words. "I was there for culinary classes, and we just went to drinks with everyone, you know. I was tipsy, and then I saw you. You know by now I had a giant crush on you at school, so it felt like a chance, you know? To dance with you, maybe to flirt. Or something." I shoot her a glare at the mention of 'something.' "We started talking. But you were pretty drunk, so it didn't feel right, you know. But then you told me that you'd just lost someone, and I couldn't leave you alone. Then we started drinking. And some more." She shrugs. "And I don't remember much after that."

Yes, I remember the part about losing someone. It was

one of my moles. Someone I'd gotten close to and who had given me tons of useful information. I let him down, and he got killed. It's when I slipped back into drugs.

"Did you black out too?" I ask.

"Sort of." She winces. "I don't remember what exactly happened, but I remember we went to your hotel room, and I snuck out in the morning because I was so nauseous and embarrassed. I didn't want you to wake up and see me like that. When I came back to the hotel the same evening, you were gone."

I was gone, she's right. I went down a very dark path after that.

"Why didn't you find me after?"

She takes a deliberately slow step closer to me. "No one knew where you were. And then, when I found out I was pregnant, I'd been hearing stories about you being the violent psychopath of Little Hope, and I didn't want that around my child."

Even though everything she's saying is logical, I can't stand her. I can't stand her withholding this information from me. Maybe my life would have been different if she had only told me the truth earlier.

"I see." I grab my keys and head outside.

"Where are you going?"

I'm silent.

"Jake, you can't just leave."

"I'll be outside, in the car watching you. Don't worry."

She follows me. "This is not what I'm worrying about." She grabs my arm. "Where are you going, Jake?"

I stare at her hand on me until she releases it and go outside. There is one of ours in the car parked across the street. They change shifts every eight hours or so. I walk straight to him and motion for him to roll down the window.

"Don't leave your eyes from that house. If she leaves to go somewhere, you follow her."

He nods. "And you?"

I shake my head and go to my truck. It's time to go back to my roots for one day.

Rory's bar is buzzing. There're way more people than I've ever seen.

"Jake?" she asks, sounding surprised. "What are you doing here?"

"I need a drink."

She chews on her lip. "Are you sure?"

"This is a bar, and I need a fucking drink," I reply gruffly as I sit in front of her.

She shakes her head disapprovingly but places a glass on the bar. "The usual?"

I nod.

She pours a full glass of whiskey and pushes it toward me with the words, "Think before you do it. I haven't seen you in a while and prefer not to see you here again." With that, she leaves me thinking. Something I haven't come here to do.

I'm holding my drink in my hands, searching answers in the amber color, when someone places their unwelcome ass on the stool next to me.

"Hello, brother."

"Justin."

His hand quickly moves to my drink and grabs it before I can even react. "I'll take that." He waves at Rory. "He'll have water or something."

She grabs a can of ginger ale and places it in front of me, smiling to herself.

"I need you to tell me everything."

"What? What do you want to hear?" I'm lost at what he knows and what he thinks he knows.

"Like what happened to you during those years. What shit you got yourself into." He takes a giant sip. "I need to know everything."

"It's not the time, Justin," I say, eyeing the glass with hope that he'll stand up and leave—this is a really bad time for the conversation he wants to have.

"There's never a time, so let's make it. What happened to you while you were undercover?"

He wants to know the truth? I'll give him that. So I turn to him and explain in a low voice so no one hears. "Apparently, I've become a father."

Unfortunate Justin was making another sip when I delivered the news, so everything from his mouth goes flying onto Rory.

"For fuck's sake!" she cries out.

"Sorry, Rory," Justin apologizes sheepishly, wiping his mouth with his sleeve. Turning to me, he says, "You're a dad now?"

"Yep."

"Where is the kid?" He looks around like I'm hiding the child under my seat in a damn bar full of drunk idiots.

I find his gaze and hold it. "With his mom." I hold a pause. "In the apartment above the bakery."

His eyes go wide. "No fuckin' way. Brodie is yours?" I nod, and he whistles. "When did you find out?"

"Ten minutes ago."

He pushes the half-empty glass to me. "You need it more."

I take the glass and start turning it in my hands, knowing that a sip will dull the ache inside my chest. But it will be a setback for me and all I've been through. So I push the glass back with a shake of my head.

"I can't." I swallow before admitting something only a handful of people know. "I'm an addict."

"An alcoholic?" His brows shoot up. "I never thought I'd hear you admit it out loud."

"A drug addict," I reply, staring at my ginger ale, and scared to look my brother in the eyes. I've disappointed him enough as it is.

But I don't need to look at him—the heavy silence is loud enough. He takes the glass, and I expect him to down it with the news. But he pushes it and waves for Rory to come.

"I'll get a ginger ale too."

With a subtle smile on her face, she places another can in front of him and goes back to wiping the glasses.

"You don't have to. It's not like I'll get jitters if you drink around me." I shrug one shoulder. "It's sort of like a replacement when nothing else works."

He shakes his head. "Nah, I'm good." Nursing the can in his hands, he slowly spins it around.

I do the same with mine, and soon we are both emerged into a silence which doesn't taunt me in the slightest. I don't remember when was the last time we were able to just sit like this.

"That time," he finally begins, "after the shooting."

"Freya's ex?" I ask which shooting he's talking about because I've been at a few. I just don't remember which ones he knows about.

"Yeah. That. Did you really go to therapy?"

I laugh sadly. "No. Training. I wish it was fuckin' therapy."

"What about the money Freya spent on it?" There's no

snark in his question. Just a genuine interest to put every-thing in its place.

"Donated to the women shelter in Springfield." That was the only thing that felt good from that pretty dark period of my life.

He nods his head and keeps spinning the can.

"Have you seen her?" His tone is careful. Probing.

"Who?"

"Kayla's mother."

I take a sip of my buzzless drink. "No. I got pulled out before that."

He sighs. "We can't tell Kayla. She'll never recover. She's always had this feeling in the back of her head that she's not good enough, and knowing that her mother is a fucking drug lord—" He shakes his head in obvious disgust. "I see how you might have thought that, I do. I just," another shake, "can't even imagine how you could believe something like that."

"I've seen a lot of shit, Justin. It made me a skeptical man."

"Alright." He turns to me. "How long have you been off that shit you've been using?"

That's the question I don't want to answer, but he deserves it anyway. So I decide to go with the full truth on it. "Since I came back with Olivia. She got me through with-drawal in some shitty motel on the way here."

"Damn. That woman saw you puking your guts out and still stayed with you?" He sounds impressed.

"I guess she didn't have a choice," I say, smiling.

Justin cackles. "Somehow, I can't see that happening. She's a force, and if she didn't want you around, you wouldn't be."

My mood instantly darkens. I would have hyped up his

Olivia-related enthusiasm an hour ago, but not now. She's been lying to me for so long.

"I can't fucking believe you are a dad."

"You and me both. I don't know what I'll be doing now."

"What do you mean?" He looks at me with widened eyes. "The same thing you're already doing every day. You're pretty much family at this point. And now it's just official. I'm glad she told you because it would have been embarrassing to learn from someone else."

I level him with a stare, and his smile slowly drops. "Oh, shit. She didn't tell you, did she?"

I shake my head.

"And you didn't even think that the kid could be yours?" He laughs. "I mean, I know you're not the brightest bulb, but the math is pretty simple."

"I don't remember," I mumble, embarrassed to admit it.

"Don't remember what?" After my death stare, he smacks his hand on the table and keeps laughing.

"Are you done?"

"I mean, phew," he pats his chest, "I could imagine her saying so. But you? I don't know." He continues his not funny hysterics.

"I was drunk. Barely remember that weekend at all. I lost someone that day and wanted to get shitfaced. Happy now?"

His face turns sour. "Sorry, bro."

Sorry, bro. I forget when the last time was that I heard it. That just made my allergies flare up or some shit, because my eyes are embarrassingly itchy now.

"Turns out I don't know a lot about you," he announces after a pause. "Doesn't mean you aren't the same little shit."

"Just probably bigger," I add with a smirk.

"Yeah, a much larger pile of shit for sure." The smile leaves his face. "Kayla told me about your talk."

I look at him questioningly, not knowing why he sounds so astonished by it. "You asked me to talk to her yourself."

"I didn't know you actually would, you know? And," his face stretches into a wide smile, "she said you made her realize that she actually wants a wedding. So I owe you one I guess." He looks so happy, I'll take it as a giant win. Especially after all the stunts I've pulled.

"That's awesome, man." I smack him on the back. "When is the date?"

"We are still figuring it out."

"Good," I say sincerely, hoping that someone is getting their happily ever after.

"What about you? Are you going to do something about Olivia now that you know Brodie is yours?"

"I don't want to be with a woman only because she has my kid."

He looks taken aback. "But I thought—" Then he adds, shaking his head, "Never mind."

"What never mind, Justin? What?"

"We all thought you had something going on. You both light up like Christmas lights when the other comes into the room. It's disgusting."

"I thought so too until I knew she was lying to me while I was living with her under one roof."

His brows are pinched together in concentration, so I ask again, "What?"

He's watching me carefully as he speaks. "I mean, you're pretty violent. I wouldn't want you around my kids if I had any."

The muscle on my jaw starts ticking. The desire to burst into the same violent creature he's describing is strong, but it would just prove him right. And everyone else.

"Besides that, she probably didn't feel compelled to tell you the truth when you were puking your guts out, you know?" He shrugs. "You're not exactly a father figure."

"And you are?"

"It's not about me. It's about you. Besides that, I don't have any." The following pause is heavy and painful. Somehow, I'm learning about my brother during this time more than I would if he was talking nonstop. "You don't even know how lucky you are," he says, shaking his head. "I'd give everything to have a little Kayla running around. But I don't. And you have this opportunity to become a real father. To actually raise a little human. Sucks that you don't love his mom though. This love shit makes everything ten times brighter, I'm telling ya." He takes a sip of ginger ale and winces. "I'll pretend it's whiskey."

"Why don't you have kids?" I ask, even though I know I probably shouldn't.

He sighs and starts swirling the liquid inside of his can. "Kayla doesn't want any."

This knowledge stuns me if I'm honest. "Why? I've always pictured she'd want to have a football team."

"Nah." He scratches his chin. "She says she's never had a good example of a mother, so she doesn't believe she can be a good one."

I let out a loud laugh, making his forehead wrinkle with too many emotions. "Such a load of shit. Kayla has such a nurturing nature, it's hilarious she thinks otherwise."

Justin blinks at me with wide eyes like he just saw a ghost. To the point he makes me question if he's okay.

"What?" I bark.

"Funny you out of all people think that way."

I turn my whole body toward him, showing that I need his full attention to my upcoming honesty. I'm tired of beating around the bush, and if I want to be in my child's life, I'd better make good with people, so it doesn't reflect on him.

"Listen, I admit I was a dick. I know that. But you told me that Kayla was the reason the cops got you. You put that in my head. Everything went downhill from there like a snowball. I believed it was her fault." I press my hand to my chest. "I nurtured this hatred because I couldn't fuckin' hate my own brother for not making it to Alicia on time." His face pales, but he doesn't interrupt me. "But then we learned the truth, and I was supposed to change my opinion of her, but I already knew some shit about her mother. They're family, Justin. How was I supposed to know that Kayla hates her? I mean, look at our family. We used to be tight, so I thought everyone was the same. When I figured out Kayla wasn't involved, I was too deep into shit with everyone else that they couldn't see I was actually trying to change my ways. So I just stopped trying, you know?" I shrug. "What's the point? I was too far gone for anyone to change *their* ways about me."

"I'm sorry," Justin croaks.

"For what?" I ask.

"For not being there. For withdrawing and shit. For not knowing that you needed help."

"Water under the bridge," I say, waving for Rory to get me another ginger ale, which appears in front of me out of nowhere due to her bartender magic.

"It's not though if it's still here," he waves his hand between us, "in the air. If I was there, you probably wouldn't have to go through, you know, drugs."

My chuckle is dark. "Don't blame yourself about that part, Jus. It happened, and it's my fault and no one else's."

"Are you getting into rehab?"

"No. Yeah." I rake my hand through my hair. "I don't know. When everything is over, I'll have to step back and see what I want to do with my life. If the cravings will be an issue, I'll check into rehab. For Brodie."

Justin nods. "What about Olivia?"

I dig the heels of my palms into my eye sockets. "I don't know."

"Do you love her?"

I drop my hands on the table. "I don't know. I mean, I thought I loved her. But then I thought I needed her, like I was holding on to her like a lifeline, you know? But now I see I don't actually need her. I don't even know if I can look at her the same after learning she lied to me. I mean, I can't even *look* at her. When I look at her, all I see is all these months I've lost seeing my kid being born and smiling for the first time. I don't think I can forgive her. I hate her too much for that."

"Good to know."

The sullen voice behind us makes us both jump in our seats and turn.

"I've always wondered what you thought of me, and now I do. Thanks for the clarification."

With that, Olivia turns around and walks outside.

A grilling on the side of my face makes me turn toward Justin and find him with a concerned look on his face.

"I don't think you can get get back if you don't go after her now and tell her how you really feel."

"He's right," Rory chimes in from behind the counter when no one asked her, as usual.

"That is how I feel, and she knows it now." I plant my

ass firmly on the stool, showing everyone I'm not moving from here. I've told her before I was in love, but I don't feel it right now. All my feelings are clouded by this rage at her. It's burning hot and bright, not leaving space for anything else.

After a few silent, judgmental minutes, Justin goes back to questioning me about the past years of my life. And to my surprise, I ask him back about his. Every story he tells makes me want to ask more. And every question he asks makes me want to answer more.

We stay in the bar until closing.

And all this time, I ignore the lead feeling in my chest. My fast-beating heartbeat. The acid in my throat. And all of it because of Olivia. I just don't know if it's because I hate her so much now or if it's something else.

Chapter Forty

A
lmost two years ago

Olivia

Am I dreaming or am I really seeing Jake Attleborough getting shitfaced at the bar in Chicago? I squeeze my eyes shut and open them again only to find Jake still here.

He's alone, and his whole posture screams to stay away. Naturally drawn to assholes, I say goodbye to my buddies from class and head over to him.

"You look like you could use some company," I start lamely, planting my ass on the seat next to him.

His head slowly turns to me, and I'm met with the saddest eyes I've ever seen on a human.

"Not interested," he croaks and turns back to his drink.

This would be a good time to go. The right time. I'm not

wanted and should definitely go. I glance at my friends who are watching me curiously. I can just go back to them and have a good evening together, but then I look at Jake. His shoulders are bunched forward. He has a few days-old beard. His cheeks are sunken deep into his skull. He doesn't blink. He doesn't move. He just stares in his glass.

Oh, fuck it. I'll regret it later.

I gesture for the bartender to give me the same drink Jake has and angle my body toward him a little.

"Want to talk about it?" I offer, not knowing what else to say. My flirting game has never been strong, but he also doesn't need any of that now.

He slowly turns his face toward me. "Are you a therapist?"

"I can be," I reply with a shrug. "I can be anyone if it makes you feel better."

A spark shows up in his eyes. A sign of life. That's all I need.

"Yeah?" he drawls.

"Yep." I nod enthusiastically and down the drink the bartender places in front of me. My eyes instantly burn with tears and my throat is about to give up. "Oh," I sigh out loudly, making him chuckle.

"Want another one?" he asks.

"Sure. Keep them coming." I smile with as much enthusiasm as I can. After all, we can both get shitfaced and forget about our sorrows. Even though he looks like he's got more of those now. Jake gestures for the bartender to never let our glasses dry, and it marks as the beginning of the end.

I've never been a heavyweight in drinking, and right now I'm alive and standing—well, sitting—only by my sheer steely willpower.

Jake seems happier. He doesn't chat much, but nods at

the right moments when I talk. And I talk a lot of nonsense. I'm sure he doesn't even know what I'm talking about because even I'm not sure about that.

My phone buzzes with a message. My friends are asking me if I'll be okay if they leave. I shoot them a grateful message, saying I met an old friend. They ask one more time if I'm sure and then after my confirmation, they leave.

"Let's take a selfie!" I cry out, bouncing on my stool like a happy baby. This might be my only chance to take a picture with Jake. We've never been exactly friends back in our hometown. He agrees with a nod, and I bring my face to his. We start snapping shots, getting closer and closer together. I even brave myself enough to press my lips to his cheek in one of them.

An old country song suddenly bumps through the speakers, and I jump to my feet. "I love this song! Let's go!"

I grab his hand, and he obediently follows me. I've never been one to dance in a club like I have no care in the world, especially considering I have a class tomorrow. But this is Jake, and this is me. I might never get this chance in my life again. Through the haze of my barely coherent consciousness, I get a ping of remorse about lying to him about my identity. But I shove it down with a giant kick and start dancing.

Someone pushes into me, and Jake's arms come around me. I am in Jake's arms. My teenage fantasy is coming alive.

So are the last three glasses I downed without a pause. It was a bad idea because I'm quickly losing grip on reality. Jake's face is pressed into my hair. He's barely alive too. In fact, I don't even think he understands what I'm saying.

Whoa! I didn't even know I was speaking.

"Let's go," he says into my ear.

"Where?" I pull away to yell for him to hear me.

"To my hotel. It's across the street."

His eyes are glassy and sad. His body is hard and warm pressed to mine. He's the dream I've been having since I was a teen. I'll never be back in Little Hope. What can one night of fun do to us? Only the good stuff.

I nod in agreement, and we head outside.

The hotel is really across the street. It's not fancy, but I wouldn't recognize fancy even if it hit me in the face.

The closer I get to the main entrance, the less I'm able to stand on my own feet. I feel like Jake's having the same problem because when he's trying to catch me from falling, he's barely able to catch himself too.

The moment we're in the elevator, he presses me into the wall with his body and presses his hot lips to mine. Alcohol paired up with arousal takes out the remaining working brain cells I had left, and I don't remember anything after that.

When I wake up, I'm hit with the worst nausea of all nauseas, and I instantly run to the bathroom. I'm not in a familiar place, but there is only one open door, and it looks like a bathroom. I wretch every single drop of alcohol I have left in me and crawl into a fetal position on the floor.

I lie like that for some time before I'm able to peel myself off it and drink some water right from the sink.

Someone moves.

Shit!

I slowly come out to look outside the bathroom, holding the wall because I feel like shit, and I find a man in a bed. A very tangled bed. And a very naked man. There were some crazy activities going on there. Then I look down at myself.

I'm naked too. I was in that bed.

My mind's slowly trying to put pieces of yesterday evening together and—

Jake! I'm in Jake Attleborough's hotel room! I slept with Jake. *Shit!*

I start carefully moving around the room, trying not to make a sound while collecting pieces of my clothing. I slept with Jake Attleborough, and I don't even remember.

I slip out without him waking up. Pressing my back to the wall, I take a deep breath. I need to get the hell away from here.

A few hours and five cups of coffee later, I'm eaten by guilt. I should have told Jake who I was from the beginning. I feel like I used his vulnerable state just so I could live out my fantasies.

I find myself at the door of his hotel, knocking. When it flies open, I brace myself to see his face with a wide smile.

But it's not him. It's a man in his forties.

"Yes?" he asks.

"Mm, I'm here to see Jake?"

His brow goes up. "Honey," he starts talking like a pastor to me, "you shouldn't succumb to your sin."

"Sorry." I back away. "I thought it was my friend's room."

He shakes his head. "I checked in two hours go. I think your *friend*," he accentuates the word, "is gone. Think better the next time."

I offer him a weak smile and turn away to leave. I'm too late. I've missed my chance with Jake.

"Fuck," I murmur as I stare at two pink lines six weeks later. I'm pregnant. With Jake's baby. Mark is going to kill me, and then kill Jake. And then resurrect me again just so he can kill me again. I probably shouldn't tell him about the father right away and try to see Jake first. He's probably back in Little Hope; he's always been there. Planning a quick trip, I call Alicia to 'casually' chat and fish for some information about her brother. And what I find out is not exactly encouraging.

Looks like I'm not going back to Little Hope after all.

Chapter Forty-One

Olivia

It's been two days, and Jake hasn't been back into the apartment yet. I wish I hadn't gone to the bar and overheard what I did. This way, I wouldn't be feeling stabbed in the guts.

Those two weeks of us living together were something of a dream. Too perfect. Too clean. Too everything. And I lost touch with reality. I've built in my mind this perfect family neither me or my brother have had and thought I finally got one of my own. So naive of me.

I thought we were becoming something.

But Jake was right—I was just a needed distraction for him.

And it sucks because I let my stupid, stupid heart feel again. I thought I outgrew my teenage obsession with the blond god roaming school campus with the confidence of a swagger-bearer, but the moment he showed up with all his shining—and naked—glory, my poor, unprepared mind got sidetracked into the same routine of pining after a hot, emotionally unavailable guy. I'm hopeless.

It's six in the evening, and I decide to peep from behind the curtain outside as I've been doing for the past two days. Yep, Jake is there, in his truck, parked right across the street. One of the three men rotating watch around my house is behind him in his sedan. How long will this go on? It's been what, three weeks? I don't think anyone is coming, otherwise they'd be here already. Neither of them can stay outside forever, living in a car.

Even locals are noticing odd people parked outside my place. The other day, one of the yoga ladies jokingly asked if I have a stalker. I said it's one of the real estate agents working with Jonah who's looking into buying business here.

I'm about to close the curtain like the invisible ninja I've become for the past few days while snooping on Jake when I notice Mark's truck pulling up to the curb.

"I'll be back, baby," I say to Brodie who's playing in his playpen. "I'll just get your uncle."

I run downstairs to open the door and motion for Mark to come up.

When he appears in my kitchen, he looks gloomy. I can almost see dark clouds following him into my apartment.

"Hey." I try sounding cheerful, but he ignores me. With a blank stare like I don't exist, he walks to the playpen and stares at Brodie.

Oh, shit. He knows. I wanted to tell him myself but didn't know how. And now I'm too late. I'm too late to everything these days.

"Mark?" I call out, approaching him carefully like a wounded animal.

"Why didn't you tell me?" His voice is full of pain.

"Why do you think?" I shrug even though he can't see me. "Because of Jake." For some reason, saying his name out loud is painful. Like I've lost him without actually having him in the first place.

Mark's body stiffens from rage. He probably thinks Jake ordered me not to say anything—like that would *work*—and I quickly rush to explain myself better.

"I knew how you felt about him, and there is nothing I could do about it. The fact is the fact."

He looks at me with a face full of a different kind of pain. "But Jake, Olivia? Jake?" He shakes his head. "How the hell did he manage to keep it a secret?"

This, right here, is the moment I'll disappoint my brother forever. The only person always standing by my side. And it's my fault and mine only.

My shoulders drop when I start talking. "He didn't know. He just found out too."

"What?" He rears back with obvious horror. He's about to get loud and scare Brodie, when I know it's the last thing he wants to do. My brother is a protector down to his core, so hurting people—even unintentionally—brings him almost physical pain. I know that. So to avoid aggravating and upsetting him even more, I decide to tell him the full truth.

With a loud sigh to the sky, I start telling him the story of how Brodie came to life, dropping a few details on the way in a weak attempt not to traumatize my brother. My main goal is to tell the impartial truth, even if I'll see a face full of disgust. He deserves it after raising me and helping me become a person.

Even though I'm prepared for disappointment, it still

hurts to see it. But I need Mark to know that it wasn't Jake's fault and that he didn't leave Brodie. In fact, I withheld this information from him and hurt him probably more that he ever would me. Yes, I'm mad at Jake, I am, but I don't want him to suffer for something I've done—he has his own battles to fight.

I created this mess, and it's my burden to carry. The only thing I will never apologize for is having my child. He's the best thing I've done in this life, and I will do my best to raise him as a decent person.

By the end of my story, Mark's wiping his face with his hands, groaning loudly.

"I can't believe it." He sounds muffled.

"I know," I say, planting my butt on the stool next to him. "I know you're disappointed. And I know you were right when you said all those things about me. You were right about everything."

He pulls his hands away from his face. "What? What are you talking about?"

"That thing where you said I'm a bad mother? You were right, I am." No matter how much it pains to admit it, he's right. "I've done a lot of things wrong."

He watches me with slowly narrowing eyes. "Do you think that's what I'm mad about?"

I nod.

"Unbelievable." He starts pacing from side to side, nearly freaking me out. "I'm mad that you didn't tell me the truth from the beginning. I'm mad that you thought you couldn't share it with me. With me, Oli." He presses a fist to his chest. "Me who's been with you your whole life. Do you really think I'd be mad?"

I shrug.

He groans again. "I would, but not at you being pregnant, obviously." *Glad we're on the same page here*, I note mentally. "But for not telling me about the father and everything. Oli," he sighs, walking to me, "it's me." His face pains with sadness as he moves in to wrap his arms around me. I didn't know how much me keeping him out of the loop would hurt him.

"I know," I say, stepping backward. I don't deserve his hug. Even when I'm in the wrong, he still wants to comfort me. I don't deserve him.

"Oli," he sighs, pulling me into his hug. "We will be okay."

The first shudder racks my body right when he stops talking. The next follows shortly after. And now, I'm crying, clenching the front of his shirt.

"He'll never forgive me," I mumble between cries and hiccups. "Never."

Mark's body moves with the deepest sigh of all sighs. "I can't believe I'm saying this, but I think he'll come around. I hope he will. Or I will need to rearrange his face again. He's too fucking pretty." He freezes and glances at Brodie. "Oh, shit. He's the carbon copy of his father, isn't he? He'll be too pretty." Another pause. "Well, there's no such thing as 'too pretty' to think of it. He'll be fine."

I cackle, and my cries subside. It's funny how he's slowly coming to terms, reacting way better than I expected him to.

I slowly pull away, wiping my face in the process. "You didn't hear him. He was so mad."

Mark's face darkens. He looks just like he did when he came back home, beaten up by Justin the asshole when he was very young. I still can't believe Mark let him rearrange his face—I've seen Mark in a brawl, and I'd always put all the money I have on my brother.

"Did he say something to you?" He steps forward, scaring me for the first time, more than Jake ever did. "Did he do something?" His eyes are a raging storm. "Did he hurt you, Oli?"

"No," I reply in a relatively calm voice, trying to show him that he should be calm too. It doesn't work because his eyes are dark with anger, so I hurry to explain what happened. "I overheard him talking to Justin in the bar. I followed him because I didn't want him to get drunk since he just got clean, but he didn't need me there." With a still tingling nose, I walk to the kitchen sink to splash some water on my face and wash the drying saltiness. "But he didn't want me there. That was obvious." I sniffle and say in a quieter voice. "He said he hates me."

My brother is quiet, and this is very unusual. I look at him with curiosity, trying to figure out what he's thinking while he's slowly lowering himself back on the chair.

Then he finally speaks. "I'd be mad too. Especially, after meeting Brodie. This kid is everything." This is so not what I expected to hear. "But Jake loves Brodie. And he loves you. He'll come around." He shakes his head, looking disgusted with himself. "I still can't even believe I'm saying this."

"No, Mark. You didn't hear him. I don't think he wants me anymore."

He jumps from the stool and covers his ears. "Alright, you need a girlfriend for that. I'm sending Alicia here."

"I didn't mean it like that," I laugh. "I meant like in his life he doesn't want me anymore."

After giving me an angry side-eye, he says, "He *needs* you, Oli. That's all it is. For now. You'll figure out the rest later."

The most fucked-up thing is that even after I heard Jake

in the bar, I'm still nursing this stupid hope. So yeah, I'll take the *need*. I'll be his anchor, fuck it. He needs a crutch? I'll be it. As long as he stays in our lives.

"And he paid your deposit for the bakery," Mark quickly shoots in one breath, trying to deliver the news as fast as he can.

"What the fuck?" I cry out.

I've swallowed my pride—it took me a while because I didn't know I had so much of it, but I did it—and decided to try again.

Alicia begged to take Brodie to their place today because she's seriously obsessed with my kid. Which I don't complain about, she's helping so much that I feel like I have my very own sister. I've been a little wary of Alicia when I met her at first because she seemed a bit aloof and closed off, but the more time I spend with her, the more I understand how truly loyal and sincere she is. I trust her with my brother. And more than that, I trust her with my son.

Today he's spending the night at his uncle and auntie's house, so one can bet that tomorrow he'll be a little spoiled brat who'll think he can wrap anyone around his little, cute pinky. When I dropped him off an hour ago, Alicia winked at me while she was complimenting my makeup. Her smile was knowing. And approving. I didn't know I needed to see that so much.

Dressed in tight, black jeans and an almost see-through red shirt I know Jake likes, I stride toward his truck. It's not warm outside, but the cold will work in my favor and make my breasts look enticing. I hope. I'll use every weapon in my arsenal. If I could push my butt and my tits into his face at the same time, I would. I'm really desperate.

He's scrolling through his phone when I open the passenger door and plop inside, startling him. He looks at me with an unblinking stare.

"Hi!" I squeak, pulling my brown hair over my shoulder. I've read men love it when a woman plays with her hair in front of him. I've never been good at the flirting game, but I'm willing to try.

"What are you doing here?" he asks gruffly. His face is unwelcoming. His posture is closed off.

I must admit that this dampened my enthusiasm a bit, but I still manage to plant a wide smile on my face. "I just wanted to talk and see if you're not cold here, you know."

Real smooth, Olivia. I cringe at myself.

His blond brow drifts upward—he clearly noticed my stupid attempt at starting a conversation. I deflate a bit.

"What do you need, Olivia?" he repeats the question, sounding a little bored now.

I haven't been honest with him from the beginning, so he deserves to send me around the block. But just once.

"I'm trying to find a way to repair what's broken," I start off the bat. Anything else will make him angry. He knows I'm not here for small talk.

"What *you* broke, you mean?" His tone cuts deep, making me physically ache inside.

"Yes." I brave myself with the reality because he's right, secretly hoping he'll respect my straightforwardness for a change.

His low laughter is dark. "You can't repair that, Olivia. You can't bring back all those months I've lost." His voice is filled with pain. "You can't bring back the months of anticipation for my son to be born." His voice falters at the word 'son.' "You can't bring back the time of his first smile. Or his first tooth."

"It's not a fun time, so you didn't miss much," I say quietly, and understand too late that was the wrong thing to say.

Because Jake turns livid. "You don't get to fuckin' decide which moments to share and which to not. They're just as much mine as they are yours." His voice is low, but the threat in it is loud. This visibly calm Jake is scarier than any yelling person I've ever seen. "You think it's a fuckin' joke?"

I shake my head, knowing he stopped seeing reality a while ago. He's in his head now. Reliving his rage. And he has every right to it.

"I want to be there." He smacks his chest with his fist. "I want to see his life. And you took it away from me."

With every word, I press myself deeper into the seat. I'm becoming smaller and smaller to the point where I stop feeling *me*. While he just keeps on raging.

"Do you think I wanted to go on fucking assignments to who the fuck knows where? I didn't have a choice because I had nothing left." He smacks the wheel with his hands, making me jump. "I *thought* I had nothing. If I knew I had *something*, I wouldn't have done the things I've done. I wouldn't," he adds quieter.

Is he talking about drugs? Is he saying what I think he's saying?

I've never felt so small before. So guilty. So miserable.

He finally turns to look at me for the first time since I climbed inside his truck. "Do you understand what you took away from me?"

I can't face him. I just can't. I just let him talk.

"You took everything from me, Olivia," he finishes, ripping my heart to shreds. "Everything."

I nod, acknowledging everything he said, and push the door open.

"I'm sorry," I say, before leaving the electrified car. "I'm really sorry, Jake."

He doesn't say a word.

I need to go home but I can't. Everything there will remind me of what he just said, and I can't do it. I can't face the circumstances of my actions. I came here with a different intention and hopeful mood, but all of that has changed. I'm glad Brodie is with Mark today—I don't want to be around my child when I'm feeling like I'm dragging hell on my heels.

So I head to the bar.

I don't even feel the cold. Cat and Stallion is around the corner, but by the time I reach it, my nose is running.

The moment Rory's eyes land on me, she gestures for a man to free a seat at the corner of the bar and then for me to take it. Closer to the bathroom. Very convenient in case I spontaneously burst into tears. Or flames. I feel like either is possible.

While I take deliberately slow steps toward the stool, she places a glass in front of the seat and pours something into it. I don't care what it is. I just want not to feel.

I take two big gulps and nearly spit it out. It's so bitter.

"Drink it," she orders gently. "It won't give you a bad hangover tomorrow so you can take care of your kid. I'll get you one more."

I nod and give it another try. This time, it goes down smoother, pleasantly burning my throat and warming my belly.

"Did you drive here?" she asks. I shake my head. "Good. You can get wasted. I'll get you home. Brodie's at Mark's?"

I nod.

"Okay," she sighs. "Want to talk about it?"

A headshake from me.

"Alright. Let me know if you change your mind." With that, she flips a white towel from one shoulder to another and goes to refill beers to one of the new guys I've never seen here. I glance around and find the bar full. So many old and new faces. Everyone's talking and laughing. They don't know that my life is literally crumbling down as they speak.

I don't even notice how my glass has been refilled, but it's full again. And I drink. And drink. While silently watching a gray speck on the bar in front of me. It's fascinating. It's non-moving. It's heard so many different stories. It's seen so many tears spilled. I'll go and this speck will stay.

"You look like you could use some company," a low voice suddenly says into my ear. I wish I could say it startled me, but I'm in such a deep state of misery that nothing bothers me at this point.

It might be exhaustion or a drink or maybe both, but to my own disbelief, I find myself replying, "I could."

Taking my words as an invitation, a body moves closer to my back. A big, warm body. It's flush to mine now, emanating drunken and frivolous heat. It's companionship. This is what I came here for, right? I didn't want to stay home alone, so I ended up here.

"Do you want another one?" the voice asks, sounding even closer if it's even possible. Almost inside my own head.

I look up and find Rory watching me like a hawk. For a moment, her gaze slides to the side, and she smiles, returning to polishing shot glasses.

The heat of the body disappears in an instant. I wish I could say I'm cold now, but something was wrong with this heat. It wasn't hot enough. Not warm enough. Didn't smell good enough.

A body thuds to my right, making me jump. A man's face is squashed into the counter. His wailing arm knocks my drink down onto the floor. A furious mass of Jake pushes on his back.

His eyes are slits. His face is red. His jaw is the sharpest I've ever seen it. His muscles are bunched under his sweater. He's coiled like a cobra, ready to strike. *Wait, he's already striking.*

He leans closer to the man. "Touch her one more time, and I'll fucking break your limbs. All of them. Slowly. Several times." His voice is menacing. Tone promising. "To think of it, I'll break it anyway."

I blink in astonishment, not understanding why Jake threatening bodily harm to a man makes my panties dampen. Maybe I'm already too drunk and need to go home.

"I was just being friendly," the man explains, his voice defensive. "She was alone. I didn't mean to step on someone's toes, man."

Jake's eyes shoot to me. When he meets mine, his turn into furious slits. He probably hasn't found enough disgust in them toward the man, but the dude really was just being nice. I'm sure he'd step away if I asked him. I just didn't get the chance.

"Let him go," I mouth, hoping he'll understand. I came here to not think about it and being the center of a scene is the last thing I need. "Please," I add when I see my words mean nothing.

His jaw moves while he presses the man harder. A few

seconds and two controlled breaths later, Jake finally releases the man and pulls away. The man scatters toward a table where another man is staring at us with wide eyes. Before my failed companion takes a seat, he glances at me like I'm a poisonous snake and disregards me with obvious disgust. How did I manage to anger another person by just sitting here trying to get drunk?

When I finally shift my attention back to Jake, I find him positively murderous. Like I've wronged him. I probably have, but Jake doesn't have any right to behave this way. He said what he thinks and now he can fuck off. I've tried apologizing. I've tried changing his mind. It didn't work. Moving on.

The curious looks stop after a few moments when everyone goes back to their own drinks and conversations where they probably will talk about how unstable Jake really is and how much of a whore the new baker turned out to be.

Jake's gripping the edge of the counter with hands so hard his knuckles turn white. His head hangs low while he's trying to take slow, controlled breaths.

Good thing he's working on himself because I'm sure as shit far from being calm.

"What was that?" I hiss, demanding an answer. "You're a freaking Neanderthal."

His head slowly turns to me. Very slowly. Like in horror movies. I half expect him not to stop when he faces me and just do a three-sixty.

"What did you just say?" His voice is threatening. Gruff. Barely human.

"You heard me." I lean closer to get into his face. "What the hell do you think you are doing?"

His mouth clamps shut. His chest rises and falls with big, deep breaths.

"You told me everything I needed to hear. Now I'm drinking. In a bar. Like you do." I lean even closer, now almost touching his nose. "And now I'm going to finish my drink." A hair closer. "Get another one." Closer. "And then I'm going to go and get back the guy you just assaulted and kiss his booboo better."

I can see the exact moment he snaps. His pupils dilate faster than a blink. His nostrils flare with a fast exhale. His shoulders draw back with a snap. I've managed to release the beast everyone has warned me about. I wish I was scared, but I feel nothing.

Jake slowly rises to his full height, looking even taller than he is. Then he grabs my forearm and puts it behind my back in one swift motion. It looks like a police hold, so I expect pain. None comes. He's just firmly holding me like that, making me very obedient, and starts moving. Toward the bathroom.

I press my feet into the floor, trying to stop the walk, but he growls into my ear, "Don't." And like a stupid, eager girl, I do as I'm told.

He pushes me into the bathroom and locks the door behind us.

He's on me a moment later.

My back is pressed into the door with his body pushing onto me.

He smacks his hands against the wall, framing the sides of my face, and I understand in the back of my mind that I probably need to be scared. But I'm not. Caged between his arms looks like a safe place to be.

He brings his face closer, and due to our height difference, he needs to lean down. Making it more thrilling. Making me drip in fear and excitement like a psycho.

"Tell me again," he hisses, "what you were going to do."

I swallow a lump of excitement down. "Which part?"

His nostrils flare again. "You know which part." His face is so close to mine, his breath's fanning my forehead. I wish he would move a little lower and touch my lips. They're tingling in anticipation.

I feel reckless. And adventurous. Or maybe it's just the alcohol talking. "The part where I was going to kiss him better?" I know I'm playing with fire. But I need this fire to burn all my guilt down to ashes.

A low growl makes my eyes widen. *Did he just—*

"Never." He brings his mouth to my ear. "Never will you fuckin' kiss someone else." I feel his body shaking. "I will be the only one these lips touch." He brings his finger to my lips and presses them not so gently, pushing them open. "Try to kiss someone else." He moves it into my mouth, and I meet it with the tip of my tongue. "And see what'll happen to him." He presses his nose into my cheek while moving his digit inside my mouth. "I promise you that, Olivia." He gently bites my jaw. "Fuckin' try me."

My panties are about to dissolve into nothing from the fountain of wetness that is my pussy. It's clenching like it's trying to get a hold of the last life vest on a ship.

I push his finger out from my mouth with my tongue and say, "You said you don't want me."

He grabs my jaw with his hand. "I never said that. I said I hate you." He lifts my face up. "But I still fuckin' want you."

I feel a tear slipping down my cheek. "You can't have both," I whisper.

His gaze follows the tear until it disappears under my chin. "It's all I can give you."

I expect him to kiss me, but he doesn't. Instead, he brings his face back to my ear and bites the lobe. While his hand snakes down my body to unbutton my jeans. A moment later, Jake's big hand covers my drenched pussy. He lets out a loud, shuddering exhale I feel in my own body.

His thick finger slips inside me and pushes deeper, instantly finding the right spot. I gasp and nearly lose my footing. Jake brings his other hand to my lower back and supports me while he's pumping his finger in and out. Faster. And faster. While he bites and licks my ear and neck. No mercy. No gentleness.

I want him to kiss me, so I try to angle my head to face him, but he nudges me back. Soon, I can't fight him anymore because the feelings are too strong. The bliss only Jake can deliver is close. He knows it and speeds up his movements. He curves his fingers more. He bites and sucks my skin harder.

When I fall apart in his arms, he pulls his face away and watches me until I come back to reality. When I'm able to stand on my own feet, he steps backward in total silence.

I expect us to be a little closer after he delivered me into sweet oblivion, but it feels the opposite. There are oceans between us. Cold like his eyes.

Suddenly, I feel used. After one of the best orgasms of my life, I feel like chewed gum under someone's shoe. There's probably one of those on the dirty floor of this bar bathroom.

I push him away to get to the mirror where I fix myself the best I can and rush outside, ignoring his quiet calling of my name.

He told me all he can do is hate me and basically fuck me sometimes, and I quickly agreed to that, giving him access to my body, unguarded. Like an idiot, I let him lead me by my vagina. Have I no respect where this man is concerned?

Shooting past surprised-looking Rory, I rush outside. Once I'm out, I take in a lungful of cold air, hoping to clear my head. It doesn't work. So I run down the street toward my house. The quiet of my home and lack of people seem like a giant plus right now. I don't know why I decided to go and look for adventures before.

Déjà vu hits me when I round the corner. A hand wraps around my mouth and waist, yanking me backward. A strong body pulls me into an opened car and pushes me inside the back of something that looks like a van.

They've come for me.

Chapter Forty-Two

J^{ake}

I call her name, knowing she won't stop. Why would she? I just acted like an animal and finger fucked her in a dirty bathroom.

I didn't think. I couldn't.

When I saw a man on her back, bringing his arms around her and pushing his mouth into her ear, I saw red. I wanted to kill. For the first time, I really wanted to end someone's life. I'm eager to fight. I love fighting in fact. But I've never wished to end someone's life so badly, and I've seen fuckin' scams in my life.

I needed to take him away from her. I needed him to feel pain. The same I did when I saw them cozying up.

When I pushed him on the table, I looked at her face, hoping to see disgust. Fear. Anything that would show me that she didn't want him there. That it was unwanted.

But I saw none. Only the pleading to let him go.

I don't know how I got control back and released my hold on him. I thought I was like a Staffordshire terrier with a choke hold that can be released only if I lose my breath. I wanted him to be in pain.

I wanted her to be in pain.

That's why I took her to the bathroom.

Or was it because she baited me? Yes, that. She knew what she was doing. She wanted me to snap.

I didn't know I cared so much if I'm honest. I thought I was telling Justin the truth when I said I can't forgive her and don't need her. That I just want my son. Without her.

A fool.

When I saw another man next to her, it became clear. I need her too. I hate her but I need her. And I want her. To own her and punish her for what she did.

Or so I thought. Until I saw her face when she came down from the high. All this disgust. With herself. I can deal if she feels it toward me, but I can't see her hating herself. It gave me more pain than seeing the man next to her. My chest's still aching when I close my eyes and recall her face. So broken. So sad. She doesn't deserve that.

I need to fix it. I have to. I need her to forgive me.

I rush out of the bathroom after I give myself a moment to collect my thoughts together and bring my raging hard-on down. When I'm back in the bar, I'm met with a hot, accusing stare. I face it. Rory's ready to jump over the counter and kick me in the nuts. High chance I'll let her if she decides to proceed.

I look around and don't find Olivia anywhere. No surprise here. I rush outside. And this is where I get a feeling. A really bad feeling in my stomach. It gets heavy. Aching. Longing.

I run toward her apartment.

She's not there.

The door is locked. I'm retreating back the same way while keeping my eyes on the ground. Any clues. Signs. I need anything.

And I find it. A cupcake-shaped charm from her keychain. Right at the corner to her street. I pick it up and look around. There are many footprints around, it's a busy street, but in one particular spot, it seems more crowded and fresher.

Fuck! She was taken.

I run to the guy still parked next to the bakery. He's asleep.

"What the fuck."

I pull on the door handle and find it open. Not good. I shake his shoulder. Nothing. I check his pulse. Slow, uneven. He's been drugged.

I pull out my phone.

"Yes?" Silent answers on the second ring.

"They took her. Dickson is out. They drugged him."

"Fuck. I'm on the way. Be there in about twenty, twenty-five." Good, so he's around. I could use all the help I can get.

"Did you hear anything new?"

"Adams was seen leaving Canada. We lost track of her. She might be there."

"Anything else?" Please give me something else.

"Nothing. Everything's been quiet. No other move-ments." He sounds apologetic. For the first time in six years I've known him.

"If something happens to her—"

"I know."

I hang up and call 911, giving them info about a drugged agent and address. I shoot a voice memo to

Kenneth while I run back to my truck and tell him to go to Mark's house to watch after Brodie. If they know who Olivia is, they know she has a child. They can use him. They will.

Once I'm in my car, I grab the steering wheel and close my eyes. *Think, Jake. Fucking think.*

Where can they take her? Where would they go?

Who was sent here? Have I met them? I need to know their minds. Their patterns. I've spent fuckin' years with them. I know them. *Think, Jake.*

There was a man who was always quiet. Never got into brawls or verbal fights. He was calculated and careful. Always watching.

Every time I was moved up the chain, he was there. Every time.

Every fucking time.

The last time he wasn't there though. I was told he'd meet me after. I didn't see him, even though I checked my surroundings before the deal. Could it be that he was there too and witnessed everything? Did he see Olivia? How the fuck did I miss that?

Think, Jake.

If it was him, present at every move up the ladder, he was higher than the pawns pushing actual drugs. He might be working for Kayla's mother who was seen leaving Canada per my handler's words.

He's here. She might be here too. I was the first one who got so close to her. To them. She'd want to witness my fall herself.

She'd be seen in town. People would recognize her. She left a long time ago, injuring someone in a hit and run. People remember that. She wouldn't dare show her face on the streets.

Where would she go? Where?

The trailer park would be too obvious, but that is the place where people can hide some big shit. No, too obvious.

Who else?

There was another name that was unclear in all the years we've been looking. We haven't found anything—they are squeaky clean. Too clean. Too rich. Justin's ex-girlfriend's family. The bitch who called the cops on Justin when he got arrested. I've seen her a few times around town, and she was jumpy every time I was nearby. No wonder, she might have thought I was out for her for the call to the cops.

Was she?

I call my handler again. He picks up right away.

"The name of Ashley's family here . . . Are they still in the clear?"

A pause. *"We haven't kept tabs on them for the past few months. No resources."*

"The fuck? While I was out of town, you could have had someone check on them." My voice is full of fury.

"Hold on." The sound of his car engine quiets down. He probably just parked. Then keyboard clicking. *"Two hours ago, they received a big sum and haven't moved it to another account."*

"How much?" I squeeze the steering wheel.

"Enough for what Adams might have in mind."

"They're there."

"ETA fifteen minutes."

I shift into gear before he finishes talking and take off toward their house which is conveniently located on the side of town leading up the mountain in the woods where Alex Crawley's cabin is.

I shut off the headlights and park far. Then I take off

running. I have only one clip with me, but it should be enough. I need only one bullet for one target. I don't miss.

There are three cars behind their house. Giant SUVs. Two have Canadian plates.

I go to the window and peak inside. Careful not to be seen. They haven't closed the curtains, not thinking about someone looking inside. Very stupid on their end, and I'm grateful.

I see her. Only her. Olivia. She's sitting on the couch. A string of blood comes from her nose down to her chin. Her lips are bloodied.

I can't breathe. My vision gets clouded. I head toward the door to burst inside and kill fucking everyone who hurt her.

I pause just in time to think. They'll kill her. I can get a few of them, but one will get to her for sure.

I crawl back to the window and look inside again. Olivia is on the couch. Adams is standing in front of her with her hands on her hips. Her voice is loud. She's asking her questions. About me. Olivia's lips are pressed together. After a few moments, Adams hits Olivia's face, and I feel the pain in my stomach. It stings. It's killing me. But I control myself. I'm waiting.

The man I've seen at the deals is here too. Silent in the corner, watching the room. He's the most dangerous one. He won't hesitate to kill. And he'll go for Olivia first.

There are three more men in the room. All of them look like thugs. They came together obviously.

Ashley's two parents are standing by one wall. Ashley, with her arms crossed over her chest and a sneer on her face, leans her ass on the dining table. She looks like she's actually enjoying all of it.

I need them out one by one. I can't take them all at once without risking Olivia's life. I need a distraction.

The bush at the back by the parked cars rustles, and a moose's head pops out. Fuck, I'll take it. I move toward him, trying not to make a sound. He's waiting. Hopefully for me, because I'm about to put all my faith into a fucking moose and pray to God he's as smart as people make him out to be.

"Frank," I whisper when I crouch next to him, trying to hide behind one of the SUVs. "I need your help, buddy." He tilts his head to the side, making me think he looks curious about what I'm saying. I can't fucking believe I'm doing this. I'm a stupid fuck. "Remember the gorgeous brunette in my car before?" He doesn't move, and I keep whispering. "She's in trouble. She is inside." I point at the house. "And I need your help, buddy." I'm insane talking to a moose. But I don't have a choice. My handler could be too late. "I need a distraction. Can you be loud? Like really loud." I wave my hands in the air, trying to show what he needs to do. "Make them come out. Can you do that?"

His giant, brown eyes blink at me for a few moments before he strides out of the bushes far from the house. *Fuck, there goes my hope, back to the woods.*

When I'm about to go back to the house and think of another plan, Frank pauses and turns around. I freeze too, trying to figure out what he's about to do. He lowers his head, pointing his antlers ahead, and takes off. Toward the furthest SUV parked in the lot.

Shit, he's doing it.

I hide behind the car and wait. When Frank hits the SUV, the siren goes off, and the back door bursts open.

"What the fuck was that?" A female voice yells from inside to one of the men who's standing by the door with a gun pointed outside. It's dark, but Frank's a very obvious and big target.

"Hide, Frank!" I hiss, and he quickly moves toward the back of the car. Only his antlers are popping up over the top.

"It's a fookin' moose," the man yells back into the house.

"Get him away and shut off that sound. Don't shoot, for fuck's sake. The whole damn village will be here in a second," the same female, smoked-up voice orders. It's Adams for sure.

The man holsters the gun and walks up to the car. "Get the fook away!" He waves his arms at Frank who's still hiding behind the car. Right next to me.

Once the man is there, I hook his neck with my arm while I cover his mouth with another hand. I squeeze until he goes to sleep. Then I hide his body in the bush.

Frank's watching me. An unmoving Robin to my Batman. I nod for him to do the same.

He goes farther away, lowers his head, and does the same thing, making the siren wail.

The second goon comes out, looking around.

"Can someone shut these things down?" Adams yells from inside the house.

The very same thing happens again. Frank lures him out, and I knock him out. By now, I'm sure I'm the Robin in this story. I owe this hero a sweet-twig-and-moss subscription for the rest of his life.

The third goon comes out right when I climb out from the bush after hiding the second body. Frank doesn't get a chance to hide, so the goon rushes toward him. I can't show my face or I'll be made. But Frank doesn't need my help. He charges the man with his antlers and knocks him to the ground. I've never seen a moose-man brawl, but I'm betting my money on the moose.

I quickly move past them toward the back door and meet Ashley's father face to face. He doesn't get a chance to yell a warning because I smack my fist into his face, knocking him out. I also don't get a chance to grab his body to make sure he doesn't make a sound. He goes down like a sack of shit with a loud thud.

I grab my gun and press my back to the wall next to the opened door. The quiet inside is warning enough. They know. They're ready. I bet Olivia's in the hands of the man from the corner.

I see my boss a second later. He's silently moving toward me with a gun in his hands. He looks twenty years older than when I've seen him before, and he's only about thirty-five. He gives me a short nod and stops behind the door.

"Come inside, or we'll shoot her brains out," Adams yells from the house.

Another nod, and I move inside first. They don't know how many are out there.

When Olivia's eyes find me, they widen. Her mouth falls open, and she makes a move toward me. But she can't. Because the man is holding her by her throat with his hand. Her back is pressed into him. He's not very tall. Unfortunately. Her head almost hides his.

"The other one too," he orders, but my partner doesn't make a move or sound. The man squeezes Olivia's neck, making her cough. Then he shakes her until she stops coughing.

I can't fuckin' breathe. My eyes are clouded with rage, but I force myself to stay calm. Olivia's life depends on it. I can't afford emotions. Feelings are dangerous now.

My partner comes out, gun in his hands.

Ashley's sitting on the table now, her feet hanging. She looks excited. The bitch will go down today. To jail or forever, I don't fucking care. She goes down.

Her mother is still by the wall. Her hands pressed into the surface behind her. She is the only person who looks to be out of place.

Adams is sitting on the chair with a gun pointed at Olivia. While the man's gun is pressed to her temple.

Olivia's lips tremble. She's scared. I look away because I can't let emotions overcome me.

"Look who's here," Adams starts, crossing one leg over another. "I've had a feeling there's something shady going on. I just didn't know you had it in you." She watches me with an evil smile.

I don't respond.

She laughs. "How long you've been after me?" She looks at my partner. "Years? You've even aged." She laughs louder. "I've made you run around the block a few times, haven't I? And now I've got a Christmas gift early this year. You, and you, and even your little whore." She turns her attention at Olivia. "When I erase you, I erase your unit. After all, you can't waste so many resources on one person. Am I right?" Another laugh. "When you're gone, I'm free. Lost in the ocean of big fish. Free of your ever-looming presence. I mean, I love the attention, but yours is getting a bit annoying."

"Just get it over with," Ashley chimes in from the table with a gleeful voice. "I'm tired."

Adams looks at her with a newfound interest. "You're bloodthirsty, are you? I think I'll need your help here. After all, Jake over here," she points a gun at me, "took my very promising protégé away from me six years ago. Didn't you,

Jakey? Now, I'll take everything from you." She leans forward. "And I'll make you watch." Her wide smile is psychotic. It also tells me she'll do what she says.

My partner understands it too. "You or me?" he whispers, barely audible.

"Quiet!" Adams yells.

"I'm a better shot," I whisper back. "On two."

On the count of two we both shoot. His bullet hits Adams in the arm, making her drop her gun with a loud cry.

My bullet hits the man's head on the left. Right where it's poking out from behind Olivia. I have a crippling fear that his finger will jerk, but I see a moment before I shoot that his finger moved a little backward from the trigger. Only the tip of it was touching. It wouldn't be enough for the muscle spasm to have enough power to move the bullet.

It shouldn't be enough.

I don't breathe. I can't.

His hand shoots up. Muscles make his arms flail as he falls backward.

Olivia's still standing. Her eyes are round with shock. She looks terrified.

Ashley's mother is yelling.

"Make sure she stays down," I say, as I take off to Olivia. I don't need to look behind to know he's heard me. He'll take care of Adams.

My woman is my priority.

I grab her into my arms and press her into my body, trying to shield her from pain.

"You're okay," I whisper into her hair. "You'll be okay." I can't stop touching her.

She doesn't cry. Doesn't say anything. I know it's shock. I hope it is.

"I love you, Oli. I love you so fuckin' much," I say as I breathe her in.

She lets out a shuddering exhale and pushes her face into my neck.

"J-J-Jake." Her voice is unstable. She's stuttering. "Jake."

"I'm here. I'll always be here, Oli," I promise, as I'm feverishly roaming my hands over her body, trying to figure out if she's hurt somewhere. "I love you."

"Jake," she repeats again like the sound of my name makes her grounded.

"I'm here."

"Is Brodie okay?" Her voice dips with fear.

"Yes," my partner says from behind my back, clearly cuffing Ashley while she's cursing him with very interesting threats. "He's with your brother and the sheriff. He's fine."

"Th-thank you," Olivia breathes out with relief and lets me hold her until the rest of our unit arrives.

Chapter Forty-Three

J^{ake}

The medics arrive shortly after Kenneth. He left Jennica at Mark's place and came straight here.

Our unit is on the way too.

"No one touches the body," Silent orders everyone, flashing his badge to Kenneth who, to my surprise, doesn't object. He cuffs the men from the bushes and brings them to the porch.

Brad, the new addition to the police station, comes to a stop with a screech, making everyone alert. When we see it's him, we relax. He rushes toward Kenneth.

"Where do you want me?" Brad asks him, and I note how far he's grown since I last saw him.

"Put them in the cruiser and make sure they don't leave." He nods at Adams and Ashley who are restrained on the ground. They're tied by a very masterful knot my boss knows. I've always wondered what his deal is, and I'm thinking I might not want to know it after all. The satisfaction I saw in his eyes when he tightened the knot, making Ashley cry out in pain was a little unsettling.

"Silent," I call him. "Well, she lived," I refer to Kayla's mother.

"Unfortunately." He winces. "But we need her to give us names. Someone will come to replace her once she's out of the picture. When she learns about that, she'll sing like a fucking songbird."

Makes sense. When one head of a hydra is cut, two pop up. The goal of this operation has always been to annihilate the whole thing from the roots. Whatever he needs to do, I'll testify. I'll say whatever needs to be said. He was right, I don't have problems with bending the rules. If the bad guys can do that, so can I.

"I'll be back," I announce, and walk outside where Rachel, the local medic, is checking Olivia's vitals. With a silver blanket wrapped around her, sitting in the back of the ambulance with her knees pressed to her chest, she looks small and defeated.

I go straight to the vehicle and kneel in front of her. Rachel instantly steps away. Olivia's eyes slowly move to my face while I take her cold hands in mine.

"I would never have missed. I hope you know that." I need her to know that I'd never risk her life if I wasn't sure. I was sure. I calculated the risk and outcomes. This was the best decision. The only one.

"I know," she replies quietly. "The whole time I was there, I knew you'd come."

"I didn't mean what I said." My voice falters at the end.

"I know." Her throat works in a swallow. "When they got me, I knew you'd come. I knew it."

I press my face to her hands and cover them with kisses. Even after me being an asshole, she had faith in me. She believed in me.

"I love you, Olivia. I love you so fuckin' much I can't breathe."

Her index finger presses on my chin to force me to look at her. "I love you too, Jake. I've always loved you."

A strong shudder shakes my whole body. My throat closes up, and I move on my knees forward, pressing my face into her neck. I breathe her scent in, letting myself *feel* for a little. It's not the time yet, but I can allow myself this luxury. Just for a moment.

When I pull away, I find her eyes. "We will need to give Benson a statement. The DEA will be there too. Since two agents were present, they won't require much from you. I'm sorry you have to relive it. I'm sorry, Oli." I fix a lock of her hair behind her ear. "I promise it's the last time."

"It's okay," she says with a small smile, and I take it as a good sign of her slowly coming back to herself. "Can you call Mark and tell him I'm okay?"

"Already done." I nod. "He said he'll keep Brodie until you're back."

"Okay." She wipes her nose. Thank God Rachel cleaned the blood from it, or I wouldn't be so calm right now. The bruise on the left side of her face is triggering enough. "I don't want him to see me like that. He'll get scared. He's very sensitive."

"Of course," I nod quickly. "We'll get him tomorrow."

A sudden sound coming out of the bushes makes every person draw a gun.

"Frank!" Kenneth rolls his eyes, holstering his. "Not now."

"Who are you talking to?" Silent asks, joining us all outside.

"Him." Kenneth points at the moose.

"The moose?" Silent asks, sending me a funny look.

"Yeah," Benson sighs. "Come later, Frank."

But Frank doesn't leave. Instead, he's watching me with his big, brown eyes. Too understanding for an animal. Or I might be going insane. We're all waiting for him to move, but he doesn't. He keeps staring at me until I become squirmy.

Fucking hell.

"She's fine, Frank," I mumble, feeling a quizzical look on myself. "Thank you. You can go now."

And then I do something I never pictured myself doing.

I drop my chin with a curt nod. At the moose.

He blinks, turns around, and disappears in the bushes.

The stare on the side of my face intensifies, and I finally look at Silent. His eyes are round. I don't think they were this round when he found me shot on one of the assignments. He definitely was less impressed then.

"What?" I ask, tired of his intense stare.

He shakes his head in obvious disbelief. "I shouldn't have left you alone for so long."

"Fuck you," I reply with a smirk, making him snort. Because I'd rather him believe that I went insane than that I'm talking to a moose.

Kenneth, watching the whole situation unfold, glances between me and the bushes and asks, "I will love your statement, won't I?"

It's my turn to snort because I'm sure as fuck going to mention Frank's heroic role in everything.

Benson, to my utter surprise, walks up to smack me on

the shoulder. "Welcome back to Little Hope, Attleborough."

I'm not fuckin' choking on the air here.

The DEA team works along with the local cops. They take statements and pictures. Soon, I'm in the clear to take Olivia home. I can stay and help them more, but Silent knows I'm not in the right state of mind for that. All I want is to be next to my woman and be sure that she's safe.

At home, I help her take a shower and dry her with a towel. She lets me. I make her drink hot tea and put her to bed. She lets me. I tuck her under my arm and wrap myself around her. She lets me.

I feel like a fuckin' hero. She always does that.

When she falls asleep, exhausted, I carefully unwrap myself from her and quietly pad to the bathroom. Where I turn the water on to muffle unhuman sounds coming out of me while my body racks with silent cries.

I could have lost her. I could have never seen her again. Never felt her again.

She would have never known how much I love her. I let myself *feel* as my body quakes with emotions.

This is the only time I let myself do that. When I shut off this faucet, I will turn into her hero again. For the rest of our lives.

The next day I expect to be unpredictable. No one knows how a victim of a situation like that will behave. I'm ready for anything.

But Olivia surprises me again. She wakes up like nothing happened. The only reminder of yesterday is a purple bruise on her cheek. She's so fucking strong, it's unbelievable.

I offer to make her some breakfast, but she refuses and agrees only to a giant cup of coffee, saying that she's too exhausted to eat. This is the only indication that she remembers what happened yesterday.

"Are you ready?" she asks.

I pause the mug halfway. "For what?"

"To meet your son."

My throat closes up. A bundle of nerves activates in my stomach, and with a suddenly shaking hand, I put the mug down.

"Now?"

Her brow lifts up. "Scared?"

"A little," I reply, almost honestly. Because I'm scared shitless.

Her face softens. She walks up to me and cups my face with her hands. "You'll do great, Jake. Brodie will be proud. His father is a hero."

I swallow the damn lump in my throat, which refuses to disappear, and nod.

My steps falter when I walk up the stairs of Mark's house. Yes, I've spent time with Brodie before, but I didn't know he was my son then. Everything is different now.

Mark opens the door and swallows Olivia in a bear hug. His body shudders, and he pulls away. His nose is red. His eyes are bloodshot. I texted him last night after I came out from the shower and told him she was fine. He wanted to come and check on her, but I convinced him it's better if we just leave her asleep and let her body deal with everything on its own. He agreed but wasn't happy about that. I understand. I would want to see my sister too if something happened to her.

Lost in my thoughts, I don't notice Mark stepping close to me. I suddenly find myself squeezed between his arms. The fucker is giving me a hug.

Giving me another squeeze, he silently steps away, letting quietly crying Alicia come to me.

But she's not alone. She's holding Olivia's kid in her arms. My son.

My eyes sting, and I sniffle, trying not to look like a damn pussy meeting my son officially for the first time. But I fail. A few rogue tears escape my eyes, but I'm not ashamed of them. I don't think.

I take him from her, and she gives me a quick hug and quickly moves to Olivia.

I'm holding him in my arms. I thought I loved him before. He was Olivia's kid. He was a part of her, and I loved them both. But what I'm feeling right now is different. My whole being is singing. My soul and body are high. This is the highest I'll ever get. No drug will replace it. Never.

I extend my arm toward Olivia, inviting her to join. With an understanding smile, she steps over to us.

This is it. This is my family.

I leave a few days later to finish years of work. Silent told me I should be there if I wanted to. I wanted to, but I have a family to consider now. After talking to Olivia, we decided that I should go.

I spend a whole month away from them, but I'm videochatting them every time I get a chance. There's no more undercover jobs for me, Olivia put her stubborn foot down, and I don't blame her.

Kayla's mother starts singing a week after being arrested.

We close this chain of drugs thirty-six days later. Along with the deep roots and all branches of that rotten tree.

A few months later, Adams gets a life sentence. Kayla is present during the court on the side of the prosecution with Justin holding her hand through the whole process. Her back is straight, she's getting justice for herself too.

Ashley gets thirty years without possibility of parole. We've discovered her involvement in moving drugs in Springfield among other things. Her father gets twenty years. Her mother is the only one who walks away because she's truly not involved.

When I come back to Little Hope after this trip, I'm met like a hero by everyone. The story made it to the national news due to the large drug cartel being shut down. It's weird. I'm used to being a villain and I've gotten used to it.

The only ones whose opinions truly matter are Olivia and Brodie, but he's still too small. Oli has always been calling me her hero, and for Brodie I'll become one because I sure as hell will be staying in their lives.

And this ring on her finger is the proof. I came back with one from the trip and asked her to marry me right away. We eloped on a short getaway with just the three of us. It was the best week of my life. I'll get her a beautiful celebration of an anniversary, but I couldn't waste any more time with her and my son. I had to make sure they were mine.

Little Hope is slowly getting back on track, but the talk of the local family being involved in serious drug trafficking brought some weird people to town. So Kenneth asked me to take my badge back. I didn't know how much I needed it. I've always wanted to help people, just at some point, the way I was helping them took a weird turn. It happens no more. I wear the badge with pride. I will not let my beautiful family down. I'm not a villain anymore.

Except when I'm alone with Oli. Turns out, she loves my mean and jealous parts, so she puts a lot of the male population in danger by making me jealous. And I love to fuck her in the bar bathroom. At some point, Rory said she'll be charging us rent.

I'm fine with that. As long as she lets the villain get the girl.

Epilogue

A *few months later*

Olivia

"Jake, you look too guilty," I warn him as I fix his hair with my hands.

"Of course I do!" he explodes. "I'm about to kidnap a person!"

"Calm down." I press my hand on his chest. "Deep breaths."

With a lopsided smile, he pulls me toward him. "Who's the villain now, huh?"

I swat his hands away. "Focus, Jake. Or you'll be late."

"Fine," he pouts and pulls a white shirt on, covering the gorgeous tattoo Kayla inked on him. It's a giant phoenix wrapped around his shoulder with one wing on his chest and another on his back. Its head resting on top of his shoulder, moving every time he does. It looks alive. I don't think the phoenix would suit anyone more than him. Risen from the ashes into a new life. My villain turned hero. She also added a small dandelion on his left butt cheek as retribution for him being a dickhead toward her. I love it.

Jake looks hotter with it if that's even possible. His masculinity is so profound, a cute flower on his ass won't ruin it.

"Wish me luck," he says, giving me a last kiss before he leaves.

"You don't need it! You're strong and brave. You're the best kidnapper in the whole world."

His loud laughter is his only reply.

While Jake's going to kidnap Kayla, I run to grab Brodie and drive to Marina's diner where everyone should be gathered soon.

When I open the door to the diner, I'm met with the strawberry smell. Justin says it's his favorite scent in the world because Kayla smells like it. So the strawberries are everywhere. Literally. They are implemented into bouquets on the tables and appetizer dishes scattered all over the place.

Justin has gone all in with this wedding. He wanted to rent a giant restaurant, but Marina talked him out of it. She said her wedding should be where it all started. And this is how we found ourselves as a part of this scheme.

Everyone Kayla holds dear is here. And everyone is nervous because we all rely on Jake's Oscar performance.

"Do you think he'll do it?" Alex asks Justin who looks very pale and about to throw up.

"He will. He's my brother. He won't let me down like that," Justin replies with zero doubt in his voice. It makes me happy to hear that. For the past few months, they both have been working hard on rebuilding their relationship, and I'm proud to see them both coming together.

Alex smacks his back with a nod and moves his toddler from one side to another. He's been visiting our apartment awfully often, always needing something from Jake. I thought Jake would get tired of that, but it's actually the opposite. He seems to light up every time he comes to our place, and they can spend hours discussing stuff I don't bother to get involved with. Let boys be boys.

Mark practically lives at our place because Alicia's pregnant and she always wants something sweet. So he often finds himself in our kitchen begging me to give him an éclair. He's currently watching his wife stealing a chocolate-covered strawberry from the fruit tower with the happiest look on his face I've ever seen on him.

Freya and Josie are chasing their kids around while Kenneth's repeating his speech. He's the officiant today who will seal the deal. He looks super nervous, and it's adorable. He's talking to himself, repeating a mantra under his breath.

Mary gives a soft kiss on her husband's cheek and walks up to me. We've been slowly trying to repair our relationship, but it's not there yet. I brace myself for the impact when she's near.

"I've always wondered who will be brave enough to take on my son," she starts. "I'm glad it's you. I don't think anyone else could have pulled him out of that dark place he was in." Her voice falters at the end. She finds my hand and takes it. "Thank you, Olivia. Please know I'm here for whatever you need. I would have come sooner, but I didn't know if you were mad at me."

"I was," I admit. "At first, I was."

"I know," she sighs. "I was wrong to push you to tell the truth. I should have let you do it on your own terms."

I whip my face toward her so fast my neck crinkles with pain. "What truth?"

Her brow slowly rises up. "Do think I didn't know it was my grandchild?" she stuns me into stupor. "He's Jake's copy when he was his age. We both knew that the moment we saw him."

I recall the first dinner at their place and how Jake's father was staring at Alicia. Or so I thought. Turned out, he was staring at Brodie.

"You knew?"

She nods. "Yes, and I just wanted Jake to know it too. I didn't mean to accuse you of being a bad woman, you know. I just wanted to be able to officially spend time with my grandson."

"I'm sorry," I say quietly. "I'm sorry for taking this time away from you."

She shakes her head. "You had your reasons, dear. Thank you for bringing me my son back." She quickly gives me a very unexpected kiss and departs to Marina who's running around like a madwoman, trying to make finishing touches. It's her almost-daughter's wedding day, and it makes me happy seeing her so nervous. That's what real moms do, don't they?

Jonah is following Marina on her heels, telling her to take a deep breath every few seconds and getting smacks a few times for that. It doesn't stop him though. He keeps telling her to chill out or her foundation would melt down to her décolletage. I think this is the only thing that makes her slow down a little.

"They are here!" Kenneth yells in a falsetto I didn't know he possessed, running away from the window. People start panicking. Literally every single person. They start moving around like people stung by bees. It's pure chaos.

Leila, Alex's sister, steps into the middle of the diner and loudly claps her hands. "Everyone! Stop!"

I didn't know she had so much authority in that small body of hers, but the panic stops. Which can't be said about her husband, Archie, who's leaning on the back wall with a child in his arms. The girl looks like a tiny version of Leila, and I can tell Archie is smitten with them both like they're still in the newly dating stage.

"Get ready, people. Chop-chop!" She claps again, and everyone takes their assigned spots like well-trained soldiers. *Damn, woman,* I think, *remind me to invite you to a dinner one day.*

"Here," Jake's voice comes in when he opens the door and drags Kayla inside, "Marina said the leak is awful. The poop is everywhere, and she doesn't know what to do with it."

"Oh, crap!" Kayla exclaims.

"Crap, indeed," Jake confirms, and I roll my eyes. Jake will always be Jake, and I love that about him.

When she steps inside the diner, she freezes. Her eyes go round as she takes all of us in. Justin, swallowing so loudly even I can hear, pushes people aside and walks up to her.

"Now?" he asks, sounding like a begging puppy.

Her scared face softens when she takes his hands in hers. "Now," she replies with a nod.

"Thank fuck!" Cherry, Archie's business partner from Boston comes to take Kayla's hand and drag her away. "Let's go, we need to get you ready."

She pushes Kayla to go first and follows her while her eyes are glued to Kayla's ass. Interesting. When Justin notices it, he says, very loudly, making everyone chuckle, "Don't even think about it, Cherry."

She chuckles, giving him her middle finger without turning back.

We wait for Kayla to change into a dress Justin asked Freya, Josie, Alicia, Leila, and me to help him choose. It's red. Kayla's favorite color. And very expensive. In fact, I'm sure my brand-new SUV Jake bought for me costs about the same as this dress. He really went all in.

"Hey," Archie's voice sounds to our right. Jake turns toward the voice, and me with him because his arm is wrapped around my shoulders. He's holding Brodie in his other arm, sniffing his baby hair from time to time. I've noticed he does it a lot. Maybe even more than I do.

"Hi," he replies.

"Daddy," the girl in his arm says. "Who that?"

"That's the man who saved your daddy's life," Archie explains, kissing her chubby cheek. She doesn't understand what he means.

But we do.

He's referring to the time when Jake saved Archie's life by shooting his attacker and giving Archie CPR until the ambulance arrived.

"I've never gotten a chance to say thank you." Archie's voice is quiet but meaningful. "Thank you. If not for you, I'd never have met my daughter. And never married Leila. I owe you. Till the rest of my life. I'm sorry it took me so long to come and say it." He chokes at the end, making my eyes turn misty.

We haven't spent much time together with Archie, if any. He just stops by to pick up pastries for Leila and chats about random, polite things. All my information about him is from stories of others who know him better. And all I've heard so far indicates that he has a tough-guy appearance and fuck-off attitude, but also that he helps everyone any way he can. I don't see a tough guy right now. All I see is the man who's grateful to be alive.

Jake tenses around me, and I quickly press my palm to his chest, grounding him. It always helps when he spirals.

"I'm the one who should be thanking you," Jake says unexpectedly. "I was in a really tough patch. Dark. Helping you was what kept me going. You saved me too."

Archie nods with acknowledgment, understanding something I don't, but it feels beautiful. When he smacks him on the back with the words "We will be fine," I smile. We will be.

The wedding is amazing. Kayla is the most gorgeous bride I've ever seen. Justin made sure that every single food she's ever liked is on the table. That every person who means something to her is here. The tough tattoo parlor owner, TJ, who was one of the first ones who noticed her talent, is here too. He even sheds a tear, wrapping his arm around his wife.

When the official part is done, we move our celebration outside because there is not enough room here for everyone. The whole street gets closed, and half the town is here.

I look around. Surrounded by familiar, smiling faces, celebrating the start of a new chapter in everyone's life, I feel like the decision to move back to Little Hope was one of the best ones I've ever made. Little Hope is home.

Bonus Story

Well, here is the end of the story.

Oh, wait!

It's not exactly. If you want to read a very super-mega-duper extended epilogue about happily-ever-after from EACH couple POV, you can do so by going to Ariana's website www.arianacane.com and then proceeding to the EXTRA'S page. Under the Little Hope series tab, you'll see the link to the story.

If you are reading this from a mobile device, please follow this link to download your copy.

Happy reading!

Acknowledgments

If you want to read an extended epilogue about each couple, it's on the AFTERWORD page. Don't miss it!

This is the hardest part where I'm trying not to forget anyone over the years. It's going to be long, so bear with me. It's the end of an era after all. There will be a bunch of names, and the order doesn't matter. I'm sure I'll forget someone because I'm too nervous right now, so please don't get offended if you are not here!

Thank you, my dear husband, for believing and pushing me to continue. And sponsoring my books, of course . Thanks for that too!

Thank you, Sarah. My PA who's been with me from the beginning, before I even published my first book. I wouldn't be here if it wasn't for you. A note to new authors: Find yourself a PA who believes in you more than you do. Find yourself a Sarah.

Thank you, Lauren, my editor whom I wish I found earlier. Your professionalism is beautiful.

Thank you, Books and Moods, for making the covers I didn't know I needed. You've rebranded my whole name.

Thank you, V., for letting me make Jonah out of you. And thank you for letting me borrow your joke. And your pornstache.

Thank you, Jennifer a.k.a. Jenny for being you. You are the most positive person I've ever met.

Thank you, Priya, for your unconditional love for Justin. It makes me want to write more, I swear.

Thank you, Steph, for listening to me complain on the phone, ha-ha.

Thank you, Meaghan, for being my friend.

Thank you, Tricia, for hyping me up.

Thank you, Janine, for believing in my craft. You sure do more than I do, ha-ha.

Thank you, Rach, for explaining addictions to me. You're very brave, and I'm honored you've shared your story and knowledge with me.

Thank you, my Patreons, for sticking with me and supporting me. I hope your Jakey boxes won't disappoint you. I've spent so much time researching what to put in those. I didn't know I loved making those boxes so much until I actually started doing it for you.

Thank you, my street team, for spreading the word about me!

Thank you, my arc team, for being so excited to read my books and finding time in your schedules to actually read them and post reviews!

Thank you to those who sent me messages about how much you loved my books or how it helped you overcome certain things. You have no idea how much those messages mean to me.

And of course, thank you, readers. Thank you for sticking with the series and its characters. Thank you for believing (or not) in Jake. If you are reading this, that most likely means you've been around for a while. Jake has been a thorn in my side since book one, and I couldn't wait to tell his story. But then, after whispering into my ears for a year, he quieted down. I got scared that he'd never be back. So I posted a question on my Instagram about what you're most excited about Jake, and you guys haven't disappointed. Your answers made Jake talk again. Thank you! He happened because of you!

And, thank you, Little Hope! It's been a fun ride!

Now, moving on to the next chapter! See you again, Maine!

With love,
Ariana